LEGEND

LEGEND

by Barry Maher

Lindisfarne Books

Published by Lindisfarne Books
400 Main Street
Great Barrington, MA 01230
www.lindisfarne.org

An earlier edition of this book was published by
Garber Communications in 1987.

ISBN 1-58420-008-1

Maher, Barry.
Legend / by Barry Maher.
p. cm.
ISBN 1-58420-008-1
I. Title.
PS3563.A3558 L44 2002
813'.54-dc21

2002003267

10 9 8 7 6 5 4 3 2 1

Book design by Jason Brown/BMA studios

To Tom and Tom.
I miss you both.

Contents

Prologue

Near the end of a long day of site evaluation, the archaeologist discovered the door. He wasn't surprised when it started talking; he'd often said that just as surely as primitive civilizations surrounded their cities with walls, "more advanced" peoples surrounded themselves with machines that talked. His old fingers fumbled briefly with the familiar switches on his computer before he managed to activate it and it began translating:

1

Martin

… Besides, it wasn't as if being a bureauer was something Martin had ever wanted.

"Questions are for philosophers; *we* do our job," Brodwich had said, even before Martin had a chance to ask what his new job was supposed to be. He assumed it was a good job. Any job was good compared to the hungry life of the street folker that he'd just left.

And he didn't want to complain, especially not to Brodwich, his immediate Better. Yet Martin had been at his job here in his office every day for the last three weeks, and until Brodwich had shown up that afternoon, he hadn't had anyone to talk to but the door. He still hadn't been given anything to do.

And now Brodwich was leaving. Obviously pleased with the aptness of the bureauers' age-old motto as an exit line, he pivoted his lumbering bulk around on his heel and stepped smartly to the door. Unfortunately, since this was the door of a young and extremely low-level bureauer like Martin 37037-927-8048, and probably a little defective, like everything else in the city, it was much slower to react than the doors to which Brodwich was normally accustomed. For long silent seconds, he was left anticlimactically staring into its mirrored upper surface at his own reflection. After a moment, he reached a hand to his head, as if he would adjust one of its tattooed strands of hair. Finally the door opened itself for him and he was gone.

Alone again in his tiny, windowless office, Martin went over and sat down carefully in the noisy swivel chair behind the desk. One of the chair's legs was always falling off, and fixing it had been about the only work Martin had found for himself since becoming a bureauer, a person with a job, part of the government instead of the governed.

It occurred to him that he didn't even know what "philosophers" were. He wondered if even Brodwich knew. Maybe "philosophers"only existed as a word in another one of those unexplained formulas that bureauers seemed to haul out whenever they deigned to comment on why there weren't enough fare-well coupons for the food units again this month, or why the bureauer policers went out of their way to crush rubble homes with their tanks, or why, for that matter, the construction of rubble homes was forbidden, when there weren't nearly enough inhabitable rooms in the city. And far too many unsheltered folkers.

Feet up on the scarred desktop, leaning back recklessly in his ancient chair and blowing tunelessly into the pocket instrue he always carried, Martin was still pondering "philosophers" a good while later, when the door clicked itself open and announced, "quit-time," in the warm and motherly voice that Martin found so disconcerting. Amazed that for once some work time had passed quickly, he rose and started toward the door, no longer afraid that it might click shut before he got to it and lock him in the office overnight. It was only three steps from his desk, and he was almost there when he heard thunder.

He went back and grabbed the unfamiliar brown cloak of

the bureauer rankenfile from the nail behind the desk. Since he hadn't shaved his head or his body, it was the only thing that set him apart from the folkers when he made his way home through the crowded roads in the evening. He was always forgetting it. The thin cloak had little value as weather protection; it was mostly a badge of office. To most bureauers, that made it far more than just clothing; to Martin, that simply made it hard to remember. Possibly the only bureauer ever who hadn't been born and raised for that position, he had been brought up with a folker's regard for the practical.

He threw the cloak around his shoulders with a self-mocking flourish, and as he did, he happened to tilt his head upward. There was a hole in the ceiling. A hole that hadn't been there before. Taking a position directly underneath it, he looked up, but could see nothing but the dim daylight on the other side. Something crunched under the tread of his cloth-bound sandals, and he bent down to discover tiny pieces from the ceiling tile amidst a film of sawdust.

The door made its announcement a second time. Slightly less patiently too, he imagined. The problem of the hole would have to wait. Thunder boomed again, as he stepped out of the office into the twilight of the hall. It sounded closer this time and made him wish for the thick folker cloak that old Moohna had stitched together for him out of salvaged odds and ends. His eyes, as yet unaccustomed to the comparative darkness of the corridor, took several seconds to register the huge purple mound coming into focus against the background of the buckling hardwood floor. The thing possessed an enforced stillness, like a photograph, a suspended millisecond of motion. Though frightened, and excited by a complex blend of emotion, Martin wasn't actually surprised by the bloated purplish face, or the livid tongue vomited from the dead mouth. Around the throat, a finely made sash cut deeply into the fatty flesh; it might have been trying to redefine a neck that had been buried long before under the successive strata of fat that marked Brodwich's various promotions up the bureauer hierarchy to the rank of Big Eater. Behind Martin, an explosion split the silence. He wheeled around. Even as he realized the explosion was merely the office door automatically clicking itself shut, he found himself staring into the eyes of Brodwich's killer.

A naked woman was responsible for Martin becoming a bureauer. Totally naked, no shoes or anything.

For the first twenty years of his life, Martin had been just another average folker. Raised in a food unit of six women and fourteen other children, he might have been considered odd at times, but none of the others had ever considered him anything special. Not even Moohna, who was probably his biological mother. But then no folker child was anything special.

He'd always done his share of the work, and maybe a bit more, if no more willingly than the rest of the children, at least not all that much less. And like all the others, he'd played the hard, violent games of folker children: brick fights, king-a-the-heap, rat baiting, and, of course, poke 'em, the gambling game whose losses were taken in cuts and bruises on the hands and arms, or, for high-stakes players like Martin's huge brother Mengra, on the face. Martin was all of twelve before he'd sexed his first female, a bit late perhaps, and he'd had to be goaded on by Mengra to do it then, but he'd never really been all that much for group activities.

What he really did enjoy from the time he was eleven or twelve was combing the ruins and rubble of the city, searching for artifacts from the Age of Origin, collecting junk that had been regarded as useless by untold generations of scavengers. And no one in the unit could understand that.

It had started one day when the unit was searching the remains of an old, burned-out building, hoping to find enough fireburn to cook their evening poorage. As it got late, it got chilly and damp. Their prospects seemed to be limited to cold poorage and an even colder night, and everyone was doing a lot of yelling at everyone else. Suddenly, one of the children had literally fallen through the ground into a covered-up old room. What a find! They knocked each other over getting down there. Rooms were priceless; uninhabited rooms were virtually unheard of. And this one was large and reasonably dry, though with enough holes in the roof for light to filter in. And it had only the one accidental entrance that they easily concealed behind natura-looking piles of mortar-encrusted blocks. The opening itself they hid with a rusty car hood. The little girl who'd plunged through to the room had broken her spine. Moohna had to strangle her.

Inside, on a shattered shelf, Martin found a stack of paper. The sheets were in bundles, folded and stapled together, and all covered with pictures, apparently of the Age of Origin. While the rest of the unit was still absorbed with the room, Martin grabbed the pictures and climbed back outside to examine them before he lost the light.

They were almost magical. Some were in color so intense it seemed almost luminous. There were broad fields and green parks filled with towering plants, most larger and all more colorful than anything Martin had ever imagined could come out of the ground. And there was the city, glowing in color. At night, it lit the darkness with a million distinct beacons of light. In the daytime, its towers soared off into a clear and boundless sky, their windows reflecting and amplifying the sunlight, a light that, in contrast to the almost constant overcast of the present-day city, seemed so warm and benevolent that Martin later made the mistake of describing it to Mengra as "loving."

He'd heard about *that* for years.

Martin had wondered if the world was really so much brighter then, or if the color had somehow been added to the pictures. The black-and-white photos looked more realistic. Yet even in black-and-white, the dress of the Originals seemed more colorful than the faded and washed-out multicolor of the folker cloak. Similarly, even in the stillness of the photographs, the Originals appeared more animated than what passed for life in the world around him. The Originals! He'd thought of little else for the next several days. They were giants: they filled the earth with the splendor of their creations as easily as their almost godlike beauty filled their strange clothing. Their vehicles reduced time and space to a function of their wills; they zoomed across vast expanses of virgin tarmac that stretched out after eternity as if they even spanned the waters around the city. These Originals had drunk deeply of that wondrous sun: tanned men and women, strong and healthy, often smiling. He imagined that they had never known want or hate. It was hard to believe that they were not somehow a race apart from the bent and battered souls who were now cramped into that drab and tattered remnant called the city.

At first the rest of Martin's unit considered the pictures merely useless. Then it occurred to Mengra that, bound as they were, they were approximately indistinguishable from the sacred books of the disciples, and so the women decided that they probably were dangerous. All that prevented them from being turned into fireburn immediately was their condition; damp and moldy, they were very hard to ignite. When, over Martin's prone body, Mengra managed to get a few burning, it produced so much smoke that the tiny draft they'd rigged was inadequate to keep the room from filling, and the white plume that rose into the sky above their new home signaled an invitation to passing prowlers and to any homeless unit that might be either strong enough or desperate enough to mount an attack.

So the pictures had remained for a while. At least some of them had. When he wasn't looking at them, Martin kept them hidden away, but the children seemed to take even more delight in destroying them when they had to hunt for them first. They did this without malice. Mengra, who usually led the hunt, was Martin's friend, but destruction was another game that gave folker children a real sense of accomplishment.

Because of his private window into it, it almost seemed to Martin that the Age of Origin belonged to him and him alone. There he found his heroes, his models. The men there weren't fat, yet many of them were obviously leaders and all of them seemed more vital than any bureauers he had ever seen. He never lost his sense of awe, touching pages that hadn't been touched since the time of Jefuson, since the long-dead hands that built the city had passed from the earth. Often the images, almost as much as the unknown symbols under several of them, seemed to speak of things he couldn't understand. Things that were a bit frightening; things that became more sacred because of their mystery. But the more important they became to him, the more he wanted to solve that mystery, and so he became a collector of anything that might have a remote connection with the Age.

Of course a young folker had other demands on his time besides something so frivolous. Children were the labor of any unit, and the older Martin got the more it seemed the women of the unit expected of him. Besides gathering the fireburn and trash, hunting rats and birds, grubbing for insects, helping to braid reweave for clothing (something he was abominable at), and all the other tasks he shared with the unit, Martin had the responsibility for rationing out both poorage and fireburn, and he bartered with the reaper drivers when the unit turned in the trash they'd collected. And it was Martin the unit usually turned to if a map had to be drawn, for his were clear, with just enough detail, and he'd always take into consideration the alleys and streets that tended to be safer than most. Or if a map had to be interpreted. This last could be especially tricky. With nameless streets and wordless maps, the user had to rely heavily on counting the number of roads and determining their relative positions to the various bends in the River, something that was hard enough with the maps the criers occasionally provided and could be almost impossible with those drawn by folkers.

It's also possible that Martin did a bit more than his share of guard duty when the rest of the unit was out; his leper imitation was perfect for keeping intruders away from the room. Guard duty was usually brief, often too brief for Martin, who didn't mind the occasional opportunity to be alone.

No special recognition ever went along with any of these extra chores; to the unit Martin's mental power was less a talent worthy of respect, like Mengra's great size and obvious strength, than a curiosity. And he was more a curiosity after he began imitating his pictures of the Originals, wearing his hair pushed back and trimmed to shoulder-length or less, and later even shaving his face with his rusty, broken-off knife, a painful and bloody process.

"The boy actually seems to find pleasure in being different," Moohna often said, with an indulgent yet concerned smile. When the rest of the food unit made that observation, which was more and more frequently as he grew older, they were more apt to take offense that Martin seemed to be going so far out of his way to be unlike them.

One of the things he was best at was disappearing, usually to go off exploring some debris heap that had long ago been stripped of fireburn and anything else that might have been of any conceivable use to anyone, and he'd seldom return until long after the time the unit was usually all asleep. Still, as often as not, he'd find Moohna, bustling about, rekindling the fire, warming a little poorage that she'd hidden away from the ravenous appetites of the others so that he might have a bite of dinner. Then she'd shake her once-pretty head and click her tongue in amazement at the "crazed refuse" that Martin had retrieved: some broken piece of metal, a headless figurine, or a "plastic whatever," that had obviously been shaped to do *something*.

And "crazed refuse," or not, it was always Moohna who'd helped him to keep the other women from throwing out his things, or, if possible, from burning them the moment his back was turned. She'd set that square jaw of hers and point out that they never seemed to be nearly as anxious to clear the real refuse from their room or even to see to it that the children took care of the crap boxes that were constantly on the verge of overflowing. They all respected her; they could all remember times when Moohna's strength was just about all that kept the unit together. And it wasn't so much that they had anything against Martin as that any odd behavior could be dangerous for a folker, and they were afraid of being linked with it.

The most difficult of Martin's tasks was determining how much poorage they could eat at each meal and still have their coupons last nearly until it was time to get more. Since they never knew exactly when the coup-calls were going to come, once they even had a few coupons left over (and Mengra'd accused him of trying to starve them to death and had practically broken his arm).

That's where the naked woman came in, all dark and gleaming and incredibly clean. After seven or eight years, she was the last remnant of his stack of pictures of the Age. Though Mengra might have condemned the rest as tools of the disciples, he'd confiscated this one for his own. If it was a tool of Satan, apparently it was one he could live with. His original warning, "Rip this and I'll rip you," had been sufficient to preserve it even after he'd long since lost interest. In fact, it was several years after both Mengra and Martin had left the unit before Martin rediscovered it during a visit and changed his life forever.

The picture was mounted on heavy paper and had several number-filled pages stapled underneath; the whole thing resembled the number sheets that hung on the wall of the safeway, only with the woman above the pages instead of some fat face.

Like all folkers, Martin had learned his numbers from the fare-well coupons, and with a bit of observation, he'd gradually come to understand the function of these calendars. After a lot of time and even more trial and error, he'd gotten his to work so that he was able to predict the day of coup distribution for the 900-M series food units, enabling his old unit to be at the safeway even before the criers announced the distribution, getting them in and out of there before the coups were gone, or even before any of the real violence started, before the policers got there, swinging their long clubs, shooting their weapons, rounding up a few hungry women and children and maybe a prowler or two for the Free-Kill. The policers were always careful to see to it that food riots were not encouraged, and pushing and shoving in a crowded safeway could be considered a minimal food riot on weeks when they were low on their Free-Kill quota.

Martin's predictions worked three times running, but the next month, when the unit, relying on Martin, missed the crier's announcement, they reported a day late and got no coupons at all. Before the next distribution, one of the children took sick and died. Thereafter, even though he kept adjusting his calendar to the one at the safeway, sometimes it worked and sometimes it didn't, and no one relied on it.

The unit was between generations. Moohna's shrinking body now shook with palsy. Her thick dark hair had faded into gray, and her strength had faded with it. Several of the other women were well past childbearing age, and the children of the younger girls were still too small to be of much help. Martin was certainly aware of how much an accurate calendar could benefit them. But even beyond that, he wanted to see the calendar of the Originals working again *because* it was the calendar of the Originals, as if its revival would bring back a little of the vanished glory, a little of the magic of the lost Age into an oppressively mundane world. Then perhaps settling for the life of a prowler would be easier.

He tried to work at correlating his sheets to the bureauer calendar only when the safeway was crowded and all the bureauers were busy talking to their machines about the various food units. But he must have gotten careless, because one day he was caught by the young female bureauer with the sad smile and the dark mustache, the one Mengra had always claimed was dying to sex him (though Mengra thought all women were dying to sex him). She'd looked at Martin very strangely, and he was sure that he'd done something very wrong since he'd certainly done something very different. He'd expected to be sent to the Free-Kill then and there, but, possibly because there'd been a food riot earlier in the day and the Free-Kill quota was overfilled, all she did was take his picture and let him go. Even so, Martin had been terrified: folkers weren't photographed. The only present-day photos he'd ever seen were the ones that were used to identify the offices of certain bureauers. After that, Martin told Moohna that the food unit would have to pick up its own coups from then on, but Mengra, in his vain and dangerous lust for the female bureauer, had volunteered. (Somewhere he had heard that bureauer women were more passionate than folker females.)

Subsequently Martin merely told his brother when he thought the coups were to be expected and let him handle it.

Less than three months later, the bureauer with the brown cloak came to the entrance of the unit's room, claiming he had a message for Martin. Everyone was impressed, even the children. Bureauers simply didn't soil themselves searching the dirt and debris of the city for anything as insignificant as a folker. Overseers drafted labor crews, policers grabbed criminals that were handy, but for specific individuals the daily crier would just call out name and number and let the greed of the other folkers do the work. Besides, anything else would have been much too difficult.

Since folkers tended to attribute far more knowledge to the bureauers than they had, or needed, or even wanted, no one asked how the bureauer had known where the unit lived, or how he had known that Martin would be there that day. Most grown prowlers almost never visited their old food unit. Oddly enough, and unfortunately, Mengra was there too.

"I'll kill the bureauer scum," he boasted in an angry whisper, the scars on his face pale against the red flush of his ire. "The room's not safe, now he's discovered it."

The others didn't really need to stop Mengra; one simply did not kill a bureauer. It was widely known that all of them were implanted with alarms that summoned policers to their exact locations the moment their hearts ceased to beat. And when a bureauer was found murdered, the policers would either destroy immediately — or put up for Free-Kill — everyone of lesser rank than the deceased (which meant at least all the folkers, since folkers had no rank at all) who was within an area of one half to several blocks from the body, or had been within that area near the time of the killing. The distance depended upon the rank of the deceased and the mood of whomever was commanding the policers. Mengra was not stupid, merely young: "straining at his manhood," and "flexing his mouth," as Moohna put it. He would soon shed his vestigial pride or he would not survive.

When Martin arrived at the entrance, his brother was glaring fiercely down at the bureauer (he was a good head taller), though from a distance of several good-sized paces. The thick ball of wiry blond hair that covered Mengra's face and head was like a policer's battle helmet, only much larger. Martin stepped in between them immediately.

"*I* am Martin," he announced. He was confused and nervous, yet curiously excited by this unexpected attention.

The bureauer, though all hairless and smelling odd from the oil they smeared upon the "hair" tattooed on their skulls, was not much older than Martin. His head was very round, the roundness almost undisturbed by his features: the suspicious pale eyes peered from shallow indentations, the nose appeared too tiny to breathe through, and his chin was merely the completion of the circle. And, considering his low rank, he was quite fat.

"Martin 37021-927-8048?" he asked, clearing his throat with the question.

"Just Martin 927... eh ... 8048. I'm a folker," Martin gestured to the decimated area of almost uninhabitable ruins around them, immediately feeling ridiculous. No one could possibly take him for anything other than a folker. He sensed the blood rushing warmly into his face and was grateful that Mengra was behind him so his blush would remain unnoticed. But Mengra, fists clenched tightly at the sides of his ratskin robe, head quivering, almost throbbing with rage, had eyes only for the bureauer. Even for Mengra he was overreacting.

"Yes," the bureauer said, his face gleaming with sweat, as well as oil, under Mengra's unblinking scrutiny. "You are the folker who made the calendar?"

"I meant no harm."

In response to a clattering behind him, Martin turned in time to see Mengra, his visual threat delivered, disappearing back down into the room. He was relieved that his explosive brother had gone, yet he felt very alone in the face of official power.

"I really meant no harm," he repeated. "The figuring was..."

"You *figured?*"

The bureauer's reaction was not reassuring. Martin knew of no specific law against what he'd done, but to a folker, a bureauer was law: he decided what was and what was not legal, often spontaneously. Many times people spoke of "violating the will," instead of breaking the law. The will they were referring to was the will of the bureauers.

"Not very well," he offered, and a thrill ran through him at the deceitful implication that he could really figure at all. A very dangerous assertion for a folker to make to a bureauer, he knew, but as he spoke the words he could almost taste the increase in his stature as if they were flavored with it.

"You can figure!"

His figuring, after blackening the pages with charcoal numbers changed time and time again, had finally been reduced to just copying the sheets at the safeway.

"Only a little," said Martin, almost confidentially, in a manner that implied he could actually figure quite well. And even as he spoke, he was telling himself to stop this foolishness before it got him killed. But it did feel good.

"It is of no concern to me," the bureauer said coldly, attempting to regain his rightful position of superiority. "I come from the Bureau of Knowledge. I am Tantor L.A.C. II 34129-301-6112, assistant to Brodwich L.A.C. III 2346-666-6767. You, Martin 927, must be aware that you deserve to be Free-Killed. Instead you are to become Martin 37037-927-

8048. You should be very flattered; you're to be a bureauer. Very low level, but for one of you people, it is wondrous. Truely wondrous…"

The last few words were spoken to himself in a tone more appropriate for recounting the sun rising in the middle of the night or the second coming of Jefuson. Plainly Tantor was merely a messenger, one who neither understood nor approved, anxious only to transmit the necessary instructions about when and where Martin was to start his new life and then leave. But it took several repetitions before Martin, whose mind was racing trying to grasp the implications of what he'd just been told, was capable of absorbing any more information. It turned out not to matter, however, as unexpectedly the bureauer returned again the next day, this time along with another man. Tantor gave Martin a brown work smock and a brown rankenfile cloak, and the other bureauer pulled out an old straight razor. It was well-known that bureauers left no hair anywhere on their bodies, equating hair with the filth and vermin of the folker, so Martin assumed he was going to be completely shaved and perhaps even get his hair tattoo, like other male bureauers. But the man merely shaved his face cleanly and, working from instructions or a diagram he kept hidden in his hand, trimmed his hair, changing the shape of his hairline slightly with the razor's edge. He did douse Martin's hair with a foul-smelling liquid that changed its color to a somewhat lighter brown, and then he tied it back, carefully draping it over Martin's ears. Tantor showed it to Martin in a mirror and instructed him to always continue to keep his face clean-shaven, and to wear his hair tied like that from then on. In spite of the fact that his new number was much longer than the old one, the ID number on his face was left unaltered. (He found out later that most bureauers only wore their last two number groups, their "personal numbers" and not their "job numbers" on their faces.) No mention was ever made of implanting Martin with any device to summon the policers if he were killed.

"Don't forget, you report in three days," Tantor said as he left. "You'll know it's the right building: it's empty."

A few seconds later, he was back, handling Martin a simple map which Martin used to scout the indicated area the day before he was to start his job. The building was easy to find, still in the folker outer ring of the city, but in a block very close to the no-folker zone that separated the folkers from the Gov-Cent, which was the main abode of the government and most of the bureauers who ran it. The building was the only structure in sight that was much more than rubble. Four stories high, with all its windows actually bricked up (with real old-fashioned mortar), it seemed so luxurious that Martin wondered what the government was saving it for. And why.

He spent his last night as a folker visiting his old unit. A few of them got on him about the fact that they wouldn't be seeing him anymore, which was true, but it wasn't that they were afraid of missing him so much as that they just resented his sudden elevation to bureauer.

After the fire had burned low and the others were asleep — no one sharing their warmth with the new bureauer — Moohna left behind the makeshift crutch she'd needed recently and crawled over to where he lay. His head was filled with himself and his thoughts of the next day, but he pretended to listen as she rambled on and on, unusually garrulous in spite of a large and probably very painful sore on one corner of her mouth. She spoke of Martin's childhood for a bit, and then for some reason she got onto the subject of Pavle, whom no one had seen for years and years. Pavle was the only grown man in Martin's recollection who had ever stayed with the unit for longer than it took to sex one or two of the women and grab a quick bowl of poorage. It was Pavle who'd carved the pocket instrue that Martin had carried with him since he was a small boy. Though he'd never learned to play it properly, it was his most cherished possession, his Age of Origin artifacts notwithstanding. The sound was always sweet and evocative of a distant warmth. Pavle: tall, gray-bearded, fading around the edges of memory; a fabulous storyteller and craftsman, who could take a piece of charcoal from yesterday's fire and, like magic, sketch anyone in the unit.

A deep, dry cough racked Moohna's hunched-over body and temporarily distracted her. When she continued, she began insisting that Pavle had once had a job and apparently had claimed it was vital to be there early. Since only bureauers had jobs, and no one had ever heard of another folker who'd been made a bureauer, Martin was aware that Moohna was confused again. She was nearly fifty now, and not surprisingly her mind was going. Recently she'd begun telling everyone that she was "the only girl around who'd never been sexed and never would be."

Before she'd fallen asleep that night, with her head rather uncomfortably on his chest, she'd pressed three or four small fare-well coups into Martin's hand, calling him father and insisting that he accept them because she had plenty. Their worth being negligible, he stuck them into the pocket of his cloak. Briefly he thought of Pavle again. He felt strangely saddened.

Martin himself didn't sleep that night. At that moment it seemed to him that he'd always expected more from life than just being a folker; it even crossed his mind that perhaps becoming a bureauer had always been his destiny, but he didn't really believe that.

The next morning, he got up at dawn for the long walk across town. Arriving at the empty building, he climbed the three steps to a front door that looked like a recent addition. It swung open for him (as if yielding to a conqueror, he allowed himself to observe). After a flight of well-grooved but sturdy stairs, he turned left down a dusty corridor. Around the first corner, he found his office. Or rather it found him.

"Twoday, 27th, sequence 4,933," said a door on his left. The corridor stretched out ahead of him, and ten or twelve body lengths down it, another corridor went off to the right, but the door left no doubt that this was to be his office.

"Martin 37037-927-8048, on time," it recited, slowly opening to reveal an empty office. "Have a good work, Martin." At least he was reassured that he was in the right place.

Tantor had explained that a work week was Twoday through Forthday, 10:30 until the door called "quit-time" at about 15:30. Martin knew all about weeks from the calendar and he let the door take care of the hours. After a couple of days, Martin stopped answering it when it spoke, but it remained just as friendly.

When he got to the office in the morning, Martin would take off his new brown cloak that had only two or three very small holes in it and hang it on the hook. Then he'd sit down carefully in the swivel chair behind the desk. Along with the luxury of a flush box in the corner, these were the only pieces of furniture in the room. There was also a phone which he didn't know how to use. After the first day Martin had tried to move his desk so that he wouldn't be staring at himself all day in the mirrored upper panel of the door, but the thick metal legs of the desk seemed to be embedded in the floor, so he'd settled for moving the chair a little to the side. He soon found himself constantly recentering the chair, which left him, once again, staring at his own face with its brown hair (by now familiar) and its uncommonly regular features. Most people might have considered that face bland; with secret vanity, Martin believed it was similar to those of the Originals. He just didn't like looking at it all day.

After sitting down, he would brush off the dust from his desk with his sleeve. Then he had nothing to do. He'd glance around the office and pick the remains of the first real fruit he'd ever eaten out of his teeth. He hadn't gotten paid yet but with a bureauer's cloak on, he found that he could walk out of the food section of a safeway carrying poorage, or even real-food like fruit or bread and no one ever even asked him for monies or fare-well coups.

Sometimes Martin would spend the whole day with his feet up on the desk, imagining what his unit would say if they could see him in such isolated splendor. He soon noted that there were fourteen groups of ten brown tiles in the floor, and twelve groups of ten gray tiles in the ceiling with seven and a half extra. For a few minutes he'd found the discrepancy interesting, especially since he was a bit proud of the feat of mental dexterity it had taken to discover it. Tantor had mentioned something about a promotion from within, and occasionally, he wondered if maybe someday he would get an office with a real window, which would at least give him something to look at. Once in a while, he got a twinge of guilt about having nothing to do: as if it was due to some error or inadequacy on his part that was bound to be discovered eventually.

Finally the door would click open and he would go home.

By the third week, he was getting up late, around 7:30, and he still made it to work by 10:25 usually, though once he was late, arriving at 10:41. To his surprise, the door didn't seem to care. He'd figured it out carefully: the walk to work took two hours, plus or minus a few minutes. Going home took longer. Maybe the folkers weren't quite so quick to get out of his way in the evening.

Martin was no longer a folker, but his new home still wasn't in the Gov-Cent. Tantor had advised him to buy a weap, but he hadn't received any monies yet, and weapons weren't bought on fare-well coups. Besides, he was hardly about to go around blasting his way through folkers. Not like some.

His new home had been hard to find. Though the door had been quite specific about how to find it, it hadn't provided a map. And while Martin was following the contortions of the outer ring streets, he'd run into Mengra, who told him how a bureauer had blown Moohna apart with his weap. Apparently in senile confusion over what happened to Martin, she'd walked up to some strange bureauer and insisted that she was his mother. Naturally he'd taken it as an insult. For some reason, her death took Martin by surprise; in spite of her palsy and her advancing age, she'd seemed so solid, almost eternal, as if she were part of the city itself.

He loved the new room. Over a body length wide and almost twice as long, and it was all his! Pale green paint was still visible in some places on the walls. And it was quiet; though the noises from the road just outside the window opening never really ceased, at least the opening was covered. And he had his own door here too to wake him in time for work in the morning. Martin would sit on his sleeping pad, marveling at a personal room that was larger than the one used by his old unit of twenty-one people. It was hard not to feel that this was the start of his real life, a life with at least some of the magic of the Age of Origin. It might have been much less than the stuff of his childhood dreams, but it was much more than he'd ever really expected he'd have.

Once he tried some of the bureauer juice he found on his doorstep every third or fourth evening. But he found the sensation of losing control of his own mind to the juices unpleasant, and the taste was bitter. More than once, he thought of visiting the old unit, though he knew their familiarity might make them disrespectful or even worse, and he really wouldn't have known how to react.

He grew a bit lonely, he, who'd scarcely ever been really alone in his entire life. At work he would imagine someone else was in the building, though the dust was deep in the corridors and the silence was unbroken. Martin figured that he just wasn't used to so much empty space.

After a week he realized that he really wasn't alone. Someone else was in the building.

Arriving that Threeday morning, he found footprints in the dust outside his office door. They came down the hall from the interior of the building where he had never been; someone had come to the door and then gone back. Martin's heartbeat increased as he gazed off after them. He was about to investigate when the door opened and announced he was on time: the voice of authority reminding him that his job, whatever it may be, was in the office. A folker learned early how deadly any risk of official disapproval could be. He thought about the footprints for the first several hours of that working day.

There were several sets. And, most amazingly, he believed, though he couldn't be absolutely certain, *they were devoid of footwear.* That in itself was both frightening and provocative. He couldn't imagine why anyone would be walking anywhere with naked feet. Even the poorest folker was not so impoverished as to be indecent.

That day, while "working," waiting for the hours to pass, he heard noises, first down the hall, then directly over his head. Briefly he wondered if any of this was an intended part of the job. Everything else about it was so extremely … *unforeseen* that it sometimes made him uncomfortable, though he had always assumed, like the rest of his food unit, that if the bureauers kept jobs for themselves, then jobs must certainly be some sort of luxury.

The pounding started quite suddenly. Someone was hitting the door. *Were they trying to break it?* Since the door registered aggression, the thick glass mirror set itself to resist, turning a cold dark gray. Martin wished it had gone transparent; he couldn't make out even a shadow on the other side. Whatever manner of being was doing the banging was extremely fortunate that Martin wasn't bureauer enough to have any counterattack built into his door, though of course there was no way to tell that by looking at it.

The suddenness and the vehemence of the assault had taken him off guard, and by the time he had gotten to the door and figured out how to clear the panel, the noise had stopped and whoever had been making it had run off. It would have been nice if the controls to the door had been in the desk, but he knew he should probably feel fortunate to have a sensor-door at all.

Eventually the aggression meter on the door fell back within the gray safety level, indicating that Martin could have gone out and that the door would accept orders to admit anyone who approached in a normal temper. Even so, he waited several minutes before he ventured to stick his head out into the corridor. Now there was a stampede of footprints outside. He began to think that the bureauer, Tantor, might have been mistaken about the place being empty. The policers never arrived, though the criers had always left the impression that sensor-doors summoned them automatically.

When Martin left the building that evening, alone and unarmed, the hood of his cloak was up so that he might be mistaken for an older and more experienced bureauer; and he had to control the urge to leap down two or three steps at a time on the stairway. He realized it was only his imagination, but he felt like he was being observed. He didn't relax until he was well out of sight of the building, not wishing to have any truck with a whole barefoot group of anyone who would try to enter a room by assaulting the door.

The next day, Forthday, Brodwich came to the office and

got himself murdered.

He appeared with a banging and a bluster that spoke of the weight of his position and his body long before either could actually be seen. The very floor shook and perhaps Martin did too. The door, which seemed to have developed a speech impediment since yesterday's attack, did recognize the rank and swung open, revealing a quivering mountain of bureauer Big Eater.

Brodwich entered like the moon coming over the horizon, a great polished bulk offering salutations. It was the first time Martin had ever been directly addressed by a Big Eater; as a folker he'd never encountered anyone near that rank. He stood up slowly, self-consciously awkward, bedazzled by the massive chest covered with medals and fine ribbons, by the sheer size of the man. Obviously, this was a creature of power and knowledge. Now Martin would discover what he was supposed to be doing and if he was going to be punished for not having done it so far. He was glad that for once he'd remembered to tie back his hair as he'd been instructed.

The giant's cloak was purple, with gold braid, epaulets, and insignias everywhere, all of them ancient and, actually, a bit threadbare.

"Sit down," he boomed, his voice even louder than his breathing. The stairs had taken their toll. Then looking around and finding only the one chair, he quickly amended himself, "No, I'll sit down. You may stand."

"Thank you, sir," Martin tried, as the Big Eater maneuvered himself clumsily down into Martin's perilously flimsy chair, and unsuccessfully tried to get his feet up on the desk. Twice.

"Name's Brodwich," he announced, in deep, full tones. His stomach growled, sounding just like the heavy noises of the drone aircraft that used to lumber overhead, keeping an eye on the folkers, when Martin was a child. As often as not, they'd sputtered dead and flopped into the streets or clumsily soared out of control against the top floors of some building. Martin had almost forgotten about them.

"Brodwich L.A.C. III 2346-666-6767." The name was repeated as though it were obviously familiar to anyone in the city and therefore laden with significance. "I am your Better, from the Bureau of Knowledge, your immediate Better by direction of..."

He paused. Martin realized that he was still winded, and thought nothing of it.

"Rather, by transmit power command, number..." Brodwich fumbled in his cloak and pulled out a piece of paper which he read. At least he read the numbers, proceeding with great dignity and volume, punctuating his words with tiny gasps, and losing Martin completely in a morass of numbers apparently without either meaning or end. "Well," he demanded suddenly.

Obviously a response was necessary, though Martin had no idea what. He racked his brain for something innocuously appropriate to say. Fortunately, Brodwich wasn't about to wait.

"*REPORT*, I said!" the Big Eater commanded. "There's been no reports from you for three months. When I say, 'report,' you report, or you'll be right back at..."back where you came from." He finished a little lamely, exploring his left ear with a long finely manicured nail on the end of a pudgy little finger, and muttering, "wherever the hell that may be."

"I must report, sir," started Martin, thoroughly intimidated. Now it was *his* breath that wasn't coming easily. "that I have nothing to report...sir...I've only been on the job for three weeks, as assigned...And no one, or nothing, has happened...nothing except..." He was really unsure if he should mention the noises, unsure if they had anything to do with his job or not.

"Very good," interrupted Brodwich, apparently more interested in something he'd discovered in his ear than in what Martin had, or had not, said. "Keep up the good work. But don't you miss any more reports. You understand?"

"Yes, sir," Martin said meekly. Then, to his astonishment, Brodwich groaned mightily and lifted his bulk as if preparing to leave. "Sir?"

"What?" Brodwich demanded sharply.

"I don't know how to report."

That seemed to give the Big Eater pause, but only for a moment. "In the usual way, *obviously!*"

"Your pardon, sir," said Martin, trying hard to sound appropriately obsequious, but having trouble keeping a trace of anger from his voice, "but I don't know the usual way."

It turned out that the usual way was to tell whatever there was to report to the door and then ask for a transcript, which the door would supply in the form of a tiny piece of bumpy metal. The metal transcript was then to be placed, bumpy face down, into a slot in the desk, and a copy would automatically be created somewhere within Brodwich's offices in the Gov-Cent. Martin's Better was extremely careful to stress that the metal must be put in the slot face down.

"Had a man once, who put them in face up. For ten years! All we ever got was blank copies, five to ten blank copies every few weeks, like clockwork."

Martin didn't know what clockwork was. Folkers had night and day, and morning and afternoon vaguely, by position of the sun. Bureauers had doors, or other machines that would call out the time, which was imposed like an absolute on the bureauers' lives. "Like clockwork," was just another expression people rather haphazardly tacked onto certain types of sentences.

Brodwich shook his head in reminiscence. "Luckily, he finally died. Blank reports are hell to file."

"Why on earth…" Martin began forgetting himself until he saw the way Brodwich was eyeing him. "I mean…I just wondered…"

"YOU? *Wondered?*" The bureauer's yell itself was full of wonder. Sarcastic wonder. He didn't sound particularly angry, though. Yelling just seemed to be a habit with him. His stomach growled again, loudly, as if something was trying to get out.

Brodwich got up abruptly and started across the room, passing much too close to Martin, who moved quickly out of the way to keep from being bowled over.

Before leaving, he turned back toward Martin, pointing significantly to one of the patches on his shoulder. On the emblem, words were stitched in a circle around a fat Big Eaterish face. Sticking his finger skyward, as if claiming divine origin for the patch, Brodwich read (or perhaps, Martin suspected, *pretended* to read):

"Questions are for philosophers; *we* do our job."

———————————————————

The terror that seared Martin's brain, soldering his body to the spot, seemed to leap aggressively from a wellspring of horror within the eyes that confronted him, the eyes of Brodwich's killer. He tore himself away from them as a man frees himself finally from the grip of electric shock, and the creature attacked, knocking him to the floor. Fiercely they struggled; sharp claws dug into Martin's skin, tearing his back, rending the flesh of his neck. His eyes, ears, the sides of his head were battered. He could taste blood in his mouth. As much as he fought this demon that was upon his everywhere, he fought panic and the debilitating certainty that his life was about to be viciously snuffed out.

Swinging blindly, he made painful contact, and was amazed when the blow seemed to earn him an instant's respite.

The creature actually gave a bit! He wondered why his earlier punches had been so futile, and realized to his astonishment he couldn't actually remember if he'd thrown any. He lashed out again. And again, at first not believing that the force behind those awful eyes was yielding to his efforts. But the blows raining around his head lessened. And, after long moments, he realized the creature was not invincible, and that he himself wasn't being hurt all that badly. He slugged it again several times, and the fight was over.

And now he was really stunned. Crumbled on the floor like its victim was his monster. A folker. A female folker, and nothing more. Obviously hurt, she gathered herself up into a crouch against the wall opposite him, cornered, terrified. How, he wondered, had she ever managed to turn that fearsome and pompous hulk of Big Eater into an impotent, insensate blob, fit only to supplement somebody's diet? She was so…so puny.

The girl's eyes were blue, a light blue, but one that held no trace of the menace that Martin now believed must have been merely panic at his sudden appearance. They darted quickly, first one way down the hall, then the other, lingering momentarily to her left before returning to Martin's face, as if assessing her chances for escape. This added to Martin's security. After all, he was a bureauer, and she was only a folker. And a folker who was in a lot of trouble, at that.

"Ah…Youah…you," he choked, clearing his throat after the exertion. The near growl startled her, and she cowered back even farther. Her long dark hair shimmered as a sudden flash of lightning outside, momentarily supplementing the weak daylight of the corridor. The hair fell forward, as if trying to shelter in a warm cavern the delicately molded ebony face that he'd just beaten up. One of her front teeth was chipped; he wondered if he'd done it. She looked small and defeated, and Martin felt ridiculous for having been so frightened of her moments before.

Unconsciously he assumed the bluster of the low-level bureauer that he'd heard in one form or another all his life.

"Well," he tried. Then louder and harsher, making the single word a reprimand. "WELL!"

He didn't really know what he was going to do, but he did feel in command. After all, he had the murderer. And a good thing too; with the bureauer death law, if he hadn't nabbed the killer guilt-sure, he'd be marching into the Free-Kill himself before he knew it.

"You know what you've done?" he asked, rhetorically. The girl looked off to her left again, her crouch so extreme she might have been drawing herself inside herself.

"Do you know what you've done?" Again he got no response. "That was Brodwich of the Bureau of Knowledge, one of the most important men in the city. We must report this."

Turning slightly toward the door, he kept one eye riveted on the girl who kept one eye on him, but otherwise still seemed to be trying to disappear into the crack between the wall and the floor.

Martin grabbed her arm, half helping, half forcing her to her feet. He gave the door a shove with his free hand; as close as they were to it, it should have opened for him automatically. It was immobile. He pushed again. Then he banged on it. Still nothing. It was after business hours; the door was closed and locked, securing the office until the next day. But reporting Brodwich's death couldn't wait until the next day.

"Open door. This is Martin 37037-927-8048. Open." The door didn't answer. Instead there was another crack of thunder, and in the silence that followed, he heard rain washing against the building.

"Why don't you open?" he asked in a tone only slightly above a whisper, as if that could prevent the girl standing beside him from overhearing. He was beginning to feel conspicuously foolish.

"Martin," said the door in its matter-of-fact voice, "you're too early. You are not due until 10:30, Twoday, 18th shequence 4,934. You may not be admitted until 9:00, Twoday, 18th shequence 4,934."

"I have to report, door," he said trying to make it an angry command, but more for the benefit of the girl than the door, which was obviously impervious to his moods and desires.

He thought he heard a tittering of laughter behind him, but was afraid to look. It could have been the rain. He no longer felt like an important bureauer, but like a young boy pretending, surprised by an adult in the midst of a make-believe role.

"Open now…" His embarrassment was making his wrath genuine.

"Martin, you are off-duty. Reportsh are to be made only on work time. The work time of Martin 37037-927-8048, shecond grade junior underashishtant poshishion warden, Bureau of Knowledge, 1497, 900, shelected on…"

As the door ran on, the titters behind him became unmistakable. Martin whirled angrily to face his prisoner, to reassert his control. After all, she was a bureauer killer, and a captive one at that. But the laughter erupting through the hole in the tension was without either malice or scorn. And off-set by the premature darkness of the hall, the resigned light in her eyes and in her smile included him in its embrace, recognizing a kinship of impotence they shared against a universe that kept cluttering up their lives with blubbery bodies and disobedient doors. She was evidently relieved to find that the awesome bureauer who had captured her was, after all, neither god nor devil, but as painfully human as his captive.

The day before, Martin wouldn't have been able to imagine

a folker laughing at a bureauer; his first impulse was to try to decide how a real bureauer would act. But he'd been a folker himself for a lot longer than he'd been a bureauer, and, seeing himself as she must see him, as a mighty official, master of the city, unable to control a simple door, he started chuckling too. Their laughter reverberated in the narrow hallway, their voices merging easily in a common sound until it would have been impossible to say who was laughing loudest.

"Some days," the girl quoted, "you can almost walk through the limit, others…"

And that really set them into an orgasm of laughter at the old street saying that ended simply, ". . . others you're lucky if you can walk at all." Even by the paltry standards of the city, this was marginal humor, unusual only in that it didn't seek to wound.

But as if it had a life of its own, the laugh was self perpetuating. When one would manage to stop, their eyes would meet, and they'd both start up together, all over again, like two children nursing a joke when they are supposed to be trying to sleep. Once, Martin pressed his body against the door, as he'd seen Mengra do during the spiel he used to attract customers to his bone display, pantomiming someone trying to pass through the limit. And she thought he was as funny as he did.

Finally the attack had run its course. Now their eyes met and they both looked away quickly, almost embarrassed: the girl lowering her eyes demurely, Martin nervously rubbing his neck. His fingers gingerly traced the deep gashes she had cut in his flesh. And, casually, automatically, he glanced down at her fingernails.

He froze! Her pointed nails were a gleaming black, like pools of oil when they capture the moonlight. And the small finger on her right hand was missing!

"Disciple!" he cried, almost involuntarily.

No longer was this just a murderer; in an instant, she'd become something alien, something intrinsically other. He seized her roughly by the robe. Though taken offguard by his sudden turnabout, she managed to prevent the robe from gaping open. But he didn't need to see the disciple tattoo on her breast to confirm her identity.

Her eyes filled with alarm as rapidly as his had.

Snatching her cloak from his grasp, she leapt away, but Martin got a hold on her arm. Struggling fiercely, she pulled him far enough off balance for him to stumble over one of Brodwich's outflung legs and start to topple. Rather than release her arm and fight for his balance, he clutched at her with his free hand too, and then they were both falling together.

A searing pain flashed through one palm, as if it had been pierced with molten lead. And when he hit the floor, the only thing he was holding in one hand was the other.

By the time he managed to look up, she was rounding the corner, ten or twelve body lengths down the corridor.

He dashed to his feet, not even taking the time to inspect his hand, running after her in the path of the strange footprints. No folker who reached adulthood could ever be said to be slow, but by the time he got to that corner, all he could see was another empty hallway. On either side were rows of closed doors. At the far end, light streamed through a window that was only partially boarded-up. But it was too far away for anyone to have reached it in so short a time.

The majority of the footprints in front of him led to a single door, halfway down the left side of the hall, the next to the last door on that side. Sprinting to it, he grabbed the old fashioned knob, but the door was locked. He went to the next door down, tugged violently on the knob, and flung it open. And then he stopped.

He stared down at the empty room. Oddly, he realized

that he'd been expecting a crowd of people on the other side, as if he'd heard or seen or sensed something just as he'd gone to open the door. He could remember times when, absorbed in his calendar or his artifacts, he might become aware of movement off in a corner of his vision, only to turn and find nothing in sight but himself. The sensation was similar.

He was also surprised to be looking down from a height of about a story. Below was a huge hall, in itself larger than he'd previously imagined this whole section of the building to be. Though apparently totally uninhabited, it was cluttered with broken-down and overturned tables and chairs. A small podium held a few more chairs, and a rather lopsided rostrum leaned against one wall.

It must have been an ancient banquet hall, amazingly preserved unlooted from the Age of Origin. The discovery thrilled him as much as any find he'd ever made. Momentarily it seemed more important than the girl.

The door he'd opened led out onto a small railed landing from which rickety steps descended to the floor. With his eyes, he trailed a single set of footprints to the stairs and down. Then, suddenly, he was in no hurry to follow. Suddenly it was just another old room in a city full of old rooms. And a rather distasteful one at that. He knew his life would be forfeit if he lost the girl, but there seemed to be so many excellent reasons he shouldn't go down those steps. After all, the girl was a disciple, a disciple and a murderer, obviously without respect for rank. Besides, not all of the tracks by any means had entered this particular door. Quite possibly she hadn't even come this way: from the stillness of the room, it did seem that anyone who may ever have entered had long since exited.

Nonetheless he made his way gingerly across the landing and started down the stairs. They floated under his weight like the sections of the old pier down at the River.

Did he detect movement beside one of the tables? A crash rang out; simultaneously, something beneath him seemed to give way, and Martin was tumbling down the staircase.

The edge of each step punished his body individually, forcing the air out of his lungs in grunts. Down stair after stair he spun, each moment expecting to reach the floor of the hall, each moment startled by the butt of yet another step. Through the confusion, his battered senses picked up an impression that hastened to certainty: the staircase ahead had broken off. He was falling into nothingness. Frantically he clutched at the banister as it flashed by his face, and repeatedly, the momentum of the fall wrenched it from his grasp. He went over the end of the stairs and his last desperate grab held.

The abrupt halt jarred one end of the rail that was his lifeline loose from the banister. Dangling from the ominously creaking rail, he turned slowly…slowly…expecting his fall to resume at any moment. He glanced down. Panic surged through his body, the sensory equivalent of the screeching of the nails in the railing, magnified twenty times. He was twirling over an abyss! Twirling so high he could barely make out the floor of the hall that was suddenly far, far below him, with its tables and chairs and tiny, barely moving figures. Martin was higher than he had ever been before. And more frightened! Once he, Mengra, and some of the others had hung a cat from a second-story window. In the air, he thought he recognized the smell of the meat that had been in the poorage that evening.

He tried unsuccessfully to stop the twirling; the rail was pulling itself loose. Gradually, as the floor below him came in and out of view, he became aware of the people. People so far below that their upturned faces were reduced to dots. Illumination from somewhere filled the hall with huge prowling shadows. The room had been barely lit before his fall.

With an abbreviated screech like the death cry of a child crushed under a trash reaper, the rail came loose. Martin plunged toward the floor, his mouth open in a noiseless scream of his own.

2

Gena

Though Gena wouldn't have said she'd had any special powers before becoming a disciple at the age of about twenty, she did recall from childhood a feeling that was almost a taste, a sensation with an extremely unpleasant familiarity that would come to her just before a crazer or a gang of prowlers appeared, or in advance of a party of bureauers out from the Gov-Cent for sport kills, anxious for just the kind of safe prey a solitary little girl would make.

Once, when she was about nine, she'd stumbled upon the room of a food unit that had somehow gotten hold of some loaves of bread. Bread was very rare, and everyone there was absorbed in squabbling over its division. It had been two days since she'd eaten, not long enough for her digestive juices to be immune to the almost compulsive lure of the warm and somehow familiar smell of the bread. Quietly Gena slipped in among the children of the unit, working her way closer and closer to the food. It was a very perilous tactic, especially because Gena was a loner, a folker who was totally unaided in the world and therefore at the mercy of any unit or any gang. A loner might be sexed, she might be eaten, though mostly she'd be left alone. *Entirely.* Only in her earliest memories was Gena not alone, and those memories were avoided; like the aroma of the bread, they could bring nothing but a painful and dangerous hunger.

The little boy right in front of Gena, having crammed both hands full of bread, was finally moving aside when it happened. Outside, over a block away, lost in the city's steady rumble of noise, a folker had crazed out, killed a policer from behind with a brick and seized his weapon. Cutting down prowlers and staggerers, women and children, as randomly as fate, he ran up the street, muttering to himself incoherently, as if in prayer to long-lost gods.

Later, remembering the incident, Gena thought that the taste of danger had been in her mouth then; she had the impression that she'd know the crazer was coming, that she'd *known* he would seek shelter in that one particular building, even that very room, almost before the killer himself became aware that he'd chanced upon that decision, certainly before anyone in the building could have seen or heard anything amiss. Before becoming a disciple, she'd dismissed that part of the recollection as the product of a little girl's imagination.

What she couldn't dismiss was that, although she hadn't wanted to call attention to herself, all of a sudden she'd leaped up and yelled, "Go! Get out! Death!" It was an exclamation more than a warning, like someone, trapped with her unit in a collapsing building, screaming out an alarm, knowing all the while that everyone within earshot was equally aware of their danger and equally helpless, and that the stones falling around their heads were deaf and indifferent.

But the women and children in that room had looked at her as if she were the one who had crazed out. What they saw was not danger, but a loner girl trying to steal some of their precious food. An old crone with one eye tossed a curse at her futilely, distractedly, as one would shoo a pigeon away from the rotting corpse of a dead child. The other women were neither so old nor so resigned, and Gena might have been killed or seriously hurt (which to a folker, especially a loner, were often ultimately the same), but at that moment the crazer plunged into the building, his weapon spewing its own injury and death impartially, scattering the unit in a chaos punctuated by gunshots, the shrieks of children, and cries of pain. The one-eyed crone lost her other eye and her life simultaneously to the first bullet.

Gena managed to get out of there in a hurry. She found a hiding place halfway down the ladder of an open sewer hole, concealed by the smoke from the fires of the units who lived below. She wasn't so far away that she couldn't hear the crazer himself being destroyed. And she wasn't so far away she couldn't hear, right afterward, the cries of "disciple" and "kill the disciple child!" spread through the neighborhood.

For once, everyone seemed to be banding together against the common enemy: nine-year-old Gena. The bread was forgotten or even shared.

Two searching prowlers passed close by the open sewer, discussing what had happened.

"A young disciple it was. Came upon a unit. Wanted their poorage. When they denied her, she set the crazer on them."

The other didn't question how a little girl had set a crazer on anyone. It seemed only natural for someone they considered a disciple to be in league with the other incomprehensible elements in the city.

"Child or no," he said, "cut out the heart and kill the disciple. Do their horror to them so there won't be enough of 'em left to do it to you."

Gena swallowed so much smoke she nearly lost consciousness, but she hadn't been caught. Not only had she frightened others that evening, she'd frightened herself. It wasn't that she was worried about being some kind of a latent disciple. She'd heard about what the disciples believed: that one day Jefuson was going to return to restore paradise to the city, some new Age of Origin when all the buildings would be renewed, when all the junk would work again. In the meantime they apparently figured that Satan was running the world, and they worshipped him accordingly, with all manner of black acts. If they had thought about it, most folkers probably wouldn't have attributed actual supernatural abilities to the disciples (if they did, they wouldn't have admitted it even to themselves), just unknown skills, odd and terrifying practices, and an unqualified strangeness.

Gena knew she was no disciple; but she was afraid of believing in whatever it was she seemed to have sensed that evening. Life was hard enough living in the same world as everyone else: everyone else that was sane, at least. The streets of the city were filled with men who talked to invisible friends and argued with enemies that no one else could hear. Glassy-eyed men with cadaverous faces already proclaimed themselves to be Jefuson to any who would listen, which was not many. To folkers, the world should consist of what they could taste and touch; it should be run by the government, by the everpresent bureauer. There was no place for mysterious gods, except perhaps as something from the dead and distant past. Jefuson, himself, was regarded for the most part more as a hero (the supposed founder of the city) than a god. Disciples, religion, crazers, and strange tastes and powers were all of a piece to them. All were different and that was enough. Everyday, people were destroyed for far less: if not in the Free-Kill, in the streets by the folkers themselves.

In the eleven years between that incident and the time when she actually became a novice disciple, Gena had forgotten about it in the struggle of day-to-day existence. Older, knowing that certain things couldn't be done, she'd realized she probably hadn't done them. She hardly ever thought about the disciples; she certainly didn't think of them as creatures that might have anything in common with her.

Then one day, when fully grown, she'd been searching for food or something she might trade for food. Alone, as usual, she'd wandered down by the River where it flowed from the folker section across the well-cleared no-folker zone toward the distant Gov-Cent that sat in the center of the city like the last ember of yesterday's fire.

Gena was exceptional at catching fish, sometimes spearing them, sometimes grabbing them barehanded. But fish were very rare at best, and she couldn't find any that day.

She went into a building that actually bordered on the prohibited no-folker zone. It was uninhabited; though there weren't nearly enough rooms, folkers did tend to crowd together in the middle of the outer ring, more for the illusion of safety than for anything real. The area by the border was sparsely populated. Gena believed that at one time it might have been more dangerous to live closer to the zone and therefore closer to the bureauers. Now bureauers seemed equally dangerous to folkers anywhere in the outer ring.

Descending to a darkened basement two levels below the ground, she began feeling her way around gingerly, using as her antenna the collapsible metal rod that she'd found a while back next to an old auto. It was long and thin and still shiny; she thought it was an object of great beauty, and usually kept it tied to the inside of her cloak. It was a handy weapon, and she'd found many items for trade in old basements with it. Once she'd even unearthed a large supply of old cans covered with oddly colored pictures which turned out to represent the strange edibles locked inside. After she'd gotten sick a few times, she'd become used to the peculiar tastes and the incredible variety of the stuff. That find had kept her alive and in comfort for a long time.

The rickety structure she was searching that day was particularly unstable. She moved through it as cautiously and as gracefully as possible, careful not to jar any supports or shake loose anything that might cave in on her or block her exit. Instead of being open, like most basements she'd been in, this one was made up of many small rooms, and she roamed through them for a long while in the darkness, getting deeper and deeper into the dusty bowels of the building, farther and farther from the steps that led up to the open air and the comparatively bright light outside.

There was no warning. For one of the very few times in a long and precarious life of twenty years, danger took her by surprise. One moment, all was fine; the next, the world ignited and the ceiling, and presumably the building above her, were in flames. The basement filled with unbreathable smoke, so dense that, in spite of the fire, it was darker now than before. Sticking the rod back inside her cloak, she dashed from the room she was in, scarcely more than a cinderblock cubicle, scraping herself roughly against the doorway as she leapt to the next room, closer, she hoped, to the exit.

But there the smoke was even thicker, if that was possible. She heard a heavy crackling from behind the dark clouds, and then the slam of the door as it shut behind her. Blinded by the smoke, she turned and threw herself against the door, panting, sweat pouring from her body. It was metal and unyielding; even as she touched it, it was heating up painfully against her palms. She backed away. The room she was trapped in now seemed solid fire: what had been smoke a second before was now blinding flame. This was a totally new terror. Fires of this magnitude were unknown. There was little left to burn.

"*What is burning?*" thought Gena out loud, though it was obvious that everything was. Her lungs were seared from trying to breathe scalding fire, as if the air itself were ablaze. The bottom of her cloak began to flare up, kindling for her legs. As she fell to her knees, she realized the struggle was at an end. She was going to die. No more suffering the abuses of prowlers, or the chill of winter, or the unending torment of the constant and usually futile quest for food. The smell of her own flesh cooking filled her nostrils as she tried to tell herself that she might as well lie down and embrace this flaming lover. For just one moment; then she would be past all conflict and pain. Once again, she remembered the patronizing voice of a doddering old bureauer, explaining to her why the government issued no fare-well coups to groups of less than three: "If there's no one who might cause trouble when you die, there's really no reason to keep you alive, is there?" She felt her eyebrows and the hair on her head singeing. Her eyes were scorched and dry, but a great wrenching noise from above her head made her peer upward. She could barely make out the flames devouring the beam that came crashing down toward her head. The unchanging succession of horrible days was finally over. *This is it,* she thought. Then, *no, no! NO!!!* On her hands and knees, at the last second she tried to fling herself out of the path.

When she awoke, she was outside, face down, shivering on the ground. Though momentarily disoriented, an unfamiliar sensation for a woman who had awakened in a different place almost every morning of her life, she knew, perhaps by some quality of the blackness, that it was getting on toward dawn. She wanted to get up off the ground; a folker who slept into the day might never wake to see it. But it was so much easier just to lie there. She heard something above her, close, and turned to find herself face to face with a group of about six disciples.

As she jumped to her feet, they were upon her. She wrestled fiercely; their efforts to subdue her seemed restrained. The old man who led them kept telling Gena that they were her friends, even after she'd kicked him between the legs. But she was still bone weary. She was taken prisoner, her hands securely tied with thick black cords.

Rumor had it that once bound by the rope of the disciples, one belonged to them forever. Gena had heard this often enough, but it never crossed her mind that she wouldn't be free again. If she stayed alive. The leader, still partially doubled up so that the medallion on the gold chain around his neck dangled freely like a pendulum, addressed her as "Bride of the Jefuson." She laughed.

They took her down a series of roads and alleys, most of them familiar, constantly turning to avoid dead-ending into some trash heap or pile of rubble. People who saw the group approaching backtracked down a side street, dashed into the first convenient building, or, if that was impossible, huddled terrified in some doorway. A couple of the more brazen prowlers passed them, breaths held, desperately pretending that they never noticed a band of disciples leading a beautiful prisoner into the minimal daylight by the rope of night.

But though many of the sleeping bodies they passed were starting to stir, they really didn't encounter that many people up and about. Silently, they walked a long but unnecessarily roundabout way that never really took them too far from where they'd started; and they always stayed fairly close to the inner circumference of the folker ring. As she walked, Gena fell in with the tired cadence of the disciples. And gradually she began to be aware of a voice, no, many voices chanting in perfect unison:

In the beginning, the primeval darkness of Satan was upon the face of the land, enslaving the body to hunger, the spirit to ignorance. And the days of man were spent in deadly combat over morsels of food, and over the differing lies that Satan whispered to the differing cities; lies which wore the face of truth. Then Jefus, the father, descended unto earth, bringing the Salvation: loaves and fishes to feed the multitude; and, in the Book, an alternative to the Darkness. Thus did men have a path to follow toward the Light, and the time to follow it. Jefus gave man choice, and declared him accountable for what he chose. So man crucified Jefus.

Crucifixion. Gena knew what crucifixion was: all manner of death was used in the Free-Kill to give variety to the sport. But now the word "crucified" reverberated within her, filling her inexplicably with a sense of sadness and loss, and jarring loose a tiny fragment of an ancient memory. Blood. Pain. Four folkers hanging on crude crosses, one of them a woman with intimate blue eyes, linked to a chain of other unexplored childhood memories. Hearing a scream in her head, and stifling one on her lips, Gena wrenched herself away from the vision.

They walked on in silence. The words she'd heard remained with her. She'd never heard of this Jefus. Or this beginning: folkers generally assumed that everything began with the construction of the city in the Age of Origin.

After a long while, the leader of the group gave a hand signal and they turned into a doorless building and descended a flight of concrete steps. At the bottom was a broad ramp, sloping up and back out again to the city. Parked on the ramp was an ornate black carriage with huge wheels and scarlet fittings, drawn by four pitch-black horses.

The horses were the biggest and the healthiest-looking animals Gena had ever seen. She had the urge to stroke them, to rub her hands over their sleek coats. She hadn't known the disciples were so wealthy. Who had food to feed such beasts? Enough food that they could afford not to eat them. The few cows maintained for the benefit of Big Eaters never made it to maturity.

Though the doors of the coach were closed and the blinds drawn, the disciples tied a thick cloth around Gena's eyes before they hustled her inside. Like the rope, it was a satiny black. Since it was common knowledge that disciples seldom traveled by day, Gena half-expected to be waiting there till nightfall and was surprised when they galloped off almost immediately. The carriage stopped and started many times during the long ride; Gena wouldn't have thought it possible for such a vehicle to journey the disintegrating roads of the city at all.

It was much later when the coach stopped for good. She was taken out, still blindfolded, but she got the impression, perhaps from the way the voices and footfalls echoed off endlessly, that she was inside a mighty building. She imagined a fortresslike structure, although she knew there was nothing like that anywhere in the city she'd spent her life exploring. And there was no place else even for disciples to go.

They took her for another long walk: up and down long staircases that she maneuvered fairly well; through passageways so narrow they moved in single file and she bumped first against one side and then against the other; through drafty rooms and well-heated ones. Once, briefly, they went outside. Crossing a wooden bridge or ramp, she could hear a torrent of water racing beneath her, certainly much faster than the plodding River. And strange animal howls rode the air. A ponderous clanking signaled a gate closing behind them, and the group was once again inside. They walked through the rest of the day, until eventually she was given the single verbal command "Sit," accompanied by an almost gentle downward pressure on both her shoulders. She sat on a great yielding softness. Her hands were untied, but then her shoes were removed! Voices and footsteps receded in the distance, a door clicked shut, and she knew she was alone.

When she removed the blindfold, she found herself in the most, and actually the only, beautiful room she'd ever been in. A thick white rug covered the floor. The ceiling was white as well, as were the walls themselves, though three of them were hung with vividly colored tapestries, and a large mirror almost filled the fourth, barely leaving space for two doors, one on either side. Gena dashed for the doors. The first, as expected, was locked fast. She pushed open the other and found a windowless, but well-lit, little nook. Inside were more mirrors. Giving herself a friendly little smile, she noticed with no concern that she'd broken a front tooth. There was also a large box-like thing with its own door and some knobs inside; a closet; and what she recognized as a flush box. The last she unhesitatingly used, though she'd never actually seen one before. She didn't attempt to flush it; one of the disciples' most infamous practices was the squandering of organic materials. Supposedly they didn't even eat their dead.

The overstuffed bed, with its scarlet furlike covering and matching pillows, proved much too soft for comfort. She fell asleep on the floor.

AND THE LIGHT SHINETH IN DARKNESS AND THE DARKNESS COMPREHENDED IT NOT!…Jefus knew that if man had choice he would often choose evil, Satan. He offered himself up to make choice possible, so that someday man might choose good freely.

After the crucifixion of Jefus came the Dark Ages. Satan ruled, King of men and rightfully so, for man had selected him deliberately. Man got what he deserved. But Jefus is merciful. The Book was left to show the way to the self-discipline, the responsibility, and the love, necessary to prepare for freedom from Satan's slavery. And then, eventually, Jefus sent unto us his only begotten son, the Jefuson of god, to lead the Revolution '76. To

*give men the freedom to exercise the choice Jefus had shown us.
And to give us the Scroll to guide us within that freedom. Thus the
Jefuson is the Law-Breaker and the Law-Giver. And after the
Revolution came that great time of light that we now call the Age
of Origin. Jefuson was to be our model. He would help us to rule
until we were enough like him to rule ourselves. The world was
made new and clean, prosperous and open. The city was built, with
all its warmth and comforts and riches. Not only food grew freely,
but ideas. In this radiant age, truth could be tested against lie.
Openly, leisurely. Man could see for himself which was soundly
structured and secure, and which was riddled with holes the sun
exposed. Holes which would have betrayed them to the wind and
the cold. And each man could be what he would: folker, bureauer,
disciple, anything. And none were Free-Killed for it.*

"I see," said Gena as she woke up, alone and puzzled,
unsure if someone had been speaking to her or if she'd been
dreaming. But unlike any dream she'd ever had, the words
remained with her, clear and complete, though the story they
told seemed as full of holes as any room in the city. Eventually
she fell back to sleep.

The next day (or what she assumed was the next day, since
the artificial light of her chamber never varied), she was startled awake by a white-robed figure standing over her, watching.
The figure, a woman, merely bowed once respectfully, left a
tray of warm food and a thick, cold drink of something that
wasn't water, and exited. Gena raced to the door, but naturally
it had been locked when the woman left. A second quick
inspection of the quarters confirmed there was no other way out.

After escape, her first interest was in the food. The disciples had either forgotten or neglected to feed her the day
before, but then a folker is used to eating whenever he or she
has the opportunity; hunger is too frequent a companion

to be a factor.

She discovered that the box in the mirrored room would rain colored water when she turned the knobs, and that every robe in the closet was pure white and of a single material! No folker had clothing like that, only bureauers. *And disciples,* she added mentally. And some of the things were so finely made and so silky that she had to believe they were nicer than any bureauer's cloak that she had ever seen. Of course she hadn't been in the habit of hobnobbing with Big Eaters. She did know that she'd never seen anyone wearing anything that could really be called white.

She sprayed herself all over with the shower. It tingled and made her giggle, and she thought it much more fun than the River, like a private warm summer rain. She dried herself with soft white towels that were considerably darker after she was finished. She tossed them in a messy heap in a corner with her old cloak. All this whiteness the disciples had surrounded her with had seemed somehow contrived, even fraudulent; it was satisfying to add a little dirt to the environment.

Then she tried on several of the robes. They all fit perfectly. A puzzle, but a reassurance; since the disciples had provided more clothing for her than the average folker used in an entire lifetime, apparently they weren't planning on doing her in. At least not yet.

She noticed that all three tapestries on the walls depicted on the same young man. In one, he was with a woman whose skin was a richer ebony than her own. Gena wondered if she were pret- tier than the woman. Inspecting herself in the mirror, she pushed her hair from her face, tucking it behind her ears. She liked her hair, full, black, and shiny, but her face seemed small to her, and all angles. Still, her eyes were very wide, and her smile, soft and white against her skin, gave her face a beauty she thought it lacked in repose. Her self-assessment was almost impersonal, part of evaluating her position, with little vanity. Good looks were no blessing to a folker female.

When lunch came, Gena was lying down, this time on the bed. The white-robed woman entered, leaving the door ajar, and glided over to her. "How do you like the Castle, Bride?" she asked as she bent down to leave the tray. In a rapid and unbroken motion, Gena reared up and clubbed her on the back of the neck, knocking the women down and scattering food and dishes all over the floor. Darting for the door, she watched it closing with an agonizing slowness: just fast enough to shut and lock as her hand made contact with it. It didn't look like a sensor-door, but it certainly worked like one and, though she'd only encountered a few, that was enough to know that no matter how fast she moved the door would register her and secure itself even faster. She stepped over the prostrate figure on the floor and sat down on the bed heavily in frustration. She was going to be here for a while.

A few minutes later, the door opened and a group of disciples came in. Three of them, the ones in white, picked up the unconscious girl and the food while the remainder of the group, black-robed, surrounded Gena on the bed. They did their work efficiently and left without a word. The spilled lunch was not replaced. And when Gena carefully examined the floor under the bed, hoping they had missed even a trace of food, she was disappointed.

After a couple of days, Gena decided to stop overtly fighting her captors. Her quarters in the Castle were warm, the garments were comfortable, and the white-robed disciples treated her with deference. She even got used to the bare feet: apparently no one wore shoes in the Castle. And the food was easily the best she had ever eaten.

For so many years, her diet had consisted of little more than rats, poorage, pigeons, and even garbage: earned, found,

or stolen. And at first, like the canned stuff she'd found years
before, the rich real-food her captors brought her had as often
as not made her sick. But as soon as she got accustomed to it,
she found it plentiful, delicious, and regular. She doubted that
all the disciples ate this well. Since they stole all their food, they
must have to take what they could get. Perhaps they had somehow gotten into the stores of goods from the Age that the
bureauers supposedly had.

So Gena adopted a wait-and-see attitude and even post-
poned any thoughts about escape. A lifetime of enduring
almost every imaginable form of human cruelty and indiffer-
ence kept her from dropping her suspicions of the disciples and
their motives, but being fed and waited on was better than constantly struggling for just enough food to keep her hunger
alive. The horror with which the folkers had always spoken of
the disciples didn't particularly frighten her; her day-to-day life
since childhood would be horror enough to most of them. And
if, in time, the evil intentions of the disciples were revealed, that
would be the time to deal with them. In the only world to
which she might escape, the evil intentions of others were a
constant anyway.

Sometimes she thought she was even getting used to the
voice. (Actually it seemed to be several voices speaking as one.)
It came at night when she was asleep, but it also came during
the day. Often, for no reason at all, Gena would find herself
staring at a picture on the wall or her own face in the mirror or
the ceiling, and slipping into a haze, inside of which the voice
would come. Each speech was repeated just once.

*And even after the Jefuson came, men were still not ready
for freedom. Soon each man thought himself too good for the
boundaries of the Scroll, each would be his own god. They killed
the Jefuson too, thinking to make themselves more free. Then individual men used their freedom to once again enslave other men.*

Having a share wasn't enough. Each grabbed not for what he could use, but for what he could get. Those that got the most destroyed the world outside the city, in order to "keep out what must be kept out" And "what must be kept out" were men and ideas which might disrupt their greed. That was their only idea of evil.

So ended the Age of Origin. The waters covered the face of the land. Men had isolated the city, thinking they could keep Satan out. They turned to find that they had stranded themselves inside with him. Satan reclaimed the earth.

But the afternoon hazes became lighter and lighter. The voice, more and more a part of the waking world, seemed to have fewer and fewer speakers within it, and the language became more and more conversational, until finally it was almost as if someone were talking to her from just beyond a thin wall. The words, however, always remained with her indelibly.

So far Gena's only physical contact with her captors occurred when meals were brought to her, twice a day, by one or another of the white-robed female attendants, the Bride's Maids, as they were called. Extremely respectful, they might say a few words to her, never much. So she began asking questions to test their deference. Except for rare intimacies, when people might be on what was called "questioning terms," questioning an equal in the city could often be considered insulting; questioning a superior, grossly insolent. Her attempted interrogation flustered them, but of course they never answered. They just looked alarmed and either kept quiet or, if she really pressed the point, merely said, "It shall be revealed," or "Kreeops knows."

Then one day a knock came at the door. The attendants always knocked now. When they had first started, Gena hadn't understood the significance. It wasn't a folker practice; besides, she'd never had a door.

"Enter," she called expectantly, glad that, since it wasn't mealtime, this meant at least some break in the routine. The penned-in days had grown dull.

The robes of the old man who opened the door were like the standard hooded cloak worn by everyone in the city, only red and of a satiny material like the very best of those in Gena's closet. She recognized him as the leader of the gang that had captured her. The same golden medallion swung from his neck as he approached, his frame still stooping slightly forward as if bent to accommodate a weight far greater than any medallion would ever be. One bony hand was adorned by a red-stoned ring, and under one arm he carried a worn-looking black book and a rolled-up piece of paper. In the other hand he carried a bowl. Its contents were spilling over onto the rug. Weathered and furrowed, his bearded face seemed very old to Gena, but it was not the decrepit age of the folker. His rapid gray eyes were vital and alert; his visible teeth, intact though yellowed. He was smiling nervously; Gena noted a self-conscious quivering at the corners of his mouth.

"Greetings, Bride," he said formally, but she could see that he wanted to sound friendly at the same time. "I am Zaletus. Son of Ashram, son of Zaletus. High Priest, Guardian of the faith. As were they."

He thrust the bowl at her awkwardly. Gena just looked at him. He smiled again, a little more anxiously than before. His eyes darted across the room, resting momentarily on her face and moving off again, like a timid animal. He motioned for her to take the bowl.

"Kreeops has his private guard. You have your Bride's Maids. But I am not too proud to serve."

"Though you have nothing." It was obvious from his speech.

"I have my son."

Later Gena was to find out that even that was probably not his own child. The disciples preferred not to waste their energies on procreation, which explained why they appropriated most of their children the same way they appropriated their food, confirming the total hostility of folkers and bureauers alike.

"My office is hereditary," he said in a less formal tone. "We learn the sacred words. And pass them down. Father to son. The words from the Scroll, and the words from the Book." As he gestured awkwardly with the book he was carrying, she noted that, like all disciples, he was missing the little finger on his right hand.

Gena watched his black fingernails scratching fretfully against the cover of the book and tried to imagine why this important-looking man would be so flustered by talking to a loner folker girl. He hadn't come down there to tell her this dung about his father teaching him his job, she was sure. She wondered if he expected her to kick him again.

"Let me explain," he tried again. "I'm sure before you came to us you'd heard all manner of refuse about the Church of the Jefuson."

She looked at him blankly.

"The disciples," he explained, with obvious distaste for the name.

"Oh...Well, I've heard a few things that disciples do," she said as noncommittally as possible.

"The Church of the *Jefuson*," he said, stressing the name and gesturing to the rhythm of the syllables at the man depicted on the tapestries, "waits. And works. Works for the return of the Jefuson of God, the Jefuson of man. In these new Dark Ages, we study obedience and faith in a world where love and freedom are impossible. We learn to subordinate our very selves to the necessary and rightful Power of Satan, as men before us, in their error, refused to subordinate themselves to rectitude. The Will of Satan is expressed on Earth by His Regent, Kreeops. We are mere extensions of that Will. Individual willfulness and pride brought ruin upon us; so now we seek to root them out: to make ourselves worthy of freedom, to make ourselves ready for the more perfect union we've been promised when the time comes for the Jefuson to return and lead us to the New Age of Light. Then, finally, disciples, folkers, and bureauers shall walk the land together, equal and truly free."

"You worship evil to bring good to the world," Gena injected skeptically the moment he paused. No doubt he was sincere, but his words had a glibness that gave his speech an air of recitation.

"No. Only the Jefuson will decide when the time is ripe to come among us again. Until then we accept the discipline — the punishment, if you will," he lowered his voice and glanced upward, as if afraid Satan might be listening, "of living under the Dark One. A punishment that is, as I have said, necessary. And one that is also just. Twice man has murdered Beneficence."

Refuse! Gena thought to herself. Immediately, the thought was answered by a voice in her own head: *There is more to the city than you understand, little folker.* Though loud, the words were rather gentle, but Gena jerked upright as if she'd been struck. She looked quickly over at Zaletus, who was smiling in friendly amusement. The words had been his, of course; the voice, that of the central speaker from the nocturnal chants and afternoon hazes.

Disciples do have their powers, the voice came again, even gentler this time. *But so do you, Bride of Jefuson. Don't you?*

Bride of Jefuson? she repeated to herself, on the verge of speech. Zaletus answered verbally the question she didn't have the chance to ask.

"The Bride of Jefuson. The Expectant One. She's waited since last He walked the city. Though her form varies, her spirit is constant. She is with us in every generation. Sitting at the side of the Regent. Mother of the flock, she lends her strength to the coven; she helps focus its faith. She is the ambassador of the Light to the Court of Darkness, waiting to introduce her children to their Father."

ME? What a pile...But once again her thoughts were interrupted by his words. Zaletus' tone was once again animated, his gestures excited.

"For almost twenty years, since the death of Mari-tum in the second year of the reign of Kreeops, we have had no Bride. It's been 10 years since I've even submitted a candidate for Kreeops to examine." While he was remembering she sensed something within him.

"You thought he wanted no rival for power," she said. A guess perhaps, but not quite.

This time it was Zaletus who started. Then he smiled warmly again, transparently delighted. "Your power is strong. As yet untamed, but strong. Yes, you are correct. All too often, the Bride had been less a representative of goodness than an adjunct, even a subordinate, of the Regent. This was especially true under Mari-tum, who was old and rather weak. As Regent, Kreeops, or rather Satan through him, is the mind of the congregation. For now, this is as it must be. But the Bride must never forget that she is...the Expectant One. Her ultimate master is the Jefuson." He stopped, and when almost immediately he began again, his tone was lower, less stilted. It was as if the momentum of his speech kept the thoughts coming out his mouth past the intended conclusion.

"Kreeops, or rather all of us...Kreeops, myself, the flock, we tend to lose sight of the idea that we should be perfecting our servitude only so eventually we might know emancipation."

His voice seemed tired, suddenly flooded with regret. Gena could feel the confinement of the small room as it seemed to fill with Zaletus' muggy fear of his leader. She realized that in this brief time she'd been with the priest, she'd unconsciously begun receiving rudimentary perceptions in some new way. Yet it didn't feel strange. She thought of a blind man suddenly becoming aware that he was registering light: instantly it occurred to Gena how disappointed that person would be if he could ever really see the squalor of the city, how he might long to return to blindness and ignorance and imagination.

"But it *was* Kreeops who found you — " he said. " Kreeops who revealed you to us as the latest incarnation of the Bride, 'The one mortal who is immortal.' A mystery," he explained, anticipating her, rather than reading her mind, which had dismissed the assertion as silly. "Though we cannot actually read the Book and the Scroll perhaps, we have their words."

He tapped the side of his head with a long, tapered disciple fingernail, and, with just a trace of an old man's pride, continued, "From father to son, the High Priest stores the Jefuson's words. To teach the chants to the coven, to keep the faith pure, to…"

"Kreeops must have been looking for someone else," interrupted Gena. She had little interest in the priest's faith except insofar as it intersected with her life, hauling her off bodily, locking her up in cubicles, mating her with imaginary gods. Still, she looked at the figure on the tapestry with new interest. She'd never seen a picture of Jefuson before.

"Kreeops led us to you. At his direction we drove around the city that night, searching. Finally he ordered the coach to halt. He slipped into a deep meditation. When he came out of it, he said simply, 'It is she.' I got the impression you had already passed a test. Then we went to you."

She must have looked puzzled. Zaletus had given the

orders when she'd been captured. The rest of the party had seemed practically devoid of personality.

"I don't remember him," she said out loud.

"He stayed in the carriage and directed us, directed me by silent speech, the speech of thought. Flawlessly, effortlessly he led me through the devious paths of the physical world to the very spot where you lay, waiting for your call...for your consummation."

Remembering the fire, Gena realized with some surprise that she hadn't thought of it since her capture. Suddenly she ran from the bed into the little room with the mirrors. Checking herself in the glass, she confirmed what she already knew: there was no trace of the ordeal in the basement upon her! Not the slightest burn, even around her ankles where she remembered her cloak igniting. Not a singed hair, and there never had been.

"We will train you as a disciple. To bring you to your full glory," called Zaletus from the other room, trying, she guessed, to sound reassuring. Automatically she glanced to the corner where she'd thrown her old folker's cloak, though she knew it had been disposed of long before.

"Perhaps you will be the Bride who sees the coming," Zaletus coaxed, and again she considered just how little she cared about his gods and their comings and goings.

"Perhaps," she answered, stroking her unscorched eyebrows pensively. "But I wonder how anxious your friend Kreeops and his friend Satan are for that new Age of yours."

In the silence that followed, Gena was too absorbed in her own thoughts to try to guess the old man's. A tingling at the edge of her consciousness might have revealed to a real disciple his attempt to read her, but, preoccupied, her mind shrugged him off as she might flick away an insect, without even registering the action. Equally unnoticed was his happiness over his unexpected failure.

So she had become a novice disciple. It was easier than being on the street. At first she was tutored individually like royalty. After a while, she participated in classes with other novices, but even there Zaletus and his assistants never quite lost sight of the fact that they were training one who would be their better. Not that assignments were less stringent for her than for the others; if anything, they were even more difficult, more intense. More was expected of Gena, and the other novices, having been raised in the coven, had a huge head start. But the worst punishment Gena ever received for failure was a patient but tedious repetition of the lesson. Others were beaten publicly, or more often they might be removed from the group for a day or two. On return they moved with great pain and humiliation. The slowest novices just vanished, along with anyone who lacked understanding of what, in contrast to what Zaletus had emphasized, seemed to be the cardinal truth:

"Satan is the source of all power; on Earth, Kreeops is his outlet."

In one form or another, Gena's indoctrination was virtually constant. From the moment she awoke, she was taught orally and by the voice of silent speech, and the latter continued even while she slept. She learned theology and ritual, chants, a lot of meditations, and a large amount about the power and glory of Kreeops.

The disciples believed that they were all united under the Regent, and that he could see, hear, and act through any of them wherever they went. She learned that the only salvation offered by Kreeops, the only salvation the disciples believed in, short of the nebulous coming of the Jefuson, was the oblivion of a natural death. That was the honorable completion of a life of self-effacement and devotion to the Regent. Then their corpse would be taken from the Castle in the night and hidden in the ground, all its labors over. Those who for any reason incurred Kreeops' wrath would be denied this salvation. The death they found was immediate, in the bottomless pit, or being roasted alive on a pyre. It was believed their souls were absorbed into the spiritual body of Satan and enslaved for eternity.

To Gena, this was just a careless waste of edible meat. In the rest of the city, while it was forbidden to kill for food, the deceased became a source of valuable protein. The disciples, however, actually boasted of their refusal to "live off filth and decay."

Time passed quickly, or, more accurately, time distorted. Days and nights often blended together, then oddly, there were gaps, as if hours or sometimes whole days had disappeared.

She was an apt pupil, though a little slow at memorizing responses. At first she believed most of what she was taught was just superstition mixed with a few tricks and ominous-sounding spells for frightening folkers. Some of the "truths" she learned about Kreeops, and about his powers and his cere-monies, and even about territories that he supposedly con-trolled, seemed more than a little far-fetched, though no one else seemed to think so and she soon learned not to comment on it.

Still, the silent speech was genuine. And it came easily to Gena. The listening now seemed automatic, and the projecting was not difficult. A good deal of learning the art was simply dis-covering how to regulate what you projected so that too much didn't come across, garbling the message or revealing some-thing besides what you intended to reveal. After three days, no one around her could read Gena's thoughts unless she chose to let them. Yet in spite of her aptitude, she found herself holding back. She wasn't sure why; she guessed she might be afraid of proving to the disciples, or perhaps to herself, that they were right, that she really was like them. More than once she repeated to herself that, as a disciple, she was merely a conduit, she might be anyone; the real power, the will and the deed, actually did belong to Kreeops.

Then too the silent speech (and some of the chants and meditations) tired her and somehow made the world seem less stable. Once or twice, she'd became dizzy during a lesson; at times, she half-expected the walls to start moving. Despite her indoctrination, Gena was still part of the mundane world of the streets: a world of garbage and brick, where reality was something you could grab, bite, burn, or kick out of your way, where thoughts didn't fly, and the dull light that accosted your eyes was the same dingy light that shone on every other sane eye in the city. Shit, she'd had enough trouble just getting used to the bare feet.

She started seeking out the other novices more and more. For the first time in her life, she had people to talk to regularly, and she did, spending hours in conversation, both orally and through silent speech. Although virtually all the others talked about was their lessons, their company could be distracting, and their certainties were reassuring, even if Gena disregarded most of those. She discovered that, even orally, she herself possessed an unexpected facility of expression that she was at a loss to explain, unless it had come from talking to herself.

All this time she never saw the Regent, though she had dreams she associated with him that she could never quite remember. And she began to lose larger periods of time from her memory, especially those hours right before the dreams.

Late one morning, she awoke in her room with a feeling of nausea and profound terror. Her last recollection was of practicing a series of mid-afternoon chants with several other novices someplace deep in the bowels of the Castle. Unless she was mistaken, that had taken place at least one and perhaps two or three days earlier. Uneasily, she got up, dressed, and made her way to the chamber where the rest of the female novices lived. Talking to some of the ones she'd been with, she made a remark or two about the events of the afternoon before. From their responses, it was clear that they had no more of an idea of what had happened than Gena did, but when she brought this to their attention, she couldn't make them understand why she was so concerned. "As long as Kreeops knows…"seemed to be the general attitude.

Later, disturbed and deliberately rude, she put the question directly to Zaletus. She hadn't expected it, but his answer was also direct. At least for Zaletus it was direct.

"Ceremonies of Education, Bride. You and several other of the most advanced novices…yesterday and before. Through the power of Kreeops, the coven has been taking hold of your mind in these special ceremonies, and showing you what it is to be a disciple, to be one with the coven in faith. You've been very responsive; you're learning rapidly."

"*Learning?* I remember nothing," she said, frightened that she could have been functioning without recollection. She'd rather believe that she'd been drugged or even spelled. It occurred to her that he might be lying, but immediately she doubted it. She knew just how devout Zaletus was in his religion, and, oddly, that gave her a certain faith in him. *Oddly,* she mused, because the religion amounted to devil worship.

"What happens?" she asked.

"If it was something that could be explained, you probably would have remembered it." He answered verbally, though silent speech with its subtle shadings of feeling, meaning, and emphasis was usually preferable for communicating sophisticated and unfamiliar concepts. She probed for a reading of his mind, but as was usually the case, she wasn't very successful, receiving only an incomprehensible jumble of faded colors and worn-out sensations. He took her hand almost consolingly. She must have looked confused; when she wasn't projecting, he couldn't read her anymore either, not unless her thoughts were particularly uncontrolled, or if they were startled from her like a mental ejaculation.

"Patience, Bride. It's all new to you. If a man looked upon the face of God for an instant, maybe he wouldn't see Everything; maybe because Everything was there, he would see nothing." Barely pausing for breath, he slipped into another approach. "When we're infants, we see the world without understanding, without retaining. We can't possibly sort out the millions of separate sensations involved in just the perception of a single object. Is it hard or soft? How hard? How soft? What tone of which color? Warmth, depth, taste, touch, smell, the shades and degrees of even the simplest perceptions are so rich and so fleeting. But soon we learn to unite some of those sensations in an idea: poorage. After that, we identify the whole experience by a couple of sensations: if it looks and smells like poorage, then poorage it is. The rest can be ignored. A few isolated impressions can be added to the idea: it is rotten poorage. Memory is possible, because it is almost always the idea that one remembers, only rarely the genuine sensation."

"Well, I'm…"

"The ceremonies are introducing you to what it is to be one with the faithful. Ignoring part of *that* experience only serves to lessen the union. And while eventually you will remember the ideas you form about it, that in itself can be less than nothing. You shouldn't be as concerned with remembering as with learning, without the ceremonies, to reach that same communion. And learning to maintain and perfect it. For as that union becomes more perfect, so will your comprehension of the faith. You can't do it on your own, of course, but after you've gone through your ordeal of initiation and have been formally presented to the coven, Kreeops will give you the aid you require."

To Gena, this was gibberish. The memory lapses continued.

For a long while, no matter how Gena steeled herself to keep control beforehand, or how she strained to recollect afterward, all she was able to remember from these gap periods was the same sick feeling, mixed with a growing belief in the omnipotence of Kreeops. No longer did she worry about revealing any hidden disciple potential within her. Not only would any such hypothetical abilities be comparatively infinitesimal, but in any case she was becoming convinced of the absurdity of trying to keep anything from the black all-seeing eyes of Kreeops, even things she might be able to conceal from herself. And this sense of futility, of her own impotence, together with her general lack of motivation and a beginner's reticence about performing under the scrutiny of a master (even a master she had never seen), prevented her from devoting her full concentration to her studies. Much of her attention she gave to her memory, especially as the gaps, though reduced in frequency, seemed to be increasing in duration. Her frustration spurred her to greater effort, which in turn only led to more frustration and still greater exertion. She imagined herself trying to cross unseen barriers that had suddenly sprung up in her own mind. She attempted to force herself to constant attention, hoping for a habitual vigilance that would enable her to penetrate, at least partially, the fog looming ahead. Finally, when she came out of a lapse, some impressions did emerge. But they were very strange, more dream — or rather nightmare — than memory, and Gena had no faith in their accuracy.

She went through an ordeal of initiation. Apparently.

"And that's something you did remember," Zaletus told her a couple of days later. "It was very remarkable. You'd remember it still, but Kreeops bid me to give you something to help you to forget it, as novices normally do. He wanted you to be spared the pain."

But she had a missing little finger to remind her that she was now officially a disciple. The next week she was tattooed with the pentagram. Soon Kreeops was to formally present the Bride of the Jefuson to the coven.

But before that happened, Gena began to sense an indefinite strangeness in the coven. Egocentrically, she dismissed it at first as a collective excitement over the new Bride. There was a feeling of anticipation, almost of awakening, that she would have noticed even if she hadn't learned the art of reading moods. But the anticipation had an edge of fear to it.

And then there were the patrols. Now, patrols of Kreeops' private guard were certainly never a rarity; they were posted throughout the Castle and routinely moved through the city on business. She'd often seen them lined up for distribution of heavy footwear and camouflaging folker cloaks. All at once, however, it seemed like half the coven was out on patrol. She saw one group leaving the Castle, laughing and joking about how they were about to frighten some hapless bureauer out of what little reason he might possess. Then they'd gone off without footwear. The next morning, in the pre-dawn, as Gena was being led to a ritual anointing, she saw another patrol, only this one grimly serious, rushing through the same door. As if in pursuit of someone, she thought. She noticed they were carrying weapons openly: one had an ancient-looking drill that was much too large for concealment. And they too were barefoot.

Though Zaletus had once alluded to the possible planting of suggestions as a weapon against folker and bureauer minds, this was apparently something the coven would pursue in the indefinite future, when Kreeops judged them ready. For now, the survival of disciples out in the city depended for the most part upon their being able to blend in and then blend back out again.

Disciples struck terror into the hearts of the folkers, all right, but if by some chance a patrol was exposed for what they were, that very terror would often result in their being literally pulled to pieces by hysterical mobs. If they were lucky enough to be captured by the policers first, most would live until they could be brought to the Free-Kill, where their deaths would be more ingenious and in all likelihood even more brutal.

Since no folker carried a weapon out openly where the policers could spot it, and since no one went barefoot in the city, this patrol would stand out like piss in the poorage. Gena was puzzled, but she might have forgotten the incident if suddenly an overwrought Zaletus hadn't run up to the patrol, ordering them to halt. There followed a hurried argument in silent speech so well hushed that Gena could decipher little of it. But she was amazed. The disciples, even Kreeops' private guard, did not argue with authority, and Zaletus was the second most powerful man in the coven.

"I demand to know…"she heard him begin, before the noise of the barefoot party's departure covered his opposition.

Gena concluded that someone had escaped, someone important, though she had no knowledge of any prisoners in the Castle. Any *other* prisoner, she added mentally. Excitement welled up inside her. It was unexpected. She'd been allowing herself to believe that she was not only resigned to becoming an important disciple, but that she was actually *happy* about it, considering it all to be a stroke of good fortune.

That very afternoon, the Bride's Maids came to take her to be presented to the coven. It was ten or twelve days earlier than originally planned. For the second time that day, she was bathed and anointed. Then she was dressed in a beautiful white satin robe from the closet. Her face was shaded by a veil of white lace rather than the black hood of the disciple's robe she'd been wearing for the last six months. Strange-smelling herbs were laced into her hair and around her wrists, ankles, and neck. None of the attendants offered any rationale for the schedule change. She knew that they had neither been given, nor would they have expected, any explanation. Kreeops' whim was more absolute than any timetable.

Then four of the Bride's Maids led her out of her room. They turned down a long, close corridor, one she'd never seen before. She was frequently surprised by how often, even after all this time, she found herself wandering in an unfamiliar part of the Castle or being conducted through a new hallway even when she was being led to the same old places.

Bride! she heard in silent speech from a doorway in the shadows of the torch-lit corridor. She turned and Zaletus was beside her. Drawn and looking as if he hadn't slept in several days, he was dressed in his finest ceremonial red with a little red cap perched oddly on the back of his slightly balding head.

Bride! he said again. The idea was tinted with panic. *Kreeops...you are going to Kreeops, Bride. I...I...I think...*

She'd never heard anyone stutter in silent speech before. It usually flowed like thought; it was difficult to make it do otherwise.

Of course I'm going to Kreeops. Who else can present me, she shot at him impatiently. She had no interest in one of his tirades just then.

As the attendants, one on each arm, either not realizing or not caring about their conversation, hustled her down a narrow staircase, the old man lagged behind. All she got was *NO...Kreeops...this is wrong...BLASPHEMY!* The speech limped into her mind as if his very brain were panting for breath.

Then all at once it was as if the High Priest's confusion had spilled out into the world. Gena and her attendants burst into the blazing light of the throne room. It was familiar to Gena, though as far as she could recall this was the first time she had been there. The place was jammed with disciples; a feast seemed to be in progress. With extraordinary strength and more than a touch of brutality, the Bride's Maids forced their way through the still-gathering crowd, escorting her to the far end of the great room and up to a multitiered marble platform at the top level of which sat an immense canopied throne. She was taken up the stairs to a broad area just below the throne. They left her at a waist-high altar of highly polished marble engraved with intricate symbols.

Gena was aware of a very undisciple-like buzzing in the room behind her. Disciples were, above all, disciplined, subject neither to eruptions of emotion nor (their truths being provided and absolute) to the spread of idle rumor. Gena turned to face the crowd. A cheer went up! Calls of "Bride! Bride of Jefuson!" burst into the air with more spontaneity than Gena would even have imagined possible from disciples. Then a flurry of trumpets, apparently from nowhere, reminded them of themselves and the silence was immediate. An explosive flash filled it like sound, and Gena was no longer alone on the platform.

Kreeops! He looked at least twice the height of any normal man. Seeing him, she remembered, as, once it reemerges, one recognizes the forgotten menace in a recurring nightmare. And she saw why she could have never envisioned his image when she wasn't actually in its presence: a presence so incredibly, so fearsomely imminent, as if denser and more massive than the capacity of her senses to register it. Yet the figure seemed to be shimmering, making it hard to tell where the form of Kreeops ended and where the shadows that surrounded him like a dark aura began.

Completely naked, his well-muscled skin actually glowed, as if the skin, like his eyes, was illuminated by a fire from within. His huge craggy face, behind a beard that traced and sharpened his jaw line, appeared potent beyond anything Gena could have imagined. The eyes themselves, piercing, obsidian, and totally encompassing, seemed constant witness to a full spectrum of debasement, injustice, and pain. The thin lips, a glossy red, drawn back over sharp, almost delicate teeth, might have been a wound, but a savored wound. Gena felt herself draining as if her very thoughts were being sucked into the presence. She would have done almost anything to avoid meeting his gaze, though she knew within her that this was the intended effect.

"MY CHILDREN," he said. At least the figure above her moved its lips in sync to the words which seemed to rise from every corner of the cavernous room, words that were full and resonant with just a trace of a tortured scream from the depths of hell. "My children, we have been without a Bride for too long."

He paused and silence rushed into the space left by the sound, preparing them for the next sentence as hunger prepares one for a meal.

So much did every pause, like every gesture, every intonation, every physical line of the Regent's body burst forth with significance, that communication flowed as freely into the rapt coven as air flows into lungs, as impulses travel from brain to heart. Gena, again remembering the scene at other ceremonies, knew it was always thus.

"I have ruled alone too long," the voice continued, coming through their very nerves till their bodies were as full of it as their minds. "Behold, the new Bride."

The muscles in the mighty arm worked and it reached out, stopping only inches above Gena's head. The edge of a glance met her eyes, cutting into her soul. She tore herself away from it, stunned.

"The Bride of Jefuson…AND…"The word hung in the air above their heads like a gigantic bird of prey, then swooped down unfailingly to its helpless target, ". . . AND the Bride of Kreeops!"

A gasp was wrenched from the crowd in silent speech. At the end of his poised arm, Kreeops' hand touched Gena's white robe and it parted almost magically, falling from her shoulders to her feet, leaving Gena exposed before the coven wearing nothing but the veil and the herb rings.

She found herself wondering about balance: which joints and muscles in her legs must be tensed or loosened to support her body. And, as she discovered she no longer knew, she was falling. Caught by the arm, she was lowered onto the altar. *The marriage bed,* she realized recalling a phrase Zaletus once used in another context. Her mind kept repeating to itself that she was supposed to be the Bride of the Jefuson, the Expected One. Kreeops would never dare violate her. The reassurance soon struck her as ridiculous; the monster beside her obviously had even less regard for absent or nonexistent gods than she did. The room had filled with color, swirling in and out of her vision. In her mouth was the taste of danger. Idiotically, she found herself wondering if it were late or if she just hadn't noticed it before. Zaletus' face, first alarmed, then sad, then finally broken, passed in and out of view: moist-eyed, lips half-parted as if, as usual, on the verge of speech. Throughout the visual confusion, she sensed the crowd, frenzied, virtually destroyed by this sudden revision of age-old theology. She heard their wailing as an infant's confusion upon its birth into an alien world. Perhaps only their near-perfect faith in Kreeops' mastery over both the known and the unknown kept them sane.

His voice went on. The voice of reason, the voice of terror, pulsing through Gena's veins instead of her blood, usurping the place of her will within her limbs. Her body felt violated already.

"Too long has the Bride been separated from the Power that rules. If she is the spiritual mother of the faithful, and Satan is the Father, why should they be held apart?"

From far away, almost lost in the background of Gena's confusion, came a distorted though familiar scream, *Heresy!* softly, once, followed by *we must wait.* Gena looked up to see Zaletus at the end of the platform just as he was violently knocked to the floor. No one, nothing, was anywhere near him, and no one but Gena had noticed. She let her eyes close. The effort to keep them open against Kreeops' continuing speech was too great.

"Our enemies are everywhere. Soon we must destroy them, or they will destroy us. We can no longer afford the luxury of letting our strength wither away while we wait for tardy gods. Like all the rest of us, the Bride should and must devote herself fully to Satan's service."

Gena tried to run. Her body would not obey her. When she attempted to reopen her eyes, she thought she saw Zaletus, blood streaked across his face, working to raise his head from where he lay sprawled out as if crushed beneath a great weight.

The shadow of Kreeops was upon her as he moved above. His eyes, huge and black, blazed like fire in the night, only cold. Again, she tore her face away to avoid those eyes.

"I, Kreeops, Regent of Darkness, I take the Bride, the Bride of the Jefuson. I bring us union under Satan."

A touch on her forehead shot icy pain through her nervous system, and the world flared blood-red even through closed eyelids. Her body jerked spasmodically. Gena had the impression she was looking down from above, watching herself being frightened to death. She saw her own whitened face, the screaming mouth stretched past the point of pain, the bulging eyes (she was no longer sure if they were open or closed). Her body was rigid as a corpse; her heart felt like it was pounding itself to death against the cage of her chest. Long, sharp nails left a five-lined trail of blood across her exposed breasts and stomach; one huge finger twisted itself deeply, agonizingly, into her navel. She shrieked. Pain, as if from her core, radiated out in all directions, somehow telling her, plainer than words, of the orgasm of torment that awaited her as his Bride. It was a union for which only death would be the most favorable possible outcome. The hand trailed lower toward her pubic hair. She watched as the beads of sweat mixed with the blood in its wake. His loathsome body bent itself to her, now not much larger than man-size, but somehow even more intense. Its huge member came into view, swollen, pointed, red-tipped as if dipped in death. Gena was immobile with terror. The smile of Kreeops filled the world as he straddled her. She wondered why she didn't faint and guessed he was keeping her conscious.

His flesh seared her, as weight lowered itself upon her, increasing, crushing. Then, suddenly, decreasing, gone. He was off her. Gena waited, not knowing why he had stopped, dreading his next move. But now she was slightly less afraid; her mind was functioning again, if only barely. Tentatively, she opened her eyes a crack. *Had they been closed?* she wondered.

Kreeops was beside her, standing very still as if waiting or perhaps listening, momentarily more a man than a monster. Not even an especially large man, she noted with surprise. His penis, starting to descend somewhat, looked no more menacing than any of a number of prowler organs Gena had been sexed by in her time. She raised herself on one elbow, still shaking, but no longer paralyzed by the fear. Zaletus too, having gotten to one knee, was looking up, watching Kreeops. The priest's head was cocked a bit to one side as if trying to hear what Kreeops was hearing. The disciples at the tables and in the aisles were still rapt, but more like spectators at a Free-Kill than the mesmerized and willless slaves they'd been seconds before.

It was Zaletus who broke the silence, speaking the words that both he and the Regent had heard in silent speech. It was the confirming report of a patrol. A patrol that was so excited when it made its report that the priest had intercepted what was intended for Kreeops' ears alone.

"It is," he said quietly, almost to himself, more visibly shaken by this than by the attack he'd suffered earlier. Then, louder, "Jefuson!" And still louder again, proclaiming to the coven in awed triumph what he hadn't dared to hope. "The Jefuson has been found! The New Age is upon us!"

In the chaos that followed, Gena barely had the presence of mind to make her way to the guard room and find a folker cloak and a pair of sandals before fleeing through the exit she'd seen the patrols using when they were heading out to the city. Still dazed, she was moving by instinct, and even as she ran, her mind seemed to fill once again with vivid images of the monster behind her. She was oblivious to the passage-way around her, or to anything else but the memory of that face and those eyes, and the thought that he might be coming for her and that she had to hide. And when eventually she ran into Brodwich, and he tried to sex her, it had taken her a moment to realize that he wasn't Kreeops and that she wasn't back in the Castle. Then she killed him with his own sash, frantic lest the delay of his puny sexing should give Kreeops time to recover from the disruption of his plans, time to note her absence.

Dropping herself roughly from the second-story window onto the Big Eater's purple car, she escaped from that other bureauer, the odd one with the hair. She didn't mind the drop; she was only glad the disciples hadn't come up from behind while she was involved with the bureauers and cut off her escape. She blended in easily with the ragged stream of humanity in the street, trying to put as much distance as possible between herself and Kreeops without attracting attention, trying to maneuver her way through the ubiquitous, aimless hordes of folkers as they ambled casually after fireburn or coagulated in rugged groups, or just lay passed out on the pavement. It took a conscious effort to lift her feet from the muddy concrete; she felt as if the earth was trying to suck her into itself. Still, she hadn't been outside the Castle in the whole time she was with the disciples, and the city didn't seem so bad.

As she walked she scanned, mentally searching for signs of pursuit, occasionally stopping completely to do so. The disciples were probably still occupied with him, she figured, remembering with a small laugh of amusement the young bureauer with the gentle brown eyes and the generous smile. *Martin.* She wondered how she could have laughed with him like that, forgetting herself in the midst of headlong flight; she'd felt a safety with him that was totally irrational. He looked so innocent, especially for a bureauer. Still she could see the resemblance and figured that he must have been planted there by his Betters for just that reason. It was sobering to think what short work Kreeops would make of him.

GENA! Gena-gul, come back, broke into her thoughts, chillingly. The speaker was neutral and unfamiliar. *Come back now and it will go easier for you.*

She was still the Bride of the Jefuson, if perhaps the unconsummated Bride of Kreeops too. According to the beliefs of the Church, she was supposed to be the instrument for replacing the Regent when their god showed up. Having seen Kreeops, she wasn't about to let herself get in his way if she could avoid it.

If they could call her, there was a chance they could take a reading and find her. She panicked and broke into a run, becoming the focal point of too many eyes on that cold afternoon in the dying city.

3

Decision

The fall had stunned Martin badly, but he remembered being completely wrapped up in a heavy sheet of cloth and carried for a long time. He might have passed out or slept. When he was aware of light, it was coming from torches hung on the four close walls that towered upward for many stories, their wood paneling unbroken by any sign of doors or windows. It was more a shaft than a room, and without a roof. The small patch of night sky that he could see was alive with enormous stars. They were blood-red.

Propped up in one corner was Brodwich, very pale even in the torchlight, his purple tongue protruding, the sash still constricting his neck. Martin had the ridiculous but unsettling feeling that the Big Eater was staring at him. He looked away, upward. He could never scale those walls. In any case he wasn't too sure he wanted to go out into a world of red stars.

Becoming aware of a rhythmic droning, he stopped to listen, trying to pick out some sound that might give him a clue to where he was and what was going on. He listened for a long while, but the noise grew neither louder nor softer nor any more distinguishable.

He awoke next with a great thirst. Apparently it was daytime; the torches were out and the red stars were gone, though the texture of the light that came down the shaft seemed somewhat synthetic. The world felt a lot more solid than it had the night before. When he looked over at Brodwich, a rat was gnawing on one of the fat little fingers.

"Get away!" Martin yelled, the sound of his own voice surprising him. "Get out of there!"

The rat ignored him, so he picked up something off the floor and threw it at the animal, hitting Brodwich instead, but startling the rat, which dashed across the room. Brodwich settled a bit in the corner, disconcertingly. When Martin returned his attention to the rat, the damn thing wasn't anywhere to be seen.

It wasn't in the room. Martin couldn't believe it. He'd heard stories, of course, about rats having strange powers, even to the point of being able to pass the limit and go right to the land's end. And folkers did call them disciples' friends. But the rats he'd known hadn't been able to do anything except eat and be eaten. He went over and examined the wall by where he'd last seen it. Alternately pounding, prying and beating the wall, he couldn't find a crease in it, much less a hole. He stopped suddenly when he remembered the feel and the look of the object he'd thrown at the animal. Bread!

Sure enough, sitting there in the middle of the floor where it had fallen after bounding off Brodwich, was a golden loaf of real bread, such as only bureauers ate. And, what at that moment seemed even better, back over where he'd been lying when he awoke was a beaker of water. Food and drink! Neither had ever been so satisfying, and the loaf was gone and the water was nearly so, before Martin thought to conserve. *Oh well*, he figured, *if it was provided once*...He lay back against the wall, refreshed. At that moment, the shaft didn't seem all that bad a place, quite interesting actually.

"If only you were a better conversationalist," he said out loud to his dead Better, adding, with ironic respect, a belated "sir."

It occurred to him that Moohna and Mengra and the unit would never believe it if he told them about this place, and this made him uncomfortable. Reflexively he reached into his pocket for his instrue, noting as he did that his blade had been taken. He blew idly into the instrue, looking around. Moohna was dead, and he knew he would never present a story like this to the rest of the unit. Right after Pavle disappeared, Martin had begun to make up his own fantastic and heroic stories. Aside from an occasional bit of unimaginative and petty bragging, folkers neither understood nor appreciated invention, and, while Pavle had been dangerous enough to get only a minimal amount of abuse around the unit, young Martin was subject to such derision that he'd soon grown ashamed of his imagination and the stories had stopped. Shortly thereafter, he'd developed his interest in the Age of Origin, but that interest he'd always considered scientific, and over the years he had come to think of himself as a skeptical, hardheaded person, totally contemptuous of superstition, legend, and unfounded conjecture.

In any case, this place was indeed beyond conjecture. And yet the novelty of his position soon waned, and the day grew long and so uneventful Martin felt like he was back at the office. Eventually he just fell asleep again, dreaming that Brodwich was trying to answer all his questions, but all that came out when the Big Eater opened his mouth was flies.

He awoke to the sound of the droning. It seemed to be night; two of the four torches were lit, but the opening overhead was closed. Brodwich was gone. And a door had appeared in the wall across from him. It was the same scarlet as the stars.

He got up stiffly and walked over. The old-fashioned knob was silver and in the shape of a demon head. If he'd had any doubts before that he'd been captured by the disciples, they were removed. He wanted to tell them, and tell them quickly, that he wasn't really a bureauer; then he realized that he really was. At least to them he really was. He'd heard of what disciples did to bureauers (even worse than what they did to folkers), and while he was imaginative enough to be very frightened, even the fear wasn't entirely unpleasant.

Still, it did cross his mind that he might have been better off as a prowler.

Like all folker males, when he was sixteen Martin withdrew from his unit. After sixteen years the government (meaning the bureauers) stopped supplying fare-well coupons for male children, who would then drop all ties with their old unit to become "prowlers," members of one of the gangs of adult men. Women and children could do nothing for a grown man; but as a member of a prowler gang, food could be earned, stolen, or extorted, and sex would be his for the taking. Even when a gang was rounded up for labor, they'd be regularly fed, and when the overseer bureauers let them go, as often as not they'd be rewarded with fare-well coups. And since it was always easier for the overseers to grab new workers than to scrupulously guard the ones they had day and night, escape from a labor force was simple enough when one grew tired of eating and working quite that regularly.

At the time he left, neither Martin nor the unit felt any great need for the other. Mengra would brag about being "the balls of the unit," and Martin would tell him that he was only off by a couple of inches. (For awhile, Mengra wasn't entirely sure that wasn't meant as a compliment. Then he decided to fight about it, just to be on the safe side.) As for himself, Martin figured he was more like a fungus, or a growth on the side of the unit: perhaps benign, perhaps even useful occasionally, like a bunion that registers impending changes in the weather, but nothing that anyone would want to call attention to.

Unlike most other boys his age, Martin had never been all that anxious to become a prowler. And though he knew it was inevitable, he found himself putting off the day when he would join a gang. For a couple of years after leaving the unit, he roamed the city with his brother Mengra, maintaining some contact with the old unit, accepting an occasional meal from them in exchange for a little protection or some favor: maybe driving off somebody that was threatening their room or their food, or buttressing the walls of the room with old pipes. But for the most part the brothers fended for themselves, eating and sexing as the opportunity arose. Pickings were slim since a two-man force was limited, but Martin was bigger than average, and Mengra was a gigantic tank of a man who simply and unthinkingly rolled over anyone who stood in his path, even when he wasn't quite sure where that path led. So they managed to survive, though Martin often got the impression that he was only on probation with his brother.

Eventually Martin was going his own way more and more, while Mengra began devoting most of his time to a hustle he had worked out near the waters, charging gullible folkers to let them see the pile of baby bones that he claimed was what was left of the "only living person ever to make it past the limit." His huge size allowed him to get away with it; but that wouldn't help him if the policers found out, such unheard-of initiative on the part of a folker being as obvious an offense against the will of the bureauers as anything Martin could imagine, certainly far worse than building a rubble home or murdering another folker or too blatantly stealing too much of a food units' meager rations, and every day people were Free-Killed for those.

Mengra's courage, though foolhardy, was considerable. "You're either best or you're bested," was Mengra's idea of a witticism. And he just had to be best, whether he was hunting rats and pigeons, or wrestling, or sexing women. Anyone who didn't take his accomplishments as seriously as he did himself was in for trouble, as Martin had repeatedly discovered, being unable to refrain from a little joking that Mengra never considered friendly. When they fought, just as when they competed at anything else, Martin very often got the worst of it, being neither as big nor as motivated as his brother. In competition, he was usually satisfied with just doing well; second place was often just fine as long as he didn't embarrass himself — not the most successful attitude to take into a fistfight.

But Martin saw little glory to be gained in the world around him. Likewise he had no great plans for the future. Sometimes at night when he had trouble getting to sleep, he'd allow his mind to drift into fantasies of living in the past, of being a leader among the Originals, of making love to Original women. Since these dreams didn't have the slightest application to his life, the fact that he dreamed them didn't change his evaluation of himself as a person who was not only cynical but (like all folkers but his brother) unambitious. He never stopped to consider that in a world long dead, that might not have been the case.

Martin turned the demon-head knob, and, to his complete amazement, the door of the shaft room opened easily and quietly. The passage beyond seemed to be of the same dimensions as the door, with a slightly downward plane. After a few yards, it disappeared in shadow.

He listened for a moment. The droning had stopped; the darkness ahead was silent. Not seeing that he had any real choice, he started down the ramp, slowly and carefully. After a minute or two, the corridor took a sharp turn to the left. Now in total darkness, Martin inched forward, one hand against the wall on his right. When he'd started, the walls had been paneled with the same wood as the shaft, but here they were gritty and crumbling, as if the tunnel was cut in the very earth itself. Occasionally he touched patches of moisture and tiny streams that ran down the sides and across the floor. The downward grade grew considerably steeper, and the air became hotter and closer.

He reached a point where the wall on his right broke off. Groping after it, he took a step or two in that direction, waving his arms in front of him like a blind man, and hitting nothing but empty space. Trying the opposite direction, he couldn't find the other wall either. He might be in a large underground chamber, or simply at the intersection of two tunnels, but since he didn't really want to try to find his way back (though it did cross his mind that at least in the shaft he'd been supplied with food) he just took his best guess as to direction and pressed on, arms outstretched, toes testing every step before his feet made it. Just when he was convinced he was hopelessly lost, he caught the droning again. It was hard to tell where it was coming from, but it did seem to be getting louder. And at that moment a pack of bureauer-hating disciples seemed preferable to a short aimless life of blind wandering.

"There you are, love."

The quite female voice beside him startled him more than anything that had happened thus far. Reflexively he reached into his pocket for his missing blade. It wasn't there, of course, and neither was his instrue!

"I've been waiting." The tone was soothing, deliberately

so, he thought, and a bit syrupy. It made him nervous. Yet the touch of the hand that somehow found his was soft, and the tugging that bid him to follow her lead was gentle. He didn't budge.

"What…"he began.

"My name's Ryenna. And I've come down here to help you. On the mission." Her arm went confidently around his waist, and though holding back somewhat, Martin let her lead him in a new direction for a length or two. He was very conscious of her body, of her breast against his side, of her strong sweet scent, the kind the bureauer woman in the safeway had worn. He stopped walking.

"My name is *Martin*," he said, expecting her to understand she'd grabbed the wrong man.

She didn't say anything for a moment, then in a loud and slightly impatient whisper, she said, "I'm a bureauer too."

"I work for Brodwich. The Bureauer of Knowledge." He said it carefully, as if he might try to retract the statement if she clutched for it too quickly. The idea was to assure her either that he really wasn't the person she was looking for, or, if he was, that he had absolutely no idea that Brodwich had been killed.

"Well, I work for the same people Brodwich works for. Anyway, Brodwich is dead."

He stood still as a stone.

"The disciples got him," she said with as much concern as if it had happened to some minor form of vegetable life on some remote planet. "He had no business interfering with your position anyway. Of course, he told you why you were there." The voice was critical.

"No one has ever told me anything."

"Huumm…He probably didn't know. It's hard to imagine him not farting out anything that was in his mind. Anyway, I'm a bureauer, but the disciples think I'm one of them. It's very rare for someone who's not raised a disciple to be contacted, and even more rare for an outsider to be actually allowed into the coven as a full-fledged disciple. Kreeops finds me especially useful." With a harsh little giggle, she added, "So does the Bureau of Knowledge."

He got the idea she expected to be complimented. When he said nothing, she continued.

"Anyway, I've gotten close to Kreeops. There are ways," she said, tickled by the innuendo. "He's consolidating his power. He won't rest until the entire city is his."

Martin felt like asking her what difference that would make to anyone besides this Kreeops himself, and possibly a few Big Eaters, but he didn't. The world around them was lightening into streaky purples and heavy, muddy browns. Without even being aware of it, he'd been walking along with her. They were climbing slightly, apparently on a vast open field. *Where were they?* All he could get the woman beside him to say on the subject was, "Kreeops knows." As for Ryenna herself, she was slim and almost his own height. But with the hood up on her black disciple's robe he couldn't tell much else.

"Kreeops is Evil," she offered in a way that sounded like she was defining the term, as if "Kreeops" was the name for all the evil in the city.

Martin remained silent. The rough earth beneath their feet was increasingly spotted with tufts of grass. He watched his companion, hoping to get a look at her in the growing visibility. Still, he could see nothing but the hood until, clicking her tongue as if she knew what he'd been thinking and she wanted to get the irritation of his examination over with, she suddenly stopped and threw off the hood with a flourish, not unlike a Big Eater unveiling a bust of himself.

She was unexpectedly beautiful. And obviously very proud of it: posing with her head held back, her spectacularly molded features at three-quarters profile, the thick waves of red hair tossed in one well-practiced motion back from the green eyes and the pale skin. He was a little taken aback by the unveiling. It was almost absurdly egotistical, and a bit like a crazer he'd once seen strutting around a pile of debris, showing off the fine home he imagined he'd built there, stopping occasionally to brag about one of the magnificent draperies he'd hung on his nonexistent walls. Only Ryenna *was* beautiful, almost too much so; she was like the tiny dolls that children played with, carved out of bone illegally withheld from the trash reapers. He found himself searching for a flaw. No doll was created without one; it made them seem more lifelike.

She relaxed. Unlike folker women, bureauer females relied heavily on their looks and therefore tended to value them accordingly, but Ryenna sighed as if her good looks were simply a bore and a nuisance. Then she reached someplace inside her robe and removed a piece of paper which she thrust at Martin.

"Look at this," she said, sounding annoyed.

Seeing it was a photo, he felt a surge of excitement. He hoped it would be from the Age of Origin and flashed on a couple of his old pictures that had been destroyed. He had an idea, though, that it would be a picture of Ryenna.

Instead it was of a man. A rather rugged-looking man in a strange type of shirt. He was neither old nor young, but rather mature. And though the man was probably an Original, and therefore interesting, Martin would have bet he wasn't one of their best; he was just too ordinary. Martin pretended to study the picture intently, as they resumed walking.

When it became obvious that Ryenna wasn't going to

explain why she'd given it to him, he looked up at her and handed it back, raising his eyebrow in a gesture he hoped would be vague enough for her to find an appropriate meaning in.

"Well?" she asked.

He made a noise that was a sort of noncommittal hum.

"You don't find the resemblance amazing?" She shook her head in disbelief. He must have looked thoroughly confused. She thrust it back at him like she was going to stab him with it.

"It's Jefuson. And it looks just like you!"

He looked again, his interest really aroused this time, then dismissed it.

"No more so than anyone else with shoulder-length hair and no beard."

Ryenna took the picture, looked at it again, and then at Martin. She didn't say anything for awhile, and they walked on quietly.

Finally she said, "You're full of shit. Anyway, it doesn't matter." She explained briefly about the Regency and the Jefuson, concluding, "Anyway, the disciples think there's a chance you're Jefuson, come back to take Kreeops' place. *Jefuson,*" she shook the picture at him, identifying it again. "Your job is to press that claim and before you can do that you've got to make it to Kreeops' Castle."

Then with the slightest trace of mockery, she added, "A bureauer does his job."

Her words had a finality he didn't like any more than the job she described. He'd heard about the disciples' "Castle," but he'd always figured that was just a fancy name for some old building. But then the city he knew had nothing like the place they were in now. Apparently this Kreeops, these disciples, somehow had a domain of their own. The landscape

had gradually become a rather verdant pasture with pleasantly rolling hills, remarkably like the scene in one of his old
pictures. The day hadn't gotten much lighter.

"Or," she continued, "you *could* run." She gestured at the
world around them. Almost playfully.

"A bureauer does his job," he said. It was almost a question.

"It could be arranged. Tattoos can be altered. There are
lots of anonymous folkers living in the city."

She said this lightly, exactly as a policer might suggest
escape to someone he'd caught guilt-sure when the Free-Kill
was overstocked, secure in the knowledge that he had a weap
that would cut the man down the moment he moved. Oddly,
Martin realized later, he didn't really make his decision in
terms of what she had told him to do or what she could force
him to do, as most bureauers would have. Instead he thought
of the dullness and the eternal sameness of life in the city, of
gray days stretching out ahead of him and innumerable fla-
vorless bowls of poorage providing nourishment so finally
his remains would nourish someone else. He didn't know
where he was, but he knew that for the last couple of days life
had been different. He'd learned early in childhood how
mundane most wonders turned out to be upon examination,
and he fully expected that this one would too. *Eventually.*

"If it's my job, then I guess I should do it" was all he
said. But inside he was frightened and excited all at once.

"The trip is difficult." She sounded almost gleeful: perhaps she was anxious for him to try a break so she could flash
the weapon that could stop him. "Kreeops is deadly."

"Almost everyone is," he said, impatiently, afraid he
might change his mind. "Let's go."

Following no path that he could see, she altered their
direction: toward the Castle of Kreeops, he supposed.

They headed across unbroken fields. It occurred to

Martin that this land might be suitable for growing crops or raising animals. Arising from the gloom of the skyline, a solitary farmhouse appeared beside an old barn. A fairly clean tractor was parked out back, as if the farmer had just stepped inside for a quick bite to eat. Lights burned in every window of the house. Martin was delighted. Such images had more than once provided his childhood with warmth and life when the city had seemed particularly barren and hostile.

They came to a gravel road that wound over toward the house, and turned onto it. When they got closer, he could see a jack o' lantern burning in mock ferocity on the porch, among toys scattered by the play of what must have been several children. Almost the exact scene from one of his pictures! He suddenly felt sure that they were still underground.

The farmhouse was totally still. Martin had an impression of animals grazing in the distance. He'd really begun to hope that this idyllic setting might be at least a temporary destination for them and was disappointed when his guide led him past the open gate without so much as a sidelong glance. Just then he heard a door slam once, twice, and barefoot children rushed out to play on the front lawn, calling to each other and to someone in the house in a familiar tongue which Martin soon realized was a distorted, perhaps ancient, form of English. He was thrilled, and he stopped to watch the children for a moment.

"I want to play with Mommy, Bobby," he heard the little girl call over to her brother. With her sweet, immaculate face and curly locks, she was not three paces from Martin on the other side of the fence, but was totally unmindful of his presence. He thought how wonderful childhood must have been in the warm and vital days of the age.

"No," said the brother. "Mommy's no fun anymore."

"Oh, please, Bobby. Please, let's play with Mommy. Just

this once more."

"Oh, all right," relented Bobby with that exaggerated solemnity children take on when assuming an adult role. He ran over to the side of the house and picked something up. "Here, catch," he called, flinging it toward his sister.

Mommy's head was all tattered and bloody, and the little girl screamed with delight as she made what was, for a child her age, a rather remarkable catch.

The pressure of the hand at his side increased and he became aware of Ryenna beside him. A finger raised to her face bade him to remain quiet as he was led on.

The stars were red, he mused to himself, remembering his shaftlike room. He'd recognized Mommy as Moohna.

The road continued and eventually brought them to the top of a gorge. Martin had never seen the like; it was as if the land were trying to imitate the alley between two skyscrapers. He could have thrown a rope across it, but the same rope would have reached only a fraction of the way to the bottom. The river far below roared as it cut its way through the living rock while speeding onward to who-knew-where. The cliff facing them on the opposite side seemed as sharp as a prowler's makeshift knife, and the one at their feet looked nearly as sheer, although a few paces to the left he could see the beginnings of a trail broad enough for a good-sized rat. It wound downward and disappeared from sight as the cliff sloped inward beneath them.

Ryenna headed for the path, but Martin held back. He never cared for great heights; the last few years he'd avoided rooftops that were more than a few stories up. And this height out here in the middle of nowhere, and actually a part of the land itself, seemed so unnatural.

"If this is part of the job, I'm not so sure I'm cut out to be a bureauer. I'm really not agile enough," he said, trying to be funny and not succeeding in hiding his fear. She looked at him expectantly, and he remembered the grayness of the city. "Oh, refuse! Let's get it over with."

The tug she gave him in answer to those words was of such unexpected force that if she had not held tight to his hand, he probably would have sailed past her, right over the edge to be dashed to death on the rocks below, or swept off down the turbulent river like a stick in a rain-filled gutter. He started down the path, leading the way, yet feeling as if he was being herded. Though anxious to get to the bottom, he had no faith in himself in the face of this novelty; he wanted to go slowly and carefully, but Ryenna kept bumping into him from behind. At one point they rested for a moment, leaning against the cliff, of necessity pressed against each other. Martin realized he had hardly thought about sexing Ryenna since the first few minutes they had been together. It was unlike him. He was intimidated by her, but it wasn't just that. Before he could puzzle it out, she started trailing her fingers over his smooth face, giving him a surprisingly sympathetic smile. She seemed to be on the verge of saying something, but, perhaps thinking better of it, she only nodded toward the path. Disentangling themselves, they resumed their descent.

From that point on, the trail became extremely rocky, and was seldom wide enough for a man to place both feet on it together. He would have liked to have avoided glancing downward because of the dizziness, but the way was too treacherous for that, and there were occasional gaps where sections of the path had broken off, leaving only the sheer cliff and the river swirling far below. They would stretch across these breaks, their bellies rubbing against the cliff, their fingers clawing for a hold in the rock. Fortunately the cliff face was rough enough for their hands to do the work where their feet could not.

The path Z'd gradually downward until they were about halfway down. In the lead, Martin was becoming more confident with each step, knowing he was that much closer to the bottom. Then, instead of crossing back under itself, the trail rounded a bulge where the cliff veered out toward the opposite shore, and he discovered a good-sized waterfall immediately in front of them. Their way was blocked. Even if the trail picked up on the other side, there was no way, short of flight, to get over there, past the tumbling water. Martin turned to his companion behind him and shrugged, though he had little stomach for retracing his steps. But instead of backing away, Ryenna came even closer, crowding him against the end of the path as he tried to get out of her way.

"Watch out," he yelled above the noise of the water. Heedless, she grabbed onto him, putting her arms around his waist and pulling him toward her. He didn't struggle: that would have toppled them over for certain, and besides her strength seemed irresistible. Her body, so soft when they had touched before, was now unyielding, cold, and hard against his chest. Her breath was foul with the musty odor of a long disused room, the odor, he recalled, of the hall he'd fallen into back in the building where his office was. He was in her arms as she stepped off the trail, and together they plunged toward the river. Martin was too stunned even to cry out.

They were still together when they hit the surface of the water, sinking into the cold liquid farther than he would have imagined possible, judging by the rapids he'd seen from above. Water filled his mouth and his nose. His feet sought for the bottom; he knew nothing of swimming. After a few moments, his body started rising naturally. Then he was alone, carried off by the current before he regained the surface. His back smashed hard into a rock, stopping him momentarily, preventing him from grabbing any air even as his head lifted above the water and he was dragged off again downstream.

4

The Limit

She was limping slightly, but compared to the others she passed, bent as they were under loads visible and invisible, the slim figure might have been gliding through the streets of the folker ring. More than one prowler stopped to watch her small but rather luxurious body as it worked against her cloak; the disciples had always fed her well.

A woman was usually relatively safe, even alone, on these congested main streets. A solo man couldn't sex her and defend himself at the same time, and prowler gangs seldom attacked individual women that publicly. Not that they had any sense of chivalry, but with too little female to go around, the entire gang might be milling about indefinitely, an easy target for any over-seers who might come cruising the central thoroughfares, looking for a ready-made labor crew. Instead of pumping on the woman, they might find themselves pumping on energy bikes, yielding their strength to light the Gov-Cent. Besides, the first priority of folker men was food, not sex.

Still, prowlers temporarily separated from their gangs twice turned to follow the girl in the expectation that eventu-ally she would enter (or could be made to enter) some sparsely populated road or alley. There she could be sexed freely and with abandon, as prowlers believed all women should be, regardless of their personal inclinations.

However, on that drizzly afternoon, both prowlers thought better of it almost immediately, and headed off in search of other, less attractive prey. This woman, moving slightly faster and much more purposely than the others on the road, *was* somehow out of the ordinary.

So Gena-gul went unmolested. The evening gloom rose from the shadows, reaching last of all the several patches of sky visible above the crumbling skyline. Someplace Gena had heard it said that the smoky colors of twilight went better with the ugliness of the city than the light did, the same way that illusion could be considered more compatible with misery than truth could ever be. Yet twilight only led to the increased dangers of the night.

Back in the Castle of Kreeops, day and night, like light and darkness, and life and death, were the respective trappings of Jefuson and Satan. The words were on every tongue. Symbolically, the satanic ideas surrounded the disciples as if Kreeops was adjusting the universe for maximum theatrical effect. The Castle itself virtually glowed in blackness, and even its torches seemed made up of flickering shadows, more a product of the night than a restraint to it. It had occurred to Gena more than once that in the Castle, daylight, like the Jefuson, was just a vague promise for the future, perhaps just something Kreeops paid lip service to in order to keep Zaletus happy.

Skin color meant nothing in the city (though the color of one's robes might), but Gena had often wondered if the Regent had chosen her to be Bride of Jefuson because her skin was black, possibly suggesting to the disciples that even though her robes were white, her true affiliation was to Satan.

Gena herself paid little attention to symbols. The city she

knew was naturally an overcast gray, with a few days when the sun broke through and a few that were like night. Although it could never be called safe, the city *was* more dangerous in darkness. With less visibility, maneuvering through the decrepit streets, trying to distinguish shade from reality, became even more difficult. Any misplaced step might easily be your last. And the world could become peopled with enemies who weren't there, while those that were might remain undetected. In spite of her indoctrination as a disciple, it had never occurred to Gena to doubt that the greatest possible evil could happen at high noon (and without any help from Kreeops), or that the greatest good (if it could happen at all) could happen in the darkest hole in the city.

Gena had a stitch in her side, but clutching at her thoughts from a distance, she felt a pursuit she couldn't see and she knew she couldn't stop. The only escape lay in increasing that distance. So, without a conscious decision, she was headed for the edge of the city. She was fully aware that it was a dead end, yet some associations she had picked up in Martin's mind, when he'd mentioned the limit, had given her the flimsiest hope of finding a place where she would be safe from the grasp of Kreeops.

The rain grew heavier. She found it cool and refreshing, washing the day's sweat from her face. Gradually she was revived, though walking remained difficult. She bumped into a staggerer who fell aside drunkenly. The pockmarked pavement was choked with all manner of broken bricks, stones, tiny pieces of glass, hunks of concrete, tin cans, and well-rusted auto parts. Ancient cars had once populated the city's roads, had once housed many food units. Few were left that could provide any shelter, as time and folker need and greed had stripped most of them completely, leaving only remains: scattered engine and body parts and old tires — limbs and organs severed from even potential function, like the staggerers who, in various stages of unconsciousness, also littered the streets. She knew now that many of the staggerers had been raised as disciples, only to be discarded as useless after the ordeal of initiation. She wondered if they thought themselves fortunate to be away from Kreeops, or if they thought at all. The cakes that kept them staggering were one of the few things in the city that were never in short supply, and addiction was almost instantaneous.

Gena's journey was long and tedious. The folker outer ring was the largest of the three sections of the city (and the city was the world), but it was also the most congested. The city had many more folkers than bureauers, and all of these folkers lived here, along with many of the rankenfile bureauers necessary to "administer" their lives (the term "administer" being used interchangeably with "control"). The rest of the bureauers made up the population of the Gov-Cent. No one lived in the no-folker zone.

Among the bureauers who lived in the folker ring were those who distributed fare-well coups or otherwise worked in the safeways. Then there were the overseers for the labor forces that cleared and tried to cultivate the few pathetic lots that yielded less in calories than the folkers working them burned off. There were many of these overseers. The real-food was earmarked exclusively for the Gov-Cent, and they had to protect it both from the harvesters and from each other.

Large numbers of policers also lived and worked in the outer ring. They were the bureauers who maintained order by leaving the folkers in a state of restricted chaos, keeping the population far more concerned with staying alive than with interfering with the workings of the government. Their job was usually easy enough; folkers generally knew better than to put themselves in harm's way. The policers had the Free-Kill, a means of population control that was at the same time a system of rewards and punishments. A folker could be sent to the Free-Kill by any policer who felt that folker was acting in a way that might be socially detrimental. The policers also decided who would get to do the killing, how many and what type of kills they could participate in, and who would get to watch. The ranks of the killers and the spectators were supplemented by lottery, so that some of the vast majority of the folkers, who were incapable of doing the policers any service at all, might get to participate as well. It gave them something to hope for, since being in a Free-Kill was often the highlight of any folker's life. Even if he or she was the one being killed.

The criers were another integral part of the folker ring, though they actually lived with the majority of the bureauers in the Gov-Cent. At least several times a week and sometimes almost daily, the criers went into their assigned neighborhoods and told the folkers anything the bureauers wanted them to know: what number-series of food units were to receive coupons that day and how many they were to receive (always too little, so the units would have to collect trash and steal from each other), schedules for Free-Kills, the names and numbers of any who were to be spectators, killers, or killed. For a crier to ask for a man was for him to get that man. Folkers competed to turn each other in, often even within a unit; it could mean extra coups or even a kill or two. Consequently folkers were not free with their names, though each was required to wear his government-issued I.D. number, the one that had been tattooed on his cheek shortly after birth, on the front of his or her robe. Since trust was virtually impossible, communication between the different food units and gangs was minimal, and the only times people who may have lived beside each other all their lives did anything in common was when they assembled for a crier.

The criers' stories and songs were not just the only formal

education folkers ever got, they were also the main entertainment. Usually they were about some food unit or gang that had done some vile deed against the will of the bureauers and what had happened to them as a result. The stories almost always ended with the crier giving "knowledges," pithy little morals the folkers were admonished to remember, which was not difficult. Though the stories would usually differ, the knowledges were very often the same:

"Don't waste. Nothing is new in the city."

And consolingly, "Nothing is new in the city. To change her is danger, and what could be stranger."

"When you do what's right, your Free-Kill's in sight. If you're not right-willed, it's you who'll be killed."

"The bureauer works, so the folker enjoys."

More than a few food units actually lived in the main streets, and as Gena made her way along, she saw some of them preparing their evening poorage in the shadows on either side of her. She passed a prowler gang or two and innumerable staggerers asleep for the night against the sides of burned or rotted-out buildings. Most of the staggerers were too far gone even to pull their hoods up over their heads to keep off the rain. The water, mixed with the dirt of their faces, made them appear to be men of the mud, which in some areas seemed to be reclaiming the city from the concrete and asphalt.

The buildings themselves, open window holes staring at the world as empty and as indifferently vulnerable as the eye-sockets in a skull, were little enough shelter from the rain and the growing cold. A few window and door openings were covered with the faded multicolor of reweave drapes. The larger and stronger units, with perhaps ten or more women and many large male children, could stake out a part or even all of a room and hold it indefinitely, even in this particular area, where rooms were considered choice. Many of the buildings

Gena passed were nearly intact, with roofs and exterior walls, meaning, of course, they'd never contained much wood. Most of the city's wood had been burned long ago, along with nearly everything else that could be used as fireburn.

The smaller, weaker food units dwelled in lesser buildings, or dug themselves holes in the rubble (trying not to move enough dirt and debris for the policers to call it construction), or they lived in alleys, or often they had no shelter at all, like the loners.

There were three types of loners: those women and children who belonged to no unit and those few men who belonged to no gang; the crazers; and the staggerers, whose numbers seemed constantly on the increase like the shattered bricks that were always toppling from the buildings, filling up the world.

Gena-gul! she heard again, but with a fuzziness that she had come to realize meant the signal was not aimed right at her, but rather was diffuse and searching. It was like being startled by a crack of thunder rather than hit by lightning.

An alley opened to her left, its mouth partially blocked by a bank of rubble. She climbed over it, automatically scanning the alley mentally as her eyes grew acclimated to the change in light. Folkers and bureauers couldn't project anything as coherent as silent speech, of course, but neither could they protect their minds, and she was surprised by how easy it was to probe into their more immediate thoughts. She was beginning to discover, however, that often these thoughts were so confused as to be indecipherable. And this was the case with the jumbled images she picked up from a couple of staggerers just inside the alley.

She also received more solid impressions from the members of several food units that seemed to be nesting there, but even so the reading was far too generalized and too many people were thinking at once for her to understand much of it. No matter; she'd just wanted an idea of who was there, and she had that: mothers, many children, even a prowler, probably just seeking sex. She cut her probe short, realizing she was being careless; the disciples would be able to focus in on the energy of the reading.

The smell of cooking poorage mixed with the permanent odor of disease and excrement. Now she could make out a small fire farther in and the shapes of people gathered around it. As she moved forward, her adjusting eyes enabled her to pick her way over the cracked pavement and through the accumulated debris. The staggerers, both of them out from a cake or two too many, lay in the gloom, indistinguishable from the inorganic rubble. When she stepped on one of them, it was unintentional, but she was as free from regret as the occasional snow whose harsh shroud froze the life from sleeping infants.

Ahead of her were five worn-out women. The youngest was about sixteen, a slightly slobbering young thing with a rough and purple scar covering one whole side of her face; the eldest was a white-haired, stooped, and almost toothless old crone of at least forty. They were huddling in front of the fire with perhaps twenty children. A small tin pot, filled with the gray of poorage, was near to boiling. One of the children, a half-naked girl of about four, with a harelip that split and twisted her face into two incompatible halves, was standing very close to the fire, ostensibly for warmth, but perhaps actually to sneak an extra bite of food.

Gena, who just wanted a moment to take the chill off, noted with some relief that the only man present took no interest in her, merely glancing up for a moment from where he lay, hogging a good section of the fire, cloak up around his waist, scratching himself. He'd apparently just been with one or more of the women.

As Gena took a small step closer to the fire, one of the younger women cursed, "Fah you," in almost perfunctory menace.

When Gena inched still closer, a young boy on her right grabbed at her calf and sank in one of his remaining teeth with a frightening leisure that seemed unaware of the possibility of retaliation, drawing blood that trickled warmly against Gena's leg.

Without a sound, Gena drew back. In the past six months, she'd grown used to being treated with an automatic respect. She imagined the terror she'd command if these people knew she was a disciple, but she was very glad they didn't. No telling how far the collective fear of those around the fire would transmit itself. Searchers that had been unable to pick up her own thoughts might easily trace the mental scream, *Disciple!*

Reflexively her right fist tightened to conceal the missing finger until the remaining fingernails were digging hard into her palm. She'd scraped the black polish off them hours before. The most fleeting reflection upon being dragged back to the horrors of Kreeops was enough to get her moving again, and that was all she allowed herself, lest her own panic give her away. She remembered a story Zaletus had told of a novice disciple, raised in the coven but not yet initiated, who was vocally skeptical about some detail of faith. Preceding a ceremony, Kreeops had simply stared at the novice and, by suggestion, revealed to the boy what he *could* do to him. The boy had literally torn himself apart with his own hands. Gena had learned to give credence to the story.

The pot had just begun to boil, when the hungry little girl with the harelip stuck in her hand. Her screams were cut off momentarily as the sixteen-year-old woman, the scar on her face highlighted hideously in the orange and shadow of the flame, kicked the child sharply in the back, knocking her face against the scalding pot. The resemblance between mother and daughter would be increased now that the burn scar had been passed down from one generation to the next as faithfully as if it were in the blood.

The smell of seared flesh joined the other odors in the closeness of the alley as Gena walked away from the fire.

Several days later, Gena rounded a corner and saw the waters. Flat and metallic, the waters surrounded the city: water for as far as the eye could see, which was none too far, given the general overcast of the days.

Two or three body lengths in front of the waters was the limit. It wasn't much to look at, just a ring of apparently unconnected yellow poles, each about the height of a man, one every half block or so in an enormous circle around the city. Almost every pole had a sign on it, bearing the limit logo:

lim

$\overset{\text{O}}{\underset{/\backslash}{\uparrow}} \longrightarrow \infty$

No one ever made it past these poles. The limit stretched invisibly between them, severing streets, scruffy lots, and even buildings. Some folkers believed that if it was ever violated, a pestilence would decimate the city. But from the reading Gena had gotten from the mind of the bureauer Martin, it seemed possible that the limit had already been violated at least once. Somewhere someone was selling tickets to see the bones of a baby that had gotten across and was lying on the inaccessible strip between the limit and the waters. As far as Gena was concerned, that two or three length strip was the city's only hiding place.

Before becoming a disciple, Gena-gul usually stayed clear of the area by the limit, as she later found out most of the disciples did when they were moving about the city. If she strayed too close, her ears always began ringing; closer and she would get severe headaches. Her ears were ringing now. In her   desperation that was hardly a consideration. Here, she was waiting to die; if she could get across the limit to the strip, nobody could get to her. She'd probably have rats to eat. And though it was the rats' limit-crossing ability that linked them in the popular mind with the disciples, the disciples themselves could no more cross the limit than they could control or communicate with rats.

Gena followed the limit across an open field. In general, the farther you got from the Gov-Cent, the more the city seemed to be falling apart. Grass grew through the pavement, and some of the food units that lived this far out had small gardens in the exposed earth. Folkers often tried to cultivate a few food plants; they were usually scraggly and undernourished, the hair on a corpse that grows for a time after death. But the people out here actually managed to raise some significant part of their diet. They were no less hungry for that; the outskirts often got shortchanged on fare-well coups, and what safeways there were out here were even more poorly stocked than most.

Around the limit itself, the population was dense. It was one direction from which no attack would come. Once in a while, someone tried to build a rubble home beside it, letting it serve as one wall. It didn't keep out winds, or rain, or even bugs, but it kept out people.

No folker tried to understand the limit. They knew it was beyond them. A favorite game of children was to throw rocks through it, watching them sail past land's end, then disappear into the waters. If the children tried to poke at a brick or a piece of trash lying near the waters with a stick, the stick wouldn't pass through. Yet if they threw the same stick, it sailed across as if there were nothing at all in its way. This suddenly struck Gena as very strange. She'd never really thought that before, though the only explanation she'd ever heard was, "that's just how the limit works."

Although no one had any particular interest in doing so, it was well known that, just as you couldn't get through, neither could you get over or under the limit. Even the River respected the limit. The River appeared in the city through a giant metal tube that came straight up out of the ground. It flowed across town and finally forced itself down into a concrete tunnel that was barely large enough for its meager volume. Both ends of the River were next to the limit, but there was no visual evidence of the River either flowing in from the outside at the one end or flowing out at the other. And none of the flotsam or the occasional bodies carried into the tunnel by the current ever surfaced in the waters beyond the land's end. Gena had once heard a young girl speculate that it was possible that the River merely rose like a wellspring from the earth below the city, to which it in due course returned, perhaps even flowing back underneath itself, forming a huge circle. It *was* possible that the Originals could have engineered such a thing, yet it seemed to Gena a very impractical way to provide water for a city that was surrounded by it. Besides, the River water was always filthy when it left the city and fairly clean when it entered.

So rats, pigeons, and probably the River crossed the limit, but not people. Still, Gena had lived in the city too long to believe in perfection. If that baby got through, she could. Then, if she survived long enough, eventually she would be forgotten and could return.

The rest of the day she spent in search of the baby bones. Folkers didn't take kindly to people coming up to them on the street with questions, but she got herself sexed once and mentioned the baby and the limit, and managed to find an image of the place in the prowler's mind. He totally ignored her request for a map. Heading in the indicated direction, she stayed as close to the waters as possible while sticking to the main streets to keep from losing any more time getting sexed again. Not until early that evening did she find the right spot, noticing a crude picture painted on a wall which showed a small figure that may have been a child, separated from some other stick figures by a wall of dotted lines. Following the arrows beneath it to a series of similar signs, she arrived at last at a brick building. Still more signs led her up four flights of stairs. Each flight terminated in a landing with a hole in the wall letting in the twilight and with doorways on either side. She was surprised that no one seemed to be living on the landings. On every floor, voices filtered out from behind the coverings on the doorways, and the smell of poorage and excrement was, as in every enclosed area, constant.

On the fourth-floor landing, three prowlers were listening to a blond man in his late teens or early twenties. He was holding a candle; from the image in Martin's mind, she recognized the man as Mengra. He didn't seem quite as large as Martin had envisioned him, and the blue eyes above his thick beard seemed paler and duller. As he gave his spiel, his voice sounded not only bored but a little bitter, as if unsuccessfully concealing a conflict between resignation and rage.

"...and she returned to find the baby had rolled off the blanket. When she reached down to pick the child up, she was stopped by the limit. The child was on the other side! This was evil at work," he said, professionally sinister. "For the next few days, the mother and even the rest of the unit tried every way to reach him. Finally, they just watched the child die of thirst, inches away from salvation. The mother tossed food and water through, in vain of course; the infant was too young to feed itself. Before it was over, the mother had crazed out. Now you and I might see the hand of the Dark Powers of the disciples behind this evil, unnatural passage, but that woman walked all the way to the Gov-Cent and there she attacked a guardpost full of policers. They played with her for hours before they finished her off.

"Legend has it," he continued, gesturing with a huge hand toward the room behind him, "that when that baby is returned to the city, the limit will drop forever and the world will be made young again." If this was a legend, it was one Gena had never heard. "So now you can see the only person ever to cross the limit alive. For just a few coups or other goods, see the famous show!"

"We could just go in for free," said a tough-looking prowler standing right in front of Mengra.

Mengra drew himself up, thrusting out his chest, staring the older man in the eye. Then he smiled, and the smile held a self-assurance that might once have been the cockiness of youth, now turned mean. It was even more menacing than his considerable size. Mengra raised his hand and the other man covered himself, jerking both arms up in front of an often- broken smear of a nose. But Mengra merely ran his hand slowly through his thick blond hair. The others laughed and everyone, even the man with the nose, started paying, offering Mengra whatever they'd brought. He'd examine their tokens and accept slightly higher.

Gena held back, retreating part way down the stairs as the party was conducted into the room. A few minutes later they were back and, suitably impressed, made their way down past Gena, chattering loudly.

"I'da hit him if I'd eaten today," someone said.

Gena walked up to the door where Mengra stood looking at her like she was what *he* was going to eat that day.

"You wanna see the great show," he said, "you gotta have something pretty good." He looked her over then glanced to the stairway behind her, making sure they were alone, she assumed. His eyes gleamed with more than mischief. His nostrils were hairy and enormous.

"I have nothing. I'm only a loner girl. But I want to see the baby, if we can work something out."

She was quite prepared to bargain *willing* sex, if he was interested in willing sex, which was often not the case. It was all she had.

He moved the candle closer to her face. She wasn't sure if he meant to examine or burn her and stepped back.

He grinned, then he grabbed her and flung her into the room behind him. Following her in, he closed the metal door slowly, watching her reaction, savoring it.

One side of the room was open, looking out over the waters. On the other side, a small fire was burning in a real fireplace, burning though nothing was being cooked, giving the impression that he'd been doing very well at his business indeed.

He removed his cloak, displaying his naked body as if that were the "famous show." She was resigned, just hoping he wouldn't want to hurt her too much, until she saw the huge chancre on the top of his penis.

"Just a little sex disease," he laughed, reacting to her expression. "You don't mind. Life is short anyway."

The disease itself was bad enough. And anyone who had it was supposed to be Free-Killed. There wasn't a soul in the city, except some fellow sufferer, who wouldn't turn you in if they found out.

Mengra placed his candle on the floor almost daintily, and started toward her. She remembered his brother, the bureauer, and took a chance.

"When in the corsa human events," she recited slowly. "We hold these truths to be selfadent."

She smiled, stopping him in his tracks. Slowly, she spread her cloak, as if in invitation. But what caught his attention was not the beauty of her body or the texture of her skin, but the terrifying pentagram tattooed on her left breast. The breast itself, which, with its conical nipple stiffening in the cool air, might have fascinated Mengra only seconds before, was now nothing but a backdrop for the mark of the disciples.

Gena stepped forward, chanting, "In dowbada creator with certain inaliabalu right."

He bent and picked up a hunk of wood, perhaps preparing to attack, perhaps just to get something between them. In his eyes, she could see the battle between, on the one hand, his fear and good sense, which told him to get out of there, and on the other, his normal inclination to attack in the face of challenge or threat. She kept moving toward him and tipped the balance. He picked up his candle and flung it at her defiantly, but then he reached for the door, getting out as slowly as he dared, taking the hunk of wood he was holding with him. She listened to his footsteps all the way down the stairs. At first they were fairly rapid, but after a couple of floors, they slowed and the volume increased.

"You've got till morning to be out of there, disciple!" he screamed from the street outside.

She was alone. But the alarm was out. No one who heard it was likely to investigate unless they could get a mob together, but their fear, along with Mengra's, could be tasted by those who savored such flavors, by those who were listening for just that cry in the night. The fire had burned low, leaving Gena surrounded by a darkness in which anything might be approaching.

Gena-gul! The cry entered her head. The flesh on her stomach began to crawl; she felt the touch of memory in her navel. Instantly she retreated from thoughts that could be as much an enemy as Kreeops himself.

5

Kreeops' River

His arms, his legs, and his robe, swirling around him as if they were traveling down the river independently of his body, Martin was swept off, futilely fighting more water than he would have imagined existed inside the limit a few hours earlier. "Up" and "down" quickly became meaningless terms; he breathed water, then momentarily gasped at the sky before smashing into a rock and choking on air, or river, or both, again. His legs tore against rapids, dragged over them as he tried to push off and failed. The water deepened for awhile, then finally his stomach hit something and scraped against it. He grabbed desperately at a boulder. It was worn too smooth for a firm grip, but he held on anyway, panting, and spewing water back into the river. He heard laughter and as his vision cleared he saw Ryenna standing in calf-deep water directly in front of him. He'd been washed into a shallows under the cliff face.

"I could have drowned," he choked out in accusation when he could talk.

"You didn't. Come on." She helped him up, practically dragging him to shore. He spent the next few minutes lying on his back on a small grassy bank, coughing and snorting, trying to rid his body of water. For the first time in his life, Martin understood the possibility of having too much of a good thing.

After a bit, he checked his pocket one more time just to make sure his instrue was gone. He supposed it didn't really matter; he didn't know why he carried it anyway, when he couldn't even play it. It was just that Martin had heard no other instrue that sounded so sweet in the years since Pavle had gone.

During Martin's early childhood, Pavle was always appearing for a day or a week with the unit, then disappearing for a month or a year. Each time he returned his head was balder, his beard longer and grayer, his hands just a bit shakier. He'd been one of the few folkers in the city who knew how to make instrues, both the kind you blew into and the kind you plucked, and what was most amazing was that his weren't crude and misshapen, but symmetrical and beautifully finished. Pavle was always seeking out Martin and trying to teach him to play one of them. But the child appeared hopeless, though he did truly enjoy singing, and even made up his own rudimentary songs.

Most of the women in the unit thought Pavle was a fool who talked more than most people breathed, but to Martin he was fascinating. Pavle would ask the boy strange questions (though to folkers, all questions not absolutely necessary were strange), and he would sing Martin songs that he said were very old, and tell him fabulous stories. Most folkers didn't converse much, but there were a few who loved flowery and formal speeches, generally about nothing. It passed the time. They considered themselves very grand if they could sound like a crier's edict; it did seem to lend authority to their statements. Pavle had a bit of this in him for certain. But still, his songs and stories were like nothing Martin had ever heard: songs of folkers defying the policers and banding together to overcome ridiculous odds; stories, supposedly of Pavle's own youth, filled with the joy of tricking the bureauers, and with prowling through the Gov-Cent. The songs were obviously fantasies, and Martin never quite believed the tales either, knowing even as a small child that bureauers in general were to be avoided, not sought out, and no folker ever did any prowling anywhere near the Gov-Cent.

As the years passed, Pavle had grown more and more nervous. Eventually, he would jump at every little sound, including a few that no one else could hear. Then, one evening when Martin had returned from a rat hunt, Moohna had a huge bruise beginning to blacken the side of her face and bloody gums showing in the front of her mouth where two teeth had been that morning. She'd told him that Pavle had crazed out and run off. Years later, he learned that the crier had called Pavle's name that afternoon. When the folkers had come for him to turn him in, Moohna had tried to help him resist, a futile and foolhardy act that, understandably, she had been ashamed to admit. A true folker, she believed vulnerability contemptible, and deliberate vulnerability psychotic.

As Martin lay at the base of the cliff recovering, the day grew warmer and, though he couldn't see the sun, exceptionally bright. He felt silly for having imagined this entire place to be underground, just because in the dimness he hadn't noticed when they'd surfaced from the cavern. He peered up at the precipice behind him. A not entirely unpleasant thrill ran up his body as he remembered there was no way to get back up it. Not that it made much difference; he hadn't known where he was originally anyway. He closed his eyes and let the heat of the day relax his body.

"You're all right, Martin." He looked up and saw Ryenna lying on her side in front of him.

"I might have drowned," he muttered, though the warmth spreading through him seemed to mute the accusation.

"Life is danger," she said peevishly.

He was admiring the way her wet robe clung to her breasts and the swell of her hip, until feeling her eyes upon him, he glanced away quickly.

"Anyway, I was right here," she said.

"And I was out there," he answered, not reassured. "I don't imagine your Betters would be too pleased if you drowned the man who's supposed to dethrone the enemy."

She smiled. He couldn't tell if the condescension on her face added to, or subtracted from, her beauty.

"To tell the truth," she said, "I don't think they'd be as upset as Kreeops."

"Kreeops!"

"You certainly don't think that after the years I spent gaining his trust, I'd be doing this without Kreeops' approval. He thinks I'm obeying *his* orders. Anyway, in a sense, I am."

"I see. Kreeops wants me to oust him. That certainly makes sense."

"Kreeops would like to see you in hell, and may yet," she responded, unnervingly. "But the whole coven is aware of your existence. And some of them are silly enough to be on the verge of hailing you as the Jefuson; the perfection of faith that Kreeops insists on is threatened. So while he certainly wants you dead, and while many do die out here, what death is so innocent that there's no room for even a suspicion of foul play? And with the eyes of the coven upon you, if anything happens before you can be brought back to the Castle and formally discredited before the High Priest, there's a chance Kreeops might have a martyr to contend with."

"I should think he'd rather take that chance than risk losing everything to me."

Her laugh was musical, and more frightening than anything she could have said.

"Sorry, Martin, but I don't imagine he's too worried about that."

She stretched herself, her body sleek and white beside the black of her robe, her fiery hair laced with sparkling beads of water.

"Up ahead, you're going to have to survive the river. A novice disciple, after spending a lifetime in training, is taken a distance from the Castle and *of his own free will* must decide to return, to become part of the coven. In order to get back, he must ferry the river of the Regent; *that* is his ordeal of initiation. Anyway, the Jefuson must do the same. 'The Jefuson is of the disciples, of the folkers, and of the bureauers.' Like I said, many don't survive it, but everybody will be disappointed if you don't."

"Comforting." He tried to keep his voice even.

"Well, you've already chosen to come this far. From now on, every decision you make could very well be your last. There are places where choosing life may bring death and places where choosing death may bring life.

"Anyway," she paused before continuing, "you could still run, you know." And though he'd been thinking the same thing, something smug and almost contemptuous in her tone steeled him, at least in his reply.

"So could you," he said, his words practically an accusation. "Kreeops could find out you're working for the bureauers, at any time."

She laughed again. Martin felt like he was hitting a cloth hanging over a hole in a wall: one that gave with every punch and never came down.

"He knows I'm working for them. I told you, he knows everything."

His cloak was spread wide, and the work smock he had on underneath must have been gaping open. She reached inside, tracing her black fingernails over the sensitive skin of his thigh. Surprised, he jerked back as if burned.

"Kreeops thinks," she began, smiling in mock apology, "that he managed to seduce me from the bureauers, and that now I'm only pretending to spy for them."

Her fingers reached farther into his smock and found his penis. He grabbed her wrist, but let it go when she laughed at him again.

"Anyway," she continued, "even if he suspects that my real loyalties *are* with the bureauers, he doesn't care as long as I'm doing what he wants done. Like I said, the claim must be pressed. He's more anxious than the bureauers for your testing to begin."

"He knows of my mission," Martin mused. He was trying desperately not to get hard. He felt as if it would be a shameful admission of weakness. He wasn't used to having the woman sex *him*.

"Your mission is so obvious, he'd know of it anyway. With or without me." She still sounded detached, but he was getting harder as her touch grew softer, riding up and down on the shaft of his dick.

"And you're working for the bureauers and the disciples, who are working together...AHH!" he cried as her nails nipped at him. She smiled. He felt like a confused child trying to play an adult game for the first time.

"Working together against each other," she said. "Both want you at the Castle, but the difference starts there. The bureauers want you to be successful, as successful as you can be, anyway, creating maximum confusion and dissention. Kreeops, however, wants you disposed of and forgotten, and the sooner the better."

"Suppose I discredit myself. Suppose I deny the claim."

She opened his smock wide and grabbed his cock with

both hands, describing a circle with its tip. She bent forward and her tongue flipped across it. He reached out to cup one of her breasts, but she slapped his hand away.

"Deny it. Our Betters might get upset." Her head came down and her mouth was on him briefly, moist and warm. "Anyway, your face makes the claim for you."

He tried to touch her again, but again she knocked his hand away carelessly, jerking his cock painfully to one side as she did so.

"No matter what happens to me, you people win," he said.

In his mind he was trying to grab on to something that crumbled into dust like an old plaster statue whenever he touched it. Still, it was just possible that if he could get enough handfuls of that dust, maybe sooner or later he'd be able to understand what it was the plaster had once formed.

Ryenna gave him another enigmatic smile that seemed just as likely to take a bite out of him as to kiss him.

"Anything that disrupts the machinery of the disciples helps *our* side," she said, emphasizing the "our" sarcastically. "After all you *are* one of us."

"But I'm the one who gets to stick his head in the machinery."

"You could run, Martin. But Kreeops, being pretty much invincible, he'd catch up with you anyway. And the penalty for impersonating the Jefuson is death."

"I impersonated no one."

"Who got born with that face?"

"I was born with nothing."

"Well, you grew it, then. Anyway it's yours. And Kreeops is hardly about to leave a fraud running around loose with that face. And, if you run now, the bureauers will be after you as well." She flicked her fingernail against him twice, painfully. "If you aren't running, come on. Destiny awaits, O Jefuson."

"Where *are* we?" he tried again.

"Kreeops knows." Her laugh made him feel a bit nauseous.

He believed at least one thing she had said: that Kreeops was hardly about to let him run anywhere. He knew that he hadn't escaped from the shaft room, he'd been allowed to leave, and he was fairly sure that, as she'd implied, they were being observed even now. He was also fairly sure that if any disciples *were* nearby, she wouldn't be so free with her claims about being a bureauer unless she wasn't one. This seemed to be one of those times she'd mentioned when choosing life by running would certainly bring death. He didn't know just what he was going to do, or who was on whose side; he felt certain that nobody was on his. Quite possibly the only thing that had kept him alive this far was that the ridiculous idea that he might be the Jefuson didn't seem so totally ridiculous to somebody. For the moment he saw no point in convincing that somebody of their error.

His erection had gone down. Ryenna, following the river downstream, was rounding a bend without looking back. He got up and headed after her. Maybe when he met this Kreeops he could explain that he wanted absolutely no part whatsoever of his position or his power. It was an idea in which he had no faith. He hadn't noticed when, but that day had gotten colder and damper and grim again.

In silence they followed a path along the base of the cliff for hour upon hour. The way was slow and obstructed by large rocks and small slides of gravel which they often had to wade into the stream to avoid. Once they stopped to rest and Martin fell asleep for what seemed like a long while. When he awoke, he guessed it was the next day though the light was still the same. Ryenna pulled a dark loaf out from somewhere inside the folds of her clothing, and he drank a minimal amount of water from the river. After yesterday he had no great thirst. The bread was delicious.

All that day they traveled in thick overcast without a glimpse of sunshine. Once they stopped briefly for a rest and some food, the same brown bread and river water as that morning, then quickly they resumed their journey. The river seemed to be getting deeper as well as broader the farther they progressed downstream, though it varied greatly from place to place. It had slowed to the speed of a very fast runner, and the cliffs on either side had become merely hills, more dirt than rock, more swelling than steep, when late the next day, they rounded a bend and Ryenna pointed out the ferry. A heavier and more unnatural gloom was coagulating in the air around them. Martin wondered if it was dusk and felt a dread that he was unable to dismiss as silly, of a night that would develop from such a twilight.

Despite no evidence of trees for miles around them, the ferry was a raft of roughly hewn lumber without sides or anything for a passenger to hang onto. Even as it sat tied to the shore, water washed over it, and he questioned what it would be like out in the middle of that river. He'd seen pictures of some of the water craft of the Originals; they hadn't looked nearly so small or so flimsy. He remembered the sensation of being overcome by the river and carried off, remembered the suffocating water invading his nose, his mouth, his lungs.

Ryenna motioned him on board. Reluctantly he followed her, and there they stood, soaking their footwear. He started to ask what they were waiting for, but she gestured for silence. In no hurry to attempt the crossing, he didn't press the point, but he would rather have waited on the solid, dry shore. The chill from his feet spread throughout his body. The night air was not warm.

But the sky cleared, as for some reason it often did in the city at night, and he watched the full moon rise and gradually move halfway across the sky. Distant and pale, the moon gave him no comfort. Its cold, dead presence sent shadows crawling around the river bank, thickening the murk of the river; the moonlight seemed less the reflection of sunlight than its opposite, the way a friend's corpse might seem to be the antithesis of the friend, as charged with the stillness of death as the original was charged with life. The moon was a commonplace, more so than the sun. Folkers frightened their children with tales of the skull in the moon. Never had it looked so lifeless, yet so malevolent, as if death *were* suddenly an active force. Gazing at it, Martin felt as if the eyes that he believed were constantly upon them were the all-seeing sockets of that celestial skull, peering down like a logo for mortality.

After walking all day, Martin's legs were tired. He started to step off the raft so he might sit down on the brief shore, but Ryenna grabbed his arm and motioned silently for him to stay. After a while, he sat anyway, right there, getting wet. Compared to the chilling breeze that had come up, the water now seemed warm. Once he got up to relieve himself, and Ryenna again made as if to stop him until she realized what he was about and backed off almost discreetly. Noises sprang up: rustlings from just out of sight on the near bank; fierce intermittent howling from the far shore, their destination. His clothing damp where it wasn't wet, Martin tried to bounce up and down for warmth, and his efforts almost knocked them both off the unstable craft. It occurred to him that it was much harder to be in a place without people at night.

A hand on his shoulder brought him awake before he was aware of his sleep. He looked up expecting Ryenna, but the face he saw was unknown, and male, perched at an odd angle on a short, almost dwarfish body, and weathered till it looked like the bark on the raft itself. Wrinkles, filled with years of accumulated dirt, outlined each feature as the moonlight played irregularly over the face. The night had developed clouds.

Martin noticed the eyelids were lowered almost to the point of being closed; yet the fierce, black eyeballs were clearly visible as they shifted slowly across the contours of his own face without comprehension, as if they were examining not a man, but something that had sprung spontaneously from the earth, unique and unprecedented. Was the old man a staggerer? Out here? There was a very unstaggerer-like alertness about him. The hand that removed itself from Martin's shoulder had no fingers, only stubs protruding at odd angles from the palm. The other hand was out of sight someplace under the layers of ragged clothing he wore.

"Hrunchh," he said and made as if to spit, but Martin couldn't see that anything came out of the jagged mouth. "Hrunchh?" he said again. Apparently it was a question.

"We want to cross the river," Martin said, looking toward Ryenna for confirmation. But she was staring out at the opposite shore and hadn't even acknowledged the new creature on the raft.

"Hurunch," the man said, baring his teeth. His breath was foul enough to blind, but to Martin's surprise, the teeth were the white of bleached bone, and numerous. Very few his age had all their teeth, and usually what teeth they had were old and yellow, if not brown or gray. Stranger still, the teeth seemed very sharp. A trace of spittle drooled out into the malnourished beard. Martin glanced over at Ryenna, hoping to see that this old man was expected, that things were going according to plan some plan, any plan. But she seemed intent upon the river; alert, he thought, but not to them. In a way that was some reassurance; at any rate, Martin felt better for her presence. For the moment at least, he and Ryenna were both working to get him to the Castle. He figured she'd correct him if he did anything wrong, anything inconsistent with this goal.

"We wish to cross the river," he reiterated, hoping to make

it less of a question this time. He caught a gleam from beneath the rotted outer cloak the little man was wearing. The bare blade in his sash was hopefully much wider than it was sharp, but Martin doubted it.

"Hrunchh...initiate...cross the river of the Regent," the man began slowly, in the sing-song that confirmed he was a user of staggerer cakes. Martin had never heard of a staggerer who carried a knife, or for that matter did anything but fill himself with cakes. Certainly he'd never seen one that exuded the menace this one did. Usually, they just lay around, occasionally stumbling into someone's way, merely the human decay that blended in perfectly with the inorganic decay of the city.

The old man's voice continued, high-pitched and piercing. "The trip...is of precious cost...one way. Round trip...is of greater price than you may pay." He giggled at his private joke, a giggle that danced close to the brink of hysteria. It ended abruptly. "Might like to change your mind." A pause here for a response that Martin didn't make, then he demanded, "Fare!"

"I can pay for myself," Martin said, not at all sure that was true. All he had were two or three leftover fare-well coups that Moohna had slipped him when he'd left the unit, and, *in theory anyway*, the coups would be no good to anyone whose unit I.D. number didn't match the number on the coupons. The memory of Moohna brought with it a new twinge, and he tasted the guilt of one who has forgotten to actively worry over something that bothered him (though he wasn't sure just what and he had no time to puzzle it out now). He looked to Ryenna once more, hoping she would volunteer her own fare, but she never budged. The staggerer seemed as unaware of her as she was of him.

"One...hurunchh." It sounded like a confirmation, and apparently it was, for as he said it, he took Martin's right hand by the wrist, and with a "whoosh" of one sudden and well-practiced movement, drew his blade and found his target. *The little finger of Martin's right hand was cleanly severed.*

It dropped into the water that ran over the surface of the raft. After hesitating a moment on each of two or three protruding logs, it would have slid off downstream, but the creature retrieved it, in another graceful motion that was almost a bow. Grunting, "Paid: one passage," he stuck the unwiped blade and the finger someplace back inside his tattered robe.

And then Martin began to feel the pain. The blood flowed freely from his hand, some of it merging with the current and drifting off. Martin sat down hard. After another "hurunchh," and one more dry spit, the old man tossed something in Martin's lap, then picked up a pole. Bending his back, he shoved them easily out into the river.

Once they were away from the shore, the river was a flow of thick ink that made the night seem well-lit by comparison. Martin was reminded of the oily pools the bureauers filled their vehicles from. His head was swimming a bit as he watched the water separate from itself, move over the raft, and reunite. The shrill howling seemed all around him; another current, one in which they were all submerged. He heard voices in it, many voices, babbling indecipherably. Were they talking to him? For an instant, he was afraid that he would swoon and vanish into the unknown depths. There was a package on his lap. It was open; he could see the gray roundness of staggerer cakes inside. He wanted to look up; he had a memory of reflected light from the sky, but a wave of pain hit him again, so great that after a moment the pain seemed both larger and more concrete than his own body. The ferryman's face hovered in front of him, mouth gaping, pointed teeth bared as if to devour Martin. In two or three mouthfuls, that face could swallow him and his pain. The old man could handle the pain; he had his cakes. As if from long ago, Martin recalled the cakes that lay in his own lap. They seemed like little moons. The old man nodded, grinning. His arm, as long as the great distance between them, soared gracefully through the air; fluttering down in Martin's lap, it seized upon a cake and popped it delicately back into that gruesome mouth.

Martin wished that he could grasp what the voices around him were saying. His confusion merged with his pain, like his blood on the water, blending together, coloring each other, yet distinct. He didn't understand what was happening to him. And he was afraid of not knowing.

His thoughts were in the wind around him, part of the babbling. Or was it the babbling that was part of his thoughts? It all shifted in and out of focus: impressions, faces, sky, raft, pain, voices; first very close then out of reach, rolling, swelling. Ripples and swirls. A confusion of patterns either undiscerned or non-existent, certainly beyond him. He dropped his head as if to shield it from the confusion, and he saw the majestic blackness of the river: power and direction, pure in their constancy, in their dominance and certainty; an awesome, horrible, seductive, inevitability that beckoned him to slip from his confusion on the raft and surrender to the freedom of its force. The water was warm, inviting, *dry*, and absolutely buoyant. He knew he would be safe; in fact, it was tempting him with some strange type of immortality. Its life carried on forever; it would flow through him, guiding him and freeing him from his confusion, making him part of something mighty and eternal. Half submerged, he stared into the water's overwhelming power. Of course, it wasn't water. The river of the Regent was a flowing powder; beneath its surface ran a thousand different shades of dark color.

Just as he knew that once on the cakes there was no going back, Martin understood that once in Kreeops' river there'd be no getting out. But both the cakes and the river were in great supply, perhaps even more abundant than the pain and confusion themselves. With a few cakes in him, if he happened to get across the river, fine. If he crazed-out or leapt into it, that was fine, too.

The old man was oblivious to the river; though he sailed it, he was off on a journey of his own, freed from worry. Martin had a cake almost to his mouth when he let it drop. For the moment.

A dry spray was tossed up against his face. He peered over the edge and saw his own face peering back as the raft passed over the moonlit "water." Everywhere he looked that face looked back: a thousand million of him already packed into the river like bricks in an endless wall. Each identical, black-robed face fixed in its position, belonging. Together, strong and secure. He wanted to join them, yet he hesitated. Something held him back, but that something had little more force than the fear of the dark a prowler might have had in childhood, and it took a constant effort of will to keep himself on the raft. He knew it would be so much easier to just stop this effort, to simply loosen his grip and let himself roll in, the way a man toting a heavy, yet fragile burden might finally let it slip from his exhausted fingertips and smash to pieces; the way an old and befuddled prowler surrenders with well-hidden gratitude the leadership of the gang to someone else.

But there was something not quite right about those faces in the river; envisioning his own, it seemed different and original. And weak and befuddled though he was, Martin realized that part of him was still beyond the suffering and confusion, watching himself enduring them. And it occurred to him that he might well be less transitory than either. Besides, it almost seemed that just swaying with the force of those babbling winds, just testing himself against the incredible pain of the wound, was giving a balance to his body and a tone to his muscles that set him apart from those numbed faces.

"Hold on! The raft will sail clear of the pain! And you'll still be on it when the pain's gone and the finger's healed," Martin whispered to himself, or one of the voices murmured. Almost spasmodically, he managed to dump the cakes into the river, and they sank behind him. When he pulled his hand out of the "water," it was covered with a hot maroon dust that was indistinguishable from the dried blood around his wound.

Though the gusting confusion in the air still threatened to knock him into that river even if he would not go there willingly, and though it showed no signs of abating, Martin now believed that he could hold out. Even this river had a far shore. Perhaps there he would discover shelter from these winds. In any case, he could hang on, hoping for a chance to go where this river would never take him. There was a quality in the difference between his face and those in the river that he wanted to explore. (And without having to actually think it, he knew that the river would always be there to come back to.) He moved over toward the center of the raft where it wasn't as hot. He was already less afraid.

After a while, a long while, there was a tug on his nonexistent finger and a coolness entered his hand and rose up his right arm, spreading into his chest, then pulsing through his body. It reached his head, at first soothing, then, after a few minutes, clearing his mind. He lay on his back; he was almost comfortable. The raft was beached. The sky was filled with stars; the moon was gone and so was the old man. A moment later, he looked toward the gentle tugging on his finger. Ryenna was at his side, sucking on the stub. The chill that had been soothing at first was starting to become distinctly cold and uncomfortable. Eventually she lifted her head. She wiped the blood from her face slowly. His finger had stopped bleeding.

"That was the ordeal of initiation," she said.

"Which explains why the world isn't overflowing with disciples."

"Sliding into the river is the easiest thing in the world. Those that go in get fished out downstream where the river winds by the Castle. The river sweeps them right into the coven, so to speak, and they become disciples."

"I'd have drowned."

"Most don't." she said with her usual unconcern. "On the other hand, those who choose the cakes stay staggerers. We put them out on the streets with the rest of their kind and let the bureauers take care of them."

He didn't mention that she was supposed to be a bureauer. Instead he said, "You didn't throw the old man out with the other staggerers."

She looked at him blankly.

"The old man from the ferry," he explained. "The one who shoved us out into the river."

"He stays and fills his hours by hunting down and destroying those novices who decide not to try returning to the coven in the first place," she said matter-of-factly. Then, changing the subject without pausing, "In recent memory, except for you, only Kreeops and the Bride of Jefuson have made it all the way across the river. Kreeops says the Bride made it only with his aid."

He examined his finger again. It was raw and bloody, but at least for the time being the pain had stopped. Before he slept, he listened to the sound of the dark water lapping around the edges of the raft. Someplace, asleep or awake, he saw Ryenna at his side.

Martin was waiting for Ryenna to return from her trip to the nearby clump of scruffy trees. Her modesty was unexpected, due, he figured, to her upbringing as a bureauer woman.

From where he stood, he had a good view of the distant Castle. He'd never seen anything like it. Or had he? Among his pictures? Certainly there was nothing like it in the city. Which brought him back again to the question he couldn't answer: where was he now?

The Castle seemed almost an outgrowth of a stunted rise, set solidly on its top like an addition to nature, an improvement. Its towering walls, of the same granite as the surrounding hills, were topped at regular intervals with graceful turrets. On each turret was a pennant of solid gleaming black; they flapped on the breeze with the sound of giant engines.

The massive gate in the front seemed as solid and secure as the stone itself. At first the Castle seemed barren, perhaps lacking some detail. Then Ryenna came striding determinedly out of the trees, and as they got closer it seemed more complete. A drawbridge protected the entrance. It was down, spanning a moat so deep that the river inside it could only be seen from the edge of the moat or from the drawbridge itself. From what Ryenna had told him, Martin knew this was the river they had already crossed, the river of the Regent, just winding back on itself. The gusts that swarmed about the castle walls were cold, soul-chillingly cold. Ryenna's hood was up, sheltering her face. Pulling up his own seemed to help.

Suddenly Martin was certain that he didn't want to enter that fortress. Not then, not there. He felt that he'd been tricked, led blindly to just that spot at just that time. He reasoned that if he was supposed to be a god, he should choose the time, if not the place, for his confrontation with Kreeops. He held back. Ryenna tugged on his arm, softly at first, then harder. Resisting her increasing force, he managed to grab onto the rail of the bridge with both hands. But her strength was incredible.

"Come on," she said. It was an order. Her voice was unfamiliar.

"No!"

"You are to come!" she said, sounding a bit more like herself.

"Why? And according to who?"

He did feel rather silly. He wondered if he was just trying to rationalize a basically irrational fear.

He was about to be overcome by her strength when she stopped pulling. With one hand she held him securely. The other hand went to her hood, giving him his first glimpse beyond that hood since she'd returned from her trip to the trees. Though the hand blocked his view of the lower part of her face, the eyes he saw were not the hard yet beautiful eyes that he'd expected. But what eyes they were! To stare into the pit of those eyes was to descend into a black, tortured, multi-leveled hell.

If this was a woman, she must be a mother of demons. The hand at the face was large and thick, not feminine at all. Martin noticed a silver ring he'd never seen Ryenna wearing. Its black stone flashed, as abruptly the hand snatched away the hood, and Martin was gazing at a face that might have been a model of deliberate greed and sadism, a portrait of evil.

"Kreeops," Martin said, softly.

The gate to the Castle burst open and a horde of black-robed disciples flooded out. With them was Ryenna, the real Ryenna, wrapped in a folker cloak that was far too big for her, looking proud and scornful, red hair blowing, eyes flashing only briefly into Martin's: flashing in accusation, as if what she'd done was his fault.

Then he was free of Kreeops' grip. He started to run, knowing it was hopeless, knowing it was probably exactly what they wanted him to do, realizing that Kreeops, physically so much more powerful than he, had held him just long enough to bring him to the verge of panic. Very likely the Regent had only let him go so that he would have to be captured and dragged into the Castle forcibly, more like a felon than a god. It infuriated Martin to think that he was being played with like that, and before he knew what he was doing, he'd turned and was charging toward his would-be pursuers, growling and waving his arms around like a crazer.

The disciples were momentarily stunned. Even Kreeops caught himself ducking back reflexively.

"To the Castle," yelled Martin, pointing behind them as if they were troops under his command who were only accidentally heading in the wrong direction.

No one moved except five or six very large male disciples, who had surrounded the Regent instantly when Martin had leapt forward. Now, equally rapidly, they subdued Martin while the others watched. Everyone seemed very impressed by his rashness, though nobody treated him like a god.

He was half-dragged, half-carried across the drawbridge and through the main gate. Off to the side of the entrance way was an iron door. Passing through it, he was taken down a long, close, torchlit corridor. He stumbled over its rough-hewn blocks to a winding staircase that was carved out of the living rock. A long climb was followed by another corridor. Except for its well-varnished floor, this passage was crudely made, as if for servants rather than for the real presence in the Castle.

Suddenly Martin was pushed sideways through an almost invisible opening in a drapery and into an enormous hall packed with more black robes. The hall was of such splendor as would impress even one who had not spent his formative years jammed into a single room with twenty other people. As long as the distance a strong man might throw a hunk of brick, it was perhaps half as wide. The floor was made up of large squares of different colored marble, cunningly fit together so that, if not for the change in color, the cracks between the squares would have been almost invisible. Martin had the impression that the squares made up a design, but from where he stood he couldn't be sure. The walls were three stories high; black satin curtains covered their lower halves; above the curtains, mosaics of sparkling stones formed a set of pictures. From the appearance of one of the men who recurred throughout the scenes, Martin guessed that this was the story of Jefuson. Here was a resemblance even he could see. He also recognized Kreeops in a couple of the scenes. It was a bad likeness, almost a caricature.

A huge, flaming pentagram hung from the ceiling, providing the light.

At one end of the room, marble tiers led up to a huge canopied throne. Its great seat was empty, as was one of the two smaller chairs that were on the next level down and to the right. The other chair was occupied by an old man with a large golden medallion around his neck, conspicuously dressed in red robes with a tiny red hat perched on the back of his head. He was busily worrying the end of one sleeve with his fingers, as if testing the material.

Martin's captors pushed him toward the center of the room, using him to batter their way through the crowd to where a black pentagram about the size of a sewer cover was inlaid in the marble floor. It was probably the only place on the floor where no disciples were standing. His guards, who seemed to be taking care to stay out of it, positioned Martin inside, facing the throne. At his feet, three white crosses were inlaid on the field of black.

The silence thickened. Martin tried to look around, but a sharp blow to the small of his back made him think better of it. The room began to glow with a red light that got progressively more maroon. The source of the light was nowhere apparent; certainly the fiery pentagram over their heads wasn't providing nearly that much illumination.

Over the throne, about a third of the way up one of the mosaics, he noticed what appeared to be a small balcony, virtually invisible within the picture there. As he watched, he could have sworn he saw movement in a piece of the wall behind it, as if a door had closed but having closed was now undetectable.

A change had come over the room. For a moment it was so subtle that he wasn't sure exactly what the difference was.

It was a sound: low, like barely discerned thunder, off almost beyond the horizon of his hearing. Gradually, as it got louder, he realized that it was a chant, coming from the robed figures packed around him. It seemed to have words, but he couldn't tell what they were. He knew it had meaning, or at least purpose. It swept him up into its power as a windspout sweeps up the refuse in its path, swirling, tumbling; and as the urge became overwhelming, he found himself chanting too, not knowing where the sounds came from.

The song built to a crest and, in a great wave of feeling, broke abruptly, sharply, leaving Martin at the top of a wave that no longer existed, weightless for an instant, yet about to plunge smashing to the ground as the curtain directly behind the throne parted and the Power stepped into the room to receive the suspended emotion.

6

The Gov-Cent

The bones of the baby lay just out of reach, across the limit in what was left of the other half of the room. Beyond the jagged ends of the floor tiles, there was nothing. Only evening sky and, below that, the calm waters.

Gena was propped up against the far wall, exhausted, trying to regain enough energy to get out of there before the disciples arrived.

She realized the arrogance it had taken to believe she could get across here. How many attempts had been made at this very point, by the desperate mother and by half of the curiosity seekers who'd entered the room since? The ringing had settled deep in her head, underneath the monstrous headache the actual attempts to cross had given her.

Three times she'd pressed herself against the limit, her eyes fixed on a spot where the waters merged with the gloom of twilight. Three times she'd made absolutely no progress. On the last attempt, the pain had her on the verge of passing out and the ringing in her head had become such a screeching that she could almost hear the barrier commanding her not to pass. And that's when she'd seen it, so indistinct, so close to illusion, that even now she wasn't sure that she hadn't imagined it.

It may have been land; it may have been a structure. Whatever it was, it appeared to have its base in the waters and its summit in the sky. There wasn't supposed to be anything out there!

When she'd fallen away from the limit, she'd had barely enough strength to crawl as far away as the wall. She'd never heard of it affecting people as severely as it did her. To be sure, no one could get through, but most people regarded the limit as a passive force, a sort of invisible stone wall. With her, it seemed to be more aggressive, counterattacking fiercely when she attempted penetration. The excitement of her discovery drained almost immediately; even if she had seen an island, what difference did it make? If the city wasn't all there was, it might as well be, for all the chance anyone had of getting out.

One thing was certain: she had to leave that room, and soon. Still a long time passed before, with tears that were a mixture of exhaustion, frustration, and rage streaming down her face, she stumbled to her feet and out the door. She practically fell down the stairs, but it still took a lot longer than going up.

Back down in the street, she was too tired and too lost in her own distressing thoughts to notice Mengra slip from a nearby alley and follow after her. In any case it was getting dark and his hood was up. One folker cloak looked pretty much like another.

But if the hood had been down and Gena had been close enough to recognize his features, she would have seen a very different man than the one she'd frightened off earlier. The jaw under the beard was tense, his teeth working anxiously against each other. His expression was no longer resigned; it was hungry. The eyes gazed in her general direction, yet might have been focused on a more distant prey.

He advanced cautiously. He might have been stalking a

creature of incredible ferocity, but one which could deliver his most longed-for desires, and even those for which he had yet to long, a creature that could at once supply the dream as well as its satisfaction, but one which in the blink of an errant eye could turn and devour the life that dared to pursue it.

When Gena had read Mengra's brother, Martin, the image she'd gotten of Mengra was that of a willful boy, careening haphazardly through the city. When she'd run into Mengra, he'd seemed to be careening no longer, but frustrated and a bit angry, starting to sour. The big man behind her now looked older and, as he pushed his way through the crowded street, he was slow and self-controlled, and yet as unyielding as a spreading cancer.

Gena, on the other hand, was just walking. She had no place to go. Anywhere she might hide between the limit and the Gov-Cent, sooner or later, and probably sooner, the disciples would catch up with her.

The Gov-Cent! she said to herself, pondering the unspeakable. The folker disguise wouldn't help her much there, since folkers weren't even allowed in. She'd probably be killed on sight. But even that might be preferable to what the disciples would do. And they'd never think of looking for her there, or at least it might be a while before they thought of it. And more importantly, there and there alone could she hope to discover a way to cross the limit, and that was her only chance of permanent escape. She pulled her cloak around her tighter. As soon as the decision to go was made, she realized how it could be accomplished. She also realized it was like jumping off a collapsing bridge to keep from going down with it. In twenty years of solitary life, she had seldom felt so alone.

She found a sheltered doorway and tried to sleep. No sense in traveling any farther that night. Part of her mind was almost hoping she'd get caught before she could put her plan into operation, but she slept. The chill of morning came and she awoke, as did the street around her.

Those food units that had had them rekindled last night's banked fires with fireburn that the women had slept on so they might still have it in the morning. Children cried and were hit for it, and so cried all the louder. Some of the units that still had coups left sent people off to the local safeway for breakfast, and soon the familiar smell of poorage returned to the air. Gena ignored her hunger. In a doorway opposite her, a staggerer got up awkwardly, stretched and fell sideways against the wall. Without bothering to right himself, he pulled a handful of poorage from a pocket and ate it raw and dry. He reached into his robe again and popped something else into his mouth: his first cake of the day. He sat back down. No need to move. At least, not until he ran out of poorage or cakes, and even the for- mer wouldn't be critical immediately. Except for their cakes, staggerers ate almost nothing.

The day that was upon them moved from black to the usual gray. Some days made it nearly all the way to yellow. For no apparent reason, Gena had an almost overpowering urge to cry, but she didn't. She heard the clanging bells and the complaining engine of the approaching trash reaper, and she was just as happy the sun hadn't risen. It wasn't a time to feel too alive.

The majority of the wagons in the city were what the bureauers referred to as "poorage-powered," meaning they were propelled by the sweat of the prowlers who pulled them. Infrequently, cows might be used to pull meat wagons to the Gov-Cent. Only a few vehicles moved under their own power: run by steam or batteries or fueled by the oily pools in and around the giant cylinders that stood in a remote section of the folker ring. Among the motor vehicles were a few policer tanks, an even fewer passenger cars for the fattest of the Big Eaters, and these trash reapers.

The reapers were semienclosed cabs pulling long open trailers. They roamed the streets, hitting each neighborhood every day or two. Many folkers spent most of their time foraging for trash: pieces of ancient leather or rubber, tattered bits of cloth too small even for use in reweave, inedible weeds and insects, anything organic that could be exchanged for a farewell coupon or two when the reaper came around. And everyone got a few more vital coups for the waste from their crap boxes and for their garbage (usually only the nails, teeth, and the cleanly picked, demarrowed bones of dead relatives, the inedible parts of pigeons and rats, and maybe a fish skin or two).

The reapers carried all this back to the Gov-Cent, where it was processed, combined with a little plant matter and "who knows what other shit," and then distributed through the safeways to be reused as food: the poorage that fed the city. Gena had heard that some of the poisons that were removed eventually became the cakes that went to the staggerers in such abundance.

The reaper drove slowly past. Several children were hitching rides on its wide rear bumper, not going anywhere, just out for a little free fun. Gena ran a few steps, and she leapt for the one open space on the bumper at the same time as a smelly young boy of about twelve. Colliding in the air, they both missed the truck and tumbled, entangled, to the pavement, inciting jeers and laughter in the folkers who'd come down to exchange their trash.

"Likes 'em young, she does," taunted a woman.

"True desperate for it, when she has to tackle it in the street like a prowler," said another, a male this time.

Gena-gul struggled to her feet. Unfortunately part of her cloak caught under the boy and opened up, revealing her naked body from the waist down. She managed to hold the top of the robe closed, preventing her disciple tattoo from being exposed, but she was frightened of the attention she was receiving. With this much incentive, main street or no, the men present might try to sex her. She'd seen it happen where a woman, especially one who was still young and desirable, could be passed from man to man, regardless of gang affiliation, almost indefinitely. Her skin stung from the eyes upon her; the block was packed with ready men. She snatched at the cloak, but it was still caught under the boy, who was in no hurry to move.

"Not a bad idea," called someone.

The boy was scrambling up, in his eyes the first flickering of the urge that would have him jumping women of his own soon. Gena pulled the robe free and dashed for the trash reaper, hoping to get out of there before the lumbering mind of the mob had time to rouse itself to action.

"It's my seat. Go away!" yelled the boy, racing at her side, forgetting the strange new sensations and remembering what they were fighting over.

With one hand, he grabbed onto the hood of her cloak, so she was actually pulling him along behind her. She heard the well-worn fabric start to rip. He slapped at her with his other hand, but she was faster and stronger, and smashed her elbow into his face without missing a step. He went down behind her, dragging over the rough pavement for a length or so, before her hood tore free of the cloak. With a leap, she gained the seat.

She rode off to the applause of the crowd. They'd gotten a good show. With the edge of her cloak, she wiped an unexpectedly large amount of the boy's thin blood from her elbow.

The smell behind the reaper as it accumulated garbage wasn't strong enough to overcome the hunger eating at her from the inside. The stay with the disciples had weakened her in at least one way: she'd gotten used to regular meals.

A light rain began to fall. Every time they struck a particularly large obstacle or chuckhole, Gena was hit with a spray from the truck. The sprays got heavier and heavier as the trailer filled, and one by one her riding companions decided they'd had enough of this fun and hopped off. Though moving around on the bumper was awkward, and she didn't want to chance having the tattoo exposed, Gena managed to cover her head with the lower part of her cloak. This arrangement revealed quite a bit of flesh and elicited a few double-takes from those who happened to catch sight of the back of the reaper.

"Nicest pair of legs on any pile of shit I ever saw," was a typical comment. A sense of humor was a necessity in the city, but the humor was almost always low, a weapon and a vent for aggression.

Fortunately for Gena, though the truck slowed down for pickups, it hardly ever stopped completely, so it was never around any given area for too long.

The reaper was winding its way through a part of town that was unknown to her. Of course there was nothing here she hadn't seen: just more filthy roads lined by shattered buildings that were sometimes little more than towering heaps, many burned out, some just worn out by too many hopeless attempts to shelter too many hopeless generations. The people they passed were like the houses, gray and tired. Food units of several mothers and more children than they could sufficiently feed, be it two or ten, were huddled close to tiny fires that kept the streets clear of combustible litter, but gave little warmth. The truck passed one, a large unit, whose fire actually seemed to have a piece of wood in it: stolen from the walls or floor of some other unit's room, no doubt. They shouldn't have the room and the wood too, ran the argument, as the city devoured itself like an insane serpent. And the units kept growing.

The fare-well bureau was the closest thing to a father any unit had. The children got reared in common by the women. And while the male children left at sixteen, the females would stay and have children of their own. A unit that didn't produce females could be left with nothing but old women beyond childbearing age, as vulnerable, and therefore as contemptible, as loners. Many folker women had this dread, and they would scare themselves with various horrible tales, but in truth few women lived very long past the birth of their last child.

Looking at the different units during the lengthy ride, Gena was taken by how similar they all were. She'd always had some sense of herself as an outsider, accompanied by the self-inflicted judgment of inferiority that this seemed to imply. It was as if, though cut off from the other folkers, she'd nonetheless shared their values. At times she had envied them. At times she'd even hated them for what she took to be their rejection of her, though she'd always understood, at least intellectually, that this "rejection" was for the most part simply apathy. Now, covered with garbage, racing toward one horror even as she fled from another, for some reason she was suddenly thankful for her otherness, and thankful for the movement of the reaper that at once propelled her through this squalor and separated her from it. For once she didn't have the slightest desire to be part of a unit, or even to be thought part of one by this homogenous horde that seemed so much like the bland poorage that they filled themselves with. She felt alien from them, and she also felt a small and rather pleasant pity.

The trash reaper continued at a slow pace around the outskirts of the city, but before it was quite overflowing, it stopped collecting and headed for the center of town as rapidly as the congested streets and necessarily circuitous routing would allow. Gena had had more than enough of a long and uncomfortable ride by the time the reaper lumbered out of that cemetery of dead buildings, and into the vast open strip of land with no buildings, no rubble, and no people: the no-folker zone.

On either side of the road, as far as she could see, the zone was under cultivation with the squat grayish-green plants that went into the poorage. In the far distance, she could see where that poorage was produced, their destination, the Gov-Cent. Folkers, the criers implied, might occasionally be able to get special passes that would allow them into the center. Of course it was never made clear what the procedure would be for obtaining such a pass, if for some reason a folker had wanted one, which no one ever did.

The truck hit one large bump, and Gena was almost thrown off the back. Then the ride became smooth and the asphalt that whizzed by beneath the bumper was virtually unbroken, something Gena had never seen before. The familiar, homey, folker ring receded farther and farther behind her, leaving her sailing across a plain of stunted vegetation. The disciples and Kreeops and his psychotic plans for her suddenly didn't seem nearly as bad, nor as frightening as this…this strangeness…this unfamiliarity. Gena-gul had a flash of panic; she was, after all, very young. She almost leapt off the trash reaper despite the great speed it had attained. Then something within her — it might have been the disciple training — seemed to switch on, as if automatically; she regained control, focusing herself on what was happening around her, becoming very still inside and out. The reaper sped along until it was almost halfway through the zone, approaching the checkpoint in the first wall that protected "those who do the business of the people" from the people themselves.

Three checkpoints later, they entered the actual Gov-Cent. Fortunately for Gena, it had been years since the center had been under any real threat, and the guards were lax. They didn't bother to look into the trailer because they couldn't imagine that any disciple would dare try to slip into the Gov-Cent unauthorized. Or that any folker would want to: popular revolution was a virtually forgotten concept; theft was a possibility, but it was hardly likely that a folker could last long enough inside to steal very much. Besides, the bureauers were so wary of each other that their personal possessions were all well protected by sensor-doors. Government possessions were often guarded almost as jealously by officials anxious to uncover the pilfering of their own men, especially if one or more of those men coveted the official's own position. A Better could always just kill any bureauer of lesser rank, but it wasn't terribly socially acceptable unless a reason could be supplied, and the better the reason, the more credit there was in the kill. More than a few Big Eaters had gained their extra weight by gobbling up their subordinates.

The main reason, of course, why no folker would ever want to sneak into the Gov-Cent was the danger. Large numbers of policers were stationed inside, and few bureauers had the slightest qualms about killing for sport those they ruled. Bureauers in the outer ring usually minimized that sort of thing, if for no other reason than constant usage and opportunity removed most of the thrill. But the ones who never left the Gov-Cent, especially those who had no one else to lord it over, might have a very hard time passing up a shot at a real, live, unprotected folker. Especially when even the bureauers' slight concern about the possibility of reprisals from other folkers was removed. (Scandalized rumors notwithstanding, no one could remember an actual case of reprisals from any folkers anywhere.)

So no guard checked into the trailer, and no one saw the delicate nose barely sticking above the mess sloshing around back there.

The reaper made a couple of quick turns and then proceeded straight for several blocks before Gena allowed herself a peek over the edge at the inside of the Gov-Cent. To her, everything seemed to sparkle with newness. In reality, there wasn't a building in the center — including the largest and least efficient poorage processing plants which were the newest structures — that might not have been seen by Gena's great-grandmother, or even by *her* mother, had they been allowed inside, which they wouldn't have been. And most were far older. Still, almost all the windows had glass in them, and those that didn't were soundly bricked or even boarded up. The streets were not only free of holes but free of debris. And no one seemed to be living in them. The well-dressed, well-scrubbed, and well-fed pedestrians walked down the sidewalks, leaving the streets open for vehicle traffic. Later she would note that the air was free of the smell of human refuse, but from the position she was in at the moment that observation was impossible. In any case the total effect of the Gov-Cent was awe-inspiring, and intimidating enough that, even if her life hadn't been endangered, Gena would have been hard-pressed for the courage to climb out of the garbage and down into the bureaurers' part of the city.

No one in the street paid any attention to the reaper. Soon it turned down a narrow road, then into an alley. Gena couldn't see any pedestrians here, but she still hadn't worked up the courage to jump out when the truck slipped into a tunnel. Beneath the echoing of the truck's laboring engine, she could hear the clanking of heavy machinery. The reaper pulled into a large concrete cavern and took its place at the end of a line of three other trucks. On either side were open pits, and each truck drove as close as possible to the low protecting wall around them, then dumped its load sideways over the edge and moved on. Gena knew it was past time for her to leave; she didn't feel ready to become part of somebody's breakfast. The problem was, not only did the truck she was in have a driver and an attendant, but she could hear another reaper coming down the tunnel behind them. Being seen meant being killed, probably viciously with as many of these rankenfile bureaurers getting in on it as were within earshot. In her condition, she wasn't even worth sexing.

It seemed to take her forever to climb down out of the truck. She'd no sooner done so than the driver, with an efficiency seldom found elsewhere in the city, pushed his dump switch. One side of the trailer lifted while the other side opened, and the load was released.

Gena darted between the pits, squatting down so that their walls would hide her from view. The pits were irregularly spaced; she threaded her way between them, heading toward the far wall of the cavern, sometimes crawling, sometimes dashing forward in a crouching run, using her hands occasionally to keep from falling over.

She was almost to the wall when she heard voices approaching. Just ahead was a space between the last pits and the wall, and in that space was a line of metal bins. Scrambling into the closest one, she landed face down on top of the dull white jelly inside. Some of it got up her nose and into her mouth, coating them unpleasantly. It stung her eyes.

"Ready?" called a man from nearby.

"Ready," came the distant answer.

Footsteps approached. An engine started up, and under the cover of its noise Gena tried to clear her throat. She heard a clanging of metal against metal.

After a moment, there was a scraping against the outside of the bin. Afraid her breathing might be loud enough to hear, Gena held her breath.

"OK," someone said.

More machinery whirred. The bin shook and then lifted, swaying violently. In spite of herself, Gena let the air out of her lungs. The barrel rose for a while, then stopped and with another jerk began moving to the side. The swaying became a gentle rocking. She would have liked to peek over the top, to see what was going on, but she was afraid of tipping the thing over.

Then the noise of the machinery lifted to a higher pitch, and she was descending. With a splash the bottom met resistance; when she got to her feet, the drum was sinking into what looked like a huge pool of poorage, and the line that had lowered it was ascending, alone, toward the ceiling. Rapidly, the bin filled with the stuff of the pool and vanished into the depths beneath her; Gena managed to keep her head above the surface, first by climbing the side of the rusty barrel, then by thrashing her arms about in the poorage.

It wasn't actually poorage, or maybe it just wasn't poorage yet. The viscous solution that surrounded her looked like the folker food, all right, but it was much greasier, and it smelled like the decomposing garbage in the reaper. Still, the fetid air tasted sweet, as Gena cleared her eyes and carefully scanned the top of the tank a couple of lengths above her. She wasn't sure how much of her fear she'd broadcast, but she half-expected a party of disciple faces to appear at the rim at any moment (even though she knew the disciples were hardly likely to venture into the Gov-Cent, lest their meat wind up on bureauer tables and their bones wind up in these very pits).

Of course the bureauers in the area wouldn't have been able to read Gena's mental shrieks, no matter how loud. And now, she looked enough like the rest of the contents of the tank as to be indistinguishable to any casual observer from above.

She remembered the detached, almost superior way she'd dismissed the lot of the folker women that morning, and practically laughed aloud. Now, enveloped in this particular sea, unable to find any way out, being common seemed wonderful. She would have gladly traded places with any of them, the more common the better: living and dying in ignorance of disciple life and poorage pits and other extraordinary terrors, just being a simple folker, part of a self-perpetuating unit, raising babies, collecting fare-well coups, sharing mundane duties and mundane fears with the most unspecial group of women she could find—this seemed to define luxury more than all the wealth she'd witnessed in the Gov-Cent.

She discovered she could swim through the thick swill, and she headed toward the closest wall. Her progress was slow and the air no longer tasted very pure, but eventually she reached it. The concrete rose above her head, featureless, unscalable. She'd hoped the pool would be shallower at its edges, but she still couldn't touch the bottom. Working down the wall, she soon came to several pipes extending outward enough for her to cling onto and grab a little rest. There were markings on them, which, of course, she was unable to understand. As a small child, Gena had considered the ancient writing visible around the city to be a kind of talking design that had grown too old for speech, as if the talent that had atrophied was in the symbols themselves. What a surprise it had been to learn that, supposedly, at the very highest levels of government, people could still interpret them; that, in some strange and different way, the symbols still spoke; she simply couldn't hear.

While she rested, she got an almost overpowering urge to rinse out her mouth, and she suddenly found herself vomiting so violently that she lost her grip on the pipes and slipped back into the pool. Floating there on her side, she felt as well as heard a great clanging of gears. Then the level of the poorage started dropping, and dropping fast. She grabbed a pipe and held on as the gruel receded from her body. Before long, she was hanging almost completely out of it; fortunately, another pipe was revealed, over to the side a bit, at about knee level, and she was able to get a foothold on that.

In the wall adjacent to the one from which she hung, a circular hole was emerging: like a hollow sun, burnt out and used up, but nonetheless still rising over a smelly, decaying planet, as if either aware of some greater continuity or just helpless to stop. When Gena could see the entire hole, it occurred to her that it was about the size and shape of the opening in an ancient toilet. She'd seen quite a few. Toilets were a folker luxury, not for the function for which they'd originally been designed, but rather as chairs, the toilet being one of the very few objects from the Age of Origin capable of withstanding the rigors of day-to-day life in the city. Filled with dirt, it made an excellent seat, one that was difficult to steal.

Gena gathered her strength and plunged back into the pool, heading straight across for the opening rather than expending herself by working her way around the edge. It was a shame, she thought, that she couldn't tap whatever it was in the slimy stuff that would eventually provide energy for all those folkers. All she was getting from it was the suffocating odor of rotting death.

After the initial discovery of her ability to stay afloat, Gena had been too busy to question it, which was just as well. Once, back in the coven, she'd accidentally read Zaletus' mind, in spite of the screen he'd had on his thoughts.

"You're not supposed to be able to do that," he'd informed her. He hadn't been displeased.

"Well," she'd replied lightly, "nobody bothered to tell me."

Saying that, she'd remembered for the first time what had caused the small limp that always came upon her when she was exceptionally fatigued; perhaps all the hours of straining to fill the gaps in her memory had paid off, though this was something that had happened long before she'd become a disciple. And she'd begun to describe to Zaletus what had happened: how as a child of about eight, she'd tried to leap across an alley from one thirdstory window to another, knowing in advance that she wasn't going to make it, falling badly and breaking her leg. Halfway through the telling, she'd realized that the story didn't illustrate her point. Apologetically she'd interrupted herself:

"Of course, I never could have made it across that alley, no matter what." With a self-deprecating laugh, she added, "But lack of confidence didn't help."

She'd said nothing about it to Zaletus, but she'd also remembered a certain satisfaction that seemed tied to the actual fall. And for the rest of her time with the disciples, it had puzzled her. Had she jumped to put an end to a lonely and unpleasant life? With all the honesty she could muster, she didn't believe that. As a little girl, she'd always been far too concerned with just maintaining life; it would never have occurred to her to wonder if that goal of living was desirable. Rather the satisfaction that she remembered seemed to have sprung more from relief that she hadn't been able to make the jump successfully. It was the kind of relief adolescents have when they discover that they really don't have the skinniest, most ridiculous legs in the neighborhood.

After Gena'd remembered the incident, she considered it strange that she'd ever managed to forget it in the first place. It was a miracle that such a little child, all alone in the city, had even survived a broken leg. But since she'd been unable to raise any recollection at all of the recovery period, it didn't seem that she'd gone through any especially extraordinary hardship.

In any case, now, in the poorage pool, she never questioned her swimming ability. She had no reason to know whether everyone could swim instinctively or not. The source of all the city's water was the River, where any folker washing and bathing was done. But though it was broad enough, its languid, muddy waters were never over knee-deep and usually less. The likelihood of anyone being immersed in enough water for swimming being so remote, Gena-gul, at least, had never even wondered whether or not it was possible.

Now she pulled herself up to the hole in the wall and peered inside. The small concrete passageway sloped gently upward, disappearing from view. She could do no more than guess where it led — probably, she imagined, to just another pool. She slipped off the dangerous folker robe. It was soaked through anyway, weighing her down, and the narrow tunnel would be scarcely large enough for her to make her way even without the restriction of loose and sodden clothing. She kept her sandals on.

Pulling herself forward on her elbows and forearms, she went in headfirst. The slime that covered her naked skin gave some lubrication, but it was a tight fit on all sides; the rough cement scraped on her stomach and thighs; cuts opened on her knees and arms. She realized that she would be unable to turn around in the event that the tunnel proved to be a dead end. Backing out would certainly be even more difficult and more painful than going in, and might just prove impossible.

Outside somewhere, the gears were clamoring again. The tunnel being effectively plugged by her body, the noise was muted. She inched forward. The clanging might well signal another drop in the level of the tank. Or a rise. She could feel and, unfortunately, even taste the slime on the floor, the sides, and even the top of the passage. She struggled on, trying to hurry, but moving only inches at a time. Before long, her feet were just dragging uselessly behind her body, so numb that she didn't feel the poorage climbing up the sloping tunnel until it reached her calves. Her eyes strained forward, searching for another opening ahead, but there was nothing to be seen and the effort to keep her head up was so tiring that she soon gave it up, crawling along blindly instead, her cheeks brushing if not scraping the wet floor.

The fetid odor, which had never actually gone, now filled

the tunnel. And as the level of the swill rose, so did Gena's desperation. Her body slipped along easier on the slime as again and again, she threw herself forward, no alternatives left to consider.

The poorage stung as it mingled with the blood in the scratches on her face and body. She panted in a mouthful, choking violently. Awkwardly and painfully, she managed to turn herself and crawl along on her back, using her elbows and, her numbed feet being unresponsive, jamming the sides of her knees against the walls for added leverage. When she relaxed for just a moment and rested her head on the concrete, her ears filled. She shut her eyes, more against her own sweat than the slime, and pressed on. What air there was to breathe had grown so vile that she gagged on almost every gasp. The tunnel was headed somewhere; it must be. *Don't all paths have purpose?* she wondered, without wondering where she'd gotten such an idea. At any rate, maybe this tunnel was the exception: maybe for some reason it had never been finished. Or maybe, as seemed to be case with so much in the city, its path and purpose were so distant in time and thought as to have been lost, circumvented, destroyed, blocked, or just worn out in the unclocked time since the Age of Origin. Or maybe it had never really had a purpose at all: maybe those who claimed to understand the "how" and the "what" and the "why" of the world left by the Originals were as full of shit as the poorage she was drowning in. Maybe, in violation of whatever laws were supposedly decreed for man and nature, the city was nothing but a place of deadend passages without function, and orphaned girls who *could* taste the approach of menace. Maybe the bureaurers fulfilled empty positions and the disciples trained so rigorously, and neither understood either where they had been or where they were going.

Now, she was almost covered, and her efforts had bogged

down considerably. If she'd been going faster, banging her head against the wall at the end of the tunnel might have knocked from her what little consciousness she had left. As it happened, it didn't even disrupt her train of thought.

The breeze, hardly more than the faintest stirring of air against her bare breasts and stomach, was a sensation satisfying in and of itself, one to be fully savored, like a farewell kiss in the waning moments of a lifetime. It cleared Gena's head enough for her to realize that it was something more than that.

The opening was several feet short of the end of the tunnel. She would have been aware of it sooner, but her chest didn't quite reach the top of the passage. Consequently, she never touched the gap in the roof that was the gateway to a similar shaft, this one leading upward, almost perpendicular to the one she was in. Sliding down, she maneuvered herself into a sitting position, her torso up in the second tunnel. It was a bit larger. Far above her, she could detect light. A few seconds of exploring and she discovered a scoring in the cement, and, a moment later, another one above that, and then still another. She'd been provided a ladder! Though straight up, the climb might have been easy compared to what she'd just been through, but when she got to her feet they were like dead hunks of meat, and she slipped off the first rung several times before they prickled to a numbness capable of supporting her. The tunnel below her had already filled with the stuff that would soon feed the city, and it was rising.

When she'd scaled almost to the top, she chanced a reading. Finding no sign of anyone above her, she continued up and, after peering cautiously over the edge, she climbed out into a deserted but busy-looking room packed with cylindrical containers, charts, chairs, and a single table with what appeared to be the remnants of somebody's lunch lying on it. Footsteps approached, and Gena dashed back toward the tunnel, but they'd already gone past by the time she got there. More footsteps came and went. She waited, naked, motionless, poised as if her very breath might topple the walls of the room and leave her exposed. She was afraid to go outside, yet she realized what would happen if she stayed there until one of those sets of footsteps came in and found her. She tried to probe the minds of the people who went by, hoping to get an idea of the layout of the building, anything that might help her escape or even find a better place to hide. But she either couldn't understand the things she picked up or else she had no use for them, until a woman passed, on her way to the females' locker room. Only two doors down the hall! Gena waited, in the meantime bolting down the meal that had been left on the table, never even noticing the taste of the real-food. Then, once the woman had come back by and the hall outside had grown silent, she plunged through the door and raced down the featureless corridor, virtually diving into the locker room, after only the most superficial of readings.

And there *were* people inside. Luckily, they were all in other sections, using the toilets and the showers. No one saw her enter. She darted through several long lines of lockers, finally hiding in the last row, waiting for the room to clear. When it did, she checked to make sure that the lockers were indeed locked, then slipped into the showers, feeling extremely visible after the protracted mental scanning she'd done. Striving for calm, she told herself that such distant, low-level probing from such an unexpected direction would be undetectable by the disciples; she reiterated the idea several times, trying to make herself feel as well as know it.

After fooling with the knobs a bit and getting the water adjusted, she gave herself over to the shower's comforting heat and felt more anonymous. She stumbled upon the perfect place to hide a naked woman: easy enough to conceal the disciple tattoo on her breast with a carefully placed hand. But if she didn't want this to become her permanent home, somehow she had to get her hands on some bureauer clothing.

Two women came into the locker room together and eventually made their way into the shower. They were bald! Because bureauer women always wore colorful wigs instead of having tattooed "hair" like the men, Gena had forgotten that they too kept their heads and bodies shaven. She was on the verge of running, or attacking, or perhaps both, when she realized that the women had given her no more than a cursory glance. After that, women came and went, singly and in groups. And a few of them did have hair, though none of the bald ones ever spoke to those few; Gena guessed that they were the lower level of rankenfile; perhaps even too poor to afford wigs. Some of them wore sandals that were virtually as crude as Gena's. It would have been difficult to judge the relative rank of the other naked women as long as they kept quiet, though a couple of times she saw one step out of the way of another, and once or twice when it got particularly crowded, a shower was yielded. Some of the ones with hair were very young, but not all by any means. And, since rank was based on a combination of longevity and heredity, occasionally a showerful of chatter ceased abruptly and respectfully at the entrance of a woman even younger than Gena. Except for those few (often masculine) women who had risen very high in the bureaucracy (and apparently had their own shower room), fat was not considered a mark of prestige for bureauer women. They generally attempted to keep themselves thin for the men in order to be selected to mother someone's children and get out of the job market, supported for life, receiving a female equivalent of the status of the father even though they might never see the man again (especially if he didn't desire more children). Yet none of the women who came into the shower was thin by folker standards.

As time passed, Gena grew less intimidated and more impatient, waiting to be alone with someone who was in her street clothes or whose locker was open. She'd readied herself for the kill, nervous now only in that she was afraid of not getting the opportunity. For a long time, she had the shower to herself.

The woman that finally entered the room emitted weakness and confusion. Her name was Triah, and she was sick and alone, having been dismissed from work early, and her mind was on home and bed. No one would miss her; Gena read that she wasn't scheduled for work again for four days, and that there was no one else at home. Being alone was a situation the folker could understand, though it surprised her that Triah seemed to consider it normal. It also surprised her that in a way the woman was glad to be sick. Triah was thinking of the fuss her Better had made over her. In the fifteen years she'd worked in the plant, he hadn't said as much to her as he had that day. The night at home would be easier now; a glass of bureauer juice would soothe the lonely edges from her room.

Triah undressed, removing her work smock lackadaisically. To Gena, out of sight but separated from her by only a thin partition, her thoughts were a tattered filigree, as clearly visible as a spider web in the sun.

Opening her locker, Triah glanced with the barest twinge of residual concern at the pale blue street robe and matching wig hanging there. A darker blue would have been more in fashion for her rank. But this cloak was warm and, considering the strength of her patchwork, probably sturdier now than when she'd gotten it. It would be years before she'd be allowed another. Her face tingled with a guilty excitement as she pondered her secret crime, the robe she had cached away in her kitchen, shameful, treasured, like an obscene drawing. It was practically new! Once in a great while she'd even put it on and imagine...She stopped herself before she got to *those* thoughts. *Maybe tonight.*

Naked, she hesitated before reaching for the blue wig, that stylized badge of femininity that bureauer women wore everywhere. Except while working in plants like this. To Triah, that had made the job almost degrading. Perhaps the wig served no real purpose, like the useless doorknobs attached to sensordoors, or the strange pictures and symbols on monies and on the fare-well coups of the folkers, but Triah never talked to a man during work without a self-conscious awareness of its absence, and now she felt better as she tugged it on. She opened the locker door wider and examined her failing body in the jagged hunk of mirror on the back: her breasts, big and saggy, ponderously animated by the ebb and flow of her breath; her abdomen, pale, with a trace of the puffiness of unbaked dough; the thighs, getting a little out of hand in spite of the exercises she did every night. *Not the right kind of exercise, Triah,* she kidded herself, without a smile, sucking in her stomach and twisting into a pose she would never have dared in front of a man, even a lover. Recently, she sometimes caught herself thinking of her sex life as a thing of the past. She hadn't been selected for motherhood, and wouldn't be, at her age. When she might have been chosen by a man, she hadn't been sure she wanted children, but now she missed the ones she'd never had. And she had nothing else. Even in her prime, she hadn't been fantastically desirable. And since the city had an abundance of young folker women on whom many of the bureauer males had ample opportunity to feast, even her possibilities for casual sex and the minimal companionship it offered were limited. A forbidden idea played around the edges of her consciousness.

Gena, listening in, fascinated, was startled by the strength and the rigidity of the taboo against prowler men for bureauer women. She'd heard stories and occasionally had even seen parties of Big Eater women out in the folker ring, shopping openly for whatever they desired. But at Triah's level, prowler men were unthinkable — to the extent that those dirty, vile-smelling men that Gena took every care to avoid often became the sweet stuff of fantasy.

Triah removed the wig and headed for the shower. On the threshold, she hesitated. She didn't really need a shower and she *was* a bit weak. Besides, she could hear the water running; someone was inside. It might be someone she knew. She didn't feel up to making conversation. But the habit of so many years was more powerful than an edict. More compulsive, it was less coercive: compliance came easily, almost automatically, as if in accordance with some natural law. She entered the shower: if she hadn't, she would have felt dirty when she left the building.

Gena tensed to strike. The locker was ajar; with a minimum of effort the body could be safely hidden inside. Days might pass before anyone discovered it. The robe would be about the right length; the blue wig would cover Gena's tangled folkerlike hair, which hadn't been combed out since she'd left the coven. The bureauer woman would be comparatively soft and weak; in seconds it would be all over, and Gena would be disguised and gone. She never even considered simply taking the clothing and leaving the woman alive. Life wasn't like that. And a live Triah would lose no time spreading the alarm, complete with a description of her assailant and the ID number on the clothing she'd be wearing.

Once in the shower, Triah moved past Gena, giving her even less than the brief look that bureauer courtesy permitted between strangers. Gena slipped behind her, her footfalls silenced by the running water, picturing in advance the positioning of her arms for cutting the air from the bureauer's throat. A thick scent surrounded the woman's body. Her slumping posture seemed already defeated. Gena noticed three thin scratches on the white skin at the juncture of the neck and shoulder. In the steam, moisture was beading on the fine, almost invisible layer of hair that Triah hadn't bothered to remove from her body. It was time. Gena waited. Her arms lifted slowly. (She didn't like the angle; she couldn't take a chance on a scream.) And Triah turned around. Her plain face registered confusion, then comprehension, alarm, and submission, practically before she'd even completed the turn. Face to face, the two naked women froze; Gena's hands, poised in a shadow embrace, had moved only a fraction closer to that exposed throat. Abruptly now, she tensed her fingers and clamped them against the flesh, but more in threat than in strangulation. Seeing that her victim was too frightened to cry out, she held off the consummation yet another moment.

"Make a sound and you're dead," Gena hissed. She was aware that the statement was superfluous, made perhaps to appease something in herself that had no concern for anything other than expediency.

They made their way out of the plant into the evening with a studied nonchalance that probably would have been transparent if anyone had bothered to notice, which no one did. Gena, resting a comforting hand on her sick friend's shoulder, had her fingers carefully positioned next to pressure points in Triah's neck. The disciples had taught their Bride of Jefuson well. Out on the street, Gena felt incredibly conspicuous in spite of the bureauer robe. But its full length did cover a multitude of cuts and bruises; and the blue wig shadowed the two or three bad scratches on her face reasonably effectively under the artificial glare of the streetlights.

It was common knowledge among the novices that policers in the Gov-Cent had devices that would alert them instantly if a disciple ever chanced to be nearby. Of course Gena had learned a while back that common knowledge was sometimes much more common than it was knowledge: nobody confronted them, although two or three policer tanks went by, and once a single policer sauntered past close enough to spit on. Happily, this was after Gena had come to the realization that, in the bureauers' conception of an ordered universe, pedestrians did not walk two abreast; rather each held as tightly to the right of the small sidewalks as the planets held to their paths across the heavens.

Without a plan, stranded, and now having saddled herself, in the form of Triah, with a mobile alarm system that she certainly couldn't dispose of publicly, Gena anticipated only immediate apprehension and execution. For her part, Triah was so paralyzingly convinced of her own impending death she never made the slightest sound, not even as she brushed by the patrolling policer. She was still in her work smock, hood up, to conceal her lack of a wig. The fingers were no longer resting against her neck, but they felt close by.

"Show me where you live, bureauer!" Gena demanded, herself desperate to get off these terrifying streets.

The place was nearby, in a brownstone, indistinguishable from any of its long lines of neighbors on either side of the road. Gena and Triah were already part way up the front steps when Gena spotted the sensor-door. She dug her fingers into Triah's neck and pulled back.

"Nice try, bureauer refuse," she said, not concerned with whether the confused expression on Triah's face was in fact genuine, or if she'd really been hoping to get Gena close enough to the door for it to alert the policer to the aggression against one of their own. The door couldn't probe into Gena's mind, but it definitely could react to belligerence being projected toward Triah. It occurred to Gena that the bureauers had a mechanical legacy from the Age of Origin that partially compensated for some of the disciplelike abilities they lacked in such abundance.

She drew herself and her captive back down the stairs. She didn't know how sensitive these doors were. Would simply screening her thoughts and emotions the way she did with the coven get her past? She couldn't afford to risk failure. She must actually change her attitude, ridding herself of any trace of threat toward anyone who dwelled behind that door. The disciples had taught her that emotions aren't so much driven out as they are replaced, and she gathered herself mentally: steadying, calming, looking for a serenity which would wash away her belligerence, one on which she might implant an empathy for Triah stable enough to remain until she was inside. In fact (as she might have discovered earlier by scanning Triah's thoughts instead of withdrawing into her own confusion immediately upon sight of the door), this particular model was comparatively recent and very inefficient. It was likely that the shallowest of Gena's screens would have fooled the door.

Not knowing this, Gena worked on herself. She studied the bureauer woman beside her who was so different, whose life was so alien, so distant from what Gena had experienced. Gena was a woman whose entire existence had been an almost constant struggle; how could she even begin to feel favorably toward someone who'd always had everything, someone who by every act and accident of man and nature had been placed above her?

She probed Triah. Mildly. Instantly, she touched great fear, and reacted with contempt. But she continued, tensing her own muscles as she encountered the horrible knowing pressure

on the woman's neck. She saw Triah fleeing in panic across her
bureauer's mind: stumbling over sensitivities, needs, and
desires, her pride abandoned, left to drown in a pool of helplessness deeper than Kreeops' bottomless pit. Gena saw, as
Triah saw, the face of Gena the aggressor, the rampant
unknown, incarnation of a lifetime of half-understood terrors,
an evil deity that had captured Triah's every bodily function,
and that, even now, snatched away the clumsy bundles of
tomorrows stored in the woman's imagination like emergency
candles against despair, replacing them with a gruesome vision
of a lifeless Triah lying on a blood-stained floor. For Gena, the
vision popped like a strong suction when she wrenched herself
free; and it was replaced by an all too definite memory of herself, lying on an altar slab, surrounded by the black-robed servants of another unknowable power, while that power
descended inexorably upon a body *she* had lost control of.
Great as it was, Triah's fear was less than an echo of the horror
that had overpowered Gena on the altar of Kreeops.

And Gena had just spent another afternoon of fear and
impotence here in the Gov-Cent. She was jolted by this vision
of herself as a thing, a thing of force and control and menace
that threatened Triah as Gena herself had been threatened. Her
contempt for her victim had vanished, replaced by an almost
maternal desire to protect the woman, to shelter her like an
infant in her arms. Gena had been an infant herself.

She had no trouble passing the outer sensor-door to the
building, nor, after climbing three flights of stairs still somewhat in touch with Triah (though at a safer distance), did she
have any difficulty with the slightly more stringent door to
Triah's apartment.

The room they entered was small, and a streaky, subdued
blue. The plaster was almost uncracked; the window was
securely bricked up, and a naked electric bulb in the ceiling

flickered on when Triah touched a switch. A single dying plant sat in a cup on the windowsill. It was about ready for the poorage plant itself, not surprisingly, since no light ever shone through those bricks. A sleeping pad lay in one corner and an often-patched, overstuffed chair sat by a door in the far wall. The only real evidence of wealth was a dirt-colored cat that jumped lithely from the chair and prowled over to rub demandingly against Triah's legs. That explained the scratches. Gena had seen a cat before, once; it was being prepared for the pot. She hadn't gotten any, but she'd heard that it wasn't as stringy as rat or as salty as people.

Triah's fright seemed to have eased somewhat since entering her own apartment building. Whether from the illusion of safety imparted by the familiar surroundings or from some dim comprehension of the change in Gena's emotions, even she might have been unable to say. She bent to pick up the cat, stroking it comfortingly, but it hissed and twisted free, returning to its chair with a leap of graceful ease.

For her own safety, Gena tried to separate herself from that formerly necessary empathy. She wanted to see Triah as simply another obstacle that had to be removed. It was difficult. She had no belief whatsoever in a god, any god at all, much less a just one, but somehow it did seem that violating Triah's helplessness would be calling something down upon her own.

"The limit," Gena said, stating the subject as folkers habitually did to avoid the rudeness of a question. She was just a bit relieved to have a necessary reason for not snuffing out the life in front of her just yet.

"The limit?" Triah mumbled. Gena's reading picked up no single image, only chaos.

"The limit! Out by the land's end…before you get to the waters! What do you know about the limit?" The questions were sarcastic and almost violent. As an afterthought, Gena shoved the woman by one shoulder, though not really very hard. Triah was shaking her head negatively.

"The way it works, refuse. You're a bureauer, aren't you? How does the limit work?"

Finally, an image that Gena could understand gathered in Triah's mind. About all that Triah knew about the limit, aside from the logo, was that it was around the city for her protection and that it could never be penetrated. Her conception of the steely gray waters outside it was fairly accurate; but, instead of the total disorder of the folker ring, she envisioned the area as similar to what the Gov-Cent would have been like if it had been given over to savages several years back.

"Shit!" said Gena, disgusted and amazed that this bureauer knew less about a part of the city than she did herself, a completely ignorant loner.

"I don't know, believe me," Triah implored.

"Shit!" said Gena again, this time calling Triah that name. Her voice wasn't as hard as she would have liked, which angered her even more, and she flung Triah across the room. Right into the well-padded chair. The cat jumped clear just in time.

Gena stretched out on the sleeping pad, hopefully out of the range of the door. She'd forgotten all about it. Though reputedly able to monitor aggression against the inhabitant from either side, it had yet to make a sound or change in any manner. Gena figured she was still all right.

"The Bureau of Knowledge," Triah offered, not wondering why that particular place had suddenly popped into her mind, more concerned with trying to convince her captor of her desire to cooperate. She surprised Gena, who'd given up on her.

"You said…"

"The Bureau of Knowledge might have…what you want.

It seems to me they're somehow connected with the bound-aries of the city."

Gena sat upright. Not that she couldn't see immediately that, except for where it was located and what the building looked like, the woman had as little conception of the Bureau of Knowledge as she did of the limit. But Gena had suddenly remembered that the Big Eater, Brodwich, had been connected with that bureau. *Brodwich:* who the bureauer with the face of the Jefuson had referred to as "one of the most important men in the city." Where one of the most important men in the city worked, they were bound to know whatever there was to know about the limit and the waters. Even the name, Bureau of Knowledge, made that apparent.

"Poorage," demanded Gena, with less hostility now, her mind elsewhere as she settled back on the pad.

After an uncertain look, Triah got up from her chair. "The kitchen," she explained, before disappearing through the door beside the chair.

"Two rooms, hunh?" called Gena with more distaste than she really felt. "Spoiled bureauer shit. The city's jammed with folkers dying in overcrowded streets, you know. And you ram-ble around in two rooms."

Hardly outraged, Gena just felt the need for an accusation to fling at the woman. With a lifetime of sleeping on the streets behind her, Gena not only didn't see it as a hardship, she pre-ferred it to sleeping inside.

Triah prepared the food and they both ate. Gena stayed the night, tying the bureauer up loosely and sleeping fitfully herself. The next morning, they ate again, and Gena set off for the Bureau of Knowledge, tying Triah even more loosely, and muttering a few threats about coming back and doing her in if she alerted the policers. She didn't expect the threats to work. She considered attempting to plant a suggestion of strong affection for her in Triah's mind, but didn't bother, reasoning that would be even less effective than the threats. She *was* counting on the new robe she'd taken from its hiding place in the kitchen while Triah was asleep; it was a much darker blue than the one she was wearing when Triah watched her leave that morning, and, more importantly, the ID number on it was different, not Triah's number at all. She changed into it in an alley near the brownstone.

While Gena was changing, Triah was already free and in the kitchen, answering a call on the phone, getting the best proposition she'd gotten in years. Kreeops' private guard might not have been able to read Gena, but, from just outside the Gov-Cent, the panic in Triah's mind had been relatively easy to focus in on. They'd been surprised by how receptive she'd been to the suggestion they'd sent her about the Bureau of Knowledge as an answer to Gena's question. Triah'd never even considered that it might not be her own idea.

Perhaps the distance was too great for the guards to be sure of relaying the direct message from the greater power effectively; perhaps they simply found Triah's mind too fragile to handle such a contact. In any case, the party that called her that morning was not in the habit of relying on the phone, or on other such flimsy methods of persuasion. Which is not to say that he was inadequate to the task.

7

Temptation

The room fell, actually seemed to drop, into another full silence. Attention was riveted to the man in the black satin robe and cowl standing in front of the throne. No doubt it was Kreeops, though on the bridge Martin hadn't considered him especially tall, and this man towered over the red-robed figure who was stepping up to the tier below to greet him. Martin found it nearly impossible to take his eyes off the Regent.

"Hail Satan," cried the man in red.

"All hail the Lord of Darkness and His Regent, Kreeops," the practiced response came.

"Hail the Black Prince, ruler of the world," called the man.

"Keep us through the night that we may look upon the dawn."

Kreeops turned his back upon the disciples and was heading toward the seat of the throne itself, when a female voice in the crowd yelled out:

"All hail Jefuson, Prince of Peace." Martin knew that voice. He just couldn't figure out who Ryenna was working for. "Hail the Father of Independence, Molder of the Union!"

There was a moment of mute shock and then a spontaneous cheer arose from several isolated sections of the hall.

The Regent, about to sit on the throne, started and stood up, holding his hands high for order. The cheering grew self-conscious and then faded.

"Children. Be not in haste to follow the call of treachery. I, Kreeops, the earthly Regent of Lucifer, Commander of the Storm and the Fire and the Arm of Death, shall speak in rite for the Master Himself, the Dark Sun Who Creates Our Night, He who has surely held the world these last years, faithfully awaiting the promised Coming."

A controlled chanting was renewed under his words like the humming of well-tended machinery, music for his lyrics. It swelled in intensity as he finished speaking and bowed his head. Soon the very walls seemed to reverberate, and Martin imagined he could feel the tingle of the sound waves against his body. The eyes of the disciples around him were fixed on a point about two stories above the throne. He looked, but found nothing there until he realized that he was staring at the face of Kreeops: at the suspicious black eyes assailing the world from inside the cowl; at the sharp out-thrust beard and the ruddy, almost inflamed skin. But Kreeops was gigantic, so large that he blocked out most of the wall behind him.

The chant had become deafening. The great head shook itself, unleashing a noiseless explosion of black hair that was not hair, but flame, black flame, leaping and crackling around the head. Its flickering sent ripples of shade and light running across the room and the faces of the assembled coven.

The face beneath the flame transformed slowly. Still recognizably Kreeops, it became more bestial. The outline of the skull underneath the skin became so prominent that the face was like a death's head, increasing Kreeops' resemblance to his picture in the mosaics.

"Very impressive," Martin said, trying to remember that this was the same Kreeops that had backed off from him on the bridge.

He got kicked in the small of the back for his sarcasm. He stumbled forward, but not out of the pentagram, which surprised him. From the force of the kick he'd expected to be knocked halfway to the throne.

On the side wall was a mosaic of Kreeops and the Jefuson standing together on a mountain. In the glow of the flames, the sky behind them was blood-red.

The disciples sank to their knees as one being. For an instant, only Martin was standing, then, without willing it, he, too, was prostrate before the creature.

"My children," the voice boomed. It had changed also, as if chilled by the death's head. "In communion with my soul, Satan guides my words!"

A cold constriction spread through Martin's chest, a pressure that became almost a pain. He was caught up in an irrational dread that his body would no longer breathe automatically. He found himself willing each inhalation separately and forcing the air out. And doing it very poorly.

The room was thick with the rippling light. Martin's breathing grew even more labored as the voice continued like an arm slipping around a throat in a dark alley.

"We are tired in Our mission. We did not and do not ask to rule. Our rule was forced on us by the failure of the One who would be called Savior, the One whose apologists speak of the unity of man. But there was a unity of Darkness before Jefus ever set foot on this planet, a unity *He* wantonly destroyed. Jefus came, and His Son came, and both failed. Twice We were forced by Their failures to return to the rule They were so anxious to strip from us. Now the absence of Jefuson grows into an abandonment. Where is the fertile earth that He promised? Where is His Garden, where bureauer and disciple and folker walk hand in hand, beaming their benevolence like so many crazed-out old women?

"The promised Coming. There is no sign of it. *NO SIGN!* He has promised; Satan and His Regent lead the coven in the hope that promise will not be abandoned, as so many generations of men who have walked the city in constant expectation of its fulfillment were abandoned. Men who were left to find their only salvation in death. The promise has not been kept. But if it *is* ever fulfilled, *if* He ever returns, on that day you can be certain that *He will leave no room for doubt that JEF-FU-SON HE IS!!!* And until that day, beware of letting futile hope betray us. Our enemies are cunning masters of sham. Possibly, with the machines they have, and with the knowledge from the Originals, they can even create such deceits: giving ordinary folker stooges by the hundreds the sacred features of our beloved Jefuson. They have no sense of blasphemy! They eat their dead! And since death means nothing to these people, how easy is it for them to find a brave and foolhardy youth with a passing similarity to the holy, longed-for God of an entire people — or to create such a similarity — and use this charlatan, this mindless pawn, to sever the Church of the Jefuson from its rightful Head, and lead the unthinking body to their foul tables to feed their fat. Let us not be fooled. The bureauer fraud *may* have crossed the river. So have others. And even bureauer spies may be capable of rare bravery. He *certainly* comes to us from the camp of the enemy, none can deny that. And, sadly, We have also discovered a betrayal. The girl, the woman whom We entrusted so openly with Our faith, whom We sent to bring the pretender across Our sacred ordeal of initiation, that woman was a *judas*, in allegiance a bureauer, who deceived us all. Who knows what bureauer trickery and deceit she might have wielded to help this fraud across?"

"No!" came the familiar voice. "I did only as the Regent directed. The coven watched the crossing through *my* eyes. How could I…Kreeops gave me the streng…"

She was cut off in mid-word, and when Martin tried to turn toward her, he was restrained. Above him, Kreeops resumed, apparently oblivious to the outburst.

"The only way a claimant can be proven to be Jefuson is for the High Priest to subject him to the threefold test. That will make the pretender regret having come this far."

Silence. Martin kept his head bowed, his eyes studying the floor of the hall, trying to be as inconspicuous as possible. But as the silence continued, he risked a glance upward at the face and was immediately stunned by a look directed straight at him, a look of absolute and total hatred that left him wondering if his heart would stop. The beam of hate seared through his eyes into his brain. Naked to its obscene touch, he was intensely afraid, not that he would die, but that time would stop, leaving him, like a raw nerve, exposed to the face of Evil, aware only of his own contamination and of the impossibility of relief. In that everlasting moment, he would have sold himself gladly for the experience to be over. And again the voice boomed:

"Deny thy claim, deceiver, or thy life will surely be forfeit!"

The air had become a molten, throbbing orange. Martin felt as if someone was inside his head, someone or something, perhaps a knife, carefully cutting, searching. He believed that it knew he had no ambition to be deified, and that he was about to reveal that. He hoped that it would be satisfied.

"Unfortunately, Great One," the man in red called out, "we have no guarantee that the Jefuson will realize who He is, especially at first. It is said that at the Revolution '76, Jefuson had no knowledge of His true identity and, in fact, no belief in His own Father, Jefus."

The huge face was expressionless; perhaps the line of the mouth tensed just slightly before it said, "Then let the tests begin."

The pentagram Martin was standing in exploded in dark yellows and reds. In an instant, he saw phantom armies above his head smash together as mindlessly as colliding planets, leaving nothing but a powdery residue of dust that settled down over his cloak. Then the room was clear again.

"Ashes to ashes, dust to dust," the man in red recited. "He must be taken into the desert."

Martin was seized from behind.

By the time he'd gotten free of the black ropes and removed the blindfold, Martin was alone. The desert stretched out around him in every direction. It was night and cold. For warmth as much as anything else, he started walking, not going anywhere in particular, but there was nothing to be gained by remaining where he was without food or water, and his chances for survival would almost have to be better anywhere else.

So he walked. And walked. He got used to the empty spaces of the desert. But the aloneness was even stranger here than in the office. The nights were colder than any he could remember.

"Colder than Kreeops' heart," he said aloud at one point.

He didn't know if the disciples could still see or hear him. From what Ryenna had said in the throne room, he'd gotten the impression that Kreeops could use a single disciple as his eyes and ears and perhaps even show what that one saw and heard to the whole coven. He found that he actually hoped he was being watched, though he knew there was no safety in it; if anything, that would be more dangerous. He spent a lot of time continuing his earlier line of thought about where this land of the disciples was located. The disciples were in the city, or rather, when he was in the city, there were disciples who came and went. Came from here, he supposed, though everyone had always assumed they hid out someplace in the folker ring. This

was more than a hideout, and these people were more powerful than he had ever guessed. It crossed his mind that somehow
he had been taken out of the city, perhaps beyond the waters,
perhaps even to another planet, but deep down he didn't really
believe that. A youth spent roaming through almost indistinguishable neighborhoods had given him an excellent sense of
direction. His progress into this world had been almost steadily
downward. Downward! But he could see the sky. And that
moon.

The days were hot and nearly bright, though a surreal haze
covered the sun.

Eventually his mind grew muddled, his memory erratic.
The little water he could occasionally find, if it wasn't just mud,
if it was perhaps trapped in a hollow of a rock, was so filthy
even a pigeon wouldn't touch it. But he did. He had no food.
He tried to eat the sandals on his feet, but the hard pieces of
plastic that he'd been so happy to find for the soles were no
more edible than the rotten cloth binding. He cast one of them
aside in disgust, only later realizing how his foot suffered without it.

Now I've slowed my progress, he mused. He laughed again.
As if his progress mattered. He didn't have any more idea of
where he was going than he did of where he was, but he kept
moving. He was falling down a lot. Once he banged his head as
he stumbled face first into a rock formation. He tried to walk
only on the ashen sand, which was everywhere, but within it,
sharp stones and jagged slabs of shale were scattered about like
lice on a staggerer's head. He got pretty cut up. There wasn't a
part of his body that didn't ache. His vision kept blurring as if
sudden fogs were sweeping over the desert. And when he collapsed into exhausted sleep, the things he encountered there would
leave him more tired when he awoke than he had been originally.
Soon the distinction between sleeping and waking began disappearing. Often his dreams would find him roaming over arid

waste, and his waking journey would be populated by night-mare monsters and unfamiliar voices carrying on complicated conversations relating to nothing he could even begin to figure out. The idea evolved that his disordered search for a way out of the desert was a journey toward a land of beauty, a perfect place of rich green shrubbery and cool streams, where he would be welcomed as a hero because…because of the message he carried. The valuable, the priceless message for the wise leaders. The message would explain everything, enabling them to announce the truth to their noble population.

He was weak. The blazing desert scorched his eyes and stole the fluid from his body.

The light had incinerated the land and burned off its life, the way the disciples cremated their corpses, achieving nothing but ashes. But that precious light, without being dispelled or dispersed, could be transformed. Martin knew that the message was like life-giving water. A tank of it. Under the guidance of the wise, it could be soaked up by the air, moistening and cooling the atmosphere and the land; so that the unfocused light reflecting so devastatingly off the desert might be more widely and easily conferred upon it, nurturing the earth rather than devouring it.

For this place, though evil and hostile to life, was not like the city where Martin was born. The city enshrouded itself in the clouds of civilization; any sunlight that got through was soon absorbed in the labyrinth of overcrowded streets. This desert, however, had the space and the vitality to be a garden, yet wasted them in self-immolation. Martin was bent almost double under the weight of the water. Carrying such a burden made him very thirsty.

Then he realized or remembered about the enemy: Ryenna, Kreeops, Brodwich, all the disciples, all the bureauers. The ene-mies patrolled the desert just out of sight behind the dunes or boulders, watching, as enemies always watch, awaiting their chance to capture him with his precious tankful of message that they would befoul forever. The enemy was everywhere, but Martin was determined to reach the beautiful city where the lovely girl that had murdered the enemy, Brodwich, worried and waited for him with love and laughter.

Everything depended upon Martin.

He was aware that he had lost the ability to distinguish between the world around him and the world inside his head, but that didn't worry him. He did try to make things out as accurately as possible, but the world as he saw it was the world he had to live in, and that was all there was to it.

So the jumble milled around his head until, in a single instant, suffering stopped, and ripples of pleasure passed over him one by one. Everything was clear. All that was, all that had ever happened: the births, the deaths, the wars, the famines, the Originals with their doomed world of wonder, all the day-to- day minutiae, a left turn instead of a right a thousand years ago, an accidental meeting of elements before the birth of the sun; everything led up to this moment, this one march. From the beginning of the cosmos, he had been the anointed. The world held its breath awaiting the result of his mission, though the outcome could not be in doubt; it had been decided before the first atom stirred. His enemies were the enemies of the universe itself. How could they triumph, how could his body dehydrate into merely another handful of dust for Kreeops' desert, unless all that had ever happened were to have happened in vain?

Everything was so beautiful, so complete, so clear, that it never occurred to Martin to wonder what this amazing message of his was, much less why it had been entrusted to him, a man who couldn't even figure out his job as a rankenfile bureauer. In any case the reason was obvious; it was given to him because he was he, the "I" that moved over the face of the world, through whose eyes the world was filtered. The going was faster now, he was climbing over obstacles, rather than going around them.

He had another awareness of height. He understood it as a fear the enemies would use against him, as if it were a weapon, external and concrete, a spear that they could throw at him or poke him with to knock him off balance. He realized that he had climbed to the top of a high plateau. He moved back to step out of the line of fire of this weapon and found the plateau had four sheer sides; he might have been on top of a tall building rather than a mountain. That idea steadied him a bit, then made him even more nervous.

"I have weapons of my own," he said aloud to no one in particular. He knew they heard.

Below him was a sprawling city, all shining lights and sparkle, nothing like the one in which he'd spent his life. Throngs of well-fed, apparently happy people moved serenely along broad, precise boulevards, and sweet music drifted up to him on the wind. He was puzzled; it reminded him of something. Then he realized that this must be his destination. This was the wondrous place for which he'd been searching so he could deliver his message.

"It can all be yours." The words came from behind him, jarring against the idealism of his vision.

He was completely unsurprised to find Kreeops there. After all, he'd been seeing and sometimes hearing the enemy for days; though Kreeops looked *very* substantial. His cowl was down and he was wearing his normal face. A strange, out-of-place smile was stretched over the Regent's teeth; it looked irritating, perhaps it was chafing him like poorly fitting footwear.

Kreeops was staring at Martin. The eyes seemed to crawl around through the chaos of Martin's mind for a moment, then withdraw. The Regent's smugness was expressed by a further twist of his already tortured smile. He appeared at once pleased with Martin's cloudy confusion and disdainful of soiling himself with it further.

"I know your thirst. I know your hunger," his words said. "They can be satisfied."

Martin would have liked to say something, but he couldn't get a sound up his dry throat. It hurt when he tried and his lips cracked. Now that he'd seen this city, he knew once again that he was going to triumph, and he was too drunk with this delusion to be frightened. Could Kreeops go against the course of the sun, of the stars?

"This will be your domain," the Regent continued, indicating the city below with a sweeping gesture of his arm that Martin thought was very graceful. "Your world."

Something was wrong here. Things as Martin understood them weren't jelling. If this was where he was supposed to go, what he was supposed to do, why did Kreeops, an enemy, want him to go there? Martin shook his head as if that might clear it, then attempted to focus on the disciple leader.

"Food and drink," proclaimed Kreeops, and as he did, Martin's vision seemed to enter one of the fine homes below, where, all prepared and waiting to be eaten, was a sumptuous feast of real-food.

Chilled glasses of ice water, crystal-clear with beads of condensation running on the outside, were set every foot or so across the scarlet tablecloth. The table was covered with vividly colorful foods that Martin was sure he'd never seen before. While he looked, he received a memory of their names that couldn't have been a memory. And then, almost making him swoon, came impressions of their tastes, one after the other, memories like reality, not unfamiliar and vague, but as if these were the foods he'd been eating all his life. Or was it perhaps, he wondered, that their taste was part and parcel of fulfilling his destiny; perhaps he'd been waiting to eat these foods since the first day of creation. Perhaps this Kreeops really wasn't an enemy. Perhaps he understood.

Turkey, juicy and golden with thick gravy and spicy stuffing; fresh green peas soaking in butter; candied yams; apple cider like sunlight; and again those wonderful glasses of water. The only thing in Martin's stomach was a sharp, hollow pain as it responded to memories he'd never had before.

For a normal folker, this strange feast would be little temptation, he thought. *But for me...*He interrupted himself with, *Why do I think I'm different? Am I?*

Now the smile on Kreeops' face seemed genuine. How amazing it was that this man could comprehend exactly what Martin had needed all along, when even he himself hadn't known. Once again the Regent spoke, even a bit deferentially, perhaps.

"Women! All the most beautiful women, the most willing, yours to command. Anxiously they await you!"

And now Martin saw inside a bedroom. There were three women. One was raven-haired, tall and sleek, and as willowy and sensual as any Original. Another, with a blond, round nakedness, stretched herself indulgently as if under the tension of her passion. The third had red hair, like Ryenna, much like Ryenna...*Ryenna*...the name sounded in his head like a warning shot. For a moment he had trouble concentrating on the women. They began caressing each other, striping off their silvery garments to expose more soft, yielding skin; if possible, they were even more exciting, even more magical than the Original women that had populated his adolescent fantasies.

"They crave a man," said Kreeops, as they tumbled onto the bed and all over each other. "They await your pleasure."

Then Martin could see no more, the distance being once

again too great. There was something he had to remember. It was difficult. It was...

"You'll have wealth, and, more importantly, power," Kreeops continued. "The whole city will be yours to do your will upon. You'll be to them as I am to my coven."

That was it. Kreeops and his will. The enemy. Or was he? The Regent was regarding Martin with real concern; it might even be called brotherly. Martin was born for this city, but...to be like Kreeops? He strained.

But then his vision was taken to the inside of a palace. An assembled court was hanging almost worshipfully on the every word of a man who was seated upon an elevated throne. Something else tugged at Martin's mind. A golden crown was on the man's head; he was a king. He was familiar. From a painting. A wall. The king was Martin. A solitary man looking very small was kneeling in front of King Martin. The man, well-dressed and meticulously groomed, had the appearance of a Big Eater without being particularly fat. The king made a small motion with one hand and guards from out of nowhere took places on either side of the man. After removing a large purse from his belt and bringing it to their king, they dragged the pleading and wildly gesturing man from the room. On the throne, King Martin remained impassive, but as he watched, the Martin beside Kreeops was uncomfortable. Almost as if in response to that feeling, the scene changed. A group of people was brought before the king: one woman with three small children. Martin watched himself speak, and the woman began smiling and genuflecting, weeping for joy. Then King Martin tossed her the purse that had been taken from the Big Eater; it fell open at her feet, coins spilling out onto the floor. Hurriedly, as if afraid he might change his mind, the woman gathered the coins up and hustled her children out of the room, obviously singing Martin's praises with every retreating step.

On the mountaintop, Martin was rather pleased by the odd behavior of his other self below. He remembered Moohna as she had been during his early childhood: young, calm, and strong, usually sheltering one baby at her breast while taking charge of the other children in the unit, seeing to it that they were fed and as warm as possible. Moohna had been a natural arbitrator, sought out by the other women who knew their own bickering was threatening to destroy the unit and make loners of them all. But there was no arbitrating with the city. With a little help from such a king, her calmness might never have been reduced to exhaustion; in a world with a bit more justice, her wisdom might not have been overwhelmed into senility. As a boy, Martin had dreamed of being like the young leaders of the Originals. Could it be that a tidy and purposeful fate had brought him to that destiny here?

But who had ever heard of taking wealth from a Big Eater and giving it to an insignificant folker? Obviously they'd never let him do it, he found himself thinking, out of habit. And then he realized that if he was in charge there would be no "they."

"Only me," he muttered aloud.

And if he chose, he could take everything and distribute it like fare-well coups until everyone got as much as anyone else. Except for the Big Eaters who wouldn't get…

"Power, wealth, women, fame. All this can be yours," said Kreeops fervently.

Martin could see that Kreeops was so friendly and so concerned with Martin's welfare that he must be a brother king. The regal bearing is probably what makes us look alike, he thought, for the figure on the throne *had* reminded him of another figure on another throne. And this second figure cleared in his vision as, on the verge of accepting this most generous offer, he saw Kreeops react, tasting his victory. The Regent's eyes narrowed ever so slightly; the lips parted to expose sharp and vengeful teeth; the avaricious tongue flicked over them the way a beast would check his fangs before moving in for the kill. And Martin's numbed mind remembered that vulturish face back in its own context, in the throes of its own limitless greed. Other memories clicked into place beside that one, like interlocking tiles on a floor, as he recalled the world that resulted from such a rule.

Martin gazed down at the city with all its beauty. Who was he that its people should bow down to him? And what would become of him if they did? How long before his feeble wisdom would be overwhelmed by the burden of so much power? At what point would his resolve be reduced by expediency?

His mind was clearing, but he was a little lonely for the delusions he'd had in the desert.

"It can all be yours," repeated Kreeops, seeing the awe with which Martin regarded the city. The Regent was delighted and in control of his features once again.

"I should be the Kreeops of the beautiful city," Martin said wistfully and ironically, realizing he spoke the unfortunate truth. It occurred to him that he could soar off that mountain and die as the city filled up his eyes. The idea made him nervous.

"And you could make this a paradise by your efforts. Your paradise."

Apparently Kreeops was hearing what he wanted to hear, taking Martin's last statement as an acceptance. Another flicker of his tongue, and once again, momentarily, the face was transparent: small, grasping, and mean: *threatened*. His true disposition was amplified by the quickness with which he covered these emotions.

"Refuse!" said Martin, matter-of-factly, almost to himself. "If I've got to look like somebody, I sure as hell don't want it to be you."

He was weary of this nonsense. The height was bothering him. He didn't know how he got up there or if there was a safe way down short of accepting Kreeops' offer to ruin the city below.

Kreeops was obviously stunned, as if incapable of imagining anyone turning down such a proposition, especially someone half-dead like Martin.

"How do I get off?" Martin mumbled. His decision made and firm, his mind was fogging as he relaxed. His eyes wandered around the mountaintop as if no longer aware of Kreeops at all.

"Jump, you ungrateful slime! Jefuson, my ass!"

"Jefuson," repeated Martin, not knowing what that had to do with anything. *Jefuson?* He took it as an accusation.

He was about to get indignant and tell the Regent that Kreeops himself was the only one in this garbage heap of a desert who thought Martin was the Jefuson. Martin didn't even believe in the Jefuson. But that was such a lot to say and he was very tired. He lay down for a moment's rest. Just before nodding off, he recalled there was someplace he had to go and it was still a long way off.

8

Jefuson

After Gena had left and Triah finished with the first phone call, she made another immediately. She didn't recall the last time she'd used the phone; she never really had anyone to call and the machines, when they worked at all, were notoriously unreliable. This time, however, policer headquarters answered promptly and provided her with the information she needed and yet another phone number, which became the third call she'd made or received that year.

She identified herself by name and number to the policer at the checkpoint, when he finally answered.

"I'd like a pass to be issued to a folker," she said.

"To a folker?" The policer would be of a higher rank than the one indicated by her ID number. Both his question and his tone made that obvious. "Are you certain you want to do that?"

"His name is Mengra. He's coming to do some work for me. Some of the rest of his gang might be with him, bringing in cow meat for my Betters. They should reach the first checkpoint any time now."

"I'll bet he does good work, doesn't he?" The chuckling was unpleasant. Her face was burning and she was glad for the invisibility afforded by the call-phone.

The snide remarks continued, and Triah had to talk to several other policers, all of whom treated the whole thing like a dirty joke. After they tired of playing with her, the pass was issued. She didn't know it, but her ID number was never even checked. The call was obviously from a bureauer. No one else had phones. No one else wanted to sex those foul-smelling prowlers.

Within two hours, Mengra was at her door. Alone. The policers never even bothered to verify where he actually went once he was inside the Gov-Cent. After she hustled him into the room, she inspected him without meeting his eyes, trying to be impersonal, as if she really did want to find out if he would be strong enough for some specific labor, or as if she were evaluating a purchase. Her face was flushed, her heartbeat very rapid. She wondered if she was still sick, remembering for the first time the illness that had removed her from work the day before.

She had an urge to hide him, like the dress in the kitchen. Knowing how shameful it was to have him there, she half-believed the policers might arrive at any minute and take him away. But unlike the dress, her only concern was about losing him; she hardly even gave a thought to what would happen to her if anyone should discover the arrangement she'd made to get him. For the moment, she herself had all but forgotten what she'd have to do to fulfill her part of that arrangement.

"You're not a disciple," Mengra said, forcing his personality into her consciousness. Disconcertingly, it didn't jell with the conception she'd had of him before he'd arrived, that of one of the prowlers from her fantasies, big, strong, bursting with passion, yet a creature whose total existence, even in its brutality, lay in paying homage to her: to her beauty and desirability, to her uniqueness.

"Neither are you," she answered, trying for a huskiness and sounding more hoarse than husky. Daringly, she opened his robe a bit, then wider, brushing her fingers over his chest. "No tattoo."

As an explanation for her brazenness this was transparent; to some extent it was intentionally so, a cue from a fantasy. But to a greater extent, it was offered as a hedge for the audacity of her touch, and that was unsettling; she didn't want to have to excuse herself or her desires to this folker. For the first time in a life spent either performing for someone else or doing without, *she* was supposed to be getting what she wanted.

"I'm *not* a disciple," he said eventually.

She didn't like it when he talked. He sounded so unconcerned with her, just like anyone else. Just like everyone else.

"I'm just doing a little work for them," he said. "I make out all right. You too?"

He smiled at her confidently, like an equal. It was a moment before she realized an answer was required. A folker was questioning her!

"They called me on the phone," she said.

"On the phone?" he mused. After pausing, perhaps listening for a sound that wasn't there, he lowered his voice, and, as if condescending to confide a secret discovery to a fellow folker, he added, "You know, I think they lose it when they get too far away."

She didn't ask what. At that moment she was more concerned with what *she* might be losing. The voice on the phone had promised her a lot, including this folker. Still, if she got only half of what had been promised, she'd be better off. In fact she was better off already; the unceasing emptiness of her life up to that point had been worse than death.

"The girl?" he asked.

"What?"

"The disciples haven't contacted you in the last few minutes?"

She shook her head. Her wig slipped. Gena had her only decent one.

"They won't need any phone now."

Triah was bothered by the way he was acting. He was so independent. He was even taking charge. She was the bureauer. *Her* desires were supposed to be what counted. She wasn't a particularly selfish person, but she'd really never gotten anything she'd wanted and now she was wondering if her new pet was going to make her do tricks for it. She wanted to adjust her wig, but didn't.

"I told them that she went to the Bureau of Knowledge," she offered, but he ignored her.

He seemed to be meditating. At length the pensive expression left his face, and a moment later he started nodding. On the third nod he grinned.

"They told me that we're to wait here." His grin became a leer. Suggestively he added, "And that wasn't all they told me."

Then his arms were around her. She flipped off the light as he started to caress her with a gentleness that he worked his way out of, at just the right pace. Like magic.

Only for once she would have liked to have been on top.

Gena wandered around for a couple of hours, searching for a building that matched the image of the Bureau of Knowledge in Triah's mind. It was a problem. Often the mental picture that one person had of an object would be totally different from the way the thing itself appeared to someone else. She tried a few quick readings of the bureauers around her. Not surprisingly, no one was thinking about the Bureau of Knowledge. Finally she had to resort to mentioning it to   people, raising the thought in their minds herself, and none too subtly.

"The Bureau of Knowledge should be right around here," she'd announce, accosting some unfortunate pedestrian, lifting her voice slightly at the end of the sentence as people occasionally did to make a statement *almost* a question. However, they didn't do it to strangers in the street, especially not in the Gov-Cent. The maneuver earned her several very suspicious glances and no verbal response at all, but on the fourth try she did succeed in obtaining a reading that told her exactly where the bureau was: fortunately, just three blocks straight ahead.

She was halfway there when she became alert.

She sensed it in the air, like an overly rich odor. It was familiar. And menacing. *Disciples!* Realizing that she'd been waiting for them, even here, she experienced a certain relief that the waiting had ended, the never knowing which corner they'd be around, which shadow would be alive with them. She cursed herself for doing so much probing; at the same time she became aware of a growing urge to stop in her tracks and wait for them right where she stood on that sidewalk. For the first time, she acknowledged to herself that she'd never really believed she'd be able to escape from them.

Though her goal had lost all meaning, there was nothing else but surrender. Gena quickened her pace, determined to go on struggling toward the bureau until they overcame her. Yet, certain of her impending capture, she wondered, deeper inside, if this show of defiance was merely for her own benefit, to allow her to pretend that she had done all she could.

She pulled her cloak tighter around her, as if the flimsy disguise might give her some protection. She was beginning to pick up dark colors in the air. Were they simply her senses' reaction to the threatening advance, or were the colors actually there, preceding the disciples like a visual aroma? One thing was certain: she could feel the presence of the disciples throughout her body, as one feels the increase of heat from an approaching fire, or the first numbing freeze that leads the way for the coming of winter. No probing was necessary for that.

How had they gotten into the Gov-Cent? And in such numbers? They seemed to be moving rapidly. Disciples seldom moved faster than a walk; they were always totally controlled.

The air seemed to reek with the smell that had come from Kreeops' body when he'd descended on her, the smell of burnt hair. Winds had sprung up, billowing dark reds and deep oranges, like a firestorm rushing through the canyons between the buildings of the Gov-Cent. The Gov-Cent. The criers had always claimed that someday the Gov-Cent would reach out to crush the coven.

Gena was awed by the display. The bureauers themselves continued their orderly journeys, apparently oblivious to the multicolored chaos swirling around them. Gena searched for an escape, but there was no way into the long concrete building on her right, and the motor traffic on the street to her left was fast and frequent. Contrary to her first impression, she'd learned that only a few of the roads of the Gov-Cent were maintained for vehicles. Right now it looked like every car in the city was speeding down this particular street.

The building for which she'd been hunting was just ahead and across that street. She fought to keep from breaking into a run as she saw the double doorway of the bureau, both sensor-doors open, a neat line of bureauers flowing in the right-hand door to match the line flowing out the door on the left. Apparently the shifts were changing.

Of course, being out of sight wouldn't protect her. As a disciple, she'd developed more than the usual nonvisual contacts with the world outside herself. Hiding from view might provide an illusion of safety to a person who relied more heavily upon sight; Gena wouldn't even have that illusion. Yet she hoped, probably vainly, that the disciples might shun the obvious display of arrogance necessary to march right into the belly of a bureauer office building and drag out a cursing, protesting woman from amidst a throng of bureauers. It would be a deliberate taunt to those who claimed to be the government of the city.

A chill rode the colored breeze. It seemed to seep into her brain like concrete into a form, solidifying around the movement of her thoughts. As if to shake it off, she leaped out of the pedestrian flow, straight into the vehicle traffic.

A car whizzed by her, neither veering nor slowing down, not making the slightest allowance for the human fact in the street: people weren't in the street, not in the Gov-Cent; people were on the sidewalk or crossing in the prescribed way at the prescribed time. After a stunned hesitation, the other pedestrians reacted. Many stopped in their tracks, cries wrenched spontaneously from their throats, not entirely understanding what they perceived, beyond the realization that it belonged to what they regarded as the virtually homogenous and definitely frightening class of things that weren't done.

Though the drivers, most of whom had never driven anyplace beside the Gov-Cent, were unable to adjust instantaneously, Gena had been born and raised in folker roads and had therefore become an expert at removing herself from the paths of both people and objects. None of them had traveled at this speed, however, and as she darted clear of one car, a second missed her by the thickness of a staggerer's breath, actually brushing her cloak. Hearing the yelling around her and relating it to the deepening of the colors in the air, Gena assumed the bureauers were yelling about the arrival of the disciples. She dashed blindly across the remaining distance to the far side. By a miracle, she wasn't hit. The confusion she created on that sidewalk, moving first in the wrong direction, and then forcing her way into the building through the "out" door was unprecedented, but the bureauers were well-conditioned. Even those most upset by her charge, even those she'd banged into and one rather dignified gentleman whom she'd actually knocked down, were nonetheless determined to keep from disturbing the flow themselves. If Gena had been able to see better through the colors that, apparently only for her, crowded the day, she might have seen that within a very short time all those who had witnessed her impropriety had moved off out of the area, and that all but the most flustered had stopped muttering even to themselves about it. And bureauers did not talk to other bureauers in the street.

Once she was a little way inside the Bureau of Knowledge, the fiery colors did thin out. A large floor plan was diagrammed on one of the lobby walls. The various sections of the bureau were indicated by differing colors and a few stick pictures. The incoming crowd quickly shoved Gena past the diagram: the only thing she noticed was that the building had just the one way in. Or out.

She attached herself to one of the lines of people headed for different parts of the building. With them, she climbed two flights of stairs and probably would have climbed a third if she hadn't been suddenly reminded of her reason for coming to the bureau.

On a door across the hall from the third-floor landing was a large portrait of Brodwich. A rather flattering portrait at that. The eyes were less bovine and much more forceful; the slack puffy skin was taut and healthy-looking. But it was Brodwich, hanging there like a gauze-covered window into some overfed past. In spite of the improvements upon the original, the painting obviously hadn't been put there for decorative effect. To a bureauer, a snapshot of himself on his office door was much more impressive-looking and more convenient than just an ID number. A painting wouldn't be as valuable as a photo, certainly, and if Brodwich was supposed to be so important…But then no photo would be that size; Gena'd never seen one much larger than her palm. And no photo could make so much ugliness even that presentable.

The door was slightly ajar, which meant either it was faulty or that it had been shut off, possibly to allow others to get into the office after Brodwich had been killed. The office gave Gena a place to go. Not belonging anywhere in the bureau, she obviously wanted to avoid having to explain her presence. She felt sure Brodwich wouldn't be coming back.

Quietly she crept up on the door. Down the corridor, several bureauers were bustling around busily.

She'd be less conspicuous to the disciples if she stripped naked and stood on her head in the lobby than if she took a reading here, so she just knocked on the door and after getting no answer, she slipped inside. She left the door as she had found it, not quite closed.

Everything in the office seemed to be solid wood. The walls, the floor, the desk, even the ceiling was of the same weathered wood. It was splintery, Gena noted, touching her hand to the surface of the desk, but ostentatiously valuable. A square carpet, still fairly thick in places, covered most of the floor. It was a purple that matched both Brodwich's robe and his face when last she'd seen them. The upholstery on the chair behind the desk and on the Big Eater–sized couch was of the same shade, as were the drapes. The real glass window overlooked the street she'd just left.

Like a flash of light reflected into her eyes, something on the desk struck her attention. Amongst the litter of at least one good meal, a couple of pots, some jewelry, and two pieces of wrinkled brown fruit, she dug out two photographs and another painting.

The first photo, though crude and poorly developed, was

in color. At first glance it seemed to be a picture of the bureauer with the face of the Jefuson…and yet…it was a little older, a jagged scar slashed across one cheek, the chin was weaker, and there was a greenish mold between the teeth. The other photo, in black and white, was shaky, as if the subject or the camera operator or perhaps both suffered from severe tremors. But clearly this *was* Martin, though here his hair was darker and cut differently.

So he *had* been deliberately planted by his Betters. Of course. A twinge of pity ran through her. He'd seemed sort of a friendly bumbler. The tempest into which the bureauers had sent him adrift would swallow him up effortlessly. Her pity was jarred aside by an unexpected shock of anger at the person who had let such a thing be done to himself.

She put the photos aside and picked up the portrait. The paint was faded and cracking like the edges of the riverbed that were exposed to the summer heat when the River was low, but the faces in the painting seemed to shine through the paint. Though older, it was similar in its features to the face in the photographs; and yet it was so totally different that it had taken her a moment even to notice the resemblance, a moment in which she'd realized that this must be the original of the looka-likes. This was Jefuson, all right: the art of the disciples had hardly done him justice.

This was Jefuson and *this* was a man no one would *send* anywhere. The eyes were quiet yet firm. Gazing into them, she could imagine a self-awareness that was almost absolute, and a purpose and an understanding that might have been rooted in the primal movement that preceded creation. In that sense the man was foreign, unlike anyone she'd ever encountered, as if beyond the sum of those creatures and more human than any. There was something else, something obvious, something that permeated that unmoved, moving face. It eluded her.

The colors in the air had increased again and darkened to the point where they were barely colors at all. They hung like thick, dirty smoke, choking the room, dimming it, making her vision an effort. From outside came the clatter of hoofbeats on pavement.

Horses! It could only be Kreeops' personal coach. Tradition dictated that the coach and horses were used only for journeys made by the Regent himself. Once Zaletus had explained confidentially to Gena that disciple traditions were the weights they loaded on to give the world ballast, but she had the feeling the idea was to weigh everything down so that nothing moved at all. In any case she had seen that Kreeops, as a practical ruler, held to tradition only insofar as it served his purpose. He might consider a show of force inside the Gov-Cent beneficial, but he was hardly likely to stick his own head into the mouth of the enemy.

Gena looked out the window in time to see the six great, pitch-black horses charge around a corner, snorting steam from flared nostrils. Harnessed in black and silver, they drew the jet-black carriage down a street that now appeared deserted, though Gena could hear faint sounds of bureauer foot and vehicle traffic as an undercurrent to the chanting that now reached her in silent speech. They were coming for her.

Shut up as it had been when she'd ridden inside, the coach pulled to a halt directly beneath the window, right in front of the building's only exit. The driver dropped the reins and motioned to the disciple seated beside him. From their size, she could tell that they were from the Regent's private guard. They both wore their disciple's robes; considering where they were and the fact that it was broad daylight, their lack of disguise was unbelievably arrogant. The driver said something and they both craned their necks upward. For a tremorous moment, Gena imagined she could feel the threatening leer of their eyes upon her, and her head began to swirl as once again her mind was pulled back to Kreeops' ceremony. The chants were the same. Her skin remembered the power she could neither tap nor resist that had swept around her, leaving her psychic orifices even more exposed than her physical ones. The sweat poured from her body in recollection. Once again she felt electrified by the loathsome imminence of Kreeops; every nerve tensed against an attack so vile as to make sexing by the most brutal gang of prowlers less an affront than a baby's kiss.

She fought the memory, wrenching herself from her own mind. She had the impulse to bang on the window and scream out at the disciples below, but by this time the chanting was so loud that challenging it with her one puny set of lungs would only confirm the lonely impotence of which she was already too aware.

Below, the driver and his companion swung down from their seat, one moving unimpeded toward the front of the bureau, the other coming around to the door of the coach. As she watched that door opening, Gena was fully *aware* that Kreeops wasn't inside that carriage, and she fully *believed* that he was.

Almost involuntarily, she pulled herself from the win-dow, searching the office for concealment. She fought her panic; they would only home in on it, feeding upon it until they found her. At this distance, they probably could read any strong emotion. There was no place to hide in the office, and the one door led out into greater openness. Should she go or stay? The taste of danger that had been a constant in her mouth for so long now increased to the point of being noticeable once again. Had they seen her at the window? Had they recognized her? Could she run for it and risk the commotion she'd arouse? She waited, halfway between the door and the window, unwilling to give up her hiding place just yet. *Were those street-level doors still open for the shift change?* she wondered agonizingly.

Then she sensed the entrance of the disciples into the building two flights below. These bureauers were incredibly lax. But surely, she thought, now they would attack; surely here in the citadel of their strength they wouldn't suffer the intrusion of their enemy, they wouldn't allow him to work his will. She couldn't pick up any sound or sense of the struggle below. The disciples were on the stairway! On their way to her. Probably following her fear easier than any map. She dashed for the door. It was shut; she didn't remember shutting it. The disciples were almost to the second floor; she could *hear* them. Her hand closed around the doorknob. The door was stuck. The door was locked! Pushing, pulling — nothing happened. She punched it in frustration. They were on the final flight of stairs. Their pace was slower now, more confident perhaps: their prey was trapped. They were dragging something heavy between them.

Desperately, she dashed back to the window, trying to open it, intent on leaping out. Perhaps the damn carriage would break her fall, though she'd rather Kreeops' own body did. The window no more budged than the door. She pounded on it, and it didn't break. They were on the landing right across from the office. She turned to face the sensor-door. Could that hold them when all of the bureauers in the Gov-Cent hadn't been able to?

The door was ajar, just as it had been when she'd entered the office.

In a moment of self-indulgence, she sampled the terror that preceded Kreeops' men like a shout. To Gena, it was a message from their master. Inside this message, she felt the cold slab of marble pressed against her back as she was mounted by her satanic lover; she writhed under a thousand fingers, stroking, pinching, grabbing violently at her thighs, her breasts;

a thousand hands came alive with bestial passion as she was passed, stiff and terrified, around the throne room; she caught the glint of a blade and tasted blood. She understood this vision as a prediction, as a promise. Soon she would be the bride and the slave of an endless and unendurable gluttony.

There would be time enough for mourning, time enough for self-pity, and certainly time enough for suffering.

The disciples were coming. Though she was certain it was far too late, desperately, automatically if not instinctively, she emptied her mind: not so much to erase the emotional trail she knew they must be following as to escape for a last few moments of freedom from the torture that would soon enough be hers. She sought out and accepted sensations from her immediate surroundings: the thick purple carpet brushing her feet through the gaps in the top of her footwear; the surface of the desk, rough with the brittle atrophy of tree veins; the quiet air, warm against her face and hands, with the lightest trace of moisture; footfalls; cloth on her fingers; beneath her body, the resilience of cushions expanding against constraint (she was sitting on the chair, she didn't wonder how). She sensed herself, noting her own calmness as if it were an object in the room, not reflecting on it.

On the desk of tree, the smile of the portrait was so aware, and yet as naturally and as unconsciously compassionate as the energy that plants suck from the air. The footsteps in the room receded, but not completely; the danger went unobserved. Gena had a desire, a need, profound but unarticulated, for a reading of the man in the portrait, a reading so deep and complete that it would be a merger. It was a desire for her feet to tread where his feet trod, for her hands to touch what he caressed, for her eyes to begin to record the territory he surveyed. She wanted to immerse herself in that smile, as if to return to the source of herself, but now with awareness. Yet she sensed there was still something, something obvious, that was escaping her.

A warmth spread throughout her body, a passion so basic that it suddenly seemed to be the cause of every other desire in her life. It was as if she had always sought this man, as if he was the place that unconsciously she'd been running *to*, when her mind had been focused on what she was running *from*. She wanted to enter him as he entered her, to press herself against him until the atoms of their bodies fused, and then to bathe in the life overflowing their body. In a bead of light, she was the sun, almost pure white, in a drop of sweat upon his brow. And yet...

Paint. She could smell it, she could taste it, she could feel its resistance to a thin brush. Paint: being mixed into shadings and spread on canvas, ordered and structured to reflect patterns and purposes unknown to itself.

The face. The Jefuson. Gena was probing the portrait, all right, but what she was reading was not the Jefuson, not an actual being. Rather, she was exploring a psychic construction from the brain of the artist; magically and impossibly preserved among the hot and the cold of color; mixed, against all odds, into the hardened texture of the paint itself, and preserved across time.

The image. An idea from a human brain, from a mind she understood as shockingly less than its own idea. Now she touched the artist and found him enmeshed in pain and pettiness and fear, nearly strangled in the habitual cowardice of expediency and custom. Yet, even within the ultimate darkness of his own skull, he could envision such a portrait. And in spite of a thousand and one betrayals of himself, by himself, he could paint it.

The man with the green teeth, the jagged scar, and the weak chin had been the artist and the artist's model: commissioned to create a likeness of the Jefuson for a city which at that time had no conception of what Jefuson looked like. The artist's name was Pavle.

Gena basked for a long time in those painted eyes. The figures hustling around the room were only floundering shadows to her. For the moment at least, she had so much in front of her that she had no need to hustle anywhere.

When her attention returned to the office, the disciples had gone. Gena collected her impressions and reacted. She had seen them; but they hadn't taken her. Could they possibly have missed a fully grown woman seated behind the desk? And Kreeops hadn't been there, not in the office. She hadn't tried to read the disciples who were; her attention had been elsewhere, except for the tiniest amount necessary to record their presence.

Figuring that there was no sense in hanging around for them to come back, she rounded the desk and found the huge body the disciples had left on a sheet on the purple rug. *Brodwich.* She leaned against the desk and took a deep breath, catching the full force of the smell and screwing up her face.

Gena knew it was coming, but there was nothing she could do as the door burst open and spewed armed bureauers all over the office, as if the building had sneezed.

Firmly, but not painfully, her arms were grabbed from either side. Then another bureauer, young for the purple robes of the Big Eater, sauntered in. He inspected the scene with a self-satisfied nod of his little globe of a head. "All right, seize her!" he commanded, after the fact.

His face was round, misshapenly so, and practically smooth, as if the features had been stamped on by a worn-out die. Behind him Mengra, the young folker from the site of the baby bones, entered, and, less surprisingly, so did Triah, the bureauer woman whose clothing Gena had taken. Triah was holding possessively onto Mengra's arm. For his part, Mengra looked poised for flight; he surveyed the bureauers around him with obvious distrust and eyed Gena with caution, as if not certain the beast was securely restrained. His fidgeting made him appear far less self-assured than when she'd last seen him. Then he'd been cooler in retreat than he was now, standing his ground. He pointed at Gena.

"As I told you, Tantor," he said, "the body and the killer."

"Just so. The outer ring is hard on bureauers. Some are too weak. She wouldn't be the first to craze out. Usually they just dive off a roof. Sometimes they go after the populace, thinking they can cleanse the city. Occasionally, they take their delusions out on their Betters. Who *is* she?"

Mengra hesitated, then shook his head negatively. It was clear to everyone that he was lying.

"Like I said," he tried, "I just saw her loading the body into a cart and followed her."

"Figuring you could steal it from her?" Tantor was contemptuous but unconcerned.

"I'm only a folker, she's a bureauer. I wasn't sure she'd done anything wrong. I figured I'd follow her and find out what she was up to. Maybe get a Free-Kill."

"Just for your information, she was bringing him here," Tantor said, trying it on for size, "... so the punishment would fall on the bureau...Yes...It would decimate us. It's a good thing I caught her guilt-sure."

Gena could see that Tantor was more interested in developing a scapegoat and a plausible story than in the truth. A disciple was a far more impressive catch than a bureauer woman, but he was obviously unaware that she was a disciple. The fact that Mengra and Triah had kept her identity to themselves told Gena who they were working for, if nothing else did.

Stepping up to Gena, Tantor reached out to stroke her arm, almost hungrily. She was his catch all right. In spite of his rank and his self-importance, from the way his eyes roamed over her body it didn't seem that he caught many women. Not of their own volition. She drew her shoulders back. Her breasts were very close to him. Her right hand, held in an almost constant fist since she'd left the disciples, clenched itself even tighter.

"Just so," said Tantor again. Then, jerking his eyes from Gena to Triah, he asked Mengra off-handedly, "Where did you pick that up?" He looked Triah over from the vantage point of his position of power, slowly, suggestively, but hardly seductively.

Mengra just stared at Tantor; perhaps the folker was still occupied with another matter. After several seconds, Triah herself spoke up, tentatively, as if she was afraid Mengra would interrupt her with a contradiction.

"I got him a pass, so he could follow her inside the Gov-Cent. I've known him for a long while and…" Her words trailed off; it seemed she'd become so intent upon scratching the backs of her hands that she'd forgotten to finish.

"Keep quiet," Mengra shot at her. "Triah did nothing. The reward is mine."

"Reward?" said Tantor with feigned surprise. Quite evidently savoring the role of Big Eater, he glanced at Gena as if checking on his audience before turning to Mengra and delivering his lines, slowly and precisely. "You come to me with this absurd little tale and you expect a reward?"

"I need the treatment. I've given you the killer. Without her, you and all the other rankenfile…"

"I'm not rankenfile any longer, my lad. The very moment this buffoon disappeared, my Betters seized their opportunity to place me in his position. So be very careful." Tantor spoke with irritation. But then he smiled; his smile, a rip in the circle of his puffball face. "Perhaps you were all in on the murder together. He *was* my father, you know."

Mengra knocked Triah's arm away, ready to flee. The bureauers guarding the door stepped forward threateningly.

"Relax, my boy," said Tantor, who was scarcely any older than Mengra, though much fatter. He made a gesture that he would have called magnanimous, still keeping one pale eye on Gena, observing her reaction. "Didn't I pay you before, Mengra? Didn't you get both the coups and that funny-looking little girl at the safeway that you wanted so badly?"

"She's why I need the syph treatment!" Mengra declared bitterly, ignoring Triah's horrified expression and shaking her off as she clutched at his arm.

"You thought your brother was going to be Free-Killed when you led me to him, didn't you?" Tantor asked tauntingly.

"*He* made the calendar." It was a justification. Then: "You never told me you were going to make him a bureauer. I would have made a better bureauer; he always followed me around."

"Good practice for him," Tantor said. "What gives you the idea that all bureauers are leaders? In any case, as it turns out, he has been killed. Just like you wanted."

"Martin is dead." He didn't quite dare to make it a question. In any case it didn't sound as if he wanted to know the answer.

"Isn't that what you wanted?"

"I had no way of knowing what you'd do with…It's part of life, I guess. He was all right. It's no crime being weak."

"That doesn't sound like you."

"I didn't know what would happen to him," Mengra repeated.

"It was all very secret. Even I wasn't told what my Betters wanted with him, though naturally, they bypassed big-mouth Brodwich and chose me to run the operation. It turns out they only made Martin a bureauer so they could shove him in the path of the disciples. Never mind why. They sent down the file this morning; the case is closed. Your brother's disappeared and we've lost contact with our agent inside the coven. If the truth be known, sticking his fat face into the whole affair is probably what got that gasbag over there killed."

Gena let herself appear suitably impressed.

"I told you *she* killed him," insisted Mengra. "I get the reward. The treatment."

"She certainly did," Tantor laughed. "Our stomachs depend on it. Without the killer, the retaliation goes from that body on out. It could be blocks. Besides, no policer in the city is about to go and arrest Kreeops. She most certainly did it."

"So I get my treatment."

"You get your reward. Unfortunately, my young friend, for that disease of yours there is no treatment. So just be thankful if I don't turn you in." He smiled at Gena as if they were sharing this joke. "Folkers *should* learn to be more careful of the things they want. But I'm really too busy to discuss it."

He turned to the bureauers at the door. Over Mengra's protests and the sound of Triah's voice yelling at Mengra, Tantor ordered, "Get them out of here. The dark one stays, but take her number for the Free-Kill lists."

The Big Eater's eyes drifted slowly over Gena's body. They never stopped at her face; they never noticed that the ID number tattooed on her cheek didn't match the bureauer number stenciled on her robe.

"Leave us," he told the others.

Gena was lying on the purple couch, studying the grainy wood in the ceiling. She was going to be sexed, of course. She didn't really mind that, for although she wasn't sure she could turn it to her advantage, it was certainly better than being sent straight to the Free-Kill. Unless he killed her himself right afterwards, that is. But certainly she'd been sexed by a lot tougher than this faceless boy and lived to tell about it. He was fairly fat, very fat considering his young age. And while that might give him prestige, in his stimulated condition he'd been huffing and puffing already when he'd been called out of the room.

Gena had never been sexed by a bureauer, much less a Big Eater. In spite of herself and her predicament, she had to admit that the idea excited her. After all, now that he'd been promoted he could probably have about anyone.

Her titillation was mixed with a far greater apprehension but was not destroyed by it. Her life was already out of her control, racing toward its own final limit a lot faster than she was getting across the limit around the city. She'd heard that bureauers actually sexed naked; if Tantor removed her robe, the pentagram on her left breast would reveal her as a disciple, and her personal limit would be crossed immediately.

She could hear him outside the door, giving orders to somebody. She hadn't bothered with a reading before, she'd been tired and too many conflicting thoughts had filled the office. She didn't try one now, either. She wanted to marshal her strength for a time when it might do some good. She had powerful enemies.

She'd been impressed by Kreeops' use of the outsiders Mengra and Triah. Was he moving to expand his domination? Or had he simply decided that for this particular job those two would be more appropriate than disciples? They'd be less likely to be noticed by their prey and more familiar with the terrain. And they could set her up as a bureauer, to be Free-Killed, without attracting any special notice to her or to themselves that might alert the bureauers to extraordinary activity among the disciples.

"No special notice?" she said out loud, and for the first time she fully understood that no one else had seen the coach as it rode up to deliver the body. And no one else had seen the disciples as they carried it up the stairs and into the office. *No special notice!?!* Kreeops had prevented the bureauers from taking *any notice at all* of his guards' activities. She was awed.

"Now we won't be disturbed," announced Tantor, reentering and removing his robe.

Her cautious attempt to probe him was rebuffed by a hot wall of lust, and the lust excited her far more than his physical body, with its pale skin and rolls of flab, ever could. Fat might have sex appeal to bureauer females, but Gena had always believed that folker women who claimed to find it sexually attractive were merely sycophantic social climbers and that they were only pretending. Normally, very little aroused Gena; in fact, almost nothing. Sex was an experience to be avoided. At best it was an intrusion, someone else's impersonal assertion of control over her body. At worst it could be a mortal danger. But now, reading the bureauer's desire for her, she felt potent and rigid with excitement.

Without ever taking notice of her, the bureauers had been the force that had shaped, ruled, and provided for the world she'd grown up in. Perhaps they were basically indifferent, but they were virtually omnipotent over folkers, and they were definitely unassailable. Especially the Big Eaters in the Gov-Cent. She'd known Brodwich was a Big Eater when she'd killed him, of course, but his murder had been almost reflexive, and afterward, in her preoccupation with survival, it had been unreflected upon. Observing the effect that the murder had on Tantor and the others had been a revelation to her, impressing her in a way that being a V.I.P. among the more alien disciples never could. Like an infant discovering that thrashing its arm

would topple the doll placed beside it, Gena was learning that
even the government and its most important people could be
made to respond to her, even if the response was only to slap
her down. The corollary to this idea was that, to the extent that
she could exert power against them, her evaluation of their
abilities waned. What manner of leaders let her run free for so
long, kidnapping and murdering as she chose? She certainly
hadn't expected as much feebleness, pettiness, and confusion
here as everywhere else.

And she understood, even more fully, just how desperate
her trip to the Gov-Cent had been. She might have been charging a policer, knowing that his weap was drawing a bead on her
chest, in the hope that she could move faster than the bullet or
that a gunshot wound in the heart wouldn't be fatal. For just
that certainly had she expected to be crushed by the power
she'd envisioned in the Gov-Cent, a power different in kind
from the rest of humanity and even from the rankenfile
bureauers she'd encountered in the outer ring.

Now this Big Eater, young and foolish as he was, was actually abandoning his post, leaving who-knows-what vital business unattended to: fare-well coups undistributed, murders
unpunished, labors not assigned, all because Gena had thrown
back her shoulders and stuck out her disciple-stained chest at
him? Now she thought she understood why some women were
attracted to bureauers.

For practically the first time in her life, in the presence of
another individual, Gena wanted to be sexed, or, more accurately, she wanted to do the sexing. She was like a young
prowler, anxious to assert his manhood on the first helpless
women that appeared.

Puffing, Tantor rolled onto the couch beside her. Naked,
the pink and puckered hills of his breasts and abdomen reverberated even after the rest of his body was still. This was the

largest amount of nudity Gena had ever seen. His self-indulgent excesses had been made flesh in a fat that had taken over his body, dwarfing his erection among ponderous thighs and sagging stomachs, anchoring him on his back as he was enveloped by the softness of the huge couch. He lay beside her without touching her, trying to gather the energy that his very excitement seemed to exhaust. Sweat poured out of his over-saturated body, escaping downward in squirming rivulets and streams, as if seeking a thirst or a dryness.

Gena touched him. More a poke than a caress, more in curiosity than in passion. She heard the quick intake of air and then a slight involuntary moan.

"Let me take off your clothes," he managed, turning onto his side with great difficulty.

Gena smiled and said nothing. Instead of a probe, she tried a wordless suggestion below the level of silent speech, hoping to get him imagining how nice it would be to sex this woman while she was fully dressed. Aware of the singlemindedness of his desires, and aware that her own arousal was making mental control difficult, she had no great expectations that the attempt would work. A quick, rudimentary reading revealed that his bulky passion was unaffected, taking over his mind the way his body took over the couch. His hand trailed heavily up her leg, twitching spasmodically, peeling her robe open. The hand slid back down as she brought her leg up, twisting around to offer him her foot. He removed her sandals, smiling up at her. Gena let her robe open to the waist.

"Clothes put such a limit on things," she tried. These were almost the first words she had spoken to him, certainly the first she had initiated. Her voice held even more passion than she felt. "We don't really need any limits."

It was a lame attempt to raise the subject in his mind, and she got no coherent reading from her probe.

Like his hand, his cock was twitching involuntarily. She grabbed it hard and threw one leg over him.

"Hurry!" she cried, straddling him roughly, knocking him onto his back as she climbed on top. "Can't wait a second longer!"

"Neither can I," he muttered, not having any choice as she enveloped him.

He seized her breast, clumsily and painfully, but through her robe, without opening it. He was very inexperienced; he trembled once, immediately, and lay still. It was over. Gena wasted no time rolling off. She was more aroused now than when they had started, but she knew that, even if this was the time or the place to worry about satisfaction, there was none here; and she was anxious to keep his hands from straying once again to her tattooed breast. Tantor looked at her, a little shyly, a little inquisitively. His bluster was gone; with his round, hairless head, he resembled a child.

When she reached for his thoughts she was surprised. No male folker was ever interested in the woman's satisfaction. If they measured sexual prowess at all, it was strictly quantitatively. Tantor, however, was more than a little concerned with having "done it right," and with Gena's impression of his sexing. He seemed so young.

It didn't hurt her any, so she told him how strong he was, how masterful, even how handsome. She was monitoring his thoughts carefully, a bit wary of laying it on too thick. But his suspicions about her credibility yielded easily; he really needed to believe the things she was saying, and they meshed so well with the way he liked to see himself. As she talked, she watched his mind trying to crawl out from under another conception that he had of himself, one that he despised, a conception more closely in line with the way his father, Brodwich, had seen him.

Apparently, in Tantor's childhood, Brodwich had been the

distant and unseen ideal of manhood that his mother had always thrown up at him. Once apprenticed to his father's office, Tantor had worked hard. And while not especially talented, and openly contemptuous of his father, he'd advanced rapidly, probably because of his parentage, but definitely not because of Brodwich himself. Brodwich, when he'd remembered his relationship to the misshapenly moon-faced Tantor at all, had treated it as a personal insult from nature. And he'd tended to make his son the object of his humor, publicly. Tantor was "as mindless as he is faceless," or "my worst spermy come wriggling back to remind me of some fourth-rate sexing. Usually I can piss better than that," or "the price of sodomy."

Now, as Brodwich's death rose to his son's consciousness, Gena encountered no sense of loss. Rather, Tantor felt released, free from his father's image of him, ready to try to impose an image of Tantor, Big Eater, upon the world. But although it was out of her reading at the moment, Gena was sure that the Brodwich conception of Tantor would be an enduring legacy. Better to have had no father. Like her.

Talking with Tantor and playing bureauer, Gena spoke carefully and a little bit formally. Not that there was much difference between the way bureauers spoke and the way most of the rest of the city did; it was just that folkers sometimes imagined there was, because of the odd sounds of some of the edicts that the criers recited. Many of the edicts were older than any of the bureauers.

After awhile she dropped her probe until she could get "limit" back into the conversation. That would have to be soon. When this audience ended, so did her life.

"Hadn't you better take your powder?" Tantor asked suddenly.

At first, she didn't realize what he meant.

"You aren't assigned motherhood, are you?"

"Oh." She understood.

Among the bureauers, motherhood was strictly regulated to keep the population stable. If selected by a man to be the mother of a child, a bureauer woman could apply for motherhood status; others were simply assigned it and left to their own devices. Population control for folkers was left to more natural causes, including violence among themselves and sport kills by the bureauers, as well as fearsome diseases and starvation and accident. For all the children the folkers managed to produce, they weren't very fertile, probably no more so than the disciples or the bureauers. They just worked at it harder: sexing being a major diversion for the males, and the females needing the children to get more coups. Unless, of course, the females were loners, like Gena: a unit of two got no coups. Her only birth control had been abstinence. As much of it as possible.

"Well..."she began.

"Oh, I forgot. You won't be around that long, will you?"

Any sympathy she may have been developing for Tantor disappeared. He had a very unpleasant laugh. Desperate to avoid the topic of her fate, she shifted the subject abruptly and awkwardly.

"I've been thinking about babies lately. You know that folker, the one who accused me of the murde..."She took a deep breath, then plunged on, blindly, in spite of the confusion on his face and in his mind. "I do *know* him. I remember now. He used to have a business out near the edge of the city by the...".

"*A business?*" For a folker to have a business was unheard of, far more socially detrimental than the common forms of impertinence like rioting in the safeways or stealing growing food. It smacked of anarchy. Tantor had been sleepy before, now he came wide awake.

"Oh, no, not really a business." She didn't want him to get sidetracked; getting Mengra Free-Killed beside her wouldn't help. "He just shows people to this room by the waters. The limit passes through the…"

"He shows people? Who? Does he charge?" Tantor, Big Eater, was back.

"No. I don't know. It's just for folkers. I heard…I mean, I did stop by once. He didn't charge; he just lets people look. I think he lives there. It's not a business; he just lets people look into his room. The limit goes through it, and there's a baby on the other side…between the limit and the waters: baby bones. It's truly amazing, and I've never know anyone before who was Big Eater enough to explain it to me."

"Hummh." An acknowledgment of his importance. A little disappointed. Then he brightened. "It really doesn't matter, you know. About the business. Every year there's less poorage for the folkers. And there's an additive left by the Originals, called vit-immunes, or vit-inimo, or somesuch; every batch needs a little. Hardly any left. No poorage, no folkers." He voice was sleepy. He was totally unconcerned. He wanted to nap.

"Then it's true."

"What?"

"About the baby." Gena had too many problems at hand to waste time on future apocalypses, no matter how imminent. "About the baby crossing the limit."

"Oh…I guess it's true. Of course. *There are records.* We know all about that sort of thing."

"And…"

"What?"

"Well, it's just that everyone knows that the limit can't be crossed."

"That's true."

"Then how did the baby get to the other side?"

The sheer affrontery of the question, combined with the threat to his image if he didn't know the answer, had him off balance. She realized that if he'd been a little more secure as a Big Eater, or if he had really known the answer, he wouldn't have felt the need to provide it. But he wasn't and he didn't. Bitterly disappointed, Gena didn't waste her energy probing him as he slipped into cliché.

"The limit," he quoted, "is for the protection of the citizens. It cannot be crossed and there is no reason it should be."

"I know," she said, trying to sound rankenfile and stupid, instead of contemptuous, in the increasingly vain hope that he might reveal some information that might help her stay alive a little longer. "But I could never figure out how the baby crossed."

"Well," he said. "It's quite simple actually, once you understand how the limit works and all. I'm afraid it's probably quite beyond you, my dear." This had a finality that was meant to terminate the conversation.

"But you understand all of that," Gena tried, her voice full of a wonder appropriate for a "my dear."

"Well, Big Eaters have to know nearly everything so we can do our job…so we can keep the city running at *peak efficiency*." He paused, pleased with the term. "We work closely with all the different bureaus, including the Bureau of the Boundry."

There it was! Instantly she was in his mind again.

"I didn't even know there was a Bureau of the Boundry." Her excitement registered in her voice more than she would have liked.

"Of course there is."

And, to her relief, she got the image: an old building with no windows and five great concrete columns out in front.

"It must be far away. I've never seen it." Shamelessly blatant.

Quickly, the relationship between their location and the Bureau of the Boundry slipped into his mind. She saw the streets of the Gov-Cent radiating toward it like spokes into the hub of a wheel. He said something she didn't quite catch. Now that she had what she needed, she yawned and stretched out drowsily on the couch. Actually, she wouldn't have minded a nap, after all this mental exertion.

"You probably *have* seen it," he said, then yawned back. "Average bureauer doesn't even know what it is."

He stroked her leg without interest. She yawned again and closed her eyes, hoping his passions wouldn't be reawakened. A suggestion she planted, of how nice sleep would be, may have worked; he also seemed to have some idea that a nap might be customary after sex. In any case, following her lead, he relaxed beside her and shut his eyes. After a moment, he looked up and tossed one arm over her, smiling as if in inspiration.

"It's classified," he said. "How the baby got across the limit is *classified*. That's why I can't tell you."

That being a satisfactory answer, he rolled over and went to sleep, muttering as he went, "Never heard so many…"

He wasn't concerned with Gena: if you had a bureauer woman's number, you had her. There was no place for her to run. She'd never even consider trying to blend in with the people in the folker ring. Even if she wouldn't have been certain that she'd stand out like a pearl on a pile of shit, a bureauer woman would have regarded mingling with the folker and his filth as worse punishment than the Free Kill. Still, if Tantor had remembered it, he would have reactivated the sensor-door, resetting it to keep Gena inside.

9

Violence

Zaletus' braided beard was starting to unravel at the ends. Martin cursed him mentally. It sounded like the High Priest was arguing Martin's case again.

"The Jefuson," said Zaletus in his speechmaking voice, "is of the folkers and of the bureauers, as well as of the faithful. He is the folker who shall replant the earth, the bureauer who shall reunite the city, and the disciple who shall make each man a leader."

"My name is Martin. Not only am I not your Jefuson, I don't even believe in him." Martin lifted both arms, shaking the black disciple's cloak he'd been given to wear as if to indicate that it was what he didn't believe in.

"Blasphemy!" cried Kreeops with what seemed to be well-calculated scorn. "As long as the forces of Satan are in control, you shall be punished for such…".

"Hold, Kreeops!" commanded Zaletus. "You are Regent. But *only* Regent. And if the Jefuson has come, your time has past."

The discussion had a rather formal air, as if for public consumption, though, except for the three of them and the two guards beside Martin, there was no one on the brown, lifeless plain for as far as the eye could see. A barren tree stood alone several lengths behind them. To Martin, who'd never seen a real tree before, its branches appeared twisted and deformed.

Kreeops' closed carriage had brought them here from the Castle, but they hadn't traveled very far. Martin was tired, with less than three days rest from his ordeal in the desert, but otherwise nearly back to normal. During those days, he'd been tended by Zaletus and "protected" by Kreeops' private guard. In theory he'd had the run of the Castle, but physically he hadn't been able to run anywhere. Mostly he'd slept and eaten and listened to Zaletus drone on about his religion. While they were alone, Zaletus had been scrupulously noncommittal about whether or not he believed Martin might be the Jefuson. But once, late in the afternoon of the second day, near the end of a long, rambling diatribe about the murder of Jefus, the father, his tone had changed, becoming almost pleading:

"The strong, you see, crucified him so they could continue to lord it over the meek...without guilt. The meek went along...perhaps because they only understood the Satanic violence of the strong, the awesome momentary strength of the holocaust. Such they had always known and therefore thought natural. They simply were not able to comprehend Jefus' humble strength, the patient power of the grass which no fire, no violence, no concrete, no evil, can drive from the earth."

It had almost sounded as if Zaletus were apologizing to Martin for mankind.

"Or perhaps," the priest had added, no longer apologetic, but with just enough bitterness to underscore an old man's resignation at what seemed to be a relatively fresh disillusionment, "perhaps the meek went along because they were unwilling to extinguish their own feeble fires, the embers that they too might someday nurture into fearsome infernos of their own...Thus the crucifixion."

Since, either by constraint or inclination, Zaletus spoke about precious little except religious dogma, generally Martin had paid little mind to his words. Still, as the old priest had predicted, Martin's recovery had been spectacular. Kreeops, anxious for the tests to continue, had assembled the disciples in ceremony on two different occasions to speed his recuperation. Martin gave more credit to sleep and to the real-food he'd been provided for meals.

Now Kreeops came over toward Martin and the guards yielded. Once again, the Regent was just a man, powerful certainly, but neither the superhuman giant he'd been in the throne room nor the somewhat surrealistic tempter from the mountain. And Martin noted a web of very human-looking wrinkles around his black eyes.

"I should be the first to hail Jefuson, and the happiest," Kreeops said. "But this bureauer impostor is a false god. To follow him is to surrender our church to our enemies."

"That is for the High Priest and the Bride to decide," Zaletus said. "Not for you. Nor for him. With the Bride..." The priest let his gaze linger on Kreeops, not quite in accusation, and finished heavily, "*missing*, it falls entirely to me."

"Is it likely that Jefuson would return in the absence of a Bride? After all, the second test..."

"I know the law, Kreeops. Let us move on to that test. You have no need to concern yourself about impostors. No one but the Jefuson could triumph over all three trials."

"Satan and I seek only to lay down our scepter." The Regent looked miffed. Martin couldn't tell whether it was at Zaletus for his refusal to decry Martin's legitimacy, or at Martin for existing.

"Let the second test begin," proclaimed Zaletus.

A small hooded figure stepped out from behind the denuded tree. Zaletus and Kreeops moved toward it, and

Martin followed behind. Arriving there in the lead, Zaletus turned and, once again as if addressing a throng of unseen spectators, projected his voice like an old and dignified crier.

"When undergoing his initiation into the coven, the candidate not only crossed the river instead of blending into it, he did it with full consciousness and even retention. This is as it should be. God is not a common disciple to be spared the memory of his ordeal: God can no more forget his decisions than he can avoid their consequences."

"I went across *and* with retention. Am I a god?" Kreeops laughed derisively.

"Then there are the three tests," Zaletus continued, ignoring the interruption. "To pass the first, the candidate chose to persevere though tempted by the greatest imaginable personal gain."

"Paltry," announced Kreeops, "when compared to the power and the glory of absolute rule over the Church of the Jefuson."

"The second test is the Revolution. The champion of the candidate, in a fight to the death, must overcome the champion of the Dark Powers, known as the Inquisitor, and the champion of the bureauers, the Hessian. Thus is it asserted that the candidate is independent of their control. Normally the Bride is asked to be his champion, but nowhere does it say that she must be. If she accepts and wins, she rules by his side, if and when he passes the test of rebirth. If she accepts and loses, she will have gained the candidate honor, in that such an exalted personage was willing to lay down her life for his independence. But if the Bride refuses, or is, for any reason, unable to fight the Revolution, the candidate must contest it himself. And none have ever done so, successfully."

"I'm not going to fight anybody," Martin declared. A lash cracked against his shoulders, cutting him off. It didn't quite knock him from his feet, and he looked behind him to see a whip in Kreeops' hands.

"Your god's a coward," the Regent spat at Zaletus, obviously delighted.

Martin wondered if his shoulder bones were broken and felt less and less like playing this game, though he could see that, between the disciples and the bureauers, if he wanted to avoid it, he'd practically have to create his own world, like a crazer. Well, he thought, it just may come to that. He was sick and tired of being a weapon in every hand but his own.

"The time has come, Kreeops," said Zaletus, "to bring forth your champion, and the one who has been obtained from the bureauers."

From the way these two were bellowing, Martin was absolutely certain that somehow, somewhere, all the disciples were watching.

"Because the candidate is without benefit of champion," Kreeops pronounced, "the Bride having been taken from our midst (in all likelihood being held captive by the bureauers to prevent her from denouncing the fraud), and because it is the policy of the Dark One and myself to speed these proceedings to their inevitable conclusion, I, personally, have selected one champion who shall serve to represent both Satan and the bureauers."

He gestured toward the figure now slumped against the tree: "Ryenna: disciple and bureauer spy."

Zaletus looked first to Kreeops then to Martin, but said simply, "Then there is to be one fight only."

"To the death!" Kreeops reminded them with relish.

"Places," said Zaletus.

The guards led Martin toward the tree, while Kreeops rather awkwardly maneuvered Ryenna to a spot opposite Martin, about five lengths away. She kept her face in the shadow of her hood, out of view: perhaps from embarrassment, Martin figured.

Kreeops' choice of the girl had Martin off balance. Partially he was relieved. He wondered if, for some motives of his own, Kreeops wanted to let him win this second test. He couldn't imagine any rational reason why the Regent should, but rationality had little bearing on the recent events in his life. He knew Ryenna was very strong for a woman, but he would have expected to be facing the toughest giants the Regent could muster.

Still, the words, "to the death," were giving Martin trouble. If this was Kreeops' way of executing Ryenna, he wanted no part of it. His mind was racing, hoping to discover some way of stopping the fight, short of killing her, and still be victorious.

Then Kreeops drew the hood back from her head, and Martin realized that the Ryenna he had to fight had already been killed.

The head bobbed forward at a sickening angle: her once beautiful bureauer face was ashen, her expression one of permanent wild-eyed horror, as though molded by years, not moments, of continual suffering. A yawning, bloodless gash, through which her life had drained, was a fixed smile under her chin. Martin groaned and turned away, his mind remembering the aggressive passion of those battered and swollen lips. He was sick to his stomach there on the ground.

"Get up, weakling," Kreeops jeered. "Take heed to our justice. She was a very ugly bureauer when I bestowed beauty upon her in exchange for her allegiance. When she rescinded that allegiance, my guards merely repossessed that beauty. Your crime, stealing the face of our God, is far worse. And you have a duel to fight."

The horror that had once housed a thinking, feeling woman slowly lifted its arms into a ghastly parody of a greeting.

"Fight or die!" said Kreeops lightly, "as you will." Harshly, almost triumphantly, he turned to Zaletus. "It is time. It is past time. Start them or I will."

Martin never heard if Zaletus gave an answer or not. As he looked up, the monster was upon him. The stench of spreading decay assaulted his nostrils, and he thought he would have been sick again if he'd had the time. Or perhaps he was sick but too distracted to notice.

The creature was on his back, its teeth chattering wildly in his ear, tearing viciously at the side of his neck, passionately trying to do to him what had been done to it. It wasn't breathing, but ghastly grunts and rattles escaped from its throat excitedly as it broke the flesh; he could feel its swollen tongue, forcing itself into the wound, expanding it, ramming itself as deep as possible, while his warm blood lubricated the way. The monster had grabbed him around the waist. Its strength was enormous, but his repulsion was also strong, if close to panic, and he managed to tear himself away long enough to get turned around. They grappled face to face and fell to the ground. The being hit him hard, and in return he struck that face repeatedly, but aside from knocking out several teeth and flattening its nose, he made little impression. It didn't bleed from the mouth or nose.

He tried strangling it, his fingers fitting neatly into the gash on its neck, but though the throat gave and gave under his pressure, the punishment its fists were inflicting upon him never slowed for a minute. Giving up on strangling what didn't breathe, he tore at its wound, enlarging it, and, as if mirroring his actions (*does it think?* he wondered), its fingers dug painfully into the wound on his neck.

How can I kill something that's already dead? ran through his mind and was unanswered.

Its hands pounded his head and body: blows that knocked

the air from his lungs and made the world dim and threaten to go black. He smashed at its face and back and gouged at its eyes. The right eye popped out: hard, dry, and round in his hand. He thrust his fingers into the socket, searching for the brain. Whatever he reached crumbled to his touch, sprinkling out like dust from the empty hole. Its hands never faltered, though all that seemed to be left of Ryenna was the violence that had been inflicted on her. Was she taking her revenge for it upon him? He found that even now, part of him pitied this horror that was killing him, and would have been willing to surrender to unconsciousness rather than have to watch what was going on. He knew that he'd be more aggressive, more violent if he could tap some of the hate that his opponent seemed to possess in such overabundance. Was it his own softness that was killing him?

Then Kreeops moved into his vision, grinning, and the hate did well up in Martin. He smashed at the monster again and again. The hands might have slowed momentarily, as if taken off guard, but in an instant they were battering him even harder than before. And she was kicking him at the same time, almost in frenzy: not just reflecting but magnifying his own fury. His anger swelled in turn; he hit her harder, and once again she returned it with interest. Thus they thrashed about on the ground in an increasing furor, each feeding off the other's aggression, pummeling the other harder and harder, but only Martin feeling pain, only Martin suffering real damage. Finally, realizing he was defeating himself, he stopped completely for a mo-ment, and, an instant later, so did Ryenna. In the respite, he saw a delighted Kreeops bent almost double with laughter. The Regent hadn't yet noticed the calm, and when he did, slowly, steadily, inevitably, Ryenna started in again. Martin was virtually exhausted, and he was unable to restrain the hands as they closed around his windpipe. His blows were futile.

Kreeops was pacing around them, watching carefully now, apparently keeping himself in a position to enjoy Martin's face during the kill.

All this time Martin had been holding Ryenna's eyeball unthinkingly in his fist. Not wanting to appear broken (as Kreeops expected him to, and as Martin suddenly believed the Regent himself would have appeared in defeat), Martin tossed it over toward Kreeops: a last gesture of defiance, of independence even in death. He tried to call out, "catch," but the word that left his obstructed throat was unintelligible.

Startled, the Regent threw himself out of the way, momentarily confused. Certainly he had no idea what Martin had thrown. For a split second the fingers on Martin's neck loosened and even with his waning strength, he was able to knock them away, and desperately fling himself away from the creature long enough to grab a couple of quick breaths and gasp at Zaletus.

"The fight is...over...over...I won!"

"What?" said Zaletus, coming into view.

"I—"

"Like you're Jefuson, you win," scoffed Kreeops, actually spitting at Martin and hissing "Let the Revolution continue."

With these words, Ryenna, still lying across Martin's legs, slugged him painfully in the kidney.

"Wait," commanded the High Priest, reasserting his control over the testing. "Stop the fight. We will hear his claim."

"Refuse!"

Ryenna collapsed on Martin as if she'd been switched off. He crawled entirely free of her, remaining on his hands and knees, attempting to force lungfuls of air through a blood-raw throat that felt permanently constricted to the size of an anthole.

Not about to let him get any strength back, Kreeops sent him sprawling with a rough kick squarely on the seat.

"What's your claim now, fraud? This fight is to the death and you don't look dead to me."

"But...she...*is*," he managed painfully. "I win."

"She...she hasn't been defeated."

"She's dead." He looked to Zaletus. "A fight to the death."

Zaletus smiled. Martin thought the priest might have even chuckled if he hadn't checked himself. Then a long thin finger thoughtfully probed the hair bushing from his ear.

"What garbage," jeered Kreeops. "Let the fight continue!"

"The claim must be considered...a duel to the death." Zaletus' voice was serious now, if bemused. He mumbled the phrase, "to the death" several times, turning the words over on his tongue, examining them as if they held the answer. "This is an important matter. Later will be too late. The Revolution is suspended pending judgment."

"Shit!" screamed Kreeops at Martin where he lay on the ground. But his second kick seemed like a maiden's caress, so grateful was Martin for the rest.

It seemed only moments later that Kreeops was kicking him again and calling, "Up you go, turd face."

Ryenna, hooded again, was standing in readiness. Martin had never expected his feeble appeal to work. It hadn't. Zaletus helped him to his feet and led him over to approximately where he'd started before, again facing the monster. *Some duel,* Martin thought. *What chance have I got?*

"Wait!" he cried, still trying for some measure of control over what was happening and remembering something he and Mengra had seen at a Free-Kill when they were boys. "In a duel, the one who's challenged — me — gets his choice of weapons."

"Why don't you just go out there and die?" said Kreeops. "Weapons? What weapons!"

"I'm not sure you aren't the challenger here, Martin," Zaletus said, not unkindly.

"Go ahead," Kreeops said, "let them have weapons. Any weapons. What matter? She'll just finish him off that much sooner."

"I choose swords."

To Martin's sorrow, one of the guards produced two identical swords almost immediately. Zaletus let Martin select one, then handed the other to Ryenna. Kreeops was adjusting her cloak, and she remained motionless for long moments before moving her right arm to grasp the weapon. Her one remaining eye stared off in Martin's general direction. He imagined it locked on the last image it had ever seen, seeing no face but its murderer's everywhere it looked.

"Commence," Zaletus ordered. And Ryenna charged. But with the sword, her awkwardness was emphasized; she'd been more effective just falling upon him, covering him like a pack of rats. Now he was able to keep her at a certain distance. He slashed at her, cutting deep and broadly into her left arm. Again, the wound did not bleed, though tendon, muscle, and bone were exposed. She remained on the attack.

He meant to hack Ryenna to pieces, figuring it was his only chance. He crashed his sword against hers, hoping to disarm her, but her grip was too sure and her sword slid off his, biting into his right shoulder. A shock of pain jarred through him, and he backed off quickly. Raising her sword over her head, she charged. More coordinated he slipped aside while at the same time swinging his sword with both hands, his full weight behind it. Again it sliced into her arm. She stumbled sideways a step. Elated, he swung again and severed the arm from her body. It fell to the ground. He heard a gasp escape from a thousand voices and remembered they were being watched.

Ryenna hardly seemed affected by the blow. But she had hesitated a split-second later as the crowd reacted.

"I am the Jefuson," Martin cried, swinging his sword dramatically and painfully. "To stand against me is vanity."

It sounded silly to him, but he figured that he might have a better chance of fooling the disciples than of beating this indestructible remnant of a woman. It was just possible that if he could get some of the disciples to really believe that he was a god, and a god who was angry at this testing, then they could get Kreeops to stop trying to kill him for a day or two. If Martin had known more about the coven's absolute subordination to the Regent, he probably wouldn't have wasted his time.

But just for an instant, Ryenna seemed to waver, the arm with the sword began to descend, lowering as if in response to his cry.

"He is a fraud and his destruction is ordained in the Book and in the Scroll," yelled Kreeops, and the monster rallied, advancing on Martin again, though possibly slower this time.

Martin parried two blows and wondered if there was a bit less energy, a little less determination behind them.

Then he screamed in pain and clutched at his ankle where fingers were threatening to crunch the bones. *The severed arm was still alive!* And it had his leg. He cursed and hacked at its forearm with his sword. Ineffectually.

"The minion of Satan is complete. He has no effect on it. He is a fraud!"

At Kreeops' words, Ryenna renewed the attack, her onslaught at full force once again. The wild thrusts and slashes might have been inelegant, but they would be nonetheless deadly if they got through Martin's guard, and anything he offered in return only seemed to increase her fierceness, though he cut her repeatedly, if bloodlessly. He buried his sword into her stomach; he tore violently at her bowels, not even slowing her down. His own leg was gashed, not too deeply, but he had to break off for the moment.

"I am the Jefuson," he cried for lack of any other plan, bluffing again. Taking his lead from Kreeops, he attempted a godlike voice, but it sounded puny to his own ears. "Who dares to align themselves with those whose time has passed? With those who would kill their god once again? For each man who holds blindly to the darkness in the presence of the light must be held to blame, must know that it is he who preserves the evil that lingers around us."

Neither Zaletus nor any one else intervened on his behalf, but the creature coming at him halted dead in her tracks, her sword slowly lowering. Once, twice, she started to raise it, then it would fall as if some support had snapped in the machinery of her arm. The hand around his ankle loosened. Martin, unsure of what was happening, made no move to detach it. The creature started forward but stopped in midstep, then actually pulled its foot back, as if she was capable of confusion and was now undecided about her foe. Martin took a deep breath and lowered his sword, hoping his nervousness didn't show. He stretched himself to his full height, standing straight and tall in spite of the leg wound that almost made him scream in pain as he put weight on that leg. Kreeops was yelling to the air.

"Don't listen to the words of the false one! They are full of deceit and trickery. He would steal your faith, rob our will, and deliver us unto our enemies. He must be destroyed."

As if listening, Ryenna began to swing her sword.

With less than a half-formed idea of what he was doing and no time to think it through, telling himself skeptically that it was never going to work, Martin threw down his swords and raised his empty hands.

"The Jefuson has come to bring peace. Not strife. I bear no weapon. I am no enemy. If I were a fraud and an enemy, I am only one man and easily disposed of. But I am not, and each one of you is free; each one of you must choose whether you would defy your savior. This second test, this Revolution, is a test of *you*, not of me, designed not to see if I am genuine, but if *you* are ready, if you can proclaim *your* independence from those who would strike down the Prince of Peace once again. Those of you who fail, each one individually, will be called to account for denying Jefuson to the world."

And again the monster had halted in its tracks. Encouraged, he went on.

"This creature is dead, and its power is the violence that creates only death. In the name of life, I, Jefuson, command it to yield its place on earth to the living, as Kreeops himself must yield his before me."

"Don't listen to him," Kreeops yelled. But the creature crumbled as if in response to Martin's command. Kreeops was apoplectic. "FOOLS! He has slain nothing, nothing. You are letting him poison your faith. He is riddling our strength with doubt!!! Arise!" He lifted his arms to the heavens. "The creature of Satan will arise and destroy the blasphemous impostor!"

On the ground the arm twitched, the legs moved; as close as Martin was, he could see the muscles of the body contracting, tensing, gathering power to get up and have at him again.

"It is over, Kreeops," he called with a triumph he didn't feel in the slightest. "You have no life to give it. The test is over."

Martin turned his back to Kreeops and Ryenna, contemptuously, standing very still for a moment, playing to the crowd, bracing himself, trying not to shake visibly from his exertion and tension. He started walking, as erect as if he were both victorious and invulnerable. Behind him he heard a thud, as if the body on its way up had fallen to the ground again. But he didn't dare look back, though he more than half-expected to feel a sword burying itself in his back at any moment. He could almost hear a cheering deep inside his head, and that — and some nervous energy from some deep reserve he was unaware he possessed — kept him putting one foot in front of the other.

"You shook him to the foundation of his power."

Zaletus was following behind him. Martin didn't stop, but he slowed his pace to allow the old priest to come along side.

"He's back there trying to restore enough of their faith to make his monster walk again," Zaletuus said. "You've sown great division, but he's a master. He'll make believers of them again," This was said tentatively, almost questioningly. "And in all likelihood at your expense."

"You don't believe?"

"I believe that Kreeops is the rightful ruler until the Jefuson appears."

"But Kreeops' power isn't from Satan?"

"Satan chose him to rule as Regent. But where does any ruler get his power? It is the power of the disciples, united as one in their faith in him. He is the mind that directs the strength of the body. *For now*, at least."

Martin looked at him, realizing how much the old man wanted to believe in him, and wondering if he had any chance of bluffing him.

"The last test is the test against death." the priest said, searching for a reaction. "No one can pass that, not unless he really is God."

"Are you so sure that I'm not?"

There was no reply.

10

Beyond

It was well into the night, after an afternoon and evening of wandering the streets and circling the various buildings of the Gov-Cent, when Gena finally spotted the concrete columns of the Bureau of the Boundries. Actually, it did look quite like the mental picture she'd gotten from Tantor. She literally breathed a sigh of relief: as the foot traffic on the sidewalks died down, she'd been getting more and more conspicuous. In contrast to the folker ring, there was little bureauer activity in the streets at night (except for just before and just after shift changes). She wondered how long it would be before Tantor woke up and, finding her gone, unlike the nice bureauer girl she'd pretended to be, started asking himself questions about the woman he'd arrested that afternoon and her uncommon curiosity.

Gena climbed up the concrete steps and passed through the columns into the cavelike portico. In front of her, heavy chains hung from all four sets of steel doors. She rattled a couple of them in frustration, frightening herself as she shattered the stillness around her. Not a light, not a sound came from within. Feeling especially exposed, she chanced a reading but discovered no more that way than with her other senses. Looking for a window or any other possible entrance, she crept around the corner to the unlit alley at the side. Another quick reading, just a flash to determine if it was empty, then she merged into the safety and invisibility of the alley, the way she'd slide into the refuge of sleep after an overly strenuous day.

She kept close to the wall. After a few steps, she heard a crunch and felt a grittiness underfoot as if she were walking on broken glass. If that's what it was, it must have come from the building across the alley; the wall on her right seemed to have been built without an opening of any kind. This was the first time she'd encountered rubble in the Gov-Cent; broken windows here seemed rarer than unbroken ones outside. She'd become aware of the rumble of a vehicle, off in the distance.

As Gena had begun to suspect from the huge black form gradually taking shape at the farthest extreme of her vision, the alley dead-ended in the high brick wall of another structure. In front of it was stacked a pile of crates and junk that was almost worthy of the alleys in which she'd grown up, except, incredibly, the crates were made of wood. Suddenly, the sound of that car engine, which had seemed so distant, chugged around a corner and was very close, alarming her, sending her dashing back into the crates for cover. She banged into one of them so heavily that the whole pile shook and threatened to tumble, but she did manage to get out of sight just as the front of the alley was flooded with the jaundiced light from the policer vehicle that was crawling down the street. Before the light moved on, Gena saw an iron ladder attached to the side of the Bureau of the Boundry. Its lowest rung was at a height that must have been well up into the second story, but it led all the way up to the roof. She was amazed at her good fortune at finding the ladder together with the crates that could enable her to reach it. As she straightened up, her shoulder barely nudged a steel barrel piled on one of the crates, sending it crashing to the pavement and rolling several lengths down the alley with what must have been the loudest noise Gena had ever heard. She didn't need the sound of the engine or the blood-red glow of the backup lights to know that the policers were returning.

The car backed slowly past the alley. Then, moving forward again, it turned in. To Gena, a felon against the power behind them, its feeble electric lights appeared to be more revealing than daylight. Sputtering, perhaps draining their batteries, the lights traveled toward her hiding place as inexorably as any dawn. And she was only partially hidden, afraid to move farther back for fear of upsetting the precarious pile behind her once again. She considered running out and hailing the policers, wondering if she could make up some story: maybe she could be a female bureauer, dragged into the alley against her will. Of course she wasn't sure that kind of thing happened in the Gov-Cent. And even the most cursory check would expose her, if they weren't already looking for her in the first place.

The ladder, caught in the circle of the advancing light, was so close, an unbroken stairway out of there. But out of reach as well. She remembered the cat in Triah's apartment. It wouldn't even be challenged by a leap of only twice its height. It would be gone almost before they could see it, its sleekly compressed energies carrying it instantly, noiselessly, to the ladder and up. It might even make it undetected, while a policer head was turned, while an eye blinked shut for a split-second cleansing.

Just as Gena was about to be revealed by the light, she moved. Bounding out of her cover, momentarily hit by the glare, she ran silently, on the balls of her feet, increasing her pace with each step, coiling, then springing, feline herself, full with the smell, the taste, the grace, and the life of the cat. For an instant, she was soaring naturally. She grasped the second rung of the ladder and pulled herself up; there was just moment's hesitation as she shifted her balance, and then she scaled easily to the roof. The policers in the car below had seen almost the entire movement. One of them swore, and the other replied, "Damn cat." The vehicle stopped its forward progress, noisily shifted gears, and slowly backed out of the alley.

On the roof, Gena got even farther out of sight. She didn't know what they'd seen, but she knew she had never changed. Her form was all too plainly that of a woman, and she wasn't anxious for them to catch a glimpse of her and find that out. She lay down, pondering what had happened, as her heart recovered from its wild beating.

The way she figured it, trying to get to that ladder she must have been concentrating so hard that it was picked up by the policers. Simple suggestion, actually, merely a little stronger and a lot more complete than silent speech. It was a possibility that seemed to tickle something in her mind, as if it had loose threads that should be connected to other ideas. She would have liked to have spent some time linking them all up. It would have to be later.

Right now it wasn't the projection she was interested in. She had reached the ladder! Easily. Though it was clearly a physical impossibility. How had she done it? And what had even given her the idea that she could? Was there something hidden in the memory of the little girl who had broken her leg trying just that sort of feat? Suddenly she was drained. She sat down abruptly and rested for a long while before getting up again.

The roof she was on was flat. At three stories high, it was below the level of the Gov-Cent streetlighting, so she could see fairly well. A few feet from where Gena sat, a rather skeletal tower resting on four legs rose to a sharp point far above the building. It looked to be in a horrible state of disrepair, with huge gaps in the framework, and supports and wires dangling every which way. The roof itself was strewn with twisted girders which apparently had been shed from the tower. Among them she saw a sign with the limit logo upon it. The rust on the girder she was sitting on decomposed on her hand as she shifted position.

It's a wonder the limit works at all, if this has anything to do with running it, Gena said to herself. Rising only to a crouch, even though she was well out of view from the street below, she picked her way carefully over to the base of the tower for further examination.

Under its center, she found an opening in the roof through which a thick bundle of cables and piping came from the interior of the building and traveled up the middle of the tower. A ladder climbed this spine upwards. A circular metal stairway without a railing wound around it going down, disappearing inside the bureau. After bouncing on the top step a couple of times to test it, a precaution she almost never bothered to take among the far more obviously precarious staircases of the outer ring, Gena started down. Idly, she wondered what was done to keep the rain and snow from entering the same way. She was halfway down to the top floor when she decided to chance another quick reading, her third in the same immediate area. She was pressing her luck. It was negative. No one was around.

In spite of the ventilation in the roof, the building smelled heavily of machinery. She stepped off the stairs onto the floor, which was actually a metal catwalk, and it resounded like a huge gong. She considered removing her shoes, but the very idea of bare feet under these circumstances gave her such a sensation of vulnerability that she decided to make due with merely walking carefully, no matter how ineffectual that might prove. She knew what she had to do. If she couldn't find out how to cross the limit from someone or something here, she hoped to damage it just long enough to get across. As a last resort, she would try to destroy it; if that island she had seen was real and if she could get to it, Kreeops might be unable to recapture her anyway.

Apparently there were several skylights in the roof as well as the hole under the tower. All around her, she could make out gigantic machinery, filling the entire floor, hulking, immobile, and very dirty. Cobwebs hung from every surface, clinging to her as she wandered around the dusty catwalks. The only sounds were her own footsteps and her breathing. She had the certainty that no one had been up on that floor for a very long time, and reaching another ladder, she slipped down to a lower level. Hoping for offices, she found more machinery, only dimmer and dirtier; the thick dust entered her lungs and made her cough. Underneath her here, the floor was wooden. She seemed to be at the base of the same machines that she'd seen above. A wooden stairway led to the next level down. At the end of it, a sensor-door blocked her way, but it opened inward when she pushed. Closing it behind her, she found that not enough light survived the trip down there for her to see the end of her nose, much less the area around her, so she reopened the door to let a little in and saw a set of switches like those Triah had used to turn on the bulb in her apartment. Not really expecting anything, she flipped one, and there was light. She closed the door. If no light could get in, it seemed a safe bet that none could get out. Gena'd be as invisible to passing policers as the inside of a crazer's mind.

This floor, ground level, was broken up into cubicles, spreading out on either side of her, and one large room lined with metal panels straight ahead. As she wandered through the cubicles, they seemed to have been long empty. One or two still held a desk or a rusty file cabinet, but the drawers of these were as barren as the rest of the offices. No one and nothing. She felt foolish. She didn't know what she'd expected to find. Even if she had found a book or a chart revealing the secrets of the limit, she wouldn't have been able to read it.

Still, many of the machines of the bureauers functioned automatically without anyone, and if that were the case here, she had only to stop that functioning and steal across the limit before repairs could he made.

In the last few days she'd gotten so accustomed to thinking of herself as locked in rather than protected by the limit that Gena now regarded damaging or even destroying it as little more than a necessary and natural step. Her survival depended upon it; it was amazing she'd lasted this long. She was far more concerned with *if* she could sabotage it than she was about any slight uneasiness she may have had about doing so: of course, most people would have been horrified at the prospect, but then most of them would never even know that it wasn't functioning. Not unless it stayed off forever. People weren't going to start plunging into the waters and drowning. And she doubted that any of the "whatever must be kept out" could reach the city, even if there was any of it left after all this time.

On her way back to the room with the panels, she was overcome twice by fits of coughing. In that room, the panels stretched across the base of an entire wall. Each was marked with a different red number and covered with gauges and buttons that reminded Gena of the controls inside an ancient car. Above them all was a great map. A double line, marked every so often by the limit symbol, circled the map, and this double line in turn was divided into sections stamped with red numbers that corresponded to those on the panels. Apparently, each section of the limit was controlled by a different panel.

If Gena could shut down just one area and leave the rest

of the limit intact, she might gain a lot more time before anyone noticed anything amiss. She checked her bearings on the
map; it was difficult. The path of the River was the common
reference point in both folker maps and the maps that the
criers gave out when they were sending units to distant safeways because of food or coupon shortages, or when they were
instructing a folker on how to get to the Free-Kill. She found
the River, all right, and she assumed that the large dot near the
center of the chart was the Bureau of the Boundry. But
nowhere could she find the no-folker zone; there didn't seem
to be any indication at all of a separation between the outer
ring and the Gov-Cent. Instead the whole map was checkered
with streets. A number of them, radiating from the center, went
all the way out to the waters.

Wasting no time puzzling it out, she moved right to the
panel with the same number as the section of the limit closest
to where the River came up. She flipped a toggle switch at ran-
dom. No gauge budged; all of the lights remained unlit. She
flicked another with the same results. None of the machinery
upstairs stirred.

She switched every switch, pushed every button in that
panel. She tried a few from the panels on either side, and several more up and down the length of the wall. Never did she
receive the faintest indication that any of the controls had any
effect at all. An almost dormant intuition, embryonic for
longer than she knew in some obscure furrow of her brain, was
coming to term. If she was right, her problems might be over;
if she was wrong, she was dead.

"Lovely simplicity," she muttered sarcastically.

She hurried up the stairs and out of the building.
Lowering herself down the ladder from the roof, she dangled
from the last rung for a moment before dropping. The pavement below would be very hard. But just as she let go, hands

clasped at her legs and ankles, and she fell into them. They were all around her, at every part of her body.

Tantor kept her locked in a basement room for several days, feeding her very little, periodically coming down to scream at her for her "betrayal." Once he slapped her face. He was almost entertaining to read, almost funny.

People were the great mysteries of Tantor's universe. All he could really see was that they were menacing, and that they all seemed to be beyond most of the anxieties that plagued him. He hated them for that superiority. And Gena discovered that, although he seldom acknowledged his basest motivations to himself, he constantly found those very motives in the people around him. And without the mitigating factors with which he could excuse himself. Trying to see himself as Tantor, Big Eater, he liked inflicting a little pain in order to confirm his importance. He wasn't usually aware of this. But he had absolutely no problem seeing that Gena's impersonation of a bureauer, and her subsequent escape, was a deliberate effort on her part to establish *her* importance by making him look foolish and inflicting pain on him.

Any pain that he might cause he saw as incidental, necessary, and, at worst, understandable. After all, he was surrounded by people who deserved it, people like Gena who were out to hurt him, who were selfishly trying to raise themselves above him. The pain Gena caused was vicious and unforgivable. It hurt. The implication seemed to be that, after he'd befriended her, a decent person would have gone politely to the Free-Kill.

Yet she found out he would have despised her if she had done so; still in touch with the view of himself as Tantor, genetic burnout, he would have understood any docility only in terms of his own cowardice. Apparently, however, he desperately wanted to despise her. It would have made him feel better about himself.

He made an interesting probe, but a lousy captor.

Gena knew she was going to be Free-Killed, probably agonizingly. Yet when they finally came for her one afternoon, it was almost a relief. She was shoved into a cage on the back of a cart that was pulled slowly and unsteadily by six prowlers. Two policers gave commands from the driver's seat. They traveled almost the entire night. Since virtually all the prisoners condemned to die in any given Free-Kill were from the folker ring, they were usually kept in cells out by the waters near the Free-Kill itself. That night Gena was the only one coming from the Gov-Cent, and she was impressed that they'd bothered with this special trip just for her. She guessed it was because she was a disciple.

Lying down in the back, she watched the sky full of stars through the mesh of the cage. The ride seemed even rougher than her ride in the trash reaper. It certainly took longer, even traveling a known, cleared route. Once they got to the outer ring, they were constantly stopping to remove some obstacle or some sleeping folker from their path. Sometimes the obstruction or the folker was small enough that they didn't bother to stop, and the cart would lurch violently over the bump. Anguished cries might pierce the night; the stars got no dimmer. If anything, as they got closer to the Free-Kill, as the night darkened, each individual star seemed to grow even brighter.

She didn't dwell on what the manner of her death might be. It was as if she'd spent her life bouncing around in her cage, exposed, being dragged across a city that was as pockmarked as the streets with an almost infinite number of possible deaths. Which particular one happened to catch her, and even when, seemed at that moment almost as unimportant to her life as it was to the city.

It was still dark when they arrived at the Free-Kill, though the town was starting to awaken. Gena heard the drivers mutter with some relief that they were on time, and she thought it was silly for anyone to be concerned with such a trifle.

"Disciples die at dawn," one of them said to her informatively, explaining a feature of his job to a layman. He spoke without malice, or, apparently, even the realization that such a pronouncement would hold any special interest for the disciple who was scheduled to die then.

The Free-Kill itself had obviously once been part of a road. It was wide, over twice the width of most streets in the city, and recessed into the ground as if it had once tunneled under something that no longer existed. The walls on either side of it were concrete; the roadbed, cracked and shattered asphalt. The end where the victims were led in was closed off by a poorly-made but sturdy brick wall with a single crude gate. At the other end, a natural barrier was formed: the walled road broke off into the waters; the limit, of course, would keep any victim from plunging off after it and cheating the mob. Outside of the Free-Kill, blocks and jagged heaps of cement had been piled up over the years and arranged in irregularly-tiered seating. The whole arena (which almost nobody remembered had once been called "the Coliseum") was surrounded by a rusty, well-guarded fence to keep out unauthorized spectators. The cart that held Gena was parked just inside of the fence.

Dawn was so soon, Gena found herself thinking wistfully. Time: all at once, it was meaningful again, intensely so. It seemed to be ticking off — no, wearing out, within her. Time was in the pumping of her heart, the surging of her blood: in the tensing and relaxing of her muscles and the wear and tear upon the tissues, rather than someplace outside her in the relationship of the city and the sun. Her cage opened. It was still night, but she was taken out, stripped naked, and led through the gate in the brick wall. The Free-Kill! Above her on either side the seats were filling with folkers. They could scarcely see, and kept stumbling over each other and the makeshift seating, aggressively but almost playfully: excited; proud; winners all.

Two ropes were looped around Gena's waist. On the end of each, at a safe distance from her, was a policer. Thus secured, she was led to the far end of the long pit. When they stopped, her ears picked up a ringing; she was very near the limit. She looked toward the waters, but all she could see was night sky. Held between the policers on the taut ropes, she could barely move a step, either forward or back.

At the other end, where she'd just come from, a gang of prowlers was filing into the pit. Laughing, waving to the crowd above them, they seemed delighted with their celebrity. The elect. A couple of overseers were stretching a chain across the roadway in front of them, fastening it on either side to the concrete walls. To restrain them from the kill. Temporarily.

On one of the walls, a crier called for attention, then announced:

"First offering today. A disciple. For a solo torturing, followed by an unarmed mob rending with optional devouring. The elect are a prowler gang chosen for their magnificent labors on the generators, pumping the power that fills our batteries, the power that illuminates the glory of our Big Eaters who work so hard to keep us all fed. The gang gets one kill only, at dawn, for she is a choice young disciple. And the torturer is to be selected from their ranks."

"Stop!" It came from the seats to Gena's right. "*I* was to be torturer. Tantor gave it to *me!*"

Gena looked up as Mengra forced his way up to the edge of the pit. Right behind him was Triah, futilely pounding on his back, attempting to get him to sit down. In amazement, the crowd shifted its attention to the strange couple. Folker men were almost never seen publicly with bureauer women; they certainly were never seen defying them.

"Who is to inflict the torture?" called the crier to the gang, ignoring Mengra, although the folker was actually the louder of the two.

"It's me," Mengra screamed, shoving Triah backward and right on top of the folkers seated there, incidentally creating a barrier that kept a policer from reaching him. Several other policers were also moving toward him.

"Are you part of the gang?" the crier asked him.

"No, but Tantor promised."

"And I promise you will take her place in the torturing if you don't shut up."

In the laughter that followed, Mengra allowed Triah to lead him away; his protesting becoming quieter as he caught sight of the policers. Perhaps his use of the name "Tantor" had prevented his arrest.

"Time is short," continued the crier to the gang, "and the sun is almost upon us. Let the man you have selected come forth."

Three men stepped forward to the chain and, seeing each other, immediately began arguing among themselves; each picked up vocal supporters from the gang behind them.

The crier cursed to himself, audibly. Then he called out, "You, old man. You are chosen. Come quickly."

The sky was lightening rapidly. Flamboyantly, the torturer acknowledged the cheers and ducked under the chain. Gena was giving most of her attention to the increasing pace of her heartbeat. She wanted to slow it down, as if her life was a song with a predetermined number of beats, a song that would last longer if played slower.

The old man, the torturer, swaggered across the pavement

with an off-balance gait that made it appear as if all his insides had shifted to one side of his body. He lumbered up to Gena and stuck his ravaged brown face under hers; at first, she thought he was going to bang their heads together. Filthy tufts of hair and beard were randomly scattered over his bony face and head. Jagged, broken teeth pointed in all directions at once, like a signpost at a crossroads in hell. His nose was equally jagged, and, worst of all, a festering sore opened like a blind third eye in the middle of his forehead.

"Hurry, old man," said the crier. "What torture do you choose?"

The old man let loose a happy little high-pitched laugh, paused for a bit of contemplation, then squealed out, "The crown!"

The crowd reacted, in separate voices, calling out their approval or disapproval, or the name of their favorite torture.

From the wall, the device was thrown to one of the policers beside Gena, who caught it without letting go of the rope and brought it over to the old man. Gena was familiar with the crown, sometimes called "the crown of thorns," or just "the hat." It was a metal half-globe studded with screws. With reverence, the old man turned it over in his hands. He was shorter than Gena, and both policers stepped up beside her to help him when she struggled. Resistance was so obviously futile that, before they grabbed her, she lowered her head, offering it to the torturer, bending down far enough for him to slip on the crown. The spectators cheered. She could feel her pulse in each of her fingertips and against the cold metal at her temples. It was slower now; she had brought it somewhat under control. She could taste the predawn moisture in the air. Dew was forming on the weeds growing through the asphalt roadbed. It seemed a miraculous sign of life, sweat on the skin of a body long presumed dead. Under her feet that body was stirring; she almost believed she could probe the planet like a person as it turned slowly in its sleep prior to waking, moving the stars even as they faded before the sun that was arriving to overhang her death.

There was a pressure that grew into a spray of pain. It let up for a single heartbeat, then returned as a flood, forcing a cry from her mouth. The old man was tightening the screws on the crown around her head. Dew, or was it tears, was beading on her face. She was on her knees, stunned, wondering if the top of her head had been sheared off, and if her thoughts were escaping out of the opening to fade away among the dying stars.

Huge and unstoppable arms came down to the screws on the crown: the arms of a malicious god, intent upon strangling her brain. The pain took over and Gena felt herself disappearing, forced out of her own body. And gone.

Someone was lying face down on the asphalt below. A mob delighted in her destruction, as if it could in no way be connected to their own flimsiness. Beside the body, a pathetic little man danced gleefully. Spittle hung on his beard; for an instant the drops looked larger than the stars. His glee could be probed. He was an infant, standing on wobbly knees, as erect as lightning, enchanted by his vision of himself as a cause and a mover, as a creator of mortality. As if that placed him beyond it, even as his only actual distinction, a malformed artery burst like a rotten pipe. (Perhaps the genetic accident responsible for the defect had occurred even before the ancient light that provided his last sensation left its star.) He fell dead beside the woman he thought he had killed.

This was observed; then there was the impression that a great deal of time had passed. The world was in agony. No, she realized, *I* am in agony. There was something she had to remember. The awareness of who she was, of where she was, of her life up to that point that normally would have rushed back to her upon awakening was momentarily blocked by the pain. Then, seeing and hearing the prowler gang, she remembered, first where, then who, she was. *She was about to die.* She was bitterly disappointed at that realization, as if the world was a better place when she was unaware, as if she wouldn't have been killed if only she hadn't remembered. She would have liked to return to that ignorance: then there was hope.

But the knowledge had to be dealt with. Seeing the old man, she knew he was dead. She fumbled with the screws on the side of the crown and managed to loosen them and remove it. The crowd applauded her every movement. The chain tensed as the prowlers in the pit with her pressed against it; she saw how aroused their faces were.

She got to her knees, then staggered to her feet. Immediately, the policers tightened up on the ropes that bound her, as if she had someplace to run. She just wanted to be standing when the prowlers took her. Gazing over her shoulder to the foggy waters, it was easy to imagine more shapes out there. She looked back to the spectators and to the gang. *I could probably free them,* she thought. *I probably could. And they'll destroy me for a moment's distraction from the emptiness of their prison.* She savored a quick disgust for them, in their smug, suffering complacency, in the completeness of their surrender of their lives and of their minds. After they killed her, they would live on, dead and buried in their ignorance.

"Not me," she said out loud, and even as she spoke, she was aware of her own lie. *Yes me,* she corrected. We share the same small city; we have the same suicidal pettiness. Her very disgust with them was deadly, burning up the few moments of precious life she had left before the prowlers tore her apart.

The gang was greedy for a share of the blood they had been promised. The chain would restrain them no longer.

Overcome with passion, for once in their lives they defied the will of the bureauers, ducking under, leaping, and climbing over the chain. And charging for Gena.

I will be different, she thought. For one instant, I will be what I can be: free of this filth and hunger, free of this reverberating fear and hate, free of everything everyone "knew" to be true. The incredible pain had become insignificant, or perhaps it had become so great as to be beyond recognition. She saw it as just one more excuse for submitting to the easy way, for being too busy or too afraid or too lazy, for resting herself even unto death in the gutter of "common knowledge": as if reality required a majority vote, as if a consensus of madmen constituted sanity.

She lifted her arms slowly, her eyes blazing. The gang screamed, picking up speed, closing in on her. The chain was on the ground though no order had been given. The bureauer whose job it was to release it was desperately trying to climb out of the pit, but the rope ladder that was supposed to help him up the wall hadn't been lowered yet.

Gena took it all in. The gang was less than twenty body lengths from her. Eyes bulging, mouths hanging open, they fought each other viciously for position: as if the man struck were really so much different from the man doing the striking, who in turn was being clawed by another man beside him. As if it would make any difference to Gena's death, or to their lives, or to the still unseen sun, whose teeth tore her body or whose fingers gouged away the female organs of the Bride of the Jefuson. She took a deep breath.

Light was easing into the sky, faintly throbbing. Soon it would be settling down to earth, its life passing through everything that grew or crawled or flew, filtering down to the poorage and then to the folkers. And this is what we do with that life, she thought. The cracks in the pavement beneath her were stained red with the blood of a thousand like her, of a thousand like the killers. *How many killers later became the killed? How many of their children?*

(The policers who were holding the ropes let them go and fled for the wall. The mob was almost on her.)

Light. The stars. Gena stretched for them. They were so intense, though the brightest, even now creeping over the horizon, was blinding the crowd in the Free-Kill to the million suns beyond its brilliance. She stretched for those suns, seeing them, feeling them each clearly against her skin, throwing back her cloak letting them touch her. Her nostrils flared as if she could smell their light on the faint breeze.

(Casually, the way a man steps a few paces to remove an obstacle from his view, Gena stepped across the limit. The gang halted, spellbound.)

And Gena gazed upon the spaces between the suns, the still visible, black, dead void. Eternal night; the primordial negativity. Death. According to the logic of Kreeops' mythology, such consummate black should be a womb of demons. Yet it generated no dark sunlight to nourish any world of evil. This was death all right; yet it was no sinister malignity, but a vacuum, the nothing from which everything had somehow sprung. And as she searched it more closely, she could sense that the vacuum was filled, the death was alive, with an undifferentiated spectrum of energy in transit from the million suns. Light unreceived, unperceived; the void was dormant soil awaiting a seed.

The whole universe seemed well-lit, charged with the colors of the stars, and alive, energy dispersed throughout. Bright, dark; day, night; life, death; all seemed not so much realities in themselves as mere products of narrow and fragmented perception, moments improperly isolated, in their own way as arbitrary and theatrical as the darks and the lights in Kreeops' castle.

Moments that had as little independent existence as the frozen two-dimensional beings who peered out of photographs.

Gena felt the light racing through her like blood, powering her brain, which in turn sought the source of light, as if to complete a more perfect circuit. Then the energy was all; she saw herself as one of its organs, formed in a struggle toward self-awareness.

She was Gena, clean, strong, weightless, free, a radiant star: a unique and integral link in an infinite system. She considered the mob. They could see only the moment, called "Mengra," or "Triah," or "food unit," or "city," or just "me." Their individual energy was left to dissipate. Or else it was focused as if through a lens, on too small an area; and in the name of warmth, comfort, and illumination, that energy ignited the greedy holocausts that would eventually devour the remainder of the city and those individuals themselves.

She felt she was sucking in the vast energy the crowd in the Free-Kill was discarding, as well as the energy from the stars. The vibrating within her was becoming an ecstasy. The energy she was absorbing from all sides had absorbed her entire life, she transformed into light that she projected back across the limit to the crowd and to the heavens. Everything was immediate: the faces of the gang members that gazed up stunned into hers, as well as the other stars that lit the morning sky. She felt herself expanding. Focused on what was beyond her reason — on what was susceptible to infinite evaluation — reflection vanished from her head. All was experience and reaction, a flowing circle encompassing her greatest perceptions and beyond: because what was beyond was so immediately a part of what she touched here.

She was aware of it, but she was unimpressed by the fact that she was floating a length or so off the ground. Facing the crowd, she spoke to them, in the energy she emanated, of the possibilities she explored. Some of the gang stood just on the other side of the limit, hands pressed against it as if it were a huge pane of glass. In their confusion, a few of them were pounding on it noiselessly. Most of the gang and most of the spectators were immobile, stricken, crude, lifeless models of the type of being that floated unattainably just out of their reach. Their eyes were all fixed on that being, the formerly crushed and naked disciple, gloriously soaring beyond the death they had brought for her, as if she were immortal. To their perception, her body was enveloped in white and surrounded by an aura of light that grew brilliant almost beyond endurance. No one looked away.

Each one of the rapt crowd thought she was staring right at him or her. Some of them were beginning to notice shapes in the waters and in the sky behind Gena. All of them were gazing upon a suddenly incomprehensible world, incredibly, totally other than the one they'd been living in right up until that moment.

And yet, for many of them, it was the first time in their lives that they were unafraid.

11

Golgotha

The next thing Gena remembered, she was leaning against what was left of an ancient wall, out of sight of the Free-Kill. Around her were roads and buildings much like those in the city, only sparser and possibly in better shape. There were no waters; the land was continuous. And though the folkers couldn't see it, the road that led to this spot stretched back to the Free-Kill, uninterrupted except by the limit.

The limit: even before she'd stepped through it, she'd begun to see what was on the other side. The limit itself had been no problem. Probably self-powered like a sensor-door, it *did* still work, although it didn't really do much; crossing it she'd noticed, almost subliminally, a tiny discomfort projected at her for an instant, and then she was over. Apparently the limit was nothing more than a psychic warning signal, but one that people had learned to obey so well over the generations that for them it had become an impassable barrier. A warning signal. To keep them from stumbling into the waters that weren't there.

There was no evidence of people on this side (at least not for as far as she could sense). Just ahead of her was a tower, one of a line of towers running parallel to the Limit, each identical to the one on the roof of the Bureau of the Boundary. With difficulty, she roused herself and walked over, passing back and forth between two of them several times. The wiring on the towers was tattered and frayed; much of it was completely disconnected. There had been no power here for a long time. In the Bureau of the Boundry, she'd figured that something was no longer functioning; at the time she'd assumed it was the limit.

She was tired, but the world had opened for her. Ahead the buildings thinned out. In the far distance, she could see the green of hills and what looked to be a whole city of huge trees. She heard rats around her, and saw a few pigeons, fluttering around rooftops. A dog rounded a corner, one of the few she'd ever seen. It seemed well-fed, and had, in fact, some small animal she didn't recognize in its mouth.

Food, shelter, and growing plants. And no Kreeops. She'd be free and safe. It was far better than she could have hoped. She'd been a loner all her life, but her decision had already been made, and she didn't even hesitate before turning and walking back to the people and to the city. She was more free than she had ever been.

As she returned, the spectators inside the Free-Kill struggled for a view of her, in order to watch her walk across the waters. ("Is there something in the air beside her?" "Do you see a road?") At a spot just outside of the fence around the Free-Kill, she came back through the limit. The folkers outside the arena made way for her, silently. Not one of them followed as she passed, still garbed in some kind of whiteness, limping slightly. But two figures, hurrying from the arena, trailed at a distance.

"Can you contact Kreeops?" asked Triah.

"He contacts me, fool. We may be too far away. He may be

busy with other matters." Mengra was so edgy he was almost throbbing.

"Well, he'll sure want to know about that last trick. I never saw anything like it."

"Shut up. You never saw anything like it because it's impossible. She was *obviously* using some black art, so Kreeops *obviously* knows all about it, doesn't he? But she isn't dead and we'll get the blame, so I wouldn't be so anxious to inform Kreeops if I were you. If it was up to me, I would have killed her ourselves after she escaped from those fools the first time."

"You told me Kreeops wanted the bureauers to kill her," she insisted, beseechingly.

"But nobody killed her, did they, fool? And now he'll kill us. Or worse. He *should* kill just you. *You* got the policers."

"I was afraid. Besides, you agreed." But she sounded con- trite and guilty. She sighed, then said, "I'm really very hungry, Mengra."

"After we finish her."

"Finish...how can we finish anyone who can do what she did?"

"All right then, my fine bureauer lady, why don't you just tell me what choice we have?"

So they followed as Gena worked her way through the back roads, and it was only a few blocks before she started weaving as if she were sick or drunk on staggerer cakes. The foot traffic around her was sparse; in spite of her condition she was miraculously left unmolested. Once she fell and managed to pick herself up only with the greatest difficulty. She was obviously exhausted. The next time she went down she didn't get up. Instantly a prowler was hovering above her, but Mengra rushed over and pushed him roughly away.

Gena was sprawled face-down on a pile of shattered cin- der blocks, naked.

"What happened to her white robe?" Triah asked, but Mengra merely told her to grab an arm and gestured toward a nearby alley.

"We'll make it look like a band of prowlers did her in. That should please Kreeops." He sounded almost pleasant; his relief was obvious.

Triah was huffing and puffing by the time they got Gena far enough into the alley to suit Mengra. She wiped the sweat from her face; it left her hands grimy. Mengra was staring at Gena's body. Though scratched and damp and filthy, it was still strong and beautiful.

"This might be fun after all," he said, fingering one of Gena's breasts and getting a very nasty look from Triah. He started to remove his cloak.

"What are you doing?" Triah was horrified. She grabbed his arm as if to restrain him.

"Shut up! And stop touching me, old woman."

"You can't spread your disease all over the city."

"*She's* not going to be passing it on.

"Shouldn't we talk to Kreeops before we do anything?"

"He's busy and so am I."

As if on cue, *WHERE IS THE GIRL?!* boomed simultaneously inside both their minds. And, almost together, they dropped to their knees clutching their heads, so awful was the transmitted anger.

Is she dead yet? arrived, slightly less in volume and in pain.

"No…no, Regent," said Mengra out loud, his words sharp with fear. "But she soon will be. She would have been Free-Killed, but she got away from the bureauers twice. But we stayed with her, as ordered, and we have her again. We're just about to finish her now."

You have done well, they heard, though the words didn't sound pleased. *But do not harm her now. And do not let the bureauers harm her. You will be picked up.*

They both received an image of another location near the outer edge of the folker ring, though only Mengra knew where it was. He knew because it was the alley he had fled to when Gena had frightened him out of the room with the baby bones. It was the spot where Kreeops had first contacted him, the Regent's guard having been near enough to read Mengra's fear and transmit Kreeops' offer.

If any harm befalls her, both of you will measure the depths of the bottomless pit.

"Of cour — yes, sir," said Mengra, but the presence was no longer with them. Refastening his robe, he scolded Triah, "Stop cowering and let's get going. I don't know why you have to be so afraid of everything."

"And I don't know what kind of bravery it is that made you piss all over your cloak like that." He hadn't really, fortunately for her.

It would have taken them hours to drag and carry the unconscious Gena to the assigned spot, especially since they didn't bother to cover up her nakedness until they'd already gotten into one fight for her body and had narrowly avoided a couple of others. When Triah suggested dressing Gena, Mengra scoffed at the idea as a waste of time, but it was he that cold-cocked the first old woman that came along, and he that stole her clothing. Shortly after, long before they were anywhere near the meeting place, several men tugged a hand cart up to them and identified themselves as members of Kreeops' guard, offering right hands that were lacking small fingers as the proof that neither Mengra or Triah had considered demanding. Gena was bound and put onto the flatbed of the cart; as instructed, Mengra and Triah climbed up beside her. Then the whole bed was covered up.

"I think we're going to get an extra reward for this," said

Mengra as they bounced along.

"If your smell doesn't smother her," Triah retorted.

Later, when the covering was removed, they were inside the Castle. Gena was taken one way, and they were led another, into an anteroom. They were admiring the furnishings when Kreeops made his entrance. Though they'd never actually seen the Regent, they had experienced his power, and the contrast between what they'd expected and what they found was startling. Even Mengra, who rarely noticed anything he couldn't eat, sex, or sell, was struck by how much older and how much more tired-looking Kreeops was than was the vision of the Regent that he'd received when he was first recruited to follow Gena.

"You have done well," Kreeops told them.

Triah bowed respectfully.

"And you mentioned to no one, especially to no disciple, your original orders?"

"To get her killed?" asked Mengra, to Triah's horror.

"Shut up!" she cried.

"He asked." Sounding well-pleased and magnanimous, he admitted to Triah, "You know, I'm a bit hungry myself, bureauer." He struck himself on the stomach with the flat of his hand for emphasis.

"Not for long," said Kreeops graciously. "I thank you for bringing the Bride of Jefuson back to the faithful, for rescuing her from the murdering bureauers. She will be instrumental in exposing a little fraud they've been trying to perpetrate on us."

"And for our reward..."Menga began.

Kreeops nodded.

"A bureauer told me there was no cure," the folker said.

"My powers are less restricted. There is a cure."

Kreeops pointed to the floor at their feet, and it vanished. The smile was stillborn on Mengra's face as they dropped into a chasm without end: falling and falling noisily. Half-human horrors plummeted beside them, tearing at their flesh. The screams of the demons as well as their own reverberated in their ears and fed their terror; their bodies alternately froze and boiled, until their overstrained hearts finally gave up beating.

Kreeops rang to have their corpses removed from the floor of the antechamber, which was as far as they had fallen: the bottomless pit that had killed them being inside themselves.

Any sense of power that Martin had gained by surviving the second test dissipated quickly when his guards led him into the Castle, down a short flight of stairs, and then shoved him back into the shaftlike room with the red stars. He couldn't believe it: he'd been in the Castle to begin with! All that awful trip with Ryenna had accomplished was to get him back where he'd started.

The red stars blazed against the dark sky above him, unconcerned by the fact that it had been day when he'd entered the Castle, moments before. He half-sat and half-collapsed to the floor. He struck the wall beside him with his fist, not hard, but hard enough to reawaken the pain in his wounded shoulder.

"Here's your bride, Jefuson," he heard, and the black girl who'd murdered Brodwich was roughly thrown into the shaft. She was unconscious.

He made no effort to revive her and she didn't wake up, though she tossed and turned fitfully, groaning occasionally. He was fairly certain that she must know more than he did about where they were and what was going on here, but he wasn't certain anymore that he was all that eager to be enlightened just yet. What if she told him that, as he now half-suspected, everything that had happened (down to the smallest detail and including Brodwich's death, Ryenna's "treachery," and any victories Martin may have scored) was actually all in accordance with some elaborate plan masterminded by Kreeops, or even by the bureauers, in pursuit of strange and unfathomable goals.

Still, learning something like that might be preferable to finding out that what was happening was in accordance with no plan at all. Not by anyone.

In any event he was too discouraged to go through the hassle of deciding if anything she did reveal might really be true. After a while, he just dozed off.

When he awoke, it looked to be morning, though he didn't take that too seriously. He didn't know how it was done so realistically, but after all he'd been through he wasn't going to be disconcerted by any cheap lighting effects. The girl was sleeping peacefully; her expression was almost serene. He ate the bread and drank the liquid that he found, saving half of each for her, and spent the rest of the morning watching her sleep, chuckling about how much more enjoyable that occupation was than watching Brodwich being eaten by a rat.

Scratched face, chipped-tooth innocence and all, she was one of the most physically appealing women he'd ever seen. And, perhaps because he'd been through so much alone, her presence gave him an impression of strength that was reassuring even though she was apparently as much a captive as he. Then too, the tattered rags she wore kept opening in different, interesting ways each time she shifted position.

Eventually she blinked and stretched and blinked again, gradually rising to consciousness. Martin had expected her to be surprised or confused upon awakening in the cell, but if she was, she gave no indication of it. On the contrary, her expression was more like that of someone who had found exactly what she was seeking. He told himself that if she was there to spy on him, she'd have the good sense to act momentarily confused.

She sat up without a word, staring at Martin as if inspecting his face for flaws.

"You're in Kreeops' Castle," he said, more to say something than because she seemed to need the information. He smiled. "We're both prisoners here, I guess."

She nodded, looking through him.

"I'm Martin." He felt foolish. He wasn't sure why.

"Gena-gul," she said.

She stretched mightily, and when she finished she seemed even more relaxed than she'd been in sleep. And, with life shining through her eyes, she also seemed stronger: less vulnerable, yet more mortal; less an example of the impersonal childlike beauty of sleep and more an individual. Her nose was crooked. It had once been broken. A small scar crossing her jaw line puckered the skin. She was extraordinarily attractive. She smiled and the smile struck Martin as a deliberate attempt to transfer some of her relaxation to him, as if she'd decided that whatever she'd found in his face was favorable.

"I'm the Bride of the Jefuson," she said with a full note of irony and another little nod.

"Cozy. I'm Jefuson."

She lifted an eyebrow skeptically.

"Well," he said, "Kreeops thinks so. I mean Kreeops doesn't think so. But somebody must think…I think." He grinned, trying to turn it into a joke.

She smiled again. "I was here when they found you…in…". She stopped. Then she looked around her, staring at the walls, perhaps a bit confused now.

"They found me where I worked," Martin finished for her, helpfully, and received that stare again.

When he was a child, he'd always wanted to see all the people and all the scenes that hovered just beyond the borders of his pictures: the whole vast civilization that stood as an assumption behind the fragment represented on the flat and glossy paper. When Gena's eyes were on him, he had the feeling that she could do just that with the things he said, that she could absorb the unspoken thoughts and details behind every word. Perhaps he was only imagining it because he knew that disciples were supposed to be able to enter minds. In any case, he definitely felt exposed.

The door burst open. Two guards seized her and hustled her away. She didn't resist. But very soon she was returned.

"Kreeops just wants me to know that he's too busy to see me," she explained.

She went over and faced one of the walls, very gently placing her left hand against the paneling. One of her breasts was revealed; he watched it rising as the muscles in her chest tensed momentarily. For a second, he thought that she was missing a finger or two from her left hand as well. But when he looked at it directly, he saw that he was mistaken.

She turned to him, lifting another eyebrow.

"You didn't kill Brodwich," he announced.

"I did."

"Oh," he said, feeling naive.

He realized that the killing made little difference to him, though now he understood just how ready he'd been to believe in this woman, to accept her uncritically as an ally, in fact as even more than an ally, as an authority, a guide.

"You can probably trust me," she said, startling him, "but you'd better rely on yourself."

Then she explained to him how she'd been reading him, and all about silent speech.

"Because you're a candidate," she said, "no one's supposed talk to you that way or to probe your mind. The idea is to protect you from undue influence."

"I don't feel very protected."

"Why should a god need protecting?" she laughed. "You know, you think very loudly. And with your face as well as your mind."

He soon discovered that he was telling her everything that had happened to him. Orally. When he hesitated, she led him as she might help an old man remember the details of his life: not condescendingly, but with patient, perceptive questions that made it easier to sort it all out. He concluded the story with his conquest of Ryenna and his return to this room that he'd started from.

After he finished, she was quiet for a long while, just gazing off into space. Once she started to say something, but stopped herself. More time passed, and then she spoke, tentatively, as if testing what she was saying as she said it.

"Do you understand Kreeops' power?" she asked. They were on questioning terms already, and for some reason it seemed natural.

"I'm not sure...I'm not even sure if I actually managed to beat him in those tests."

"You can be sure that you did. Kreeops claims loud and long that he is the source of the coven's power, but I think Zaletus was right when he told you that actually the coven is the source of Kreeops' power. The disciples are psychically gifted. Their lives have been spent developing their abilities, but they don't believe in themselves, and any strength they find in themselves they interpret as merely a gift from Kreeops. They *do* believe in him: with a rigid, almost absolute faith that they've been building for generations. And they've disciplined their minds to react instantaneously to his control. As if he were god, he tells them what is true and they believe."

"You mean about him being the Regent of Satan and unbeatable?"

"Much more than that. But one of their main 'truths' *is*

that he is all-powerful. So all he has to do is plant the slightest suggestion in their minds that he is flying and so strongly do they believe what he suggests that they actually see him fly. If he suggests he is growing to enormous heights, they watch him grow. He suggests that he is bringing a corpse to life, and before their very eyes it dances. Their faith made them see it dance, and, seeing it, that faith is confirmed once again."

To Martin, the flaw in this line of reasoning was so obvious that it was embarrassing that she didn't notice it.

"But Gena, I saw him do it myself. Ryenna fought. And with the strength of ten...well, five, men. I saw it and I felt it, and I'm not one of the faithful."

"These disciples have powerful minds. They talk among themselves without words. And collectively their faith is so strong that it can easily overwhelm your sense of reality, or the physical reality of any one individual. That faith surrounds them like an aura; I can feel it as we are sitting here. And once you were within that aura, you were seeing things as the disciples saw them. Kreeops grew into a giant, and you believed, didn't you?"

"He didn't really grow?"

"But he made you think that he did."

"Wait a minute, please. According to that theory," Martin said, with just a trace of sarcasm crawling into his voice, "Kreeops can't kill me? He can only make me think that he can?"

"He can kill you, as any man can: especially a man who's an absolute ruler over a goodly number of people. But as for the corpse you fought, I'm sure that it was real, but I doubt if it was alive and moving except in the minds of those who witnessed the test."

"The wounds were real," he reminded her, touching his shoulder as if to confirm that, and grimacing at the very real pain.

"Because you saw its sword slash into you and you believed. And if you'd been overcome in that way, she probably could have killed you. With weapons in your own mind."

"I'd be just as dead," he said, certain of that, and noting the return of the novel feeling that had been growing in him for a while now: the feeling that understanding might not actually improve things.

He relaxed his struggling mind; it had only been tightening into a knot of confusion. With relaxation, he turned himself from his inner turmoil to the outer world, and the knot slackened. For the first time he noticed the way Gena's other breast, dark and alive, had almost come free of the rags she was wearing.

"Dead you would be," she said, affirming his last statement, yet laughing lightly and pleasantly. "And that would be a great shame. You've come so far."

Apparently catching a glimpse of his mind, she glanced downward at her bare breast. She pulled the rags closed, then looked into his eyes and smiled. In complete control, and yet with what he hoped was just a trace of regret, she said, "Perhaps. In time. But now they're coming to take me to Kreeops. I've had a weak shield on both our thoughts; if anybody asks, I've been examining you about your claim. It's not untrue."

The door burst open again, and she was hurried out, leaving Martin alone and wondering.

The throne room was packed with excited, noisy disciples. But the instant Kreeops stepped into view it once again dropped into total silence, reminding Martin of a folker he'd once seen who'd suddenly vanished into the pavement, accidentally discovering an ancient tomb. From the top tier of the throne, Kreeops addressed the coven. Gena, Martin, and Zaletus were on the level just below the Regent and to one side.

"The Bride has been recovered," Kreeops announced and paused as, on cue, a loud but controlled ovation rolled forward from the disciples. "She was on her way to the Free-Kill itself, when I managed to rescue her; the profane bureauer would destroy all that we hold sacred."

Angry shouts against the enemy were mixed with cries of approval for Kreeops' timely recovery of the Bride. He nodded and raised one hand, palm upward, as if orchestrating the excitement, easing it past its peak before speaking again.

"To protect their fraud, the bureauers would deny us our Bride. We have had pretenders before, but never has a Bride been deceived. *Never!*"

Kreeops' gaze fell pointedly on Gena, and Martin remembered the hours that she'd been gone the night before. They'd only had a few moments alone together after she'd returned, already cleaned up and dressed in the white robes she was wearing now. And although she'd taken the time to shave what little growth there was to shave from his face, about all she would say in answer to his questions was that she thought she could keep him alive. Now she was calmly surveying the coven, apparently the only one in the hall who was unaware that Kreeops' eyes were upon her, measuring her reaction. A roll of drums stirred the air, ending in a thunderlike crack that left the hall once more alive with silence.

"The Bride of Jefuson and the High Priest will approach," Kreeops commanded ceremoniously.

Zaletus' face set itself, its muscles working against the atrophy of old age. Martin could see that the priest was in no mood to take orders, at least insofar as the testing was concerned. But after a second's hesitation, Zaletus walked over and assumed a position directly below Kreeops. Looking hard at the Regent, very slowly, very deliberately, he put one foot up on the higher level and then stepped up beside him. For an instant, Martin thought that Kreeops was going to order him down, but if he intended to, he thought better of it.

"The High Priest," Kreeops intoned, "will ask the Bride if the pretender is worthy of her trust, *of her life*, or is merely a petty annoyance sent from the bureauers, from those who would place themselves over us, who hate us and fear us and who would murder us all gleefully, as they tried to murder our Bride, so they might feed us to their vile spawn!" This was not so much an explanation to the coven as it was an order to Zaletus. And it had the sound of an accusation, as if somehow the priest were to blame.

"Where is the Bride?" the Regent added rhetorically, obviously aware that Gena had ignored his initial command to approach, instead remaining over by Martin. "The Bride of Jefuson will come forward."

"The Bride," called Gena, in a tone that fell just short of innocent helplessness, "must stay by the side of the claimant."

Rage burned across Kreeops' face; almost involuntarily, he took a small step in her direction.

"The Bride requires physical proximity for her reading to be as pure as possible," said Zaletus. Martin couldn't tell whether he was explaining ritual or merely providing an excuse for Gena's open defiance. In appeasement, the priest added, "She has not your power, mighty Regent, nor your scope or range."

"My power reads his fraud. *Clearly!*" Kreeops spat out.

"I'm sure the Regent speaks figuratively, since entering the claimant's mind is forbidden to all but the Bride. Besides, tradition tells us, and very rightly, that the heart of the Bride gives the only true reading. For, though we might know his every thought, thought only reveals what he considers himself.

She must discern what he *is*."

Kreeops' front teeth flashed as he ground his molars together. Martin was thankful for the presence of the entire coven.

"Ask the question, priest," Kreeops demanded.

Zaletus took a tiny step forward, drawing himself up importantly, which had the effect of placing the smaller Kreeops in the background. The cords in the priest's neck worked visibly even before he started to speak. The slowness of his years was still upon Zaletus, but the wrinkles in his skin, combined with the almost childlike expectancy of his manner, seemed to inspire confidence. The respect that the disciples had for him was obvious. And perhaps this wasn't so much a respect for the competence associated with experience as it was a respect for Zaletus, the High Priest, as a link to a more miraculous age. It would be very easy to attribute to him, and to that age, a profound wisdom and an understanding of reasons and methods difficult, if not impossible, to attribute to anything as immediate as today or to anyone as similar to oneself as a contemporary.

"Bride?" he asked with lofty formality.

"Yes, Zaletus," answered Gena, clearly and modestly, the purity of her voice somehow putting Martin in mind of his childhood and the large bell that used to ring so beautifully in a nearby tower. For the first time, he realized that bells rang no more in the city. There is change, he thought, but it is all loss, all reduction.

"You have been with the claimant, Bride?"

"Yes, Zaletus."

"And you have scrutinized him and his claim?"

At another time, Martin might have enjoyed the way the disciples loved to use ancient language whenever possible. He mouthed that one to himself. "Scrutinized." He'd never heard it before, though its first syllable was in common usage, possibly a derivative. If that's what it means, she can scrutinize me anytime, he said to himself, smiling at the smallness of another very small joke.

"I have," said Gena.

"Please do. Anytime," he couldn't resist whispering to her. Her expression remained unchanged, but her lips parted and her eyes showed him a warmth that made him feel his dumb remark was clever, and had him wishing they were back all alone again in that red-starred room and to hell with all this Jefuson nonsense.

"And," Zaletus boomed, nearly matching Kreeops in sheer volume, "do you, the Bride of the Jefuson, do you, the present keeper of the ever-fertile garden passed down from lonely Bride to lonely Bride since the '76, do you, wife of the Son, possible bearer of the future Son, do you, daughter of Magdalene and mother of tomorrow, do you..."He paused, momentarily flustered, then resumed his ponderous cadence. "...do you, in your special comprehension, believe that this...this one, placed in our castle in the winter of our discomfort, *this one* that has chosen to return, that has been carried on the Regent's river, and that has overcome the temptation and smitten the violence, *that this one*, O Bride, *that this one* is He who has come to bring life and replace the darkness and death that now rules the city under the glorious Regency of Kreeops, Son of Satan, *that this one* is He that has come again, Law Breaker and Law Giver? Do you believe that this robe of mortal flesh that stands beside you garbs your long-awaited husband, the Jefuson of god, the Jefuson of man, the Jefuson of the city?"

The question was so long and so full of pauses that it took Martin a moment to realize that it was over. Gradually all eyes moved to Gena. And all ears. Considering the circumstances, Martin hadn't been exceptionally nervous that morning. He'd probably still been a little relieved at having some companionship, and he'd had some difficulty relating this ceremony to his actual fate. But now he could suddenly feel the sweat actually running down his calves. And he found that he was almost more afraid that Gena would dismiss him as a pawn, and a fool, *and mean it*, than he was that she might be unable to say the right things to save his life. For just a moment, the threat of death was too vague and too unreal to him to overcome the other, all too imminent, threat.

Then he began to wonder how on earth she could explain to these fired-up disciples that he was neither savior nor enemy, that he no more wanted to be their god than he wanted to be a bureauer, and that, as a matter of fact, all he did want from either the coven or the government was to be left alone long enough to figure out what he wanted to do. Even if the disciples weren't disappointed into the violence he'd been promised if he turned out to be a phony, Kreeops obviously wasn't about to let him walk away, no matter what.

Gena had been silent a long time, apparently composing her thoughts. The tension in the room was almost tangible, and Zaletus, probably through nervousness, certainly not because he believed that she hadn't heard the question, repeated simply:

"Do you think he is the Jefuson?"

She said nothing. Martin shifted his weight, gazing out at the intent faces of the disciples, trying to pierce through the tension to gauge their underlying mood. When she gave her reply, he didn't register it at first.

"It is he who is to free us," she said.

Pandemonium erupted in the hall: deafening cheering, disciples embracing each other, spontaneous dancing. Martin literally almost fell over, bracing himself on the wall beside him. Music was playing from somewhere, practically submerged by the tumultuous roar. For a while he imagined that, in their enthusiasm, the crowd might seize him, but apparently even as they broke loose this far, the discipline that had taught them that the throne was off-limits held up. Or perhaps they were too much in awe of his person: some of them were prostrating themselves before him. From different sections of the hall different prayers were being recited in different unisons. By the time it occurred to Martin to check Kreeops' reaction, the Regent had his back to the coven.

"Yes!?" Martin finally yelled into Gena's ear. "What do you mean, 'yes'? I'm no Jefuson. Now we'll both be killed."

Twice she tried to answer, but her words were lost in the furor, so she just smiled at him, shrugged, and gave him a little kiss on the forehead. Martin didn't find that a very satisfactory response, but when the disciples saw it, they grew even wilder, applauding ecstatically, practically howling their joy. Several faces near Martin were almost bursting from the size of their unaccustomed smiles. When the uproar had subsided a bit, Martin gave them a mock wave, which brought more applause and a stomping of feet; then it seemed as if every disciple in the place was waving back furiously.

With the realization of the power he had over them, he figured that he'd discovered Gena's plan: if the disciples wanted him to be their god, then their god he'd be, and he and Gena could walk right out of there. Who'd stand in the way of a god?

He grabbed her hand and tugged. She was rooted.

"Let's go," he called through the roar. "Let's get out of here before things settle down."

She couldn't hear his words, but she read him or just got the idea and shook her head, "No." He tugged insistently, and she pointed over toward Kreeops, and then gestured around the periphery of the room. At this, the cheering increased once again. The disciples had misinterpreted the motion, but Martin hadn't. He understood. Scattered around the edges of the hall were some very large disciples, hoods and cowls up, neither cheering nor smiling: Kreeops' private guard. Martin and his face were going nowhere. He stopped pulling on Gena's arm. He didn't know if she did have a plan, but he knew that he didn't.

A smoldering doubt flared up in his mind: what made him so certain that Gena was on his side? He had no good reason to trust her. He did have a strong impression that she was no more likely than the snow to bother deceiving him about herself (though she was perhaps equally capable of mayhem). If she was working against him, she might never say so, but he really thought that something of it would shine through, communicating it, the way the light shining from her skin communicated the rich blackness of her face.

So he wasn't sure that she was with him, but he did trust her not to be against him. Or, he told himself with irony, maybe that was all rationalization and he simply believed in her because everything else was so obviously false. In any case, there was no fuel to kindle that flame of doubt, and it went out before it had really gotten started. He pressed her hand in his and smiled, he hoped, reassuringly: somehow the awareness that he trusted her made him feel a bit responsible for her.

It was a long while before the room quieted down enough for Zaletus to attempt to get order. Kreeops was seated on his throne, a study in unconcern, busily ignoring everything.

"You realize..."Zaletus began. The neat braids in his beard had come unraveled at the ends again. He was addressing Gena, but, with the intention of being audible to all, he waited. "You realize that if that is your answer...".

"That is *the* answer," came from the floor.

"The Regency is over. Jefuson lives!" someone else shouted.

Martin was sure that these interruptions were authentic, unlike when Ryenna had interrupted Kreeops to proclaim Martin as Jefuson. Ryenna couldn't have known she was setting herself up for the role of scapegoat and traitor, but Martin would have been willing to bet that she'd been acting under

Kreeops' orders. (Perhaps, if Kreeops had told her anything at all, he'd explained that she'd be demonstrating what a disruptive force Martin would be upon the well-ordered coven.) Then the disciples had been genuinely shocked at Ryenna's flagrant breach of discipline. Now only Zaletus appeared concerned. Kreeops himself remained totally impassive. His face might have been a lifeless bust of some former leader for all the expression it held.

"You realize," the priest began again, to Gena and to the coven, "the position your answer puts you in. And you realize that the candidate must still undergo the third trial."

"That is understood," said Gena, to Martin's chagrin. "And I will be at my place by his side: *to soothe his death throes and to help him back from the infinite void.* For he *shall* rise from the dead."

The tiniest and most sickening smile that Martin had ever seen twisted across Kreeops' lips as the Regent focused his gaze upon him. The black eyes were impossibly deep; Martin felt as if he was being sucked into an airless chasm. He was about to topple into those eyes and disappear when Gena grabbed his chin and pulled his face away. The disciples were celebrating again, but now it was more controlled; they were all singing something together. Martin didn't even attempt to catch the ancient lyrics. Had he no other hint of what was awaiting him in the third trial, he would have sensed the depth of his danger from that expression on Kreeops' face. Martin was very cold and afraid he might begin shaking and not be able to stop.

Gena threw her arms around him, enveloping him in her embrace, jarring him slightly. Her soft warmth took off the chill. He caught a smell he thought of as bright green and remembered an afternoon when he was very young. He and Moohna and Mengra had wandered through a place of glittering leaves and sunlight, possibly some bureauer's forbidden garden. It was probably tiny, but to his child's eye, the whole world had been covered with flowering life for that afternoon. Now as if the smell brought some of the tranquility of those plants with it, his body was quieted, no longer at the brink of eruption. Soon Gena released him.

"What are you doing?" he asked, slightly embarrassed, not sure if he wanted to pretend that nothing had been happening to him.

"Don't underestimate Kreeops. He will be bound by the rules of the ritual only as long as it serves his purposes. Then, Zaletus or not, he will have at you in any way that he can. And he can in many ways."

"No, not that…I mean about this Jefuson nonsense."

"It was the only possible answer, if…"

Martin was focusing on the danger in the words that slipped past that chipped tooth of hers out into the room, when two of Kreeops' guards seized her, cutting her off in mid-sentence. Before he could react, two more were on him.

"Take him to his room!" came the Regent's order, "and her to my antechamber. So we may confer."

"Wait!" commanded Gena with so much authority in her voice that the huge guards did indeed wait. Martin caught a glimpse of one of the bearded faces; the small ratlike eyes were tensed with confusion over two conflicting orders.

"Do as I say!" called Kreeops, coming toward them. His voice was a bit high-pitched, lacking its usual majesty.

"The Bride stays with the claimant," Gena stated with certainty.

"True," said Zaletus, "with the Jefuson…"

"Refuse, Zaletus!" Kreeops yelled, betraying his anger. "He's not Jefuson, and you had better remember that and remember who is Regent here. You may rule the tests, but the tests will soon be over."

"But they are not over yet," Zaletus replied with great, almost exaggerated dignity. "She remains with the candidate. That is the ritual. Guards, take them both to his room."

The guards were immobile for a second. Gradually they all looked over at Kreeops. Though the Regent's face was so contorted with barely controlled rage that his black eyes seemed to cloud and his flared nostrils actually quivered, he merely nodded. Gena and Martin were led away roughly, but maybe, Martin thought, a little less roughly than on previous occasions.

Once they were back in the shaft-room, Gena motioned to him to be quiet, while she seemed to be surveying the room all over again.

"We must talk," she said at last. "So I've got to shield your mind again. It's understood that I would try to do this, so Kreeops shouldn't get too suspicious. And since the ritual forbids him from tampering with your mind, hopefully he won't risk alerting me by trying to probe through that shield just to read your thoughts. He certainly doesn't want this final test voided. But my efforts must be as weak as possible; the weaker he believes us to be, the better for us. His amassed power is potentially so great that…

"No," she interrupted herself, remembering many things she hadn't been able to do at one time. "I'll do all I can. That should be enough."

Obviously she was trying to convince herself, but Martin saw nothing to be gained by attacking her or questioning her abilities.

"I'm supposed to *rise from the dead?*" he asked. He hoped she'd tell him that this was merely a symbolic manner of speaking.

"Yes," she said simply. "They'll crucify you and you'll have to rise from the dead."

He just looked at her. When he spoke, his voice was reasonable.

"I don't think I can do that."

"Well, you'd better start thinking that you can." She smiled sweetly. "You'd be surprised at what you can do."

"I *can't* come back from the dead." He still didn't really believe she was serious.

"You can't cross the limit, either. Or take a walk across the waters. But I can."

Martin made a face. Just now, he had no interest in disciple bluster.

"And so could you," she continued, "if everything that you've told yourself, plus everything that the bureauers and the disciples and everyone else have told you didn't make you so absolutely certain that you couldn't."

She was really angry with him. He began to understand that she might not be kidding.

"Beyond the limit?" he asked. "Across the waters?"

"There's nothing there to stop you. The limit is only a rather mild alarm. As for the waters...maybe at one time they were the real limit, maybe once they were impenetrable or even deadly; but they're only an illusion. The land is just as solid there as anywhere else. I walked on it. I know it's hard to believe, but there are even buildings out there."

She explained to him about her journey to the Gov-Cent, and briefly about the Free-Kill and going across. "I don't know how the illusion got started or why. I assume that those huge machines and those towers ran it at one time, but they don't anymore. Maybe it's like a mirage. And maybe it was there for so long that even after the machinery stopped, the mirage somehow kept functioning by itself. Or maybe, after generations of seeing the waters there, we all believe in them so strongly that we see them even after the machines have stopped projecting, believe in them so completely that we even manage to pass on the illusion to our children. The disciples aren't the only people in the city with a faith."

It took him a while to understand exactly what she was saying, and then all he said was: "That's ridiculous. How can everyone see what isn't there?"

"You see the walls around you?"

"Of course."

"And you saw red stars in the sky."

"Well…"

"Well!"

"Yes, but Kreeops does tha…"

"The faith of the disciples, which makes Kreeops appear to be able to give life to Ryenna, is what makes the stars red. They appear red to the coven because they all *know* that here the stars *are* red…because Kreeops and his predecessors have 'suggested' that the stars were red, and the disciples believed them. And they appear red to you because the disciples' aura of belief is stronger than your perceptions. This castle, this world you're living in right now, is the creation of their faith — and your faith too. I know, because I've seen through it."

"What?"

She simply nodded. Martin looked at the sky, but the stars weren't out, and it was deceptively normal. The world around him was stable and in its own way every bit as consistent as the city itself. He could buy that most of what Kreeops did was done by trickery or illusion; the skeptical part of him had probably always been expecting something like that. But it was very hard to swallow that so much of the evidence of his senses was a lie. He rubbed his hand over one of the walls. It was wood, as solid as the hand that rubbed it. More solid. He wondered why he found it so difficult to disbelieve the things that Gena said. She came over and grabbed his hand in both of hers. He gasped as all three hands disappeared through the wall halfway up to their forearms.

He shook his head. It hurt. His own body felt insubstantial, not the world around him. Holding each other, they sat down together and didn't move. It was much later in the day when Gena spoke again.

"Obviously Kreops is limited in what he can suggest; there are probably lots of areas where the faith of the disciples can be stretched just so far and no more. And he doesn't seem to create too much out of whole cloth; mostly, he just alters. But that alteration can make an old rag feel like satin or a closet seem the size of a cavern — or a city. He might even be able to make poorage taste good. And faith can grow. Once, in the Gov-Cent, he had his guards believing that the bureauers would see them differently than I would, and believing it so strongly that those few guards projected an aura of their own. I saw disciples; I don't know what the bureauers in the area saw, but we were all seeing the world that the guards believed in. Of course, the guards' faith in Kreops is even greater than that of the rest of the coven."

"But haven't I…"

"Caused a few doubts? Probably, among some disciples, you caused a few even at the beginning. Recently, especially, you may have weakened Kreops significantly. But it's also possible that for the most part he's simply been spreading himself too thin, chasing me and dealing with you at the same time."

"What about…how does Zaletus fit in?"

"Zaletus. I know he sees through it all. I'm pretty sure that, as Guardian of the Faith, he acts, at least to some extent, as a monitor on whatever Kreops suggests to the whole coven."

"That's all he does about it?"

"What should he do? He believes in this Church of the Jefuson stuff, even if he sees through Kreops' methods. To him, the Regent is the rightful mind of the disciples; whether Kreops is tapping their power or they're tapping his is not important. Neither is the window-dressing of castles and red

stars, though Zaletus is obviously quite ready to yell like hell if
Kreeops tries to tamper with his religion. Besides, Kreeops has
by far the strongest and the most powerful single mind in the
coven. Look into his eyes sometime if you doubt that."

"No thanks." Martin remembered those eyes.

"He's powerful, all right, but potentially, he could be so
much more. I have to think that a really powerful person in his
position could channel the collective power of the disciples to
actually change things: to erect great buildings, or to move
through space, or even to grow great harvests. But Kreeops
doesn't change the world so much as he changes what people
think it is."

"Is the crucifixion going to be an illusion?"

"Not likely. Kreeops wants you dead. Permanently, of
course. But I think we can get you through the test."

"Gena, rankenfile bureauers aren't taught how to resurrect
themselves."

"It doesn't matter."

"To me, it matters."

"What matters is that Kreeops and the rest believe that
you've died."

"Without actually dying?"

"Hopefully."

"Wonderful." He was unenthusiastic. "Hopefully" didn't
seem like the best possible answer to his question.

"We have no choice. I think that we can pull it off; I'm
stronger than Kreeops imagines. If we can't do it, we're both
dead anyway. If we succeed, *Kreeops* is finished." For the first
time, the intonation she gave the name was filled with revul-
sion. "And along with him, all these mental dungeons he keeps
people locked in."

"And then who'll lock them in, and in what?"

"Not us. Maybe people are ready to crawl out of those

dungeons and out of the city." She said this shyly, as if almost ashamed of verbalizing such an idea.

"The city stays the same, Gena. Nothing changes." He was trying to sound like a wise Big Eater, but to his own ears, he sounded like Brodwich, reciting his tired slogans. He kept watching the walls.

"Who ever *tries* to change anything?" she asked.

"Even if we got rid of Kreeops, and all I've got to do is come back from the dead to do that, the bureauers aren't going to just disappear."

"I've already publicly gone past the limit and into the waters and back. More and more will follow. The bureauers will fall with the limit."

Martin realized the truth of this statement as soon as he heard it. The bureauers couldn't control an open world, especially one whose basic assumption had just been shattered.

"But I'm not the Jefuson." He was reluctant to reveal to Gena just how far from godlike he rated himself.

"Quite probably not. And probably neither was the last Jefuson, or Jefus before him. Like the New Age, the Jefuson is only an ideal…a map of a place that we can head for, not the place itself, and a map drawn by people who've never really been there. At best they might have glimpsed it from a distance."

"We get there by deceit?"

"Deceit won't get us there. Still, we have to make our way as best we can. As best we can. Or else the rest of the world will become like the city: the limit is down."

Martin remembered standing on a mountain with Kreeops and the temptation he'd experienced when confronted with the chance for power. Power for helping, power for change, power, perhaps, to make a city with less suffering, possibly one where people like Moohna wouldn't have to die simply because they'd stumbled afoul of some well-fed mouth who rated their life and their death, their everything, as nothing. And Martin recalled the taste of power itself, and the thrill of standing tall above a prostrate crowd, just like the fat fool who'd killed Moohna.

"If we get rid of Kreeops, they'll want me to rule," he said. "I'd have to be almost a god to handle it."

"Wouldn't the Jefuson hand the power right back to them?"

"Who knows? We've never met."

He appeared to be deep in contemplation for a moment, then he brightened.

"Why worry?" he said with a resigned smile. "I don't figure we can beat Kreeops anyway."

"Just don't do all your figuring in advance. It spoils the fun."

In the silence that followed, he got to pondering how beautiful she was.

"Yes?" she asked, though he hadn't spoken.

"I didn't say anything. I was just thinking...how...how well-spoken and convincing you are."

"It comes from reading minds," she said pointedly, yet pleasantly.

He wondered if he was blushing. Either he pulled her toward him, or she came by herself. On the eve of his death, they were hardly about to limit themselves to one kiss.

The street was convoluted and narrow; the lighting, eerie and indirect as if the source were some perverted sun hiding beyond the clay structures that pressed on either side. There was little room for the spectators and less for the grim procession. With each step the weight of the cross on Martin's back was more oppressive, and he had no trouble believing that, as Gena had predicted, the cross was no illusion. His back had already been raw from Kreeops' lashes when he'd started this trek. Instead of the pain or his fears about their destination, Martin tried to give his attention to the slow, rhythmic movement of the disciples in front of him, as the smooth asphalt roadway went up and down, but mostly up, winding to Golgotha. Gena returned beside him, silent, studying his face, or more accurately, his forehead, with unbroken concentration. And he returned his own concentration to her. To a large measure, since she'd put his hand through that wall, and maybe even before, she'd been about the only stability in his world. Her face was serene now, and that helped him.

Behind him, Kreeops rode in an ancient car. Going downhill it backfired, and going up, it stalled. Martin felt certain that the car was also real: the car; the cross; the whip; Kreeops and the coven; above all, Gena. He had his doubts about the rest of the environment. Stumbling again, he went down hard, crushed between the cross and the cobblestones that paved this section of the road. The taste of blood leaked into his mouth as Gena helped him up.

"Illusion?" he whispered.

"Remember, focus on something besides the pain." But he could see a deep compassion in her eyes.

The suffering: that too was real. More real than the light here and more pervasive, marching him to his death. The onlookers tossed stones, castigating him with every vile name that came into their heads. He contemplated Gena, touching her strength as if it were a rope between them. He had the rather far-fetched idea that she could feel his suffering, and that if he could disregard it, he'd be protecting her as well as himself.

The car chugged up beside him. As Kreeops' hate-contorted face blocked Martin's view, the Regent's whip stung into his back. The burn of the lash was a distraction from the reality of Gena: it might have been a part of Kreeops that the Regent had flung at Martin the way Martin had thrown Ryenna's eye at him.

"Keep it to yourself, please," Martin tried.

"JEF-FUS-SON," Kreeops taunted.

"That's what you keep telling me. But you're the one who won't let me leave without taking your throne."

Again the whip tore the air, flashing through Martin's vision; it looked as if Kreeops' arm had been melted and stretched like plastic. Suffering increased. Martin fell again, the cross on top of him. *Why get up?*

The flame that was consuming Kreeops seemed to flare outward once more as the lash scorched across Martin's back. They both knew that Kreeops was one test away from losing a battle to Martin that Martin hadn't wanted in the first place. Martin managed to get to his feet.

He tried to study the disciples around him. The very people who had cheered him just yesterday, who had hailed him as a god, were now spitting and cursing at him. Had he hurt them somehow? Had they been kicked around for so long as individuals that the chance to kick someone else was irresistible? Or did they just hate him for dying like this, so sweaty, so undignified, so ungodlike…so much like themselves that the first decision of their new status, whether to believe in Martin or Kreeops, was no longer the sure thing it had appeared to be the day before? Like the *whoosh* of Kreeops' whip, the jeers of the crowd now seemed to be the howling of their own agony.

A stone cut his face. Accusations came as questions.

"Are you more than Kreeops? Are you better?"

"Then why aren't you crucifying him?"

Several times individuals hailed him as Jefuson and were set upon by the mob. It became very clear that the disciples didn't want to have to decide between gods, and they resented him for making them do so; everything had always been so neatly decided for them before Martin had shown up. And

Martin had actually made it a point to tell them that they'd have nobody but themselves to blame if they chose wrong. Maybe *that* hadn't been such a good idea.

"Die, fraud, die!" Something else bounced off his face. "Die, die!"

They meant it: if he failed this final test, there would be no judgment for them to make. If he survived, however…there would be…this freedom, this freedom which just then must have seemed to them like nothing but decisions and indecision, endlessly. Could he blame them for longing to hang onto Satan's slavery? He looked past Kreeops to Gena. He wanted to speak to her; it didn't matter what he said.

"DIE…die…DIE…die," became a chant, as if every disciple was fervently praying that he would fail, praying that it would be conclusively proven that the coming they claimed they lived for had never occurred.

Again, Kreeops and his jeep came between Martin and Gena. Martin concentrated on his own feet. The road was climbing steadily now.

Most of the taunting *did* depict him as a fraud. But after a time, the accusations that seemed aimed at the Jefuson himself also became more numerous.

"If you would be our god, why aren't you loyal to us who were loyal to you?"

"If you would lead us at all, lead us over our enemies. Or is it more godlike to betray us?"

The Jefuson, the coming, the New Age. Realized, it was supposed to mean freedom for *everyone*, "all men walking together on clear, clean streets in peace and equality: disciple, bureauer, and folker alike." Only they hated and feared the bureauers and folkers.

"*We* waited," someone screamed, right in Martin's ear. "*We* kept the faith while the vermin scoffed and persecuted us for it.

We are the faithful."

What did they want from him? Martin wondered. The New Age was *their* ideal.

A single disciple broke from the crowd, one of Kreeops' guard. Martin braced himself for the blow. It didn't make any difference: one more drop of water on a drowning man. But the face that peered into his was young and imploring, a down-faced boy who took Martin's head in his hands with a gentle uncertainty.

"I'm not ready, Jefuson. And I'm afraid."

Grateful for the boy's courageous display of faith, right there in front of Kreeops, and perhaps just a bit shamefaced because that faith was unwarranted, Martin felt called upon to reassure the lad as if he really were the Jefuson. He managed to speak.

"You are *brave*."

"I am a disciple, nothing else. Infidels fear me *as a disciple*...but...in the New Age..."His voice trailed off in embarrassment.

It was in the boy's face as much as in his words. Realized, the New Age was an ideal that would take from the disciples the distinction that waiting for it had given them, the distinction that had allowed each of them, as a true believer, to rate himself as better than any infidel, be he the biggest of Big Eaters, no matter how that infidel might intimidate him, no matter how effectively that infidel might deny him the city and its wealth. Without the self-esteem of being one of the elite, without the fear that the very word "disciple" could arouse and the automatic respect engendered by that fear, without the cloak of Kreeops to hide behind, what would the boy have? What would he be? If the New Age was indeed coming, he would have to walk those long-awaited "clean, clear streets" by himself, as himself. And just then they must have looked less inviting than

Kreeops' bottomless pit.

Wanting to console him, Martin could find no words. The whip cracked against his back again. He grunted involuntarily. The young man seemed startled. He wiped his hand across Martin's brow and found it covered with sweat. Ignoring Kreeops, he began to dry Martin's face with the edge of his sleeve, but another guard seized him and hauled him off. The procession continued.

"Jefuson?" It was Gena. She spoke with gentle irony. He was very glad to see her. He must speak, once more.

"Are you absolutely certain these people want to be free, Gena?"

Before she could answer, he was on the ground. He thought he'd fallen again. Faces surrounded him. Frightened faces, much like Tantor in the folker ring, like Martin on the raft. Faces contorted in hatred, pushing him violently onto the cross. Eagerly killing him. *As if I were their freedom,* he thought. Isolated, individual faces, desperate to surrender to the surest guidance available. And there was Kreeops, smiling genuinely now, ready to reassert his control once again.

A nail pierced Martin's right palm. He saw Gena react to his pain, and then there was an electric burst in his brain.

"You're killing yourselves," he tried, but almost unintelligibly now, as they pierced his left hand. To himself he added, "Then why am I the one who's dying?" and laughed.

At the laughter, the faces backed away. Even Gena appeared confused, at first. Then he felt her inside of him, nothing specific, just a warm caressing touch; and he was aware that he would be dead in a few minutes and the disciples would be alive, but it seemed that, having had that touch, he was infinitely luckier than any of them. He smiled at them, feeling pity for their lives and benign toward the world. They pounded the spike into his feet and raised the cross, and the sharp agony shot from his feet and hands and all through him, followed by the fury of every cell in his body. *How could they do this to one who was in the very process of empathizing with them?*

"Mindless refuse!" he managed to scream out, viciously: dying words of hate.

Martin thought he was back on the mountain where Kreeops had tempted him. But alone. No. Not alone. The Jefuson was there, too, staring across at him, the image of godliness in white robes with a very picturesque halo above his head. The perfect leader had arrived. Martin was a little jealous. After all, who had gone through all the suffering?

The Jefuson turned on him, mirroring his own jealous face, and Martin recognized the eyes: Kreeops! The enemy.

He remembered those eyes from the drawbridge in front of the Castle: deeper and darker than history, on closer inspection their blackness was revealed as layer upon layer of murky color. He felt himself irresistibly drawn into them, falling inward toward the center of hell, past purplish-brown clouds that poisoned the air and repulsed the sunlight, clouds that had been vomited up from fires tended by human demons, who, foul almost beyond imagining, fed the flames with limbs they cut from themselves and from each other.

The colors, through which Martin's surroundings were fragmented like light through a prism, were the true colors of the Regent. Vivid and perverse: running puces and violets; nauseating oranges, browns, and greens — all were violently at odds with any colors Martin had ever found anywhere else in the world. His body and soul were buffeted by the blast of color. And no color was uncontaminated; no beam of it touched his skin without making it feel nearly as bad as the vile light made it look. Viscous and enervating, these rays had him trapped the way bugs and small pigeons were trapped in the tarry residue of the bureauers' oil pools.

The body hung, stretched out on the cross for well into the afternoon, seldom moving, suffering, Gena hoped, little more than troubled dreams. She'd have knocked him out sooner if he hadn't had to function enough to carry out the ritual. As it was, he'd been difficult to put out. She hadn't known which button to push; it had been the first time she'd ever attempted such a thing.

She wasn't aware of the tears in her eyes. Conscious of his thoughts climbing the hill, she'd been extraordinarily proud of him. The ordeal had brought out his best, though she wished he hadn't had to endure it, or at least that her plan was slightly less desperate.

And at that moment, a blue-eyed lady slipped back into Gena's memory, and, once again, she saw her mother hanging on a cross, towering above her. The small, emaciated woman seemed to strain against her bonds one last time. The terror of her death rattle shattered young Gena, leaving her alone, the only explanation for all pain, the vicious epithet, "insurgents," on the lips of a folker. "Insurgents." The meaning was unclear, but the connotation was obviously "different," perhaps even "special." She wrenched herself away from the memory: any fear, any uncertainty, any distraction at all could be fatal to both Martin and herself. But a residue of horror remained.

Kreeops was standing off to the side of the cross, watching her, probably wishing he could read her. But the strength of her mind was no doubt what had attracted him to her in the first place. In that he would find her more like him than were any of the others.

She was anxious to put her plan into operation, but was

cautious about rushing things and arousing the Regent's suspicion. The breathing of the figure on the cross became labored; she tried to reach the flickering life in Martin's body to gauge how much torment the tissue could stand. At best, she'd be guessing. Blood leaked out both corners of his mouth and dripped from the spikes in his hands and feet. At that moment, she saw it as a forerunner of a river of blood, flowing down to the earth, seeking its own level after twenty-odd years of being forced skyward in the face of gravity, twenty-odd years of nourishing a universe that stretched boundlessly in space across the inside of a small skull and endlessly in time across a fleeting eternity. Gena, helpless to staunch the flow, remembered the pale white skin of her mother's face and heard herself wonder, *Why did I rush us here so soon?*

This is not the time for self-pity, she answered herself, harshly.

Kreeops could barely keep from laughing out loud. Such a fine day. Like summer. For once, he approved of so much bright light. Zaletus, the old fart, would have liked clouds to gather symbolically over the fool on the cross. Refuse! Let the fraud die to the rejoicing of man and nature. The significance would hardly be lost on the coven, accustomed as they were to having their emotions manipulated by his lighting effects. It should be especially disquieting for those whose doubts had led to the loss of the second trial. Good! Still, it would be a while before he removed this "Jefuson" from his cross. The Regent smiled as he toyed with the idea of delaying nightfall, so Martin could hang in the light long after his death. A warning perhaps. But no. Nothing supernatural must attend this insignificant demise. Nothing must occur that might in any way support his puny claims or those of that bitch Gena.

Kreeops was wary of her; she was more mature and stronger than before she'd run away. Certainly it was a shame that he'd have to do away with such a creature. She *was* beautiful.

The man on the cross above him appeared strangely at peace now: the tension was gone from his face and body; his expression was almost joyful. The shortish brown hair was disheveled, but in an irritating way that suggested a crown or a halo. The sweat on the still-ruddy skin made his body appear to gleam. Kreeops scowled, but finding the breathing had become so faint as to be barely perceptible, he took heart. A man who knew how all the strings were pulled, Kreeops had no belief in the supernatural; he had never even considered the possibility that this man might be a god, much less that he might actually return from the dead. The Regent's only real concern was that this would-be usurper was good and dead in the first place.

Time passed. The light in the sky changed, almost authentically, as if actually due to the motion of the sun. Kreeops noted that Gena had barely taken her eyes from the dying man for long enough to blink. No wind blew. The disciples on the hill might almost have been dead themselves for all they moved. There was very little speech and that was done in whispers.

Finally, it looked as if Martin's breathing had stopped. Zaletus started for the cross. As the shadow of it fell across his face, he was halted by a sudden sigh and then a single racking cough from the throat above him. Martin shuddered just once and was still. Gena began to cry without a sound. Several of the disciples joined her openly; more faces hid themselves in their hoods and turned away. Those few who, for this long, had held to belief in the ability of this "Jefuson" to return from the dead now had that faith profoundly shaken by the overriding and commonplace fact of death itself. At that moment, there were no believers on Golgotha.

Zaletus approached closer to the cross.

"Leave him!" ordered Kreeops. The priest halted in his tracks; his command over the test must have seemed to count for little. There certainly seemed to be no wisdom in another confrontation with the Regent.

Fiercely, as if he might attack it, Kreeops returned his attention to the corpse. Some of the disciples began to wander away from the hill. Martin hung there. The most observant of men might possibly have imagined that he could detect Martin's head jerk and the barest ripple of one more spasm pass through his body. Kreeops glanced at Gena in satisfaction.

"There." He spoke to himself.

Gena's concentration hadn't wavered; she hadn't even dried her tears. Yet the set of her features changed ever so slightly now, and she seemed older. More time passed.

"Tradition ordains," Zaletus said to Kreeops as if he were trying to be helpful, "that there can be no mutilation of the body."

With open disgust on his very human face, Kreeops regarded the High Priest and spoke in a voice so swollen with apparently genuine emotion that, though Zaletus knew him to be a master actor, he never for an instant questioned the authenticity of its weary sadness.

"No…not now." The Regent's head bowed as if in respect, the tips of his graceful fingers tracing his beard pensively.

"We await your approval to cut him down," reported Zaletus softly.

Kreeops whirled on him with contempt. "*You*, priest, are to run the trials, not I." Then he spoke to what remained of the crowd. "In the end there must be no question of their fairness. *No* question!"

He trudged off the hill alone, eyes downcast, seemingly deep in contemplation. Several of his private guard trailed after him, but at a distance. Zaletus only watched, rooted, clearly embarrassed by his public servility and the Regent's reaction to it. Perhaps to give the appearance of having made the decision himself, he waited quite some time before giving the order to remove Martin's body. It had been on the cross almost four hours. Unnecessarily, Zaletus personally checked to make certain that the heart had stopped.

The corpse was taken to a nearby cave that was to be the tomb. There, under Gena's supervision, the Bride's Maids were to prepare the body. But after they had laid it out on a granite shelf cut in one of the walls, Gena sent them away immediately, all but one who was to wait outside the closed door in order to fetch anything Gena might require over and above the articles she'd brought to the cave before the crucifixion. The Bride's Maids noticed that Gena was limping and that when she spoke it was as if only part of her was present. The talk among them as they walked off and the same door was shut was that her spirit had died with her lover.

12

More Choices

When the stone door was securely bolted, Gena collapsed and lost all contact with the corpse. Tired, sore, and nearly as drained as if *she* herself had been hanging on the cross that afternoon, she fell right on top of the body. Her head lay in a bloody gash on his side. For what seemed like a long time, she was unable to move. It had been nearly an hour since the blood in Martin's body had stirred, and only the knowledge of how quickly time was running out enabled her to tap some deep reserve and get up.

Mentally she struggled to reach him. She hadn't intended for him to die. She'd only wanted to plant a suggestion the way Kreeops did, to have the disciples see Martin as dead. But immediately after the Regent had kept Zaletus from approaching the cross, Martin's faint heartbeat had suddenly stopped as still as it had already appeared to those who watched. She wasn't entirely sure that Kreeops had penetrated her illusion: perhaps Martin's strength had run out, or perhaps Kreeops, simply taking no chances, had given the apparent corpse one last psychic shove, to make sure he was as dead as he looked.

A spasm hit her own body now, and she had to steel her

consciousness till it passed. Martin was very cold.

She'd done something to his brain when his heart had stopped. Understanding little of anatomy, she didn't know just what, but she'd felt as if she'd caught it at the last moment of life, as if she'd held it tenderly to some mental breast, feeding it a minimal level of energy from her own body to replace the nourishment its own heart had been unable to provide. The brain had lived, barely, virtually inert, but it had lived, right up until the moment when, exhausted, she'd lost contact with it here in the tomb. Now the seconds passed and she knew that if she couldn't get Martin's heart to provide for him immediately, there would be no bringing him back. Regaining her feet, she gathered her strength inside herself like a ball and shot it at the brain she'd lost hold of. Expending herself, she crumbled heavily onto the corpse once more and lost consciousness.

But he lived.

Out of the nothingness came a jolt, unknown and unseen, unlike anything in his experience, startling him alert, trying to get at him. His head snapped painfully forward: it was like receiving a blow to the top of the spine. From the inside. Or perhaps it was a blow to the soul of some long-dead ancestor. And then Martin heard the howling: a scream that was itself the screamer. Far beyond even the horror of Kreeops, this was the shriek of the nameless dread that lurks ever-threatening beyond the body, beyond the warmth and safety of the fire, beyond the visible and comprehensible city with its sturdy concrete residue and well-defined streets, beyond even the tortuous well-buttressed castles of faith. This was the shriek that comes at the arrival of "what must be kept out"; and it struck with the abruptness and patternlessness of fire from the sky, to burn and maim, to demolish the reason of the wisest of men, to topple the faith of the devoutest of priests and cloud the vision of the master illusionist himself. When the sky parts and the earth crawls over itself and the waters rise up from their bed to explode across the land, when a thousand unknown bloody-fanged creatures come rending flesh, this was the howl that leads back to the place from which all horror comes. And as Martin traveled it, it bore into his soul with an apocalyptic force that effortlessly disintegrated his will and severed the part of his mind that saw the world and thought and held jobs and planned and analyzed and believed, from the part that ran screaming through forbidden fields pursued by slippery strangers from beyond that reason never sees.

It was Martin's shriek.

As if she'd sensed it in her sleep, Gena was already aware of the minimal activity in his brain when she awoke. His breathing was very shallow; she feared that the smallest movement might extinguish it. Carefully, she set in tending his wounds, and the very work seemed to give her the energy to replace what had drained away.

After bathing him, she wrapped him in heavy shrouds to keep off the chill. The crucifixion had taken an enormous toll on the once-vigorous body; he was almost too weak to accept her energies as, gradually, afraid that another psychic shock might kill him as quickly as a bullet, she fed them to him in measured amounts. She knew without reflection that for most people this force-feeding technique would produce the opposite of the intended effect, but she also believed that this man, even though he wasn't any Jefuson, *was* something special. Besides, there was no other way he could recover far enough, fast enough.

As she worked, she ate: tremendous quantities of real-food

she'd commandeered from the table of Kreeops himself. Poorage wouldn't have been enough. As it was, she could almost see the flesh melting away from her body, such was the intensity of the effort to lend strength to Martin's recovery and to maintain herself. Still, though she lacked the time to give it much consideration, she understood that finally his recovery wasn't up to her. All she could do was help. For the first time in her life, she was betting on someone else. And, ultimately, Martin was an unknown factor.

In spite of all she ate and drank, she relieved herself only once, going over to the sand pile provided for that purpose in the corner. During all the time she'd spent with the disciples, she'd never quite been able to feel comfortable wasting organic materials, but now she had far more pressing matters concerning her.

The shrieking had stopped, and the jolt from outside had become a touch — warm, penetrating, wonderfully familiar. It set up a tingling within him, an exquisite longing that was itself a fulfillment. At first he felt as if he were basking in the sun that had shone on the Originals. Then, through a child's eyes, he saw, not the sun, but the face of a woman, still young in years, looking down at him, beaming with a magnificent concern that filled his infant universe. And he realized that it was the face of the woman who had given him the life that had brought him here: Moohna, twenty years less worn-out, twenty years less dead. Then her face vanished, but the touch remained, perhaps becoming even purer and more vital.

In the candlelit cave, Gena couldn't tell how much time had gone by: maybe the entire first night. Were there enough heartbeats left in which to perform her miracle? On the morning of the third day, Martin would either walk out, or the tomb would be permanently sealed. And, as Kreeops had been so careful to remind her when discussing the "slim possibility" that she might support Martin's claim (on the evening before she had actually done so), the tomb was quite large enough for two.

The pounding might have been going on for a long time before she became aware of it. She'd left specific orders that no one was to disturb her; still, the banging wouldn't quit. Martin had finally recovered enough to be resting easily, but Gena's body and mind craved sleep. She wasn't sure she was even capable of conversation, much less the effort it would take to project the image of Martin as an unbreathing corpse.

Eventually she stumbled to the door.

"Who?"

She wondered if she'd spoken loud enough to penetrate the heavy stone door that was prescribed, like everything else, by Zaletus' precious tradition.

"Kreeops!"

"Shit!" said Gena to herself. Then in silent speech, she called out, *Go away.*

She got no response to that. Such a direct refusal had probably shocked him. She was so tired she hardly cared, though his anger could easily precipitate an immediate end to her life and to Martin's as well. At that moment, few could have protested anything the Regent might do.

"We must speak," he said out loud, just as she'd begun to hope that by some miracle he *had* gone away. Miracles were in short supply.

*Entry is forbi...*she started to project, but instead she spoke orally. "Entry is forbidden to anyone except the Bride and her maids." That Kreeops himself had been speaking verbally was a token nicety beyond the strict requirements of the testing, which only prohibited silent speech with the actual candidate. Gena decided it would be just as well not to go into the more direct mental communication; though Kreeops could only read what she projected, having *his* silent speech in *her* head was closer to him that she wanted to get right now.

"Where is Zaletus?" she asked, her frustration at having to deal with the Regent angering her, showing her she had more strength left than she'd imagined. Yet anger would simply waste it.

"Polishing my footwear with his tongue, I would guess. Open the door. I do not require entrance, but we must have words here and now."

He was accustomed to being obeyed; it wasn't likely he'd leave soon. And she had neither the time nor the energy to squander on a prolonged shouting match. Besides, if she protested too much about the tomb being opened, he'd begin to wonder why. Kreeops was nobody's fool, and the last thing she wanted to do was to put him on guard any more than he already must be.

Moving back into the cave, she blew out the candles by the body and returned to the door. She released the bar that secured it and cracked it inward enough to peer out, hoping that she wouldn't have to try to force a projection of a corpse-Martin through the mighty defenses of the Regent's mind.

Outside, Kreeops was standing alone in the dim light that might have been predawn. The second day. Only one more left, she told herself.

"Where is my maid?" she demanded.

Kreeops jerked his thumb back over his shoulder, once again ignoring the impertinence of the question. "I sent her back to the hill."

"What do you want?"

"I want you to consider, Gena, that on your shoulders rests the future of the church. Possibly of the entire city."

He sounded like a model of sincerity. When he paused for a response, she stared at him silently, as if she were deliberately attempting to make him uncomfortable, though actually she was merely too tired to waste words.

"The disciples are split. Whether your *champion*..." If there was sarcasm behind his use of the word, it was minimal. "...was really working with the bureauers to destroy us, or whether he fell into the situation accidentally...whether he was the Jefuson or not...the church has been weakened. Neither of us can deny that."

He paused once more for a response that wasn't forthcoming, then plunged on, every inch the reasonable leader single-mindedly concerned with the welfare of his people. "The coven cannot exist in pieces, Gena. We'd be defenseless prey for those who have been awaiting just such an opportunity to annihilate us."

"The risen Jefuson will be just the thing to unite the coven...and the city." Her words were slurred; she'd wanted them to sound defeated and sarcastic. She couldn't tell how they'd come out.

For a moment he seemed to be wondering if there was any chance that she actually believed her own words. Then the voice of reason resumed, calmly, irritatingly crawling over her nerves:

"We both know that isn't going to happen, don't we? The bluff has been called, Gena. All that remains to be decided is what we can do now." His pause here was rhetorical. A slow, benevolent grin unveiled his jagged teeth. "I want you to be *my* bride. As we planned before."

"As *you* planned!" The words leapt from her with a sudden fury.

"It is our only recourse. Nothing else can bring our people back together, *completely!*" He became more intimate now, urging her passionately, "Leave this tomb immediately. Declare that you were taken in by the dead fraud. After what you'd been through at the hands of the bureauers, you were still weak, confused. You certainly look weak. No one will hold such a 'mistake' against you, we'll see to that. And to do it now, to refute him before he publicly fails to resurrect, that would show that you had seen through him. A little belatedly perhaps, but…"

He gave a shrug of dismissal, combined with a knowing little smile, magnanimous. She understood. Thus flawed, she'd be an even better bride for Kreeops, less esteemed, less powerful. It was her move.

She was pleased that he seemed so convinced that Martin was dead. But she could hardly leave Martin now. Without both the physical and psychic food that she'd been feeding him, he would in all likelihood be dead by the next day; he definitely wouldn't be climbing out of any caves. It was becoming more difficult to sort out her thoughts, and now Kreeops seemed to be surrounding her mind, closing in on it.

"I stay," she said. "The role must be played out."

She shut the door and dropped the bolt into place. Kreeops would find "the role must be played out" a poor reason for her to let herself be permanently sealed into a tomb with a dead man. If she was lucky, he might figure she was clinging to a remnant of some genuine belief that Martin really was the Jefuson. Kreeops knew the power of faith as few men did. He shouldn't be too surprised to discover it among one who'd been through so much of his indoctrination.

But the Regent hadn't gotten where he was by taking things or people at face value, and it was an uneasy rest, brimming with horrible apparitions, that Gena let herself accept for the next hour or so before resuming her work.

She tended Martin unceasingly that day, prepared to use herself up totally, too busy to be distracted by considering what awaited them if "totally" wasn't enough. Martin's breathing had become more confident; his body, though still unconscious, stirred actively. At one point Gena went to the door and ordered more food — she had completely run out — waking the Bride's Maid outside to do so. Despite almost constant eating, she was starving, and it seemed forever before the food arrived, brought by a second maid. When Gena opened the door, she discovered once again it was night. She had until dawn. An eternity away. And not enough time. Immediately squatting right down by the door, she ate and tried to quench her great thirst. Afterward she leaned back against the wall, stretching her legs out luxuriously in front of her.

Perhaps it was the old taste that woke Gena: danger, thick and gritty in her mouth. Perhaps it was a sound or a change in the lighting as a shadow crept between her and the candles. She tried to force her eyes open, but the weight of her eyelids was too great. She guessed she'd been drugged, and when, with an effort of will, she finally could see, it took her a second to grasp what was happening.

Kreeops was silhouetted in the candlelight. Even as a shadow-figure, she knew him instantly as he stole across in front of her toward the side wall where Martin lay on the rock shelf. The sword in the Regent's hand already pointed at the unconscious form.

"Kreeops!" she screamed, fear and anger flooding her awake, then vanishing instantly. The world was suddenly calm, almost slow motion. Almost disinterestedly, she considered the mighty Regent of Satan, his posture of omnipotence exchanged for the crouch of the sneak thief. Very slowly, he turned to her.

Though most of the light was behind him, she could see his bloody eyes clearly. They had a slightly glazed appearance. His growing smile was malignant and oddly proud of his imminent triumph. It was this pride, even caught in an act that was an admission of his impotence, that filled her with pity for the Regent: he was so much less than he pretended to be.

He laughed and the edge on the laughter sounded barely controlled. Then, turning back to Martin, with both hands he raised the sword as far up over his head as he could. His body tensed: fully extended, pointed like a steeple raised against the sky. His enraptured face was lifted upward, his eyes now closed as if in inner communion with the death he was about to deliver. He hung there, poised for an endless moment, then the sword came swooping down, crashing through the exposed neck, and the head that so resembled Jefuson was removed from its body.

"Goodnight, Bride. See you at the resurrection," Kreeops called. He shut the rock door solidly behind him when he left. His words bounced through Gena's head as she lost consciousness. She had done all she could.

The touch was gone. Martin was alone. He felt as if he'd been dropped. He was falling between buildings into a rut that became a crevice in the earth itself, a womb he'd reentered, at first crying out, but now undergoing a reverse gestation, an unforming of strengths and organs and consciousness that would soon come to term in the oblivion from which he'd sprung. It was so peaceful. He saw it as a choice he'd always had and, though he couldn't remember making it, he was relieved that it was finally made.

There was a cliff beside him as he fell. It intruded on the black oblivion rushing up to embrace him; the sight of it bothered his eyes, and troubled his mind with problems of recognition and classification and with questions. It disturbed his comfort, leading away from this promising death, leading back up toward the place from which he'd fallen, the place he remembered as a world of struggling and suffering, plagued with uncertainties and temptations. He wanted to ignore that cliff; it seemed easier to just smash into the cervix of the earth beneath him.

There were vines on the cliff. They were almost green. A path, steep, rocky, and hazardous, climbed upward. Martin wished it hadn't been there.

Eventually that path would lead back to this fall anyway. He had held out for so long against this sweet seductive death already. For what? Maybe he should have gone off a roof long ago. Then he would never have had to undergo...

Gena! "Gena" was a word or a vine that wrapped itself around him and stopped him short. Tangled in with it was the memory of the warmth and the tingling, and the rest of his life: the unit, the bureauers, the coven, Kreeops, and whatever was beyond the limit and the land's end. Tied to that one word, each thing that had threatened seemed less a threat than something he was losing, surrendering, even abandoning.

He hung a long time on those vines. Swaying pleasantly, his mind very clear. The vines could be climbed. Or he could slip out of their hold and....

The city would go on without him, busily destroying itself, bathed in the twisted colors of Kreeops or shrouded in the gray dying light of the bureauers, never noticing the loss of one more tiny piece of flesh.

Gena would die by the hand of Kreeops, or, at best...He remembered Moohna, broken, crippled, a prophecy of Gena's brightest future. For even Gena would eventually be shattered by the city, probably easily, as so many others had been before her.

Still, the limit was down, and changes were not only possible but inevitable. He was listening to a gut feeling that told him it wouldn't be very long before whatever was outside the city was nothing more than an extension of what was inside, when he was astounded by the realization that it was in his power to make the inside of the city as different from what it now was as he was from the bureauers. All he had to do now was climb. The Age of Origin might be gone; perhaps the city had never been as splendid as he had imagined it; in any case, he doubted if it could be rejuvenated. But suddenly it didn't seem too crazed to try to create a world to which premature death would never be considered preferable. His own death would certainly wait. And while it waited, he would do what flesh could, for Gena and the others, if not for himself. Yes, for himself, he amended, remembering the warmth and purity of that sunlike touch.

It came as no cosmic calling. He was no Jefuson. He certainly never imagined it was something he had to do. He didn't even imagine it was something he was supposed to do. But it was something he wanted to do, something which, if he could, he was going to do.

Martin started up the long, steep path to consciousness.

When Martin awoke, he was lying on the floor in a corner of what appeared to be a cave. Across from him, candles were burning low. He could hear voices from outside the cave.

"Wait!" This was repeated several times. All the speakers were unfamiliar.

"Why? Morning is upon us. There will be no resurrection. Our days still belong to Satan, Prince of the Night. The tomb must be sealed." Even muffled by the rock walls, Martin recognized Kreeops' voice.

The response was a minor, half-hearted tumult of "Wait," and "Not yet."

"It's already well past first light. In any case, a few bricks and a little mortar shouldn't bother a god whom death itself can't stop."

Martin was fully aware of where he was and of what was going on. Bracing himself on the corner walls, he pulled himself to his feet, painfully reopening the wound in his right palm.

"All right, seal it up" came from outside. Martin chuckled to himself, but he knew he must hurry. A banging and scraping began on the other side of the door.

It was then that he noticed it, on the rock shelf over by a group of candles. His head! His body! The fact that they weren't connected to each other didn't startle him as much as the fact that they weren't connected to this consciousness of them. The pain from his wounds screamed of the reality of the body he wore as he staggered over to them, trying to clear his mind of the feeling of having experienced this separation before.

The head was lying in a thin stream of gritty blood, eyes closed. The headless body looked incredibly like his own. He poked it awkwardly. It was strange, unyielding. He poked it harder, and his finger went right through the abdomen. Into sand. With a little garbage mixed in with it.

The noise at the door was growing louder. For the moment, he'd have to leave this mystery unexplained and be about his business.

He'd taken two steps toward the door before he realized that the pile of cloth lying beside it was Gena. His first fear was that she was as dead as the sand-Martin behind him, but when he got to her he could feel a pulse in her neck. She stirred soon after he touched her, shaking off her unconsciousness, surfacing.

"Gena." He would never have expected her to be in the tomb with him. "We have to get out now. They're closing up the cave."

She threw her arms around his neck, but in his weakened condition that brought him tumbling down on top of her. They both laughed.

"You're alive," she said.

"I think so. But that one over there is pretty dead."

"Kreeops killed it; he's murder on garbage. If I hadn't awakened in time, that garbage would have been you."

"You made that thing?"

"I guess so. I hardly realized what I was doing till you were over in the corner and the sand was over on the shelf. Kreeops never noticed the real you. There's quite a resemblance, don't you think?"

"Maybe *it's* Jefuson." Then he frowned, "Are our illusions going to replace Kreeops' now?"

"Sure, if we want to end up beating the hell out of sand men ourselves."

Holding onto each other, they got to their feet. The door was unbolted, but it took a bit of time for them to pull it inward. Stepping over the low wall of bricks already started across the doorway, they moved past the astonished disciples who were laying it and blinked against the light. The morning of the third day. As Martin's eyes adjusted to the light, or perhaps as the eyes of the disciples adjusted to Martin and Gena, the field in front of the tomb seemed to fade, and he could see that they were in a very old, very ordinary, and very familiar-looking building. Beyond the window hole at the end of the corridor a surprisingly strong spring sun was shining over the city. The streets were already awake and crowded.

"Jefuson! Jefuson!" disciples cried, and several lifted Martin, first up onto their shoulders, then onto one of the scrawniest cows imaginable.

"Most of them must still see it as a magnificent stallion," Gena explained. "It will take time."

With a gesture, she waved off the disciples who wanted to put her on a second wretched cow. Martin was looking around for Kreeops, but the Regent was nowhere in sight.

"All hail the Jefuson!" Was that Zaletus? For an instant, Martin caught the priest's eye, but the old man glanced away.

"My name is Martin," Martin corrected.

"It will take time," Gena repeated.

"We've got time." He reached for her hand. "And we've got work to do," he said, sliding down off the cow.

Epilogue

The legend recorded in the door ended.

Night had come and the archaeologist was tired. The way back to his craft would be difficult, cluttered with the remains of the dead civilization, and overgrown with all manner of tropical vegetation. Starting out that morning, he'd thought to himself that it was hard to regret the passing of anything that was being replaced by such beauty, but standing in that civilization's ashes and listening to the promise and the foreboding implicit within its mythology had brought an unprofessional melancholy upon him that he attributed to old age.

He shut off his computer and roused himself to his feet. The stars in the night sky had a clarity that was every bit as beautiful as the natural garden below would ever be. And maybe that beauty was what made him think that it was just possible that this civilization hadn't died here. It was just possible that its people, those descendants of Martin and Gena, and bureauers, folkers, and disciples, had merely gone on to better things, leaving the soil from which they had sprung so that it might recover from the ravages of childbirth. It was also possible, he reminded himself, that such ideas were the whimsy of an approaching senility. Anything was possible.

LEGEND

Printed in the United States
25886LVS00002B/379-396

9 781584 200086